OCTAVIA E. BUTLER
(1947–2006) was the
renowned author of numerous
ground-breaking novels,
including *Kindred*, *Wild Seed*,
and *Parable of the Sower*.
Recipient of the **Locus**, **Hugo**
and **Nebula** awards, and a **PEN
Lifetime Achievement Award**
for her body of work, in 1995
she became the first science-
fiction writer to receive the
**MacArthur Fellowship 'Genius
Grant'**. A pioneer of her genre,
Octavia's dystopian novels
explore myriad themes of Black
injustice, women's rights, global
warming and political disparity,
and her work is taught in over
two hundred colleges and
universities nationwide.

'One of the most original, thought-provoking works examining race and identity'
Los Angeles Times

'If you haven't read Butler, you don't yet understand how rich the possibilities of science fiction can be'
Magazine of Fantasy and Science Fiction

'Butler's books are exceptional'
Village Voice

'Few writers in our field are so good at blending page-turners with philosophical questions so seamlessly'
CORY DOCTOROW

KINDRED

Octavia E.
BUTLER

HEADLINE

First published in 1979 by Doubleday

First published in Great Britain in 2014 by
HEADLINE PUBLISHING GROUP

This edition published in 2018 by
HEADLINE

18

Cataloguing in Publication Data is available from the British Library

ISBN 978 1 4722 5822 9

Typeset in Sabon LT Std by Palimpsest Book Production Limited,
Falkirk, Stirlingshire

Printed and bound in Great Britain by
Clays Ltd, Elcograf S.p.A.

Headline's policy is to use papers that are natural, renewable and recyclable
products and made from wood grown in sustainable forests. The logging and
manufacturing processes are expected to conform to the environmental
regulations of the country of origin.

HEADLINE PUBLISHING GROUP
An Hachette UK Company
Carmelite House
50 Victoria Embankment
London EC4Y 0DZ

www.headline.co.uk
www.hachette.co.uk

To Victoria Rose,
friend and goad

Foreword

I discovered *Kindred* because I needed guidance and instruction, on structure and how to write a book that travels through time seamlessly. A friend who I had asked to give me a list of novels she thought might improve my own writing had recommended it, and as I worked my way through her list, I left *Kindred* until last because, at the time, I didn't think a book that some classified as science fiction could inspire me. Octavia Butler's body of work would rid me of such notions. When I finally came to *Kindred*, I began reading it purposefully, intent on excavating what could be useful. But I was quickly drawn into Dana's world and began experiencing her traumatic journeys as though inhabiting her body. Hurtled back through time on to an American plantation along with Dana, our narrator, I soon forgot that I was supposed to be reading with an eye out for techniques I could experiment with in my own writing. Instead, I was engrossed in Butler's Maryland, navigating the dark realities of slavery in the antebellum South.

Although *Kindred* is Octavia Butler's third book, some of the events that would motivate her to write a novel that foregrounds the humanity of slaves who suffered indignities designed to dehumanise them took place when she was young. In order to provide for her daughter, Butler's widowed mother worked as a maid, enduring racial discrimination at the hands of her white employers in 1950s California. Unable to fully comprehend why

Mrs Butler tolerated insults and discriminatory behaviour from her employers, a young Octavia once told her mother, 'I'll never do what you do, what you do is terrible.' Partly inspired by this experience, *Kindred* is a skilful examination of what it means to be human in a world that refuses to acknowledge that humanity. It compels readers to rethink assumptions about the past as we ultimately recognise ourselves and our times in the complex lives of its characters.

First published in 1979, *Kindred* transverses genres and defies simple classifications, at once fantasy, neo-slave narrative, historical fiction and more, the sophistication of its form matches the complexity of its narrative. It begins in a present-day Los Angeles hospital where Dana is recuperating from her most recent journey into antebellum Maryland. Dana is a writer who finds herself repeatedly thrust into the past to save the life of Rufus Weylin, a slave owner who she discovers is one of her ancestors. She soon meets her other ancestor from this moment in history, Alice Greenwood. Alice is born free but is eventually entrapped in slavery. While in the past, Dana observes her complicated family history and the horrors of slavery first hand. Through her, the reader's experience of nineteenth-century Maryland is visceral, one that collapses time while highlighting symbolic and critical connections between past and present in an unforgettable way. As we are repeatedly pulled back in time with Dana, it becomes impossible to ignore the truth that her amputation during her final journey signals – our present lives have been shaped by history in ways we cannot afford to ignore. The past isn't as distant as we often think, we carry it in our scars, our bones and the blood that flows in our veins. In many ways a timeless cautionary tale, *Kindred,* with its symbolic demonstration of the tragic truth that social progress is reversible, is especially relevant now. As our world is transformed by political shifts, we must remain conscious of this, and, like Dana, arm ourselves with all that might be needed to protect our freedoms.

Ayòbámi Adébáyò, May 2018

Prologue

I lost an arm on my last trip home. My left arm.

And I lost about a year of my life and much of the comfort and security I had not valued until it was gone. When the police released Kevin, he came to the hospital and stayed with me so that I would know I hadn't lost him too.

But before he could come to me, I had to convince the police that he did not belong in jail. That took time. The police were shadows who appeared intermittently at my bedside to ask me questions I had to struggle to understand.

'How did you hurt your arm?' they asked. 'Who hurt you?' My attention was captured by the word they used: hurt. As though I'd scratched my arm. Didn't they think I knew it was gone?

'Accident,' I heard myself whisper. 'It was an accident.'

They began asking me about Kevin. Their words seemed to blur together at first, and I paid little attention. After a while, though, I replayed them and suddenly realized that these men were trying to blame Kevin for 'hurting' my arm.

'No.' I shook my head weakly against the pillow. 'Not Kevin. Is he here? Can I see him?'

'Who then?' they persisted.

I tried to think through the drugs, through the distant pain, but there was no honest explanation I could give them – none they would believe.

'An accident,' I repeated. 'My fault, not Kevin's. Please let me see him.'

I said this over and over until the vague police shapes let me alone, until I awoke to find Kevin sitting, dozing beside my bed. I wondered briefly how long he had been there, but it didn't matter. The important thing was that he was there. I slept again, relieved.

Finally, I awoke feeling able to talk to him coherently and understand what he said. I was almost comfortable except for the strange throbbing of my arm. Of where my arm had been. I moved my head, tried to look at the empty place . . . the stump.

Then Kevin was standing over me, his hands on my face turning my head toward him.

He didn't say anything. After a moment, he sat down again, took my hand, and held it.

I felt as though I could have lifted my other hand and touched him. I felt as though I had another hand. I tried again to look, and this time he let me. Somehow, I had to see to be able to accept what I knew was so.

After a moment, I lay back against the pillow and closed my eyes. 'Above the elbow,' I said.

'They had to.'

'I know. I'm just trying to get used to it.' I opened my eyes and looked at him. Then I remembered my earlier visitors. 'Have I gotten you into trouble?'

'Me?'

'The police were here. They thought you had done this to me.'

'Oh, that. They were sheriff's deputies. The neighbors called them when you started to scream. They questioned me, detained me for a while – that's what they call it! – but you convinced them that they might as well let me go.'

'Good. I told them it was an accident. My fault.'

'There's no way a thing like that could be your fault.'

'That's debatable. But it certainly wasn't your fault. Are you still in trouble?'

'I don't think so. They're sure I did it, but there were no

2

witnesses, and you won't co-operate. Also, I don't think they can figure out how I could have hurt you . . . in the way you were hurt.'

I closed my eyes again remembering the way I had been hurt – remembering the pain.

'Are you all right?' Kevin asked.

'Yes. Tell me what you told the police.'

'The truth.' He toyed with my hand for a moment silently. I looked at him, found him watching me.

'If you told those deputies the truth,' I said softly, 'you'd still be locked up – in a mental hospital.'

He smiled. 'I told as much of the truth as I could. I said I was in the bedroom when I heard you scream. I ran to the living room to see what was wrong, and I found you struggling to free your arm from what seemed to be a hole in the wall. I went to help you. That was when I realized your arm wasn't just stuck, but that, somehow, it had been crushed right into the wall.'

'Not exactly crushed.'

'I know. But that seemed to be a good word to use on them – to show my ignorance. It wasn't all that inaccurate either. Then they wanted me to tell them how such a thing could happen. I said I didn't know . . . kept telling them I didn't know. And heaven help me, Dana, I don't know.'

'Neither do I,' I whispered. 'Neither do I.'

The River

The trouble began long before June 9, 1976, when I became aware of it, but June 9 is the day I remember. It was my twenty-sixth birthday. It was also the day I met Rufus – the day he called me to him for the first time.

Kevin and I had not planned to do anything to celebrate my birthday. We were both too tired for that. On the day before, we had moved from our apartment in Los Angeles to a house of our own a few miles away in Altadena. The moving was celebration enough for me. We were still unpacking – or rather, I was still unpacking. Kevin had stopped when he got his office in order. Now he was closeted there either loafing or thinking because I didn't hear his typewriter. Finally, he came out to the living room where I was sorting books into one of the big bookcases. Fiction only. We had so many books, we had to try to keep them in some kind of order.

'What's the matter?' I asked him.

'Nothing.' He sat down on the floor near where I was working. 'Just struggling with my own perversity. You know, I had half-a-dozen ideas for that Christmas story yesterday during the moving.'

'And none now when there's time to write them down.'

'Not a one.' He picked up a book, opened it, and turned a few pages. I picked up another book and tapped him on the shoulder with it. When he looked up, surprised, I put a stack of nonfiction down in front of him. He stared at it unhappily.

'Hell, why'd I come out here?'

'To get more ideas. After all, they come to you when you're busy.'

He gave me a look that I knew wasn't as malevolent as it seemed. He had the kind of pale, almost colorless eyes that made him seem distant and angry whether he was or not. He used them to intimidate people. Strangers. I grinned at him and went back to work. After a moment, he took the nonfiction to another bookcase and began shelving it.

I bent to push him another box full, then straightened quickly as I began to feel dizzy, nauseated. The room seemed to blur and darken around me. I stayed on my feet for a moment holding on to a bookcase and wondering what was wrong, then finally, I collapsed to my knees. I heard Kevin make a wordless sound of surprise, heard him ask, 'What happened?'

I raised my head and discovered that I could not focus on him. 'Something is wrong with me,' I gasped.

I heard him move toward me, saw a blur of gray pants and blue shirt. Then, just before he would have touched me, he vanished.

The house, the books, everything vanished. Suddenly, I was outdoors kneeling on the ground beneath trees. I was in a green place. I was at the edge of a woods. Before me was a wide tranquil river, and near the middle of that river was a child splashing, screaming . . .

Drowning!

I reacted to the child in trouble. Later I could ask questions, try to find out where I was, what had happened. Now I went to help the child.

I ran down to the river, waded into the water fully clothed, and swam quickly to the child. He was unconscious by the time I reached him – a small red-haired boy floating, face down. I turned him over, got a good hold on him so that his head was above water, and towed him in. There was a red-haired woman waiting for us on the shore now. Or rather, she was running back and forth crying on the shore. The moment she saw that I was wading, she ran out, took the boy from me and carried him the rest of the way, feeling and examining him as she did.

'He's not breathing!' she screamed.

Artificial respiration. I had seen it done, been told about it, but I had never done it. Now was the time to try. The woman was in no condition to do anything useful, and there was no one else in sight. As we reached shore, I snatched the child from her. He was no more than four or five years old, and not very big.

I put him down on his back, tilted his head back, and began mouth-to-mouth resuscitation. I saw his chest move as I breathed into him. Then, suddenly, the woman began beating me.

'You killed my baby!' she screamed. 'You killed him!'

I turned and managed to catch her pounding fists. 'Stop it!' I shouted, putting all the authority I could into my voice. 'He's alive!' Was he? I couldn't tell. Please God, let him be alive. 'The boy's alive. Now let me help him.' I pushed her away, glad she was a little smaller than I was, and turned my attention back to her son. Between breaths, I saw her staring at me blankly. Then she dropped to her knees beside me, crying.

Moments later, the boy began breathing on his own – breathing and coughing and choking and throwing up and crying for his mother. If he could do all that, he was all right. I sat back from him, feeling light-headed, relieved. I had done it!

'He's alive!' cried the woman. She grabbed him and nearly smothered him. 'Oh, Rufus, baby . . .'

Rufus. Ugly name to inflict on a reasonably nice-looking little kid.

When Rufus saw that it was his mother who held him, he clung to her, screaming as loudly as he could. There was nothing wrong with his voice, anyway. Then, suddenly, there was another voice.

'What the devil's going on here?' A man's voice, angry and demanding.

I turned, startled, and found myself looking down the barrel

7

of the longest rifle I had ever seen. I heard a metallic click, and I froze, thinking I was going to be shot for saving the boy's life. I was going to die.

I tried to speak, but my voice was suddenly gone. I felt sick and dizzy. My vision blurred so badly I could not distinguish the gun or the face of the man behind it. I heard the woman speak sharply, but I was too far gone into sickness and panic to understand what she said.

Then the man, the woman, the boy, the gun all vanished.

I was kneeling in the living room of my own house again several feet from where I had fallen minutes before. I was back at home – wet and muddy, but intact. Across the room, Kevin stood frozen, staring at the spot where I had been. How long had he been there?

'Kevin?'

He spun around to face me. 'What the hell . . . how did you get over there?' he whispered.

'I don't know.'

'Dana, you . . .' He came over to me, touched me tentatively as though he wasn't sure I was real. Then he grabbed me by the shoulders and held me tightly. 'What happened?'

I reached up to loosen his grip, but he wouldn't let go. He dropped to his knees beside me.

'Tell me!' he demanded.

'I would if I knew what to tell you. Stop hurting me.'

He let me go, finally, stared at me as though he'd just recognized me. 'Are you all right?'

'No.' I lowered my head and closed my eyes for a moment. I was shaking with fear, with residual terror that took all the strength out of me. I folded forward, hugging myself, trying to be still. The threat was gone, but it was all I could do to keep my teeth from chattering.

Kevin got up and went away for a moment. He came back with a large towel and wrapped it around my shoulders. It comforted me somehow, and I pulled it tighter. There was an ache in my back and shoulders where Rufus's mother had pounded

8

with her fists. She had hit harder than I'd realized, and Kevin hadn't helped.

We sat there together on the floor, me wrapped in the towel and Kevin with his arm around me calming me just by being there. After a while, I stopped shaking.

'Tell me now,' said Kevin.

'What?'

'Everything. What happened to you? How did you . . . how did you move like that?'

I sat mute, trying to gather my thoughts, seeing the rifle again leveled at my head. I had never in my life panicked that way – never felt so close to death.

'Dana.' He spoke softly. The sound of his voice seemed to put distance between me and the memory. But still . . .

'I don't know what to tell you,' I said. 'It's all crazy.'

'Tell me how you got wet,' he said. 'Start with that.'

I nodded. 'There was a river,' I said. 'Woods with a river running through. And there was a boy drowning. I saved him. That's how I got wet.' I hesitated, trying to think, to make sense. Not that what had happened to me made sense, but at least I could tell it coherently.

I looked at Kevin, saw that he held his expression carefully neutral. He waited. More composed, I went back to the beginning, to the first dizziness, and remembered it all for him – relived it all in detail. I even recalled things that I hadn't realized I'd noticed. The trees I'd been near, for instance, were pine trees, tall and straight with branches and needles mostly at the top. I had noticed that much somehow in the instant before I had seen Rufus. And I remembered something extra about Rufus's mother. Her clothing. She had worn a long dark dress that covered her from neck to feet. A silly thing to be wearing on a muddy riverbank. And she had spoken with an accent – a southern accent. Then there was the unforgettable gun, long and deadly.

Kevin listened without interrupting. When I was finished, he took the edge of the towel and wiped a little of the mud from my leg. 'This stuff had to come from somewhere,' he said.

9

'You don't believe me?'

He stared at the mud for a moment, then faced me. 'You know how long you were gone?'

'A few minutes. Not long.'

'A few seconds. There were no more than ten or fifteen seconds between the time you went and the time you called my name.'

'Oh, no . . .' I shook my head slowly. 'All that couldn't have happened in just seconds.'

He said nothing.

'But it was real! I was there!' I caught myself, took a deep breath, and slowed down. 'All right. If you told me a story like this, I probably wouldn't believe it either, but like you said, this mud came from somewhere.'

'Yes.'

'Look, what did you see? What do you think happened?'

He frowned a little, shook his head. 'You vanished.' He seemed to have to force the words out. 'You were here until my hand was just a couple of inches from you. Then, suddenly, you were gone. I couldn't believe it. I just stood there. Then you were back again and on the other side of the room.'

'Do you believe it yet?'

He shrugged. 'It happened. I saw it. You vanished and you reappeared. Facts.'

'I reappeared wet, muddy, and scared to death.'

'Yes.'

'And I know what I saw, and what I did – my facts. They're no crazier than yours.'

'I don't know what to think.'

'I'm not sure it matters what we think.'

'What do you mean?'

'Well . . . it happened once. What if it happens again?'

'No. No, I don't think . . .'

'You don't know!' I was starting to shake again. 'Whatever it was, I've had enough of it! It almost killed me!'

'Take it easy,' he said. 'Whatever happens, it's not going to do you any good to panic yourself again.'

I moved uncomfortably, looked around. 'I feel like it could happen again – like it could happen anytime. I don't feel secure here.'

'You're just scaring yourself.'

'No!' I turned to glare at him, and he looked so worried I turned away again. I wondered bitterly whether he was worried about my vanishing again or worried about my sanity. I still didn't think he believed my story. 'Maybe you're right,' I said. 'I hope you are. Maybe I'm just like a victim of robbery or rape or something – a victim who survives, but who doesn't feel safe any more.' I shrugged. 'I don't have a name for the thing that happened to me, but I don't feel safe any more.'

He made his voice very gentle. 'If it happens again, and if it's real, the boy's father will know he owes you thanks. He won't hurt you.'

'You don't know that. You don't know what could happen.' I stood up unsteadily. 'Hell, I don't blame you for humoring me.' I paused to give him a chance to deny it, but he didn't. 'I'm beginning to feel as though I'm humoring myself.'

'What do you mean?'

'I don't know. As real as the whole episode was, as real as I know it was, it's beginning to recede from me somehow. It's becoming like something I saw on television or read about – like something I got second hand.'

'Or like a . . . a dream?'

I looked down at him. 'You mean a hallucination.'

'All right.'

'No! I know what I'm doing. I can see. I'm pulling away from it because it scares me so. But it was real.'

'Let yourself pull away from it.' He got up and took the muddy towel from me. 'That sounds like the best thing you can do, whether it was real or not. Let go of it.'

The Fire

1

I tried.

I showered, washed away the mud and the brackish water, put on clean clothes, combed my hair . . .

'That's a lot better,' said Kevin when he saw me.

But it wasn't.

Rufus and his parents had still not quite settled back and become the 'dream' Kevin wanted them to be. They stayed with me, shadowy and threatening. They made their own limbo and held me in it. I had been afraid that the dizziness might come back while I was in the shower, afraid that I would fall and crack my skull against the tile or that I would go back to that river, wherever it was, and find myself standing naked among strangers. Or would I appear somewhere else naked and totally vulnerable?

I washed very quickly.

Then I went back to the books in the living room, but Kevin had almost finished shelving them.

'Forget about any more unpacking today,' he told me. 'Let's go get something to eat.'

'Go?'

'Yes, where would you like to eat? Someplace nice for your birthday.'

'Here.'

'But . . .'

'Here, really. I don't want to go anywhere.'

'Why not?'

I took a deep breath. 'Tomorrow,' I said. 'Let's go tomorrow.' Somehow, tomorrow would be better. I would have a night's sleep between me and whatever had happened. And if nothing else happened, I would be able to relax a little.

'It would be good for you to get out of here for a while,' he said.

'No.'

'Listen . . .'

'No!' Nothing was going to get me out of the house that night if I could help it.

Kevin looked at me for a moment – I probably looked as scared as I was – then he went to the phone and called out for chicken and shrimp.

But staying home did no good. When the food had arrived, when we were eating and I was calmer, the kitchen began to blur around me.

Again the light seemed to dim and I felt the sick dizziness. I pushed back from the table, but didn't try to get up. I couldn't have gotten up.

'Dana?'

I didn't answer.

'Is it happening again?'

'I think so.' I sat very still, trying not to fall off my chair. The floor seemed farther away than it should have. I reached out for the table to steady myself, but before I could touch it, it was gone. And the distant floor seemed to darken and change. The linoleum tile became wood, partially carpeted. And the chair beneath me vanished.

2

When my dizziness cleared away, I found myself sitting on a small bed sheltered by a kind of abbreviated dark green canopy. Beside

13

me was a little wooden stand containing a battered old pocket knife, several marbles, and a lighted candle in a metal holder. Before me was a red-haired boy. Rufus?

The boy had his back to me and hadn't noticed me yet. He held a stick of wood in one hand and the end of the stick was charred and smoking. Its fire had apparently been transferred to the draperies at the window. Now the boy stood watching as the flames ate their way up the heavy cloth.

For a moment, I watched too. Then I woke up, pushed the boy aside, caught the unburned upper part of the draperies and pulled them down. As they fell, they smothered some of the flames within themselves, and they exposed a half-open window. I picked them up quickly and threw them out the window.

The boy looked at me, then ran to the window and looked out. I looked out too, hoping I hadn't thrown the burning cloth onto a porch roof or too near a wall. There was a fireplace in the room; I saw it now, too late. I could have safely thrown the draperies into it and let them burn.

It was dark outside. The sun had not set at home when I was snatched away, but here it was dark. I could see the draperies a story below, burning, lighting the night only enough for us to see that they were on the ground and some distance from the nearest wall. My hasty act had done no harm. I could go home knowing that I had averted trouble for the second time.

I waited to go home.

My first trip had ended as soon as the boy was safe – had ended just in time to keep me safe. Now, though, as I waited, I realized that I wasn't going to be that lucky again.

I didn't feel dizzy. The room remained unblurred, undeniably real. I looked around, not knowing what to do. The fear that had followed me from home flared now. What would happen to me if I didn't go back automatically this time? What if I was stranded here – wherever here was? I had no money, no idea how to get home.

I stared out into the darkness fighting to calm myself. It was not calming, though, that there were no city lights out there. No

14

lights at all. But still, I was in no immediate danger. And wherever I was, there was a child with me – and a child might answer my questions more readily than an adult.

I looked at him. He looked back, curious and unafraid. He was not Rufus. I could see that now. He had the same red hair and slight build, but he was taller, clearly three or four years older. Old enough, I thought, to know better than to play with fire. If he hadn't set fire to his draperies, I might still be at home.

I stepped over to him, took the stick from his hand, and threw it into the fireplace. 'Someone should use one like that on you,' I said, 'before you burn the house down.'

I regretted the words the moment they were out. I needed this boy's help. But still, who knew what trouble he had gotten me into!

The boy stumbled back from me, alarmed. 'You lay a hand on me, and I'll tell my daddy!' His accent was unmistakably southern, and before I could shut out the thought, I began wondering whether I might be somewhere in the South. Somewhere two or three thousand miles from home.

If I was in the South, the two- or three-hour time difference would explain the darkness outside. But wherever I was, the last thing I wanted to do was meet this boy's father. The man could have me jailed for breaking into his house – or he could shoot me for breaking in. There was something specific for me to worry about. No doubt the boy could tell me about other things.

And he would. If I was going to be stranded here, I had to find out all I could while I could. As dangerous as it could be for me to stay where I was, in the house of a man who might shoot me, it seemed even more dangerous for me to go wandering into the night totally ignorant. The boy and I would keep our voices down, and we would talk.

'Don't you worry about your father,' I told him softly. 'You'll have plenty to say to him when he sees those burned draperies.'

The boy seemed to deflate. His shoulders sagged and he turned to stare into the fireplace. 'Who are you anyway?' he asked. 'What are you doing here?'

So he didn't know either – not that I had really expected him to. But he did seem surprisingly at ease with me – much calmer than I would have been at his age about the sudden appearance of a stranger in my bedroom. I wouldn't even have still been in the bedroom. If he had been as timid a child as I was, he would probably have gotten me killed.

'What's your name?' I asked him.

'Rufus.'

For a moment, I just stared at him. 'Rufus?'

'Yeah. What's the matter?'

I wished I knew what was the matter – what was going on! 'I'm all right,' I said. 'Look . . . Rufus, look at me. Have you ever seen me before?'

'No.'

That was the right answer, the reasonable answer. I tried to make myself accept it in spite of his name, his too-familiar face. But the child I had pulled from the river could so easily have grown into this child – in three or four years.

'Can you remember a time when you nearly drowned?' I asked, feeling foolish.

He frowned, looked at me more carefully.

'You were younger,' I said. 'About five years old, maybe. Do you remember?'

'The river?' The words came out low and tentative as though he didn't quite believe them himself.

'You do remember then. It was you.'

'Drowning . . . I remember that. And you . . .?'

'I'm not sure you ever got a look at me. And I guess it must have been a long time ago . . . for you.'

'No, I remember you now. I saw you.'

I said nothing. I didn't quite believe him. I wondered whether he was just telling me what he thought I wanted to hear – though there was no reason for him to lie. He was clearly not afraid of me.

'That's why it seemed like I knew you,' he said. 'I couldn't remember – maybe because of the way I saw you. I told Mama, and she said I couldn't have really seen you that way.'

16

'What way?'

'Well . . . with my eyes closed.'

'With your—' I stopped. The boy wasn't lying; he was dreaming.

'It's true!' he insisted loudly. Then he caught himself, whispered, 'That's the way I saw you just as I stepped in the hole.'

'Hole?'

'In the river. I was walking in the water and there was a hole. I fell, and then I couldn't find the bottom any more. I saw you inside a room. I could see part of the room, and there were books all around – more than in Daddy's library. You were wearing pants like a man – the way you are now. I thought you were a man.'

'Thanks a lot.'

'But this time you just look like a woman wearing pants.'

I sighed. 'All right, never mind that. As long as you recognize me as the one who pulled you out of the river . . .'

'Did you? I thought you must have been the one.'

I stopped, confused. 'I thought you remembered.'

'I remember seeing you. It was like I stopped drowning for a while and saw you, and then started to drown again. After that Mama was there, and Daddy.'

'And Daddy's gun,' I said bitterly. 'Your father almost shot me.'

'He thought you were a man too – and that you were trying to hurt Mama and me. Mama says she was telling him not to shoot you, and then you were gone.'

'Yes.' I had probably vanished before the woman's eyes. What had she thought of that?

'I asked her where you went,' said Rufus, 'and she got mad and said she didn't know. I asked her again later, and she hit me. And she never hits me.'

I waited, expecting him to ask me the same question, but he said no more. Only his eyes questioned. I hunted through my own thoughts for a way to answer him.

'Where do you think I went, Rufe?'

He sighed, said disappointedly, 'You're not going to tell me either.'

'Yes I am – as best I can. But answer me first. Tell me where you think I went.'

He seemed to have to decide whether to do that or not. 'Back to the room,' he said finally. 'The room with the books.'

'Is that a guess, or did you see me again?'

'I didn't see you. Am I right? Did you go back there?'

'Yes. Back home to scare my husband almost as much as I must have scared your parents.'

'But how did you get there? How did you get here?'

'Like that.' I snapped my fingers.

'That's no answer.'

'It's the only answer I've got. I was at home; then suddenly, I was here helping you. I don't know how it happens – how I move that way – or when it's going to happen. I can't control it.'

'Who can?'

'I don't know. No one.' I didn't want him to get the idea that he could control it. Especially if it turned out that he really could.

'But . . . what's it like? What did Mama see that she won't tell me about?'

'Probably the same thing my husband saw. He said when I came to you, I vanished. Just disappeared. And then reappeared later.'

He thought about that. 'Disappeared? You mean like smoke?' Fear crept into his expression. 'Like a ghost?'

'Like smoke, maybe. But don't go getting the idea that I'm a ghost. There are no ghosts.'

'That's what Daddy says.'

'He's right.'

'But Mama says she saw one once.'

I managed to hold back my opinion of that. His mother, after all . . . Besides, I was probably her ghost. She had had to find some explanation for my vanishing. I wondered how her more realistic husband had explained it. But that wasn't important. What I cared about now was keeping the boy calm.

'You needed help,' I told him. 'I came to help you. Twice. Does that make me someone to be afraid of?'

18

'I guess not.' He gave me a long look, then came over to me, reached out hesitantly, and touched me with a sooty hand.

'You see,' I said, 'I'm as real as you are.'

He nodded. 'I thought you were. All the things you did . . . you had to be. And Mama said she touched you too.'

'She sure did.' I rubbed my shoulder where the woman had bruised it with her desperate blows. For a moment, the soreness confused me, forced me to recall that for me, the woman's attack had come only hours ago. Yet the boy was years older. Fact then: somehow, my travels crossed time as well as distance. Another fact: the boy was the focus of my travels – perhaps the cause of them. He had seen me in my living room before I was drawn to him; he couldn't have made that up. But I had seen nothing at all, felt nothing but sickness and disorientation.

'Mama said what you did after you got me out of the water was like the Second Book of Kings,' said the boy.

'The what?'

'Where Elisha breathed into the dead boy's mouth, and the boy came back to life. Mama said she tried to stop you when she saw you doing that to me because you were just some nigger she had never seen before. Then she remembered Second Kings.'

I sat down on the bed and looked over at him, but I could read nothing other than interest and remembered excitement in his eyes. 'She said I was what?' I asked.

'Just a strange nigger. She and Daddy both knew they hadn't seen you before.'

'That was a hell of a thing for her to say right after she saw me save her son's life.'

Rufus frowned. 'Why?'

I stared at him.

'What's wrong?' he asked. 'Why are you mad?'

'Your mother always call black people niggers, Rufe?'

'Sure, except when she has company. Why not?'

His air of innocent questioning confused me. Either he really didn't know what he was saying, or he had a career waiting in

19

Hollywood. Whichever it was, he wasn't going to go on saying it to me.

'I'm a black woman, Rufe. If you have to call me something other than my name, that's it.'

'But . . .'

'Look, I helped you. I put the fire out, didn't I?'

'Yeah.'

'All right then, you do me the courtesy of calling me what I want to be called.'

He just stared at me.

'Now,' I spoke more gently, 'tell me, did you see me again when the draperies started to burn? I mean, did you see me the way you did when you were drowning?'

It took him a moment to shift gears. Then he said, 'I didn't see anything but fire.' He sat down in the old ladder-back chair near the fireplace and looked at me. 'I didn't see you until you got here. But I was so scared . . . it was kind of like when I was drowning . . . but not like anything else I can remember. I thought the house would burn down and it would be my fault. I thought I would die.'

I nodded. 'You probably wouldn't have died because you would have been able to get out in time. But if your parents are asleep here, the fire might have reached them before they woke up.'

The boy stared into the fireplace. 'I burned the stable once,' he said. 'I wanted Daddy to give me Nero – a horse I liked. But he sold him to Reverend Wyndham just because Reverend Wyndham offered a lot of money. Daddy already has a lot of money. Anyway, I got mad and burned down the stable.'

I shook my head wonderingly. The boy already knew more about revenge than I did. What kind of man was he going to grow up into? 'Why did you set this fire?' I asked. 'To get even with your father for something else?'

'For hitting me. See?' He turned and pulled up his shirt so that I could see the crisscross of long red welts. And I could see old marks, ugly scars of at least one much worse beating.

'For Godsake . . .!'

20

'He said I took money from his desk, and I said I didn't.' Rufus shrugged. 'He said I was calling him a liar, and he hit me.'

'Several times.'

'All I took was a dollar.' He put his shirt down and faced me.

I didn't know what to say to that. The boy would be lucky to stay out of prison when he grew up – if he grew up. He went on.

'I started thinking that if I burned the house, he would lose all his money. He ought to lose it. It's all he ever thinks about.' Rufus shuddered. 'But then I remembered the stable, and the whip he hit me with after I set that fire. Mama said if she hadn't stopped him, he would have killed me. I was afraid this time he would kill me, so I wanted to put the fire out. But I couldn't. I didn't know what to do.'

So he had called me. I was certain now. The boy drew me to him somehow when he got himself into more trouble than he could handle. How he did it, I didn't know. He apparently didn't even know he was doing it. If he had, and if he had been able to call me voluntarily, I might have found myself standing between father and son during one of Rufus's beatings. What would have happened then, I couldn't imagine. One meeting with Rufus's father had been enough for me. Not that the boy sounded like that much of a bargain either. But, 'Did you say he used a whip on you, Rufe?'

'Yeah. The kind he whips niggers and horses with.'

That stopped me for a moment. 'The kind he whips . . . who?'

He looked at me warily. 'I wasn't talking about you.'

I brushed that aside. 'Say blacks anyway. But . . . your father whips black people?'

'When they need it. But Mama said it was cruel and disgraceful for him to hit me like that no matter what I did. She took me to Baltimore City to Aunt May's house after that, but he came and got me and brought me home. After a while, she came home too.'

For a moment, I forgot about the whip and the 'niggers.' Baltimore City. Baltimore, Maryland? 'Are we far from Baltimore now, Rufe?'

'Across the bay.'

21

'But . . . we're still in Maryland, aren't we?' I had relatives in Maryland – people who would help me if I needed them, and if I could reach them. I was beginning to wonder, though, whether I would be able to reach anyone I knew. I had a new, slowly growing fear.

'Sure we're in Maryland,' said Rufus. 'How could you not know that.'

'What's the date?'

'I don't know.'

'The year! Just tell me the year!'

He glanced across the room toward the door, then quickly back at me. I realized I was making him nervous with my ignorance and my sudden intensity. I forced myself to speak calmly. 'Come on, Rufe, you know what year it is, don't you?'

'It's . . . eighteen fifteen.'

'When?'

'Eighteen fifteen.'

I sat still, breathed deeply, calming myself, believing him. I did believe him. I wasn't even as surprised as I should have been. I had already accepted the fact that I had moved through time. Now I knew I was farther from home than I had thought. And now I knew why Rufus's father used his whip on 'niggers' as well as horses.

I looked up and saw that the boy had left his chair and come closer to me.

'What's the matter with you?' he demanded. 'You keep acting sick.'

'It's nothing, Rufe. I'm all right.' No, I was sick. What was I going to do? Why hadn't I gone home? This could turn out to be such a deadly place for me if I had to stay in it much longer. 'Is this a plantation?' I asked.

'The Weylin plantation. My daddy's Tom Weylin.'

'Weylin . . .' The name triggered a memory, something I hadn't thought of for years. 'Rufus, do you spell your last name, W-e-y-l-i-n?'

'Yeah, I think that's right.'

I frowned at him impatiently. A boy his age should certainly be sure of the spelling of his own name – even a name like this with an unusual spelling.

'It's right,' he said quickly.

'And . . . is there a black girl, maybe a slave girl, named Alice living around here somewhere?' I wasn't sure of the girl's last name. The memory was coming back to me in fragments.

'Sure. Alice is my friend.'

'Is she?' I was staring at my hands, trying to think. Every time I got used to one impossibility, I ran into another.

'She's no slave, either,' said Rufus. 'She's free, born free like her mother.'

'Oh? Then maybe somehow . . .' I let my voice trail away as my thoughts raced ahead of it fitting things together. The state was right, and the time, the unusual name, the girl, Alice . . .

'Maybe what?' prompted Rufus.

Yes, maybe what? Well, maybe, if I wasn't completely out of my mind, if I wasn't in the middle of the most perfect hallucination I'd ever heard of, if the child before me was real and was telling the truth, maybe he was one of my ancestors.

Maybe he was my several times great grandfather, but still vaguely alive in the memory of my family because his daughter had bought a large Bible in an ornately carved, wooden chest and had begun keeping family records in it. My uncle still had it.

Grandmother Hagar. Hagar Weylin, born in 1831. Hers was the first name listed. And she had given her parents' names as Rufus Weylin and Alice Green-something Weylin.

'Rufus, what's Alice's last name?'

'Greenwood. What were you talking about? Maybe what?'

'Nothing. I . . . just thought I might know someone in her family.'

'Do you?'

'I don't know. It's been a long time since I've seen the person I'm thinking of.' Weak lies. But they were better than the truth. As young as the boy was, I thought he would question my sanity if I told the truth.

23

Alice Greenwood. How would she marry this boy? Or would it be marriage? And why hadn't someone in my family mentioned that Rufus Weylin was white? If they knew. Probably, they didn't. Hagar Weylin Blake had died in 1880, long before the time of any member of my family that I had known. No doubt most information about her life had died with her. At least it had died before it filtered down to me. There was only the Bible left.

Hagar had filled pages of it with her careful script. There was a record of her marriage to Oliver Blake, and a list of her seven children, their marriages, some grandchildren . . . Then someone else had taken up the listing. So many relatives that I had never known, would never know.

Or would I?

I looked over at the boy who would be Hagar's father. There was nothing in him that reminded me of any of my relatives. Looking at him confused me. But he had to be the one. There had to be some kind of reason for the link he and I seemed to have. Not that I really thought a blood relationship could explain the way I had twice been drawn to him. It wouldn't. But then, neither would anything else. What we had was something new, something that didn't even have a name. Some matching strangeness in us that may or may not have come from our being related. Still, now I had a special reason for being glad I had been able to save him. After all . . . after all, what would have happened to me, to my mother's family, if I hadn't saved him?

Was that why I was here? Not only to insure the survival of one accident-prone small boy, but to insure my family's survival, my own birth.

Again, what would have happened if the boy had drowned? Would he have drowned without me? Or would his mother have saved him somehow? Would his father have arrived in time to save him? It must be that one of them would have saved him somehow. His life could not depend on the actions of his unconceived descendant. No matter what I did, he would have to survive to father Hagar, or I could not exist. That made sense.

But somehow, it didn't make enough sense to give me any

comfort. It didn't make enough sense for me to test it by ignoring him if I found him in trouble again – not that I could have ignored *any* child in trouble. But this child needed special care. If I was to live, if others were to live, he must live. I didn't dare test the paradox.

'You know,' he said, peering at me, 'you look a little like Alice's mother. If you wore a dress and tied your hair up, you'd look a lot like her.' He sat down companionably beside me on the bed.

'I'm surprised your mother didn't mistake me for her then,' I said.

'Not with you dressed like that! She thought you were a man at first, just like I did – and like Daddy did.'

'Oh.' That mistake was a little easier to understand now.

'Are you sure you aren't related to Alice yourself?'

'Not that I know of,' I lied. And I changed the subject abruptly. 'Rufe, are there slaves here?'

He nodded. 'Thirty-eight slaves, Daddy said.' He drew his bare feet up and sat cross-legged on the bed facing me, still examining me with interest. 'You're not a slave, are you?'

'No.'

'I didn't think so. You don't talk right or dress right or act right. You don't even seem like a runaway.'

'I'm not.'

'And you don't call me "Master" either.'

I surprised myself by laughing. 'Master?'

'You're supposed to.' He was very serious. 'You want me to call you black.'

His seriousness stopped my laughter. What was funny, anyway? He was probably right. No doubt I was supposed to give him some title of respect. But 'Master'?

'You have to say it,' he insisted. 'Or "Young Master" or . . . or "Mister" like Alice does. You're supposed to.'

'No.' I shook my head. 'Not unless things get a lot worse than they are.'

The boy gripped my arm. 'Yes!' he whispered. 'You'll get into trouble if you don't, if Daddy hears you.'

25

I'd get into trouble if 'Daddy' heard me say anything at all. But the boy was obviously concerned, even frightened for me. His father sounded like a man who worked at inspiring fear. 'All right,' I said. 'If anyone else comes, I'll call you "Mister Rufus." Will that do?' If anyone else came, I'd be lucky to survive.

'Yes,' said Rufus. He looked relieved. 'I still have scars on my back where Daddy hit me with the whip.'

'I saw them.' It was time for me to get out of this house. I had done enough talking and learning and hoping to be transported home. It was clear that whatever power had used me to protect Rufus had not provided for my own protection. I had to get out of the house and to a place of safety before day came – if there was a place of safety for me here. I wondered how Alice's parents managed, how they survived.

'Hey!' said Rufus suddenly.

I jumped, looked at him, and realized that he had been saying something – something I had missed.

'I said what's your name?' he repeated. 'You never told me.'

Was that all? 'Edana,' I said. 'Most people call me Dana.'

'Oh, no!' he said softly. He stared at me the way he had when he thought I might be a ghost.

'What's wrong?'

'Nothing, I guess, but . . . well, you wanted to know if I had seen you this time before you got here the way I did at the river. Well, I didn't see you, but I think I heard you.'

'How? When?'

'I don't know how. You weren't here. But when the fire started and I got so scared, I heard a voice, a man. He said, "Dana?" Then he said, "Is it happening again?" And someone else – you – whispered, "I think so." I heard you!'

I sighed wearily, longing for my own bed and an end to questions that had no answers. How had Rufus heard Kevin and me across time and space? I didn't know. I didn't even have time to care. I had other more immediate problems.

'Who was the man?' Rufus asked.

'My husband.' I rubbed a hand across my face. 'Rufe, I have

to get out of here before your father wakes up. Will you show me the way downstairs so that I don't awaken anyone?'

'Where will you go?'

'I don't know, but I can't stay here.' I paused for a moment wondering how much he could help me – how much he would help me. 'I'm a long way from home,' I said, 'and I don't know when I'll be able to get back there. Do you know of anyplace I could go?'

Rufus uncrossed his legs and scratched his head. 'You could go outside and hide until morning. Then you could come out and ask Daddy if you could work here. He hires free niggers sometimes.'

'Does he? If you were free and black, do you think you'd want to work for him?'

He looked away from me, shook his head. 'I guess not. He's pretty mean sometimes.'

'Is there someplace else I could go?'

He did some more thinking. 'You could go to town and find work there.'

'What's the name of the town?'

'Easton.'

'Is it far?'

'Not so far. The niggers walk there sometimes when Daddy gives them a pass. Or maybe . . .'

'What?'

'Alice's mother lives closer. You could go to her, and she could tell you the best places to go to get work. You could stay with her too, maybe. Then I might see you again before you go home.'

I was surprised he wanted to see me again. I hadn't had much contact with children since I'd been one myself. Somehow, I found myself liking this one, though. His environment had left its unlikable marks on him, but in the ante bellum South, I could have found myself at the mercy of someone much worse – could have been descended from someone much worse.

'Where can I find Alice's mother?' I asked.

'She lives in the woods. Come on outside, and I'll tell you how to get there.'

He took his candle and went to the door of his room. The room's shadows moved eerily as he moved. I realized suddenly how easy it would be for him to betray me – to open the door and run away or shout an alarm.

Instead, he opened the door a crack and looked out. Then he turned and beckoned to me. He seemed excited and pleased, and only frightened enough to make him cautious. I relaxed, followed him quickly. He was enjoying himself – having an adventure. And, incidentally, he was playing with fire again, helping an intruder to escape undetected from his father's house. His father would probably take the whip to both of us if he knew.

Downstairs, the large heavy door opened noiselessly and we stepped into the darkness outside – the near darkness. There was a half-moon and several million stars lighting the night as they never did at home. Rufus immediately began to give me directions to his friend's house, but I stopped him. There was something else to be done first.

'Where would the draperies have fallen, Rufe? Take me to them.'

He obeyed, taking me around a corner of the house to the side. There, what was left of the draperies lay smoking on the ground.

'If we can get rid of this,' I said, 'can you get your mother to give you new draperies without telling your father?'

'I think so,' he said. 'They hardly talk to each other anyway.'

Most of the remnants of the drapes were cold. I stamped out the few that were still edged in red and threatening to flame up again. Then I found a fairly large piece of unburned cloth. I spread it out flat and filled it with smaller pieces and bits of ash and whatever dirt I scooped up along with them. Rufus helped me silently. When we were finished, I rolled the cloth into a tight bundle and gave it to him.

'Put it in your fireplace,' I told him. 'Watch to see that it all burns before you go to sleep. But, Rufe . . . don't burn anything else.'

He glanced downward, embarrassed. 'I won't.'

'Good. There must be safer ways of annoying your father. Now which way is it to Alice's house?'

3

He pointed the way, then left me alone in the silent chilly night. I stood beside the house for a moment feeling frightened and lonely. I hadn't realized how comforting the boy's presence had been. Finally, I began walking across the wide grassy land that separated the house from the fields. I could see scattered trees and shadowy buildings around me. There was a row of small buildings off to one side almost out of sight of the house. Slave cabins, I supposed. I thought I saw someone moving around one of them, and for a moment, I froze behind a huge spreading tree. The figure vanished silently between two cabins – some slave, probably as eager as I was to avoid being caught out at night.

I skirted around a field of some grassy waist-high crop I didn't even try to identify in the dim light. Rufus had told me his short cut, and that there was another longer way by road. I was glad to avoid the road, though. The possibility of meeting a white adult here frightened me, more than the possibility of street violence ever had at home.

Finally, there was a stand of woods that looked like a solid wall of darkness after the moonlit fields. I stood before it for several seconds wondering whether the road wouldn't be a better idea after all.

Then I heard dogs barking – not too far away by their sound – and in sudden fear, I plunged through a tangle of new young growth and into the trees. I wondered about thorns, poison ivy, snakes . . . I wondered, but I didn't stop. A pack of half-wild dogs seemed worse. Or perhaps a pack of tame hunting dogs used to tracking runaway slaves.

The woods were not as totally dark as they had seemed. I could see a little after my eyes grew accustomed to the dimness. I could see trees, tall and shadowy – trees everywhere. As I walked on, I began to wonder how I could be sure I was still going in the right direction. That was enough. I turned around – hoping that I still knew what 'around' meant, and headed back toward the field. I was too much of a city woman.

I got back to the field all right, then veered left to where Rufus had said there was a road. I found the road and followed it, listening for the dogs. But now, only a few night birds and insects broke the silence – crickets, an owl, some other bird I had no name for. I hugged the side of the road, trying to suppress my nervousness and praying to go home.

Something dashed across the road so close to me that it almost brushed my leg. I froze, too terrified even to scream, then realized that it was just some small animal that I had frightened – a fox, perhaps, or a rabbit. I found myself swaying a little, swaying dizzily. I collapsed to my knees, desperately willing the dizziness to intensify, the transferal to come . . .

I had closed my eyes. When I opened them, the dirt path and the trees were still there. I got up wearily and began walking again.

When I had been walking for a while, I began to wonder whether I had passed the cabin without seeing it. And I began to hear noises – not birds or animals this time, not anything I could identify at first. But whatever it was, it seemed to be coming closer. It took me a ridiculously long time to realize that it was the sound of horses moving slowly down the road toward me.

Just in time, I dove into the bushes.

I lay still, listening, shaking a little, wondering whether the approaching horsemen had seen me. I could see them now, dark, slowly moving shapes going in a direction that would eventually take them past me on toward the Weylin house. And if they saw me, they might take me along with them as their prisoner. Blacks here were assumed to be slaves unless they could prove they were free – unless they had their free papers. Paperless blacks were fair game for any white.

And these riders were white. I could see that in the moonlight as they came near. Then they turned and headed into the woods just a few feet from me. I watched and waited, keeping absolutely still until they had all gone past. Eight white men out for a leisurely ride in the middle of the night. Eight white men going into the woods in the area where the Greenwood cabin was supposed to be.

After a moment of indecision, I got up and followed them, moving carefully from tree to tree. I was both afraid of them and glad of their human presence. Dangerous as they could be to me, somehow, they did not seem as threatening as the dark shadowy woods with its strange sounds, its unknowns.

As I had expected, the men led me to a small log cabin in a moonlit clearing in the woods. Rufus had told me I could reach the Greenwood cabin by way of the road, but he hadn't told me the cabin sat back out of sight of the road. Maybe it didn't. Maybe this was someone else's cabin. I half hoped it was because if the people inside this cabin were black, they were almost certainly in for trouble.

Four of the riders dismounted and went to hit and kick the door. When no one answered their pounding, two of them began trying to break it down. It looked like a heavy door – one more likely to break the men's shoulders than it was to give. But apparently the latch used to keep it shut wasn't heavy. There was a sound of splintering wood, and the door swung inward. The four men rushed in with it, and a moment later, three people were shoved, almost thrown out of the cabin. Two of them – a man and woman – were caught by the riders outside who had dismounted, apparently expecting them. The third, a little girl dressed in something long and light colored, was allowed to fall to the ground and scramble away, ignored by the men. She moved to within a few yards of where I lay in the bushes near the edge of the clearing.

There was talk in the clearing now, and I began to distinguish words over the distance and through the unfamiliar accents.

'No pass,' said one of the riders. 'He sneaked off.'

'No, Master,' pleaded one of those from the cabin – clearly a black man speaking to whites. 'I had a pass. I had . . .'

31

One of the whites hit him in the face. Two others held him, and he sagged between them. More talk.

'If you had a pass, where is it?'

'Don't know. Must have dropped it coming here.'

They hustled the man to a tree so close to me that I lay flat on the ground, stiff with fear. With just a little bad luck, one of the whites would spot me, or, in the darkness, fail to spot me and step on me.

The man was forced to hug the tree, and his hands were tied to prevent him from letting go. The man was naked, apparently dragged from bed. I looked at the woman who still stood back beside the cabin and saw that she had managed to wrap herself in something. A blanket, perhaps. As I noticed it, one of the whites tore it from her. She said something in a voice so soft that all I caught was her tone of protest.

'Shut your mouth!' said the man who had taken her blanket. He threw it on the ground. 'Who the hell do you think you are, anyway?'

One of the other men joined in. 'What do you think you've got that we haven't seen before?'

There was raucous laughter.

'Seen more and better,' someone else added.

There were obscenities, more laughter.

By now, the man had been securely tied to the tree. One of the whites went to his horse to get what proved to be a whip. He cracked it once in the air, apparently for his own amusement, then brought it down across the back of the black man. The man's body convulsed, but the only sound he made was a gasp. He took several more blows with no outcry, but I could hear his breathing, hard and quick.

Behind him, his child wept noisily against her mother's leg, but the woman, like her husband, was silent. She clutched the child to her and stood, head down, refusing to watch the beating.

Then the man's resolve broke. He began to moan – low gut-wrenching sounds torn from him against his will. Finally, he began to scream.

32

I could literally smell his sweat, hear every ragged breath, every cry, every cut of the whip. I could see his body jerking, convulsing, straining against the rope as his screaming went on and on. My stomach heaved, and I had to force myself to stay where I was and keep quiet. Why didn't they stop!

'Please, Master,' the man begged. 'For Godsake, Master, please . . .'

I shut my eyes and tensed my muscles against an urge to vomit.

I had seen people beaten on television and in the movies. I had seen the too-red blood substitute streaked across their backs and heard their well-rehearsed screams. But I hadn't lain nearby and smelled their sweat or heard them pleading and praying, shamed before their families and themselves. I was probably less prepared for the reality than the child crying not far from me. In fact, she and I were reacting very much alike. My face too was wet with tears. And my mind was darting from one thought to another, trying to tune out the whipping. At one point, this last cowardice even brought me something useful. A name for whites who rode through the night in the ante bellum South, breaking in doors and beating and otherwise torturing black people.

Patrols. Groups of young whites who ostensibly maintained order among the slaves. Patrols. Forerunners of the Ku Klux Klan.

The man's screaming stopped.

After a moment, I looked up and saw that the patrollers were untying him. He continued to lean against the tree even when the rope was off him until one of the patrollers pulled him around and tied his hands in front of him. Then, still holding the other end of the rope, the patroller mounted his horse and rode away half-dragging his captive behind him. The rest of the patrol mounted and followed except for one who was having some kind of low-voiced discussion with the woman. Evidently, the discussion didn't go the way the man wanted because before he rode after the others, he punched the woman in the face exactly as her husband had been punched earlier. The woman collapsed to the ground. The patroller rode away and left her there.

The patrol and its stumbling captive headed back to the road, slanting off toward the Weylin house. If they had gone back exactly the way they came, they would have either gone over me or driven me from my cover. I was lucky – and stupid for having gotten so close. I wondered whether the captive black man belonged to Tom Weylin. That might explain Rufus's friendship with the child, Alice. That is, if this child was Alice. If this was the right cabin. Whether it was or not, though, the woman, unconscious and abandoned, was in need of help. I got up and went over to her.

The child, who had been kneeling beside her, jumped up to run away.

'Alice!' I called softly.

She stopped, peered at me through the darkness. She was Alice, then. These people were my relatives, my ancestors. And this place could be my refuge.

4

'I'm a friend, Alice,' I said as I knelt and turned the unconscious woman's head to a more comfortable-looking position. Alice watched me uncertainly, then spoke in a small whispery voice.

'She dead?'

I looked up. The child was younger than Rufus – dark and slender and small. She wiped her nose on her sleeve and sniffed.

'No, she's not dead. Is there water in the house?'

'Yeah.'

'Go get me some.'

She ran into the cabin and returned a few seconds later with a gourd dipper of water. I wet the mother's face a little, washed blood from around her nose and mouth. From what I could see of her, she seemed to be about my age, slender like her child, like me, in fact. And like me, she was fine-boned, probably not as strong as she needed to be to survive in this era. But she was surviving, however painfully. Maybe she would help me learn how.

She regained consciousness slowly, first moaning, then crying out, 'Alice! Alice!'

'Mama?' said the child tentatively.

The woman's eyes opened wider, and she stared at me. 'Who are you?'

'A friend. I came here to ask for help, but right now, I'd rather give it. When you feel able to get up, I'll help you inside.'

'I said who are you!' Her voice had hardened.

'My name is Dana. I'm a freewoman.'

I was on my knees beside her now, and I saw her look at my blouse, my pants, my shoes – which for unpacking and working around the house happened to be an old pair of desert boots. She took a good look at me, then judged me.

'A runaway, you mean.'

'That's what the patrollers would say because I have no papers. But I'm free, born free, intending to stay free.'

'You'll get me in trouble!'

'Not tonight. You've already had your trouble for tonight.' I hesitated, bit my lip, then said softly, 'Please don't turn me away.'

The woman said nothing for several seconds. I saw her glance over at her daughter, then touch her own face and wipe away blood from the corner of her mouth. 'Wasn't going to turn you 'way,' she said softly.

'Thank you.'

I helped her up and into the cabin. Refuge then. A few hours of peace. Perhaps tomorrow night, I could go on behaving like the runaway this woman thought I was. Perhaps from her, I could learn the quickest, safest way North.

The cabin was dark except for a dying fire in the fireplace, but the woman made her way to her bed without trouble.

'Alice!' she called out.

'Here I am, Mama.'

'Put a log on the fire.'

I watched the child obey, her long gown hanging dangerously near hot coals. Rufus's friend was at least as careless with fire as he was.

Rufus. His name brought back all my fear and confusion and longing to go home. Would I really have to go all the way to some northern state to find peace? And if I did, what kind of peace would it be? The restricted North was better for blacks than the slave South, but not much better.

'Why did you come here?' the woman asked. 'Who sent you?'

I stared into the fire frowning. I could hear her moving around behind me, probably putting on clothing. 'The boy,' I said softly. 'Rufus Weylin.'

The small noises stopped. There was silence for a moment. I knew I had taken a risk telling her about Rufus. Probably a foolish risk. I wondered why I had done it. 'No one knows about me but him,' I continued.

The fire began to flare up around Alice's small log. The log cracked and sputtered and filled the silence until Alice said, 'Mister Rufe won't tell.' She shrugged. 'He never tells nothing.'

And there in her words was a reason for the risk I had taken. I hadn't thought of it until now, but if Rufus was one to tell what he shouldn't, Alice's mother should know so that she could either hide me or send me away. I waited to see what she would say.

'You sure the father didn't see you?' she asked. And that had to mean that she agreed with Alice, that Rufus was all right. Tom Weylin had probably marked his son more than he knew with that whip.

'Would I be here if the father had seen me?' I asked.

'Guess not.'

I turned to look at her. She wore a gown now, long and white like her daughter's. She sat on the edge of her bed watching me. There was a table near me made of thick smooth planks, and a bench made from a section of split log. I sat down on the bench. 'Does Tom Weylin own your husband?' I asked.

She nodded sadly. 'You saw?'

'Yes.'

'He shouldn't have come. I told him not to.'

'Did he really have a pass?'

She gave a bitter laugh. 'No. He won't get one either. Not to come see me. Mister Tom said for him to choose a new wife there on the plantation. That way, Mister Tom'll own all his children.'

I looked at Alice. The woman followed my gaze. 'He'll never own a child of mine,' she said flatly.

I wondered. They seemed so vulnerable here. I doubted that this was their first visit from the patrol, or their last. In a place like this, how could the woman be sure of anything. And then there was history. Rufus and Alice would get together somehow.

'Where are you from?' asked the woman suddenly. 'The way you talk, you not from 'round here.'

The new subject caught me by surprise and I almost said Los Angeles. 'New York,' I lied quietly. In 1815, California was nothing more than a distant Spanish colony – a colony this woman had probably never heard of.

'That's a long way off,' said the woman.

'My husband is there.' Where had that lie come from? And I had said it with all the longing I felt for Kevin who was now too far away for me to reach through any effort of my own.

The woman came over and stood staring down at me. She looked tall and straight and grim and years older.

'They carried you off?' she asked.

'Yes.' Maybe in a way I had been kidnapped.

'You sure they didn't get him too?'

'Just me. I'm sure.'

'And now you're going back.'

'Yes!' fiercely, hopefully. 'Yes!' Lie and truth had merged.

There was silence. The woman looked at her daughter, then back at me. 'You stay here until tomorrow night,' she said. 'Then there's another place you can head for. They'll let you have some food and . . . oh!' She looked contrite. 'You must be hungry now. I'll get you some—'

'No, I'm not hungry. Just tired.'

'Get into bed then. Alice, you too. There's room for all of us there . . . now.' She went to the child and began brushing off some of the dirt Alice had brought in from outside. I saw her

37

close her eyes for a moment, then glance at the door. 'Dana . . . you said your name was Dana?'

'Yes.'

'I forgot the blanket,' she said. 'I left it outside when . . . I left it outside.'

'I'll get it,' I said. I went to the door and looked outside. The blanket lay where the patroller had thrown it – on the ground not far from the house. I went over to pick it up, but just as I reached it, someone grabbed me and swung me around. Suddenly, I was facing a young white man, broad-faced, dark-haired, stocky, and about half-a-foot taller than I was.

'What in hell . . .?' he sputtered. 'You . . . you're not the one.' He peered at me as though he wasn't sure. Apparently, I looked enough like Alice's mother to confuse him – briefly. 'Who are you?' he demanded. 'What are you doing here?'

What to do? He held me easily, barely noticing my efforts to pull away. 'I live here,' I lied. 'What are *you* doing here?' I thought he'd be more likely to believe me if I sounded indignant.

Instead, he slapped me stunningly with one hand while he held me with the other. He spoke very softly. 'You got no manners, nigger, I'll teach you some!'

I said nothing. My ears still rang from his blow, but I heard him say, 'You could be her sister, her twin sister, almost.'

That seemed to be a good thing for him to think, so I kept silent. Silence seemed safest anyway.

'Her sister dressed up like a boy!' He began to smile. 'Her runaway sister. I wonder what you're worth.'

I panicked. Having him catch and hold me was bad enough. Now he meant to turn me in as a runaway . . . I dug the nails of my free hand into his arm and tore the flesh from elbow to wrist.

Surprise and pain made the man loosen his grip on me slightly, and I wrenched away.

I heard him yell, heard him start after me.

I ran mindlessly toward the cabin door only to find Alice's mother there barring my way.

'Don't come in here,' she whispered. 'Please don't come in here.'

I had no chance to go in. The man caught me, pulled me backward, threw me to the ground. He would have kicked me, but I rolled aside and jumped to my feet. Terror gave me speed and agility I never knew I had.

Again I ran, this time for the trees. I didn't know where I was going, but the sounds of the man behind me sent me zigzagging on. Now I longed for darker denser woods that I could lose myself in.

The man tackled me and brought me down hard. At first, I lay stunned, unable to move or defend myself even when he began hitting me, punching me with his fists. I had never been beaten that way before – would never have thought I could absorb so much punishment without losing consciousness.

When I tried to scramble away, he pulled me back. When I tried to push him away, he hardly seemed to notice. At one point, I did get his attention though. He had leaned down close to me, pinning me flat on my back. I raised my hands to his face, my fingers partly covering his eyes. In that instant, I knew I could stop him, cripple him, in this primitive age, destroy him.

His eyes.

I had only to move my fingers a little and jab them into the soft tissues, gouge away his sight and give him more agony than he was giving me.

But I couldn't do it. The thought sickened me, froze my hands where they were. I had to do it! But I couldn't . . .

The man knocked my hands from his face and moved back from me – and I cursed myself for my utter stupidity. My chance was gone, and I'd done nothing. My squeamishness belonged in another age, but I'd brought it along with me. Now I would be sold into slavery because I didn't have the stomach to defend myself in the most effective way. Slavery! And there was a more immediate threat.

The man had stopped beating me. Now he simply kept a tight hold on me and looked at me. I could see that I had left a few scratches on his face. Shallow insignificant scratches. The man rubbed his hand across them, looked at the blood, then looked at me.

39

'You know you're going to pay for that, don't you?' he said.

I said nothing. Stupidity was what I would pay for, if anything.

'I guess you'll do as well as your sister,' he said. 'I came back for her, but you're just like her.'

That told me who he probably was. One of the patrollers – the one who had hit Alice's mother, probably. He reached out and ripped my blouse open. Buttons flew everywhere, but I didn't move. I understood what the man was going to do. He was going to display some stupidity of his own. He was going to give me another chance to destroy him. I was almost relieved.

He tore loose my bra and I prepared to move. Just one quick lunge. Then suddenly, for no reason that I could see, he reared above me, fist drawn back to hit me again. I jerked my head aside, hit it on something hard just as his fist glanced off my jaw.

The new pain shattered my resolve, sent me scrambling away again. I was only able to move a few inches before he pinned me down, but that was far enough for me to discover that the thing I had hit my head on was a heavy stick – a tree limb, perhaps. I grasped it with both hands and brought it down as hard as I could on his head.

He collapsed across my body.

I lay still, panting, trying to find the strength to get up and run. The man had a horse around somewhere. If I could find it . . .

I dragged myself from beneath his heavy body and tried to stand up. Halfway up, I felt myself losing consciousness, falling back. I caught hold of a tree and willed myself to stay conscious. If the man came to and found me nearby, he would kill me. He would surely kill me! But I couldn't keep my hold on the tree. I fell, slowly it seemed, into a deep starless darkness.

5

Pain dragged me back to consciousness. At first, it was all I was aware of; every part of my body hurt. Then I saw a blurred face above me – the face of a man – and I panicked.

I scrambled away, kicking him, clawing the hands that reached out for me, trying to bite, lunging up toward his eyes. I could do it now. I could do anything.

'Dana!'

I froze. My name? No patroller would know that.

'Dana, look at me for God's sake!'

Kevin! It was Kevin's voice! I stared upward, managed to focus on him clearly at last. I was at home. I was lying on my own bed, bloody and dirty, but safe. Safe!

Kevin lay half on top of me, holding me, smearing himself with my blood and his own. I could see where I had scratched his face – so near the eye.

'Kevin, I'm sorry!'

'Are you all right now?'

'Yes. I thought . . . I thought you were the patroller.'

'The what?'

'The . . . I'll tell you later. God, I hurt, and I'm so tired. But it doesn't matter. I'm home.'

'You were gone two or three minutes this time. I didn't know what to think. You don't know how good it is to have you back again.'

'Two or three minutes?'

'Almost three minutes. I watched the clock. But it seemed to be longer.'

I closed my eyes in pain and weariness. It hadn't just seemed longer to me. I had been gone for hours and I knew it. But at that moment, I couldn't have argued it. I couldn't have argued anything. The surge of strength that helped me to fight when I thought I was fighting for my life was gone.

'I'm going to take you to the hospital,' said Kevin. 'I don't know how I'm going to explain you, but you need help.'

'No.'

He got up. I felt him lift me.

'No, Kevin, please.'

'Listen, don't be afraid. I'll be with you.'

'No. Look, all he did was hit me a few times. I'll be all

right.' Suddenly I had strength again, now that I needed it. 'Kevin, I went from here the first time, and this second time. And I came back here. What will happen if I go from the hospital and come back there?'

'Probably nothing.' But he had stopped. 'No one who sees you leave or come back will believe it. And they wouldn't dare tell anybody.'

'Please. Just let me sleep. That's all I need really – rest. The cuts and bruises will heal. I'll be fine.'

He took me back to the bed, probably against his better judgment, and put me down. 'How long was it for you?' he asked.

'Hours. But it was only bad at the end.'

'Who did this to you?'

'A patroller. He . . . he thought I was a runaway.' I frowned. 'I have to sleep, Kevin. I'll make more sense in the morning, I promise.' My voice trailed away.

'Dana!'

I jumped, tried to refocus my attention on him.

'Did he rape you?'

I sighed. 'No. I hit him with a stick – knocked him out. Let me sleep.'

'Wait a minute . . .'

I seemed to drift away from him. It became too much trouble for me to go on listening and trying to understand, too much trouble to answer.

I sighed again and closed my eyes. I heard him get up and go away, heard water running somewhere. Then I slept.

6

I was clean when I awoke before dawn the next morning. I was wearing an old flannel nightgown that I hadn't worn since Kevin and I were married and that I'd never worn in June. On one side of me was a canvas tote bag containing a pair of pants, a blouse, underclothing, a sweater, shoes, and the biggest switchblade knife

I had ever seen. The tote bag was tied to my waist with a length of cord. On the other side of me lay Kevin, still asleep. But he woke up when I kissed him.

'You're still here,' he said with obvious relief, and he hugged me, reminding me painfully of a few bruises. Then he remembered, let me go, and switched on the light. 'How do you feel?'

'Pretty well.' I sat up, got out of bed, managed to stand up for a moment. Then I got back under the cover. 'I'm healing.'

'Good. You're rested, you're healing, now you can tell me what the hell happened to you. And what's a patroller? All I could think of was the Highway Patrol.'

I thought back to my reading. 'A patroller is . . . was a white man, usually young, often poor, sometimes drunk. He was a member of a group of such men organized to keep the blacks in line.'

'What?'

'Patrollers made sure the slaves were where they were supposed to be at night, and they punished those who weren't. They chased down runaways – for a fee. And sometimes they just raised hell, had a little fun terrorizing people who weren't allowed to fight back.'

Kevin leaned on one elbow and looked down at me. 'What are you talking about? Where were you?'

'In Maryland. Somewhere on the Eastern Shore if I understood Rufus.'

'Maryland! Three thousand miles away in . . . in what? A few minutes?'

'More than three thousand miles. More than any number of miles.' I moved to relieve pressure on an especially tender bruise. 'Let me tell you all of it.'

I remembered it for him in detail as I had the first time. Again, he listened without interrupting. This time when I finished, he just shook his head.

'This is getting crazier and crazier,' he muttered.

'Not to me.'

He glanced at me sidelong.

'To me, it's getting more and more believable. I don't like it. I don't want to be in the middle of it. I don't understand how it can be happening, but it's real. It hurts too much not to be. And . . . and my ancestors, for Godsake!'

'Maybe.'

'Kevin, I can show you the old Bible.'

'But the fact is, you had already seen the Bible. You knew about those people – knew their names, knew they were Marylanders, knew . . .'

'What the hell is that supposed to prove! That I was hallucinating and weaving in the names of my ancestors? I'd like to give you some of this pain that I must still be hallucinating.'

He put an arm over my chest, resting it on unbruised flesh. After a while, he said, 'Do you honestly believe you traveled back over a century in time and crossed three thousand miles of space to see your dead ancestors?'

I moved uncomfortably. 'Yes,' I whispered. 'No matter how it sounds, no matter what you think, it happened. And you're not helping me deal with it by laughing.'

'I'm not laughing.'

'They were my ancestors. Even that damn parasite, the patroller, saw the resemblance between me and Alice's mother.'

He said nothing.

'I'll tell you . . . I wouldn't dare act as though they weren't my ancestors. I wouldn't let anything happen to them, the boy or girl, if I could possibly prevent it.'

'You wouldn't anyway.'

'Kevin, take this seriously, please!'

'I am. Anything I can do to help you, I'll do.'

'Believe me!'

He sighed. 'It's like you just said.'

'What?'

'I wouldn't dare act as though I didn't believe. After all, when you vanish from here, you must go someplace. If that place is where you think it is – back to the ante bellum South – then we've got to find a way to protect you while you're there.'

44

I moved closer to him, relieved, content with even such grudging acceptance. He had become my anchor, suddenly, my tie to my own world. He couldn't have known how much I needed him firmly on my side.

'I'm not sure it's possible for a lone black woman – or even a black man – to be protected in that place,' I said. 'But if you have an idea, I'll be glad to hear it.'

He said nothing for several seconds. Then he reached over me into the canvas bag and brought out the switchblade. 'This might improve your chances – if you can bring yourself to use it.'

'I've seen it.'

'Can you use it?'

'You mean, *will* I use it.'

'That too.'

'Yes. Before last night, I might not have been sure, but now, yes.'

He got up, left the room for a moment, and came back with two wooden rulers. 'Show me,' he said.

I untied the cord of the canvas bag and got up, discovering sore muscles as I moved. I limped over to him, took one of the rulers, looked at it, rubbed my face groggily, and in a sudden slashing motion, drew the ruler across his abdomen just as he was opening his mouth to speak.

'That's it,' I said.

He frowned.

'Kevin, I'm not going to be in any fair fights.'

He said nothing.

'You understand? I'm a poor dumb scared nigger until I get my chance. They won't even see the knife if I have my way. Not until it's too late.'

He shook his head. 'What else don't I know about you?'

I shrugged and got back into bed. 'I've been watching the violence of this time go by on the screen long enough to have picked up a few things.'

'Glad to hear it.'

'It doesn't matter much.'

45

He sat down next to where I lay. 'What do you mean?'

'That most of the people around Rufus know more about real violence than the screenwriters of today will ever know.'

'That's . . . debatable.'

'I just can't make myself believe I can survive in that place. Not with a knife, not even with a gun.'

He took a deep breath. 'Look, if you're drawn back there again, what can you do but try to survive? You're not going to just let them kill you.'

'Oh, they won't kill me. Not unless I'm silly enough to resist the other things they'd rather do – like raping me, throwing me into jail as a runaway, and then selling me to the highest bidder when they see that my owner isn't coming to claim me.' I rubbed my forehead. 'I almost wish I hadn't read about it.'

'But it doesn't have to happen that way. There were free blacks. You could pose as one of them.'

'Free blacks had papers to prove they were free.'

'You could have papers too. We could forge something . . .'

'If we knew what to forge. I mean, a certificate of freedom is what we need, but I don't know what they looked like. I've read about them, but I've never seen one.'

He got up and went to the living room. Moments later, he came back and dumped an armload of books on the bed. 'I brought everything we had on black history,' he said. 'Start hunting.'

There were ten books. We checked indexes and even leafed through some of the books page by page to be sure. Nothing. I hadn't really thought there would be anything in these books. I hadn't read them all, but I'd at least glanced through them before.

'We'll have to go to the library then,' said Kevin. 'We'll go today as soon as it's open.'

'If I'm still here when it opens.'

He put the books on the floor and got back under the cover. Then he lay there frowning at me. 'What about the pass Alice's father was supposed to have?'

'A pass . . . that was just written permission for a slave to be somewhere other than at home at a certain time.'

'Sounds like just a note.'

'It is,' I said. 'You've got it! One of the reasons it was against the law in some states to teach slaves to read and write was that they might escape by writing themselves passes. Some did escape that way.' I got up, went to Kevin's office and took a small scratch pad and a new pen from his desk and the large atlas from his bookcase.

'I'm going to tear Maryland out,' I told him as I returned.

'Go ahead. I wish I had a road atlas for you. The roads in it wouldn't exist in those days but it might show you the easiest way through the country.'

'This one shows main highways. Shows a lot of rivers too, and in eighteen fifteen there were probably not many bridges.' I looked closely at it, then got up again.

'What now?' asked Kevin.

'Encyclopedia. I want to see when the Pennsylvania Railroad built this nice long track through the peninsula. I'd have to go into Delaware to pick it up, but it would take me right into Pennsylvania.'

'Forget it,' he said. 'Eighteen fifteen is too early for railroads.'

I looked anyway and found that the Pennsylvania Railroad hadn't even been begun until 1846. I went back to bed and stuffed the pen, the map, and the scratch pad into my canvas bag.

'Tie that cord around you again,' said Kevin.

I obeyed silently.

'I think we may have missed something,' he said. 'Getting home may be simpler for you than you realize.'

'Getting home? Here?'

'Here. You may have more control over your returning than you think.'

'I don't have any control at all.'

'You might. Listen, remember the rabbit or whatever it was that you said ran across the road in front of you?'

'Yes.'

47

'It scared you.'

'Terrified me. For a second, I thought it was . . . I don't know, something dangerous.'

'And your fear made you dizzy, and you thought you were coming home. Does fear usually make you dizzy?'

'No.'

'I don't think it did this time either – at least not in any normal way. I think you were right. You did almost come home. Your fear almost sent you home.'

'But . . . but I was afraid the whole time I was there. And I was scared half out of my mind while that patroller was beating me. But I didn't come home until I'd knocked him out – saved myself.'

'Not too helpful.'

'No.'

'But look, was your fight with the patroller really over? You said you were afraid that if he found you there, passed out, he'd kill you.'

'He would have, for revenge. I fought back, actually hurt him. I can't believe he'd let me get away with that.'

'You may be right.'

'I am right.'

'The point is, you believe you are.'

'Kevin . . .'

'Wait. Hear me out. You believed your life was in danger, that the patroller would kill you. And on your last trip, you believed your life was in danger when you found Rufus's father aiming a rifle at you.'

'Yes.'

'And even with the animal – you mistook it for something dangerous.'

'But I saw it in time – just as a dark blur, but clearly enough to see that it was small and harmless. And I see what you're saying.'

'That you might have been better off if your animal had been a snake. Your danger then – or assumed danger – might have sent you home before you ever met the patroller.'

48

'Then . . . Rufus's fear of death calls me to him, and my own fear of death sends me home.'

'So it seems.'

'That doesn't really help, you know.'

'It could.'

'Think about it, Kevin. If the thing I'm afraid of isn't really dangerous – a rabbit instead of a snake – then I stay where I am. If it is dangerous, it's liable to kill me before I get home. Going home does take a while, you know. I have to get through the dizziness, the nausea . . .'

'Seconds.'

'Seconds count when something is trying to kill you. I wouldn't dare put myself in danger in the hope of getting home before the ax fell. And if I got into trouble by accident, I wouldn't dare just wait passively to be saved. I might wind up coming home in pieces.'

'Yes . . . I see your point.'

I sighed. 'So the more I think about it, the harder it is for me to believe I could survive even a few more trips to a place like that. There's just too much that could go wrong.'

'Will you stop that! Look, your ancestors survived that era – survived it with fewer advantages than you have. You're no less than they are.'

'In a way I am.'

'What way?'

'Strength. Endurance. To survive, my ancestors had to put up with more than I ever could. Much more. You know what I mean.'

'No, I don't,' he said with annoyance. 'You're working yourself into a mood that could be suicidal if you're not careful.'

'Oh, but I'm talking about suicide, Kevin – suicide or worse. For instance, I would have used your knife against that patroller last night if I'd had it. I would have killed him. That would have ended the immediate danger to me and I probably wouldn't have come home. But if that patroller's friends had caught me, they would have killed me. And if they hadn't caught me, they would probably have gone after Alice's mother. They . . . they may have

49

anyway. So either I would have died, or I would have caused another innocent person to die.'

'But the patroller was trying to . . .' He stopped, looked at me. 'I see.'

'Good.'

There was a long silence. He pulled me closer to him. 'Do I really look like that patroller?'

'No.'

'Do I look like someone you can come home to from where you may be going?'

'I need you here to come home to. I've already learned that.'

He gave me a long thoughtful look. 'Just keep coming home,' he said finally. 'I need you here too.'

The Fall

I think Kevin was as lonely and out of place as I was when I met him, though he was handling it better. But then, he was about to escape.

I was working out of a casual labor agency – we regulars called it a slave market. Actually, it was just the opposite of slavery. The people who ran it couldn't have cared less whether or not you showed up to do the work they offered. They always had more job hunters than jobs anyway. If you wanted them to think about using you, you went to their office around six in the morning, signed in, and sat down to wait. Waiting with you were winos trying to work themselves into a few more bottles, poor women with children trying to supplement their welfare checks, kids trying to get a first job, older people who'd lost one job too many, and usually a poor crazy old street lady who talked to herself constantly and who wasn't going to be hired no matter what because she only wore one shoe.

You sat and sat until the dispatcher either sent you out on a job or sent you home. Home meant no money. Put another potato in the oven. Or in desperation, sell some blood at one of the store fronts down the street from the agency. I had only done that once.

Getting sent out meant the minimum wage – minus Uncle Sam's share – for as many hours as you were needed. You swept floors, stuffed envelopes, took inventory, washed dishes, sorted potato chips (really!), cleaned toilets, marked prices on merchandise . . . you did whatever you were sent out to do. It was nearly always mindless work, and as far as most employers were concerned, it was done by mindless people. Nonpeople rented for a few hours, a few days, a few weeks. It didn't matter.

I did the work, I went home, I ate, and then slept for a few hours. Finally, I got up and wrote. At one or two in the morning, I was fully awake, fully alive, and busy working on my novel. During the day, I carried a little box of No Doz. I kept awake with them, but not very wide awake. The first thing Kevin ever said to me was, 'Why do you go around looking like a zombie all the time?'

He was just one of several regular employees at an auto-parts warehouse where a group of us from the agency were doing an inventory. I was wandering around between shelves of nuts, bolts, hubcaps, chrome, and heaven knew what else checking other people's work. I had a habit of showing up every day and of being able to count, so the supervisor decided that zombie or not, I should check the others. He was right. People came in after a hard night of drinking and counted five units per clearly-marked, fifty-unit container.

'Zombie?' I repeated, looking up from a tray of short black wires at Kevin.

'You look like you sleepwalk through the day,' he said. 'Are you high on something or what?'

He was just a stock helper or some such bottom-of-the-ladder type. He had no authority over me, and I didn't owe him any explanations.

'I do my work,' I said quietly. I turned back to the wires, counted them, corrected the inventory slip, initialed it, and moved down to the next shelf.

'Buz told me you were a writer,' said the voice that I thought had gone away.

'Look, I can't count with you talking to me.' I pulled out a tray full of large screws – twenty-five to a box.

'Take a break.'

'Did you see that agency guy they sent home yesterday? He took one break too many. Unfortunately, I need this job.'

'Are you a writer?'

'I'm a joke as far as Buz is concerned. He thinks people are strange if they even read books. Besides,' I added bitterly, 'what would a writer be doing working out of a slave market?'

'Keeping herself in rent and hamburgers, I guess. That's what I'm doing working at a warehouse.'

I woke up a little then and really looked at him. He was an unusual-looking white man, his face young, almost unlined, but his hair completely gray and his eyes so pale as to be almost colorless. He was muscular, well-built, but no taller than my own five-eight so that I found myself looking directly into the strange eyes. I looked away startled, wondering whether I had really seen anger there. Maybe he was more important in the warehouse than I had thought. Maybe he had some authority . . .

'Are you a writer?' I asked.

'I am now,' he said. And he smiled. 'Just sold a book. I'm getting out of here for good on Friday.'

I stared at him with a terrible mixture of envy and frustration. 'Congratulations.'

'Look,' he said, still smiling, 'it's almost lunch time. Eat with me. I want to hear about what you're writing.'

And he was gone. I hadn't said yes or no, but he was gone.

'Hey!' whispered another voice behind me. Buz. The agency clown when he was sober. Wine put him into some kind of trance, though, and he just sat and stared and looked retarded – which he wasn't, quite. He just didn't give a damn about anything, including himself. He drank up his pay and walked around in rags. Also, he never bathed. 'Hey, you two gonna get together and write some books?' he asked, leering.

'Get out of here,' I said, breathing as shallowly as possible.

'You gonna write some poor-nography together!' He went away laughing.

Later, at one of the round rusting metal tables in the corner of the warehouse that served as the lunch area, I found out more about my new writer friend. Kevin Franklin, his name was, and he'd not only gotten his book published, but he'd made a big paperback sale. He could live on the money while he wrote his next book. He could give up shitwork, hopefully forever . . .

'Why aren't you eating?' he asked when he stopped for breath. The warehouse was in a newly built industrial section of Compton, far enough from coffee shops and hot dog stands to discourage most of us from going out to eat. Some people brought their lunches. Others bought them from the catering truck. I had done neither. All I was having was a cup of the free dishwater coffee available to all the warehouse workers.

'I'm on a diet,' I said.

He stared at me for a moment, then got up, motioned me up. 'Come on.'

'Where?'

'To the truck if it's still there.'

'Wait a minute, you don't have to . . .'

'Listen, I've been on that kind of diet.'

'I'm all right,' I lied, embarrassed. 'I don't want anything.'

He left me sitting there, went to the truck, and came back with a hamburger, milk, a small wedge of apple pie.

'Eat,' he said. 'I'm still not rich enough to waste money, so eat.'

To my own surprise, I ate. I hadn't intended to. I was caffeine jittery and surly and perfectly capable of wasting his money. After all, I'd told him not to spend it. But I ate.

Buz sidled by. 'Hey,' he said, low-voiced. 'Porn!' He moved on.

'What?' said Kevin.

'Nothing,' I said. 'He's crazy.' Then, 'Thanks for the lunch.'

'Sure. Now tell me, what is it you write?'

'Short stories, so far. But I'm working on a novel.'

'Naturally. Have any of your stories sold?'

'Some. To little magazines no one ever heard of. The kind that pay in copies of the magazine.'

He shook his head. 'You're going to starve.'

'No. After a while, I'll convince myself that my aunt and uncle were right.'

'About what? That you should have been an accountant?'

I surprised myself again by laughing aloud. The food was reviving me. 'They didn't think of accounting,' I said. 'But they would have approved of it. It's what they would call sensible. They wanted me to be a nurse, a secretary, or a teacher like my mother. At the very best, a teacher.'

'Yes.' He sighed. 'I was supposed to be an engineer, myself.'

'That's better, at least.'

'Not to me.'

'Well anyway, now you have proof that you were right.'

He shrugged and didn't tell me what he would later – that his parents, like mine, were dead. They had died years before in an auto accident still hoping that he might come to his senses and become an engineer.

'My aunt and uncle said I could write in my spare time if I wanted to,' I told him. 'Meanwhile, for the real future, I was to take something sensible in school if I expected them to support me. I went from the nursing program into a secretarial major, and from there to elementary education. All in two years. It was pretty bad. So was I.'

'What did you do?' he asked. 'Flunk out?'

I choked on a piece of pie crust. 'Of course not! I always got good grades. They just didn't mean anything to me. I couldn't manufacture enough interest in the subjects to keep me going. Finally, I got a job, moved away from home, and quit school. I still take extension classes at UCLA, though, when I can afford them. Writing classes.'

'Is this the job you got?'

'No, I worked for a while at an aerospace company. I was just a clerk-typist, but I talked my way into their publicity office. I was doing articles for their company newspaper and press releases to send out. They were glad to have me do it once I showed them I could. They had a writer for the price of a clerk-typist.'

'Sounds like something you could have stayed with and moved up.'

'I meant to. Ordinary clerical work, I couldn't stand, but that was good. Then about a year ago, they laid off the whole department.'

He laughed, but it sounded like sympathetic laughter.

Buz, coming back from the coffee machine, muttered, 'Chocolate and vanilla porn!'

I closed my eyes in exasperation. He always did that. Started a 'joke' that wasn't funny to begin with, then beat it to death. 'God, I wish he'd get drunk and shut up!'

'Does getting drunk shut him up?' asked Kevin.

I nodded. 'Nothing else will do it.'

'No matter. I heard what he said this time.'

The bell rang ending the lunch half-hour, and he grinned. He had a grin that completely destroyed the effect of his eyes. Then he got up and left.

But he came back. He came back all week at breaks, at lunch. My daily draw back at the agency gave me money enough to buy my own lunches – and pay my landlady a few dollars – but I still looked forward to seeing him, talking to him. He had written and published three novels, he told me, and outside members of his family, he'd never met anyone who'd read one of them. They'd brought so little money that he'd gone on taking mindless jobs like this one at the warehouse, and he'd gone on writing – unreasonably, against the advice of saner people. He was like me – a kindred spirit crazy enough to keep on trying. And now, finally . . .

'I'm even crazier than you,' he said. 'After all I'm older than you. Old enough to recognize failure and stop dreaming, so I'm told.'

He was a prematurely gray thirty-four. He had been surprised to learn that I was only twenty-two.

'You look older,' he said tactlessly.

'So do you,' I muttered.

He laughed. 'I'm sorry. But at least it looks good on you.'

I wasn't sure what 'it' was that looked good on me, but I was glad he liked it. His likes and dislikes were becoming important to me. One of the women from the agency told me with typical slave-market candor that he and I were 'the weirdest-looking couple' she had ever seen.

I told her, not too gently, that she hadn't seen much, and that it was none of her business anyway. But from then on, I thought of Kevin and I as a couple. It was pleasant thinking.

My time at the warehouse and his job there ended on the same day. Buz's matchmaking had given us a week together.

'Listen,' said Kevin on the last day, 'you like plays?'

'Plays? Sure. I wrote a couple while I was in high school. One-acters. Pretty bad.'

'I did something like that myself.' He took something from his pocket and held it out to me. Tickets. Two tickets to a hit play that had just come to Los Angeles. I think my eyes glittered.

'I don't want you to get away from me just because we won't be coworkers any more,' he said. 'Tomorrow evening?'

'Tomorrow evening,' I agreed.

It was a good evening. I brought him home with me when it was over, and the night was even better. Sometime during the early hours of the next morning when we lay together, tired and content in my bed, I realized that I knew less about loneliness than I had thought – and much less than I would know when he went away.

2

I decided not to go to the library with Kevin to look for forge-able free papers. I was worried about what might happen if Rufus called me from the car while it was moving. Would I arrive in his time still moving, but without the car to protect

57

me? Or would I arrive safe and still, but have trouble when I returned home – because this time the home I returned to might be the middle of a busy street?

I didn't want to find out. So while Kevin got ready to go to the library, I sat on the bed, fully dressed, stuffing a comb, a brush, and a bar of soap into my canvas bag. I was afraid I might be trapped in Rufus's time for a longer period if I went again. My first trip had lasted only a few minutes, my second a few hours. What was next? Days?

Kevin came in to tell me he was going. I didn't want him to leave me alone, but I thought I had done enough whining for one morning. I kept my fear to myself – or I thought I did.

'You feel all right?' he asked me. 'You don't look so good.'

I had just had my first look in the mirror since the beating, and I didn't think I looked so good either. I opened my mouth to reassure him, but before I could get the words out, I realized that something really was wrong. The room was beginning to darken and spin.

'Oh no,' I moaned. I closed my eyes against the sickening dizziness. Then I sat hugging the canvas bag and waiting.

Suddenly, Kevin was beside me holding me. I tried to push him away. I was afraid for him without knowing why. I shouted for him to let me go.

Then the walls around me and the bed beneath me vanished. I lay sprawled on the ground under a tree. Kevin lay beside me still holding me. Between us was the canvas bag.

'Oh God!' I muttered, sitting up. Kevin sat up too and looked around wildly. We were in the woods again, and it was day this time. The country was much like what I remembered from my first trip, though there was no river in sight this time.

'It happened,' said Kevin. 'It's real!'

I took his hand and held it, glad of its familiarity. And yet I wished he were back at home. In this place, he was probably better protection for me than free papers would have been, but I didn't want him here. I didn't want this place to touch him except through me. But it was too late for that.

I looked around for Rufus, knowing that he must be nearby. He was. And the moment I saw him, I knew I was too late to get him out of trouble this time.

He was lying on the ground, his body curled in a small knot, his hands clutching one leg. Beside him was another boy, black, about twelve years old. All Rufus's attention seemed to be on his leg, but the other boy had seen us. He might even have seen us appear from nowhere. That might be why he looked so frightened now.

I stood up and went over to Rufus. He didn't see me at first. His face was twisted with pain and streaked with tears and dirt, but he wasn't crying aloud. Like the black boy, he looked about twelve years old.

'Rufus.'

He looked up, startled. 'Dana?'

'Yes.' I was surprised that he recognized me after the years that had passed for him.

'I saw you again,' he said. 'You were on a bed. Just as I started to fall, I saw you.'

'You did more than just see me,' I said.

'I fell. My leg . . .'

'Who are you?' demanded the other boy.

'She's all right, Nigel,' said Rufus. 'She's the one I told you about. The one who put out the fire that time.'

Nigel looked at me, then back at Rufus. 'Can she fix your leg?'

Rufus looked at me questioningly.

'I doubt it,' I said, 'but let me see anyway.' I moved his hands away and as gently as I could, pulled his pants leg up. His leg was discolored and swollen. 'Can you move your toes?' I asked.

He tried, managed to move two toes feebly.

'It's broken,' commented Kevin. He had come closer to look.

'Yes.' I looked at the other boy, Nigel. 'Where'd he fall from?'

'There.' The boy pointed upward. There was a tree limb hanging high above us. A broken tree limb.

'You know where he lives?' I asked.

'Sure. I live there too.'

59

The boy was probably a slave, I realized, the property of Rufus's family.

'You sure do talk funny,' said Nigel.

'Matter of opinion,' I said. 'Look, if you care what happens to Rufus, you'd better go tell his father to send a . . . a wagon for him. He won't be walking anywhere.'

'He could lean on me.'

'No. The best way for him to go home is flat on his back – the least painful way, anyhow. You go tell Rufus's father that Rufus broke his leg. Tell him to send for the doctor. We'll stay with Rufus until you get back with the wagon.'

'You?' He looked from me to Kevin, making no secret of the fact that he didn't find us all that trustworthy. 'How come you're dressed like a man?' he asked me.

'Nigel,' said Kevin quietly, 'don't worry about how she's dressed. Just go get some help for your friend.'

Friend?

Nigel gave Kevin a frightened glance, then looked at Rufus.

'Go, Nigel,' whispered Rufus. 'It hurts something awful. Say I said for you to go.'

Nigel went, finally. Unhappily.

'What's he afraid of?' I asked Rufus. 'Will he get into trouble for leaving you?'

'Maybe.' Rufus closed his eyes for a moment in pain. 'Or for letting me get hurt. I hope not. It depends on whether anybody's made Daddy mad lately.'

Well, Daddy hadn't changed. I wasn't looking forward to meeting him at all. At least I wouldn't have to do it alone. I glanced at Kevin. He knelt down beside me to take a closer look at Rufus's leg.

'Good thing he was barefoot,' he said. 'A shoe would have to be cut off that foot now.'

'Who're you?' asked Rufus.

'My name's Kevin – Kevin Franklin.'

'Does Dana belong to you now?'

'In a way,' said Kevin. 'She's my wife.'

'Wife?' Rufus squealed.

I sighed. 'Kevin, I think we'd better demote me. In this time . . .'

'Niggers can't marry white people!' said Rufus.

I laid a hand on Kevin's arm just in time to stop him from saying whatever he would have said. The look on his face was enough to tell me he should keep quiet.

'The boy learned to talk that way from his mother,' I said softly. 'And from his father, and probably from the slaves themselves.'

'Learned to talk what way?' asked Rufus.

'About niggers,' I said. 'I don't like that word, remember? Try calling me black or Negro or even colored.'

'What's the use of saying all that? And how can you be married to him?'

'Rufe, how'd you like people to call you white trash when they talk to you?'

'What?' He started up angrily, forgetting his leg, then fell back. 'I am not trash!' he whispered. 'You damn black . . .'

'Hush, Rufe.' I put my hand on his shoulder to quiet him. Apparently I'd hit the nerve I'd aimed at. 'I didn't say you were trash. I said how'd you like to be called trash. I see you don't like it. I don't like being called nigger either.'

He lay silent, frowning at me as though I were speaking a foreign language. Maybe I was.

'Where we come from,' I said, 'it's vulgar and insulting for whites to call blacks niggers. Also, where we come from, whites and blacks can marry.'

'But it's against the law.'

'It is here. But it isn't where we come from.'

'Where do you come from?'

I looked at Kevin.

'You asked for it,' he said.

'You want to try telling him?'

He shook his head. 'No point.'

'Not for you, maybe. But for me . . .' I thought for a moment

61

trying to find the right words. 'This boy and I are liable to have a long association whether we like it or not. I want him to know.'

'Good luck.'

'Where do you come from?' repeated Rufus. 'You sure don't talk like anybody I ever heard.'

I frowned, thought, and finally shook my head. 'Rufe, I want to tell you, but you probably won't understand. We don't understand ourselves, really.'

'I already don't understand,' he said. 'I don't know how I can see you when you're not here, or how you get here, or anything. My leg hurts so much I can't even think about it.'

'Let's wait then. When you feel better . . .'

'When I feel better, maybe you'll be gone. Dana, tell me!'

'All right, I'll try. Have you ever heard of a place called California?'

'Yeah. Mama's cousin went there on a ship.'

Luck. 'Well, that's where we're from. California. But . . . it's not the California your cousin went to. We're from a California that doesn't exist yet, Rufus. California of nineteen seventy-six.'

'What's that?'

'I mean we come from a different time as well as a different place. I told you it was hard to understand.'

'But what's nineteen seventy-six?'

'That's the year. That's what year it is for us when we're at home.'

'But it's eighteen nineteen. It's eighteen nineteen everywhere. You're talking crazy.'

'No doubt. This is a crazy thing that's happened to us. But I'm telling you the truth. We come from a future time and place. I don't know how we get here. We don't want to come. We don't belong here. But when you're in trouble, somehow you reach me, call me, and I come – although as you can see now, I can't always help you.' I could have told him about our blood relationship. Maybe I would if I saw him again when he was older. For now, though, I had confused him enough.

62

'This is crazy stuff,' he repeated. He looked at Kevin. 'You tell me. Are you from California?'

Kevin nodded. 'Yes.'

'Then are you Spanish? California is Spanish.'

'It is now, but it will be part of the United States eventually, just like Maryland or Pennsylvania.'

'When?'

'It will become a state in eighteen fifty.'

'But it's only eighteen nineteen. How could you know . . .?' He broke off, looked from Kevin to me in confusion. 'This isn't real,' he said. 'You're making it all up.'

'It's real,' said Kevin quietly.

'But how could it be?'

'We don't know. But it is.'

He thought for a while looking from one to the other of us. 'I don't believe you,' he said.

Kevin made a sound that wasn't quite a laugh. 'I don't blame you.'

I shrugged. 'All right, Rufe. I wanted you to know the truth, but I can't blame you for not being able to accept it either.'

'Nineteen seventy-six,' said the boy slowly. He shook his head and closed his eyes. I wondered why I had bothered to try to convince him. After all, how accepting would I be if I met a man who claimed to be from eighteen nineteen – or two thousand nineteen, for that matter. Time travel was science fiction in nineteen seventy-six. In eighteen nineteen – Rufus was right – it was sheer insanity. No one but a child would even have listened to Kevin and me talk about it.

'If you know California's going to be a state,' said Rufus, 'you must know some other things that are going to happen.'

'We do,' I admitted. 'Some things. Not very much. We're not historians.'

'But you ought to know everything if it already happened in your time.'

'How much do you know about seventeen nineteen, Rufe?'

He stared at me blankly.

'People don't learn everything about the times that came before them,' I said. 'Why should they?'

He sighed. 'Tell me something, Dana. I'm trying to believe you.'

I dug back into the American history that I had learned both in and out of school. 'Well, if this is eighteen nineteen, the President is James Monroe, right?'

'Yeah.'

'The next President will be John Quincy Adams.'

'When?'

I frowned, calling back more of the list of Presidents I had memorized for no particular reason when I was in school. 'In eighteen twenty-four. Monroe had – will have – two terms.'

'What else?'

I looked at Kevin.

He shrugged. 'All I can think of is something I got from those books we looked through last night. In eighteen twenty, the Missouri Compromise opened the way for Missouri to come into the Union as a slave state and Maine to come in as a free state. Do you have any idea what I'm talking about, Rufus?'

'No, sir.'

'I didn't think so. Have you got any money?'

'Money? Me? No.'

'Well, you've seen money, haven't you?'

'Yes, sir.'

'Coins should have the year they were made stamped on them, even now.'

'They do.'

Kevin reached into his pocket and brought out a handful of change. He held it out to Rufus and Rufus picked out a few coins. 'Nineteen sixty-five,' he read, 'nineteen sixty-seven, nineteen seventy-one, nineteen seventy. None of them say nineteen seventy-six.'

'None of them say eighteen-anything either,' said Kevin. 'But here.' He picked out a bicentennial quarter and handed it to Rufus.

'Seventeen seventy-six, nineteen seventy-six,' the boy read. 'Two dates.'

'The country's two hundred years old in nineteen seventy-six,' said Kevin. 'Some of the money was changed to commemorate the anniversary. Are you convinced?'

'Well, I guess you could have made these yourself.'

Kevin took back his money. 'You might not know about Missouri, kid,' he said wearily. 'But you'd have made a good Missourian.'

'What?'

'Just a joke. Hasn't come into fashion yet.'

Rufus looked troubled. 'I believe you. I don't understand, like Dana said, but I guess I believe.'

Kevin sighed. 'Thank God.'

Rufus looked up at Kevin and managed to grin. 'You aren't as bad as I thought you'd be.'

'Bad?' Kevin looked at me accusingly.

'I didn't tell him anything about you,' I said.

'I saw you,' said Rufus. 'You were fighting with Dana just before you came here, or . . . it looked like fighting. Did you make all those marks on her face?'

'No, he didn't,' I said quickly. 'And he and I weren't fighting.'

'Wait a minute,' said Kevin. 'How could he know about that?'

'Like he said.' I shrugged. 'He saw us before we got here. I don't know how he does it, but he's done it before.' I looked down at Rufus. 'Have you told anyone else about seeing me?'

'Just Nigel. Nobody else would believe me.'

'Good. Best not to tell anyone else about us now either. Nothing about California or nineteen seventy-six.' I took Kevin's hand and held it. 'We're going to have to fit in as best we can with the people here for as long as we have to stay. That means we're going to have to play the roles you gave us.'

'You'll say you belong to him?'

'Yes. I want you to say it too if anyone asks you.'

'That's better than saying you're his wife. Nobody would believe that.'

Kevin made a sound of disgust. 'I wonder how long we'll be stuck here,' he muttered. 'I think I'm getting homesick already.'

'I don't know,' I said. 'But stay close to me. You got here because you were holding me. I'm afraid that may be the only way you can get home.'

3

Rufus's father arrived on a flat-bed wagon, carrying his familiar long rifle – an old muzzleloader, I realized. With him in the wagon was Nigel and a tall stocky black man. Tom Weylin was tall himself, but too lean to be as impressive as his massive slave. Weylin didn't look especially vicious or depraved. Right now, he only looked annoyed. We stood up as he climbed down from the wagon and came to face us.

'What happened here?' he asked suspiciously.

'The boy has broken his leg,' said Kevin. 'Are you his father?'

'Yes. Who are you?'

'My name's Kevin Franklin.' He glanced at me, but caught himself and didn't introduce me. 'We came across the two boys right after the accident happened, and I thought we should stay with your son until you came for him.'

Weylin grunted and knelt to look at Rufus's leg. 'Guess it's broken all right. Wonder how much that'll cost me.'

The black man gave him a look of disgust that would surely have angered him if he had seen it.

'What were you doing climbing a damn tree?' Weylin demanded of Rufus.

Rufus stared at him silently.

Weylin muttered something I didn't quite catch. He stood up and gestured sharply to the black man. The man came forward, lifted Rufus gently, and placed him on the wagon. Rufus's face twisted in pain as he was lifted, and he cried out as he was lowered into the wagon. Kevin and I should have made a splint for that leg, I thought belatedly. I followed the black man to the wagon.

Rufus grabbed my arm and held it, obviously trying not to cry. His voice was a husky whisper.

'Don't go, Dana.'

I didn't want to go. I liked the boy, and from what I'd heard of early nineteenth-century medicine, they were going to pour some whiskey down him and play tug of war with his leg. And he was going to learn brand new things about pain. If I could give him any comfort by staying with him, I wanted to stay.

But I couldn't.

His father had spoken a few private words with Kevin and was now climbing back up onto the seat of the wagon. He was ready to leave and Kevin and I weren't invited. That didn't say much for Weylin's hospitality. People in his time of widely scattered plantations and even more widely scattered hotels had a reputation for taking in strangers. But then, a man who could look at his injured son and think of nothing but how much the doctor bill would be wasn't likely to be concerned about strangers.

'Come with us,' pleaded Rufus. 'Daddy, let them come.'

Weylin glanced back, annoyed, and I tried gently to loosen Rufus's grip on me. After a moment, I realized that Weylin was looking at me – staring hard at me. Perhaps he was seeing my resemblance to Alice's mother. He couldn't have seen me clearly enough or long enough at the river to recognize me now as the woman he had once come so near shooting. At first, I stared back. Then I looked away, remembering that I was supposed to be a slave. Slaves lowered their eyes respectfully. To stare back was insolent. Or at least, that was what my books said.

'Come along and have dinner with us,' Weylin told Kevin. 'You may as well. Where were you going to stay the night, anyway?'

'Under the trees if necessary,' said Kevin. He and I climbed onto the wagon beside the silent Nigel. 'Not much choice, as I told you.'

I looked at him, wondering what he had told Weylin. Then I had to catch myself as the black man prodded the horses forward.

'You, girl,' Weylin said to me. 'What's your name?'

'Dana, sir.'

He turned to stare at me again, this time as though I'd said something wrong. 'Where do you come from?'

I glanced at Kevin, not wanting to contradict anything he had said. He gave me a slight nod, and I assumed I was free to make up my own lies. 'I'm from New York.'

Now the look he was giving me was really ugly, and I wondered whether he'd heard a New York accent recently and found mine a poor match. Or was I saying something wrong? I hadn't said ten words to him. What could be wrong?

Weylin looked sharply at Kevin, then turned around and ignored us for the rest of the trip.

We went through the woods to a road, and along the road past a field of tall golden wheat. In the field, slaves, mostly men, worked steadily swinging scythes with attached wooden racks that caught the cut wheat in neat piles. Other slaves, mostly women, followed them tying the wheat into bundles. None of them seemed to pay any attention to us. I looked around for a white overseer and was surprised not to see one. The Weylin house surprised me too when I saw it in daylight. It wasn't white. It had no columns, no porch to speak of. I was almost disappointed. It was a red-brick Georgian Colonial, boxy but handsome in a quiet kind of way, two and a half stories high with dormered windows and a chimney on each end. It wasn't big or imposing enough to be called a mansion. In Los Angeles, in our own time, Kevin and I could have afforded it.

As the wagon took us up to the front steps, I could see the river off to one side and some of the land I had run through a few hours – a few years – before. Scattered trees, unevenly cut grass, the row of cabins far off to one side almost hidden by the trees, the fields, the woods. There were other buildings lined up beside and behind the house opposite the slave cabins. As we stopped, I was almost sent off to one of these.

'Luke,' said Weylin to the black man, 'take Dana around back and get her something to eat.'

'Yes, sir,' said the black man softly. 'Want me to take Marse Rufe upstairs first?'

'Do what I told you. I'll take him up.'

I saw Rufus set his teeth. 'I'll see you later,' I whispered, but he wouldn't let go of my hand until I spoke to his father.

'Mr Weylin, I don't mind staying with him. He seems to want me to.'

Weylin looked exasperated. 'Well, come on then. You can wait with him until the doctor comes.' He lifted Rufus with no particular care, and strode up the steps to the house. Kevin followed him.

'You watch out,' said the black man softly as I started after them.

I looked at him, surprised, not sure he was talking to me. He was.

'Marse Tom can turn mean mighty quick,' he said. 'So can the boy, now that he's growing up. Your face looks like maybe you had enough white folks' meanness for a while.'

I nodded. 'I have, all right. Thanks for the warning.'

Nigel had come to stand next to the man, and I realized as I spoke that the two looked much alike, the boy a smaller replica of the man. Father and son, probably. They resembled each other more than Rufus and Tom Weylin did. As I hurried up the steps and into the house, I thought of Rufus and his father, of Rufus becoming his father. It would happen some day in at least one way. Someday Rufus would own the plantation. Someday, he would be the slaveholder, responsible in his own right for what happened to the people who lived in those half-hidden cabins. The boy was literally growing up as I watched – growing up because I watched and because I helped to keep him safe. I was the worst possible guardian for him – a black to watch over him in a society that considered blacks subhuman, a woman to watch over him in a society that considered women perennial children. I would have all I could do to look after myself. But I would help him as best I could. And I would try to keep friendship with him, maybe plant a few ideas in his mind that would help both me and the people who would be his slaves in the years to come. I might even be making things easier for Alice.

Now, I followed Weylin up the stairs to a bedroom – not the same one Rufus had occupied on my last trip. The bed was bigger, its full canopy and draperies blue instead of green. The room itself was bigger. Weylin dumped Rufus onto the bed, ignoring the boy's cries of pain. It did not look as though Weylin was trying to hurt Rufus. He just didn't seem to pay any attention to how he handled the boy – as though he didn't care.

Then, as Weylin was leading Kevin out of the room, a red-haired woman hurried in.

'Where is he?' she demanded breathlessly. 'What happened?'

Rufus's mother. I remembered her. She pushed her way into the room just as I was putting Rufus's pillow under his head.

'What are you doing to him?' she cried. 'Leave him alone!' She tried to pull me away from her son. She had only one reaction when Rufus was in trouble. One wrong reaction.

Fortunately for both of us, Weylin reached her before I forgot myself and pushed her away from me. He caught her, held her, spoke to her quietly.

'Margaret, now listen. The boy has a broken leg, that's all. There's nothing you can do for a broken leg. I've already sent for the doctor.'

Margaret Weylin seemed to calm down a little. She stared at me. 'What's she doing here?'

'She belongs to Mr Kevin Franklin here.' Weylin waved a hand presenting Kevin who, to my surprise, bowed slightly to the woman. 'Mr Franklin is the one who found Rufus hurt,' Weylin continued. He shrugged. 'Rufus wanted the girl to stay with him. Can't do any harm.' He turned and walked away. Kevin followed him reluctantly.

The woman may have been listening as her husband spoke, but she didn't look as though she was. She was still staring at me, frowning at me as though she was trying to remember where she'd seen me before. The years hadn't changed her much, and, of course, they hadn't changed me at all. But I didn't expect her to remember. Her glimpse of me had been too brief, and her mind had been on other things.

'I've seen you before,' she said.

Hell! 'Yes, ma'am, you may have.' I looked at Rufus and saw that he was watching us.

'Mama?' he said softly.

The accusing stare vanished, and the woman turned quickly to attend him. 'My poor baby,' she murmured, cradling his head in her hands. 'Seems like everything happens to you, doesn't it? A broken leg!' She looked close to tears. And there was Rufus, swung from his father's indifference to his mother's sugary concern. I wondered whether he was too used to the contrast to find it dizzying.

'Mama, can I have some water?' he asked.

The woman turned to look at me as though I had offended her. 'Can't you hear? Get him some water!'

'Yes, ma'am. Where shall I get it?'

She made a sound of disgust and rushed toward me. Or at least I thought she was rushing toward me. When I jumped out of her way, she kept right on going through the door that I had been standing in front of.

I looked after her and shook my head. Then I took the chair that was near the fireplace and put it beside Rufus's bed. I sat down and Rufus looked up at me solemnly.

'Did you ever break your leg?' he asked.

'No. I broke my wrist once, though.'

'When they fixed it, did it hurt much?'

I drew a deep breath. 'Yes.'

'I'm scared.'

'So was I,' I said remembering. 'But . . . Rufe, it won't take long. And when the doctor is finished, the worst will be over.'

'Won't it still hurt after?'

'For a while. But it will heal. If you stay off it and give it a chance, it will heal.'

71

Margaret Weylin rushed back into the room with water for Rufus and more hostility for me than I could see any reason for.

'You're to go out to the cookhouse and get some supper!' she told me as I got out of her way. But she made it sound as though she were saying, 'You're to go straight to hell!' There was something about me that these people didn't like – except for Rufus. It wasn't just racial. They were used to black people. Maybe I could get Kevin to find out what it was.

'Mama, can't she stay?' asked Rufus.

The woman threw me a dirty look, then turned gentler eyes on her son. 'She can come back later,' she told him. 'Your father wants her downstairs now.'

More likely, it was his mother who wanted me downstairs now, and possibly for no more substantial reason than that her son liked me. She gave me another look, and I left the room. The woman would have made me uncomfortable even if she'd liked me. She was too much nervous energy compacted into too small a container. I didn't want to be around when she exploded. But at least she loved Rufus. And he must have been used to her fussing over him. He hadn't seemed to mind.

I found myself in a wide hallway. I could see the stairs a few feet away and I started toward them. Just then, a young black girl in a long blue dress came out of a door at the other end of the hall. She came toward me, staring at me with open curiosity. She wore a blue scarf on her head and she tugged at it as she came toward me.

'Could you tell me where the cookhouse is, please?' I said when she was near enough. She seemed a safer person to ask than Margaret Weylin.

Her eyes opened a little wider and she continued to stare at me. No doubt I sounded as strange to her as I looked.

'The cookhouse?' I said.

She looked me over once more, then started down the stairs without a word. I hesitated, finally followed her because I didn't know what else to do. She was a light-skinned girl no older than fourteen or fifteen. She kept looking back at me, frowning. Once she stopped and turned to face me, her hand tugging absently at her scarf, then moving lower to cover her mouth, and finally dropping to her side again. She looked so frustrated that I realized something was wrong.

'Can you talk?' I asked.

She sighed, shook her head.

'But you can hear and understand.'

She nodded, then plucked at my blouse, at my pants. She frowned at me. Was that the problem, then – hers and the Weylins'?

'They're the only clothes I have right now,' I said. 'My master will buy me some better ones sooner or later.' Let it be Kevin's fault that I was 'dressed like a man.' It was probably easier for the people here to understand a master too poor or too stingy to buy me proper clothing than it would be for them to imagine a place where it was normal for women to wear pants.

As though to assure me that I had said the right thing, the girl gave me a look of pity, then took my hand and led me out to the cookhouse.

As we went, I took more notice of the house than I had before – more notice of the downstairs hall, anyway. Its walls were a pale green and it ran the length of the house. At the front, it was wide and bright with light from the windows beside and above the door. It was strewn with oriental rugs of different sizes. Near the front door, there was a wooden bench, a chair, and two small tables. Past the stairs the hall narrowed, and at its end there was a back door that we went through.

Outside was the cookhouse, a little white frame cottage not far behind the main house. I had read about outdoor kitchens and outdoor toilets. I hadn't been looking forward to either. Now, though, the cookhouse looked like the friendliest place I'd seen since I arrived. Luke and Nigel were inside eating from wooden bowls with what looked like wooden spoons. And there were two younger children, a girl and boy, sitting on the floor eating with their fingers. I was glad to see them there because I'd read about kids their age being rounded up and fed from troughs like pigs. Not everywhere, apparently. At least, not here.

There was a stocky middle-aged woman stirring a kettle that hung over the fire in the fireplace. The fireplace itself filled one whole wall. It was made of brick and above it was a huge plank from which hung a few utensils. There were more utensils off to one side hanging from hooks on the wall. I stared at them and realized that I didn't know the proper names of any of them. Even things as commonplace as that. I was in a different world.

The cook finished stirring her kettle and turned to look at me. She was as light-skinned as my mute guide – a handsome middle-aged woman, tall and heavy-set. Her expression was grim, her mouth turned down at the corners, but her voice was soft and low.

'Carrie,' she said. 'Who's this?'

My guide looked at me.

'My name is Dana,' I said. 'My master's visiting here. Mrs Weylin told me to come out for supper.'

'Mrs Weylin?' The woman frowned at me.

'The red-haired woman – Rufus's mother.' I didn't quite catch myself in time to say Mister Rufus. I didn't really see why I should have to say anything. How many Mrs Weylins were there on the place anyway?

'Miss Margaret,' said the woman, and under her breath, 'Bitch!'

I stared at her in surprise thinking she meant me.

'Sarah!' Luke's tone was cautioning. He couldn't have heard what the cook said from where he was. Either she said it often, or he had read her lips. But at least now I understood that it was Mrs Weylin – Miss Margaret – who was supposed to be the bitch.

The cook said nothing else. She got me a wooden bowl, filled it with something from a pot near the fire, and handed it to me with a wooden spoon.

74

Supper was corn meal mush. The cook saw that I was looking at it instead of eating it, and she misread my expression.

'That's not enough?' she asked.

'Oh, it's plenty!' I held my bowl protectively, fearful that she might give me more of the stuff. 'Thank you.'

I sat down at the end of a large heavy table across from Nigel and Luke. I saw that they were eating the same mush, though theirs had milk on it. I considered asking for milk on mine, but I didn't really think it would help.

Whatever was in the kettle smelled good enough to remind me that I hadn't had breakfast, hadn't had more than a few bites of dinner the night before. I was starving and Sarah was cooking meat – probably a stew. I took a bite of the mush and swallowed it without tasting it.

'We get better food later on after the white folks eat,' said Luke. 'We get whatever they leave.'

Table scraps, I thought bitterly. Someone else's leftovers. And, no doubt, if I was here long enough, I would eat them and be glad to get them. They had to be better than boiled meal. I spooned the mush into my mouth, quickly fanning away several large flies. Flies. This was an era of rampant disease. I wondered how clean our leftovers would be by the time they reached us.

'Say you was from New York?' asked Luke.

'Yes.'

'Free state?'

'Yes,' I repeated. 'That's why I was brought here.' The words, the questions made me think of Alice and her mother. I looked at Luke's broad face, wondering whether it would do any harm to ask about them. But how could I admit to knowing them – knowing them years ago – when I was supposed to be new here? Nigel knew I had been here before, but Sarah and Luke might not. It would be safer to wait – save my questions for Rufus.

'People in New York talk like you?' asked Nigel.

'Some do. Not all.'

'Dress like you?' asked Luke.

'No. I dress in what Master Kevin gives me to dress in.' I wished they'd stop asking questions. I didn't want them to make me tell lies I might forget later. Best to keep my background as simple as possible.

The cook came over and looked at me, at my pants. She pinched up a little of the material, feeling it. 'What cloth is this?' she asked.

Polyester double knit, I thought. But I shrugged. 'I don't know.'

She shook her head and went back to her pot.

'You know,' I said to her back, 'I think I agree with you about Miss Margaret.'

She said nothing. The warmth I'd felt when I came into the room was turning out to be nothing more than the heat of the fire.

'Why you try to talk like white folks?' Nigel asked me.

'I don't,' I said, surprised. 'I mean, this is really the way I talk.'

'More like white folks than some white folks.'

I shrugged, hunted through my mind for an acceptable explanation. 'My mother taught school,' I said, 'and . . .'

'A nigger teacher?'

I winced, nodded. 'Free blacks can have schools. My mother talked the way I do. She taught me.'

'You'll get into trouble,' he said. 'Marse Tom already don't like you. You talk too educated and you come from a free state.'

'Why should either of those things matter to him? I don't belong to him.'

The boy smiled. 'He don't want no niggers 'round here talking better than him, putting freedom ideas in our heads.'

'Like we so dumb we need some stranger to make us think about freedom,' muttered Luke.

I nodded, but I hoped they were wrong. I didn't think I had said enough to Weylin for him to make that kind of judgment. I hoped he wasn't going to make that kind of judgment. I wasn't good at accents. I had deliberately decided not to try to assume one. But if that meant I was going to be in trouble every time I

76

opened my mouth, my life here would be even worse than I had imagined.

'How can Marse Rufe see you before you get here?' Nigel asked.

I choked down a swallow of mush. 'I don't know,' I said. 'But I wish to heaven he couldn't!'

4

I stayed in the cookhouse when I finished eating because it was near the main house, and because I thought I could make it from the cookhouse into the hall if I started to feel dizzy – just in case. Wherever Kevin was in the house, he would hear me if I called from the hallway.

Luke and Nigel finished their meal and went to the fireplace to say something privately to Sarah. At that moment, Carrie, the mute, slipped me bread and a chunk of ham. I looked at it, then smiled at her gratefully. When Luke and Nigel took Sarah out of the room with them, I feasted on a shapeless sandwich. In the middle of it, I caught myself wondering about the ham, wondering how well it had been cooked. I tried to think of something else, but my mind was full of vaguely remembered horror stories of the diseases that ran wild during this time. Medicine was just a little better than witchcraft. Malaria came from bad air. Surgery was performed on struggling wide-awake patients. Germs were question marks even in the minds of many doctors. And people casually, unknowingly ingested all kinds of poorly preserved ill-cooked food that could make them sick or kill them.

Horror stories.

Except that they were true, and I was going to have to live with them for as long as I was here. Maybe I shouldn't have eaten the ham, but if I hadn't, it would be the table leavings later. I would have to take some chances.

Sarah came back with Nigel and gave him a pot of peas to

shell. Life went on around me as though I wasn't there. People came into the cookhouse – always black people – talked to Sarah, lounged around, ate whatever they could put their hands on until Sarah shouted at them and chased them away. I was in the middle of asking her whether there was anything I could do to help out when Rufus began to scream. Nineteenth-century medicine was apparently at work.

The walls of the main house were thick and the sound seemed to come from a long way off – thin high-pitched screaming. Carrie, who had left the cookhouse, now ran back in and sat down beside me with her hands covering her ears.

Abruptly, the screaming stopped and I moved Carrie's hands gently. Her sensitivity surprised me. I would have thought she would be used to hearing people scream in pain. She listened for a moment, heard nothing, then looked at me.

'He probably fainted,' I said. 'That's best. He won't feel the pain for a while.'

She nodded dully and went back out to whatever she had been doing.

'She always did like him,' remarked Sarah into the silence. 'He kept the children from bothering her when she was little.'

I was surprised. 'Isn't she a few years older than he is?'

'Born the year before him. Children listened to him though. He's white.'

'Is Carrie your daughter?'

Sarah nodded. 'My fourth baby. The only one Marse Tom let me keep.' Her voice trailed away to a whisper.

'You mean he . . . he sold the others?'

'Sold them. First my man died – a tree he was cutting fell on him. Then Marse Tom took my children, all but Carrie. And, bless God, Carrie ain't worth much as the others 'cause she can't talk. People think she ain't got good sense.'

I looked away from her. The expression in her eyes had gone from sadness – she seemed almost ready to cry – to anger. Quiet, almost frightening anger. Her husband dead, three children sold, the fourth defective, and her having to thank God for the defect.

She had reason for more than anger. How amazing that Weylin had sold her children and still kept her to cook his meals. How amazing that he was still alive. I didn't think he would be for long, though, if he found a buyer for Carrie.

As I was thinking, Sarah turned and threw a handful of something into the stew or soup she was cooking. I shook my head. If she ever decided to take her revenge, Weylin would never know what hit him.

'You can peel these potatoes for me,' she said.

I had to think a moment to remember that I had offered my help. I took the large pan of potatoes that she was handing me and a knife and a wooden bowl, and I worked silently, sometimes peeling, and sometimes driving away the bothersome flies. Then I heard Kevin outside calling me. I had to make myself put the potatoes down calmly and cover them with a cloth Sarah had left on the table. Then I went to him without haste, without any sign of the eagerness or relief I felt at having him nearby again. I went to him and he looked at me strangely.

'Are you all right?'

'Fine now.'

He reached for my hand, but I drew back, looking at him. He dropped his hand to his side. 'Come on,' he said wearily. 'Let's go where we can talk.'

He led the way past the main house away from the slave cabins and other buildings, away from the small slave children who chased each other and shouted and didn't understand yet that they were slaves.

We found a huge oak with branches thick as separate trees spread wide to shade a large area. A handsome lonely old tree. We sat beside it putting it between ourselves and the house. I settled close to Kevin, relaxing, letting go of tension I had hardly been aware of. We said nothing for a while, as he leaned back and seemed to let go of tensions of his own.

Finally, he said, 'There are so many really fascinating times we could have gone back to visit.'

I laughed without humor. 'I can't think of any time I'd like to go back to. But of all of them, this must be one of the most dangerous – for me anyway.'

'Not while I'm with you.'

I glanced at him gratefully.

'Why did you try to stop me from coming?'

'I was afraid for you.'

'For me!'

'At first, I didn't know why. I just had the feeling you might be hurt trying to come with me. Then when you were here, I realized that you probably couldn't get back without me. That means if we're separated, you're stranded here for years, maybe for good.'

He drew a deep breath and shook his head. 'There wouldn't be anything good about that.'

'Stay close to me. If I call, come quick.'

He nodded, and after a while said, 'I could survive here, though, if I had to. I mean if . . .'

'Kevin, no ifs. Please.'

'I only mean I wouldn't be in the danger you would be in.'

'No.' But he'd be in another kind of danger. A place like this would endanger him in a way I didn't want to talk to him about. If he was stranded here for years, some part of this place would rub off on him. No large part, I knew. But if he survived here, it would be because he managed to tolerate the life here. He wouldn't have to take part in it, but he would have to keep quiet about it. Free speech and press hadn't done too well in the ante bellum South. Kevin wouldn't do too well either. The place, the time would either kill him outright or mark him somehow. I didn't like either possibility.

'Dana.'

I looked at him.

'Don't worry. We arrived together and we'll leave together.'

I didn't stop worrying, but I smiled and changed the subject. 'How's Rufus? I heard him screaming.'

'Poor kid. I was glad when he passed out. The doctor gave

him some opium, but the pain seemed to reach him right through it. I had to help hold him.'

'Opium . . . will he be all right?'

'The doctor thought so. Although I don't know how much a doctor's opinion is worth in this time.'

'I hope he's right. I hope Rufus has used up all his bad luck just in getting the set of parents he's stuck with.'

Kevin lifted one arm and turned it to show me a set of long bloody scratches.

'Margaret Weylin,' I said softly.

'She shouldn't have been there,' he said. 'When she finished with me, she started on the doctor. "Stop hurting my baby!"'

I shook my head. 'What are we going to do, Kevin? Even if these people were sane, we couldn't stay here among them.'

'Yes we can.'

I turned to stare at him.

'I made up a story for Weylin to explain why we were here – and why we were broke. He offered me a job.'

'Doing what?'

'Tutoring your little friend. Seems he doesn't read or write any better than he climbs trees.'

'But . . . doesn't he go to school?'

'Not while that leg is healing. And his father doesn't want him to fall any farther behind than he already is.'

'Is he behind others his age?'

'Weylin seemed to think so. He didn't come right out and say it, but I think he's afraid the kid isn't very bright.'

'I'm surprised he cares one way or the other, and I think he's wrong. But for once Rufus's bad luck is our good luck. I doubt that we'll be here long enough for you to collect any of your salary, but at least while we're here, we'll have food and shelter.'

'That's what I thought when I accepted.'

'And what about me?'

'You?'

'Weylin didn't say anything about me?'

'No. Why should he? If I stay here, he knows you stay too.'

'Yes.' I smiled. 'You're right. If you didn't remember me in your bargaining, why should he? I'll bet he won't forget me though when he has work that needs to be done.'

'Wait a minute, you don't have to work for him. You're not supposed to belong to him.'

'No, but I'm here. And I'm supposed to be a slave. What's a slave for, but to work? Believe me, he'll find something for me to do – or he would if I didn't plan to find my own work before he gets around to me.'

He frowned. 'You want to work?'

'I want to . . . I have to make a place for myself here. That means work. I think everyone here, black and white, will resent me if I don't work. And I need friends. I need all the friends I can make here, Kevin. You might not be with me when I come here again. If I come here again.'

'And unless that kid gets a lot more careful, you will come here again.'

I sighed. 'It looks that way.'

'I hate to think of your working for these people.' He shook his head. 'I hate to think of you playing the part of a slave at all.'

'We knew I'd have to do it.'

He said nothing.

'Call me away from them now and then, Kevin. Just to remind them that whatever I am, they don't own me . . . yet.'

He shook his head again angrily in what looked like a refusal, but I knew he'd do it.

'What lies did you tell Weylin about us?' I asked him. 'The way people ask questions around here, we'd better make sure we're both telling the same story.'

For several seconds, he said nothing.

'Kevin?'

He took a deep breath. 'I'm supposed to be a writer from New York,' he said finally. 'God help us if we meet any New Yorkers. I'm traveling through the South doing research for a book. I have no money because I drank with the wrong people

82

a few days ago and was robbed. All I have left is you. I bought you before I was robbed because you could read and write. I thought you could help me in my work as well as be of use otherwise.'

'Did he believe that?'

'It's possible that he did. He was already pretty sure you could read and write. That's one reason he seemed so suspicious and mistrustful. Educated slaves aren't popular around here.'

I shrugged. 'So Nigel has been telling me.'

'Weylin doesn't like the way you talk. I don't think he's had much education himself, and he resents you. I don't think he'll bother you – I wouldn't stay here if I did. But keep out of his way as much as you can.'

'Gladly. I plan to fit myself into the cookhouse if I can. I'm going to tell Sarah you want me to learn how to cook for you.'

He gave a short laugh. 'I'd better tell you the rest of the story I told Weylin. If Sarah hears it all, she might teach you how to put a little poison in my food.'

I think I jumped.

'Weylin was warning me that it was dangerous to keep a slave like you – educated, maybe kidnapped from a free state – as far north as this. He said I ought to sell you to some trader heading for Georgia or Louisiana before you ran away and I lost my investment. That gave me the idea to tell him I planned to sell you in Louisiana because that was where my journey ended – and I'd heard I could make a nice profit on you down there.

'That seemed to please him and he told me I was right – prices were better in Louisiana if I could hold on to you until I got you there. So I said educated or not, you weren't likely to run away from me because I'd promised to take you back to New York with me and set you free. I told him you didn't really want to leave me right now anyway. He got the idea.'

'You make yourself sound disgusting.'

'I know. I think I was trying to at the end – trying to see whether anything I did to you could make me someone he wouldn't want anywhere near his kid. I think he did cool a little toward me when I said I'd promised you freedom, but he didn't say anything.'

'What were you trying to do? Lose the job you'd just gotten?'

'No, but while I was talking to him, all I could think was that you might be coming back here alone someday. I kept trying to find the humanity in him to reassure myself that you would be all right.'

'Oh, he's human enough. If he were of a little higher social class, he might even have been disgusted enough with your bragging not to want you around. But he wouldn't have had the right to stop you from betraying me. I'm your private property. He'd respect that.'

'You call that human? I'm going to do all I can to see that you never come here alone again.'

I leaned back against the tree, watching him. 'Just in case I do, Kevin, let's take out some insurance.'

'What?'

'Let me help you with Rufus as much as I can. Let's see what we can do to keep him from growing up into a red-haired version of his father.'

5

But for three days I didn't see Rufus. Nor did anything happen to bring on the dizziness that would tell me I was going home at last. I helped Sarah as well as I could. She seemed to warm up to me a little and she was patient with my ignorance of cooking. She taught me and saw to it that I ate better. No more corn meal mush once she realized I didn't like it. ('Why didn't you say something?' she asked me.) Under her direction, I spent God knows how long beating biscuit dough with a hatchet on a well-worn tree stump. ('Not so hard! You ain't driving nails. Regular, like this . . .') I cleaned and plucked a chicken, prepared vegetables, kneaded bread dough, and when Sarah was weary of me, helped Carrie and the other house servants with their work. I kept Kevin's room clean. I brought him hot water to wash and shave with, and I washed in his room. It was the only place I could go for privacy. I kept my canvas bag there and went there to avoid Margaret Weylin when she came rubbing her fingers over dustless furniture and looking under rugs on well-swept floors. Differences be damned, I did know how to sweep and dust no matter what century it was. Margaret Weylin complained because she couldn't find anything to complain about. That, she made painfully clear to me the day she threw scalding hot coffee at me, screaming that I had brought it to her cold.

So I hid from her in Kevin's room. It was my refuge. But it was not my sleeping place.

I had been given sleeping space in the attic where most of the house servants slept. It apparently never occurred to anyone that I should sleep in Kevin's room. Weylin knew what kind of relationship Kevin was supposed to have with me, and he made it clear that he didn't care. But our sleeping arrangement told us that he expected discretion – or we assumed it did. We co-operated for three days. On the fourth day, Kevin caught me on my way out to the cookhouse and took me to the oak tree again.

'Are you having trouble with Margaret Weylin?' he asked.

'Nothing I can't handle,' I said, surprised. 'Why?'

'I heard a couple of the house servants talking, just saying vaguely that there was trouble. I thought I should find out for sure.'

I shrugged, said, 'I think she resents me because Rufus likes me. She probably doesn't want to share her son with anyone. Heaven help him when he gets a little older and tries to break away. Also, I don't think Margaret likes educated slaves any better than her husband does.'

'I see. I was right about him, by the way. He can barely read and write. And she's not much better.' He turned to face me squarely. 'Did she throw a pot of hot coffee on you?'

I looked away. 'It doesn't matter. Most of it missed anyway.'

'Why didn't you tell me? She could have hurt you.'

'She didn't.'

'I don't think we should give her another chance.'

I looked at him. 'What do you want to do?'

'Get out of here. We don't need money badly enough for you to put up with whatever she plans to do next.'

'No, Kevin. I had a reason for not telling you about the coffee.'

'I'm wondering what else you haven't told me.'

'Nothing important.' My mind went back over some of Margaret's petty insults. 'Nothing important enough to make me leave.'

'But why? There's no reason for . . .'

'Yes there is. I've thought about it, Kevin. It isn't the money that I care about, or even having a roof over my head. I think we can survive here together no matter what. But I don't think I have much chance of surviving here alone. I've told you that.'

'You won't be alone. I'll see to it.'

'You'll try. Maybe that will be enough. I hope so. But if it isn't, if I do have to come here alone, I'll have a better chance of surviving if I stay here now and work on the insurance we talked about. Rufus. He'll probably be old enough to have some authority when I come again. Old enough to help me. I want him to have as many good memories of me as I can give him now.'

'He might not remember you past the day you leave here.'

'He'll remember.'

'It still might not work. After all, his environment will be influencing him every day you're gone. And from what I've heard, it's common in this time for the master's children to be on nearly equal terms with the slaves. But maturity is supposed to put both in their "places."'

'Sometimes it doesn't. Even here, not all children let themselves be molded into what their parents want them to be.'

'You're gambling. Hell, you're gambling against history.'

'What else can I do? I've got to try, Kevin, and if trying

means taking small risks and putting up with small humiliations now so that I can survive later, I'll do it.'

He drew a deep breath and let it out in a near whistle. 'Yeah. I guess I don't blame you. I don't like it, but I don't blame you.'

I put my head on his shoulder. 'I don't like it either. God, I hate it! That woman is priming herself for a nervous breakdown. I just hope she doesn't have it while I'm here.'

Kevin shifted his position a little and I sat up. 'Let's forget about Margaret for a moment,' he said. 'I also wanted to talk to you about that . . . that place where you sleep.'

'Oh.'

'Yes, oh. I finally got up to see it. A rag pallet on the floor, Dana!'

'Did you see anything else up there?'

'What? What else should I have seen?'

'A lot of rag pallets on the floor. And a couple of corn-shuck mattresses. I'm not being treated any worse than any other house servant, Kevin, and I'm doing better than the field hands. Their pallets are on the ground. Their cabins don't even have floors, and most of them are full of fleas.'

There was a long silence. Finally, he sighed. 'I can't do anything for the others,' he said, 'but I want you out of that attic. I want you with me.'

I sat up and stared down at my hands. 'You don't know how I've wanted to be with you. I keep imagining myself waking up at home some morning – alone.'

'Not likely. Not unless something threatens you or endangers you during the night.'

'You don't know that for sure. Your theory could be wrong. Maybe there's some kind of limit on how long I can stay here. Maybe a bad dream would be enough to send me home. Maybe anything.'

'Maybe I should test my theory.'

That stopped me. I realized he was talking about endangering me himself, or at least making me believe my life was in danger – scaring the hell out of me. Scaring me home. Maybe.

I swallowed. 'That might be a good idea, but I don't think you should have mentioned it to me – warned me. Besides . . . I'm not sure you could scare me enough. I trust you.'

He covered one of my hands with his own. 'You can go on trusting me. I won't hurt you.'

'But . . .'

'I don't have to hurt you. I can arrange something that will scare you before you have time to think about it. I can handle it.'

I accepted that, began to think maybe he really could get us home. 'Kevin, wait until Rufus's leg is healed.'

'So long?' he protested. 'Six weeks, maybe more. Hell, in a society as backward as this, who knows whether the leg will heal at all?'

'Whatever happens, the boy will live. He still has to father a child. And that means he'll probably have time to call me here again, with or without you. Give me the chance I need, Kevin, to reach him and make a haven for myself here.'

'All right,' he said sighing. 'We'll wait awhile. But you won't do your waiting in that attic. You're moving into my room tonight.'

I thought about that. 'All right. Getting you home with me when I go is the one thing more important to me than staying with Rufus. It's worth getting kicked off the plantation for.'

'Don't worry about that. Weylin doesn't care what we do.'

'But Margaret will care. I've seen her using that limited reading ability of hers on her Bible. I suspect that in her own way, she's a fairly moral woman.'

'You want to know how moral she is?'

His tone made me frown. 'What do you mean?'

'If she chases me any harder, she and I will wind up playing a scene from that Bible she reads. The scene between Potiphar's wife and Joseph.'

I swallowed. *That woman!* But I could see her in my mind's eye. Long thick red hair piled high on her head, fine smooth skin. Whatever her emotional problems, she wasn't ugly.

'I'm moving in tonight, all right,' I said.

He smiled. 'If we're quiet about it, they might not even bother to notice. Hell, I saw three little kids playing in the dirt back there who look more like Weylin than Rufus does. Margaret's had a lot of practice at not noticing.'

I knew which children he meant. They had different mothers, but there was a definite family resemblance between them. I'd seen Margaret Weylin slap one of them hard across the face. The child had done nothing more than toddle into her path. If she was willing to punish a child for her husband's sins, would she be any less willing to punish me if she knew that I was where she wanted to be with Kevin? I tried not to think about it.

'We still might have to leave,' I said. 'No matter what these people have to accept from each other, they might not be willing to tolerate "immorality" from us.'

He shrugged. 'If we have to leave, we leave. There's a limit to what you should put up with even to get your chance with the boy. We'll work our way to Baltimore. I should be able to get some kind of job there.'

'If we go to a city, how about Philadelphia?'

'Philadelphia?'

'Because it's in Pennsylvania. If we leave here, let it be for a free state.'

'Oh. Yes, I should have thought of that myself. Look . . . Dana, we might have to go to one of the free states, anyway.' He hesitated. 'I mean if it turns out we can't get home the way we think we can. I'll probably become an unnecessary expense to Weylin when Rufus's leg heals. Then we'd have to make a home for ourselves somewhere. That probably won't happen, but it's a possibility.'

I nodded.

'Now let's go get whatever belongs to you out of that attic.' He stood up. 'And, Dana, Rufus says his mother is going out visiting today. He'd like to see you while she's gone.'

'Why didn't you tell me sooner? A start finally!'

Later that day, as I was mixing some corn-bread batter for

89

Sarah, Carrie came to get me. She made a sign to Sarah that I had already learned to understand. She wiped the side of her face with one hand as though rubbing something off. Then she pointed to me.

'Dana,' said Sarah over her shoulder, 'one of the white folks wants you. Go with Carrie.'

I went. Carrie led me up to Rufus's room, knocked, and left me there. I went in and found Rufus in bed with his leg sandwiched between the two boards of a wooden splint and held straight by a device of rope and cast iron. The iron weight looked like something borrowed from Sarah's kitchen – a heavy little hooked thing I'd once seen her hang meat on to roast. But it apparently served just as well to keep Rufus's leg in traction.

'How are you feeling?' I asked as I sat down in the chair beside his bed.

'It doesn't hurt as much as it did,' he said. 'I guess it's getting well. Kevin said . . . Do you care if I call him Kevin?'

'No, I think he wants you to.'

'I have to call him Mr Franklin when Mama is here. Anyway, he said you're working with Aunt Sarah.'

Aunt Sarah? Well, that was better than Mammy Sarah, I supposed. 'I'm learning her way of cooking.'

'She's a good cook, but . . . does she hit you?'

'Of course not.' I laughed.

'She had a girl in there a while back, and she used to hit her. The girl finally asked Daddy to let her go back to the fields. That was right after Daddy sold Aunt Sarah's boys, though. Aunt Sarah was mad at everybody then.'

'I don't blame her,' I said.

Rufus glanced at the door, then said low-voiced, 'Neither do I. Her boy Jim was my friend. He taught me how to ride when I was little. But Daddy sold him anyway.' He glanced at the door again and changed the subject. 'Dana, can you read?'

'Yes.'

'Kevin said you could. I told Mama, and she said you couldn't.'

I shrugged. 'What do you think?'

He took a leather-bound book from under his pillow. 'Kevin brought me this from downstairs. Would you read it to me?'

I fell in love with Kevin all over again. Here was the perfect excuse for me to spend a lot of time with the boy. The book was *Robinson Crusoe*. I had read it when I was little, and I could remember not really liking it, but not quite being able to put it down. Crusoe had, after all, been on a slave-trading voyage when he was shipwrecked.

I opened the book with some apprehension, wondering what archaic spelling and punctuation I would face. I found the expected f's for s's and a few other things that didn't turn up as often, but I got used to them very quickly. And I began to get into *Robinson Crusoe*. As a kind of castaway myself, I was happy to escape into the fictional world of someone else's trouble.

I read and read and drank some of the water Rufus's mother had left for him, and read some more. Rufus seemed to enjoy it. I didn't stop until I thought he was falling asleep. But even then, as I put the book down, he opened his eyes and smiled.

'Nigel said your mother was a school teacher.'

'She was.'

'I like the way you read. It's almost like being there watching everything happen.'

'Thank you.'

'There's a lot more books downstairs.'

'I've seen them.' I had also wondered about them. The Weylins didn't seem to be the kind of people who would have a library.

'They belonged to Miss Hannah,' explained Rufus obligingly. 'Daddy was married to her before he married Mama, but she died. This place used to be hers. He said she read so much that before he married Mama, he made sure she didn't like to read.'

'What about you?'

He moved uncomfortably. 'Reading's too much trouble. Mr Jennings said I was too stupid to learn anyway.'

'Who's Mr Jennings?'

'He's the schoolmaster.'

'Is he?' I shook my head in disgust. 'He shouldn't be. Listen, do you think you're stupid?'

'No.' A small hesitant no. 'But I read as good as Daddy does already. Why should I have to do more than that?'

'You don't have to. You can stay just the way you are. Of course, that would give Mr Jennings the satisfaction of thinking he was right about you. Do you like him?'

'Nobody likes him.'

'Don't be so eager to satisfy him then. And what about the boys you go to school with? It is just boys, isn't it – no girls?'

'Yeah.'

'Well look at the advantage they're going to have over you when you grow up. They'll know more than you. They'll be able to cheat you if they want to. Besides,' I held up *Robinson Crusoe*, 'look at the pleasure you'll miss.'

He grinned. 'Not with you here. Read some more.'

'I don't think I'd better. It's getting late. Your mother will be home soon.'

'No she won't. Read.'

I sighed. 'Rufe, your mother doesn't like me. I think you know that.'

He looked away. 'We have a little more time,' he said. 'Maybe you'd better not read though. I forget to listen for her when you read.'

I handed him the book. 'You read me a few lines.'

He accepted the book, looked at it as though it were his enemy. After a moment, he began to read haltingly. Some words stopped him entirely and I had to help. After two painful paragraphs, he stopped and shut the book in disgust. 'You can't even tell it's the same book when I read it,' he said.

'Let Kevin teach you,' I said. 'He doesn't believe you're stupid, and neither do I. You'll learn all right.' Unless he really did have some kind of problem – poor vision or some learning disability that people in this time would see as stubbornness or stupidity. Unless. What did I know about teaching children? All

92

I could do was hope the boy had as much potential as I thought he did.

I got up to go – then sat down again, remembering another unanswered question. 'Rufe, what ever happened to Alice?'

'Nothing.' He looked surprised.

'I mean . . . the last time I saw her, her father had just been beaten because he went to see her and her mother.'

'Oh. Well, Daddy was afraid he'd run off, so he sold him to a trader.'

'Sold him . . . does he still live around here?'

'No, the trader was headed south. To Georgia, I think.'

'Oh God.' I sighed. 'Are Alice and her mother still here?'

'Sure. I still see them – when I can walk.'

'Did they have any trouble because I was with them that night?' That was as near as I dared to come to asking what had happened to my would-be enslaver.

'I don't think so. Alice said you came and went away quick.'

'I went home. I can't tell when I'm going to do that. It just happens.'

'Back to California?'

'Yes.'

'Alice didn't see you go. She said you just went into the woods and didn't come back.'

'That's good. Seeing me vanish would have frightened her.' Alice was keeping her mouth closed too then – or her mother was. Alice might not know what happened. Clearly there were things that even a friendly young white could not be told. On the other hand, if the patroller himself hadn't spread the word about me or taken revenge on Alice and her mother, maybe he was dead. My blow could have killed him, or someone could have finished him after I went home. If they had, I didn't want to know about it.

I got up again. 'I have to go, Rufe. I'll see you again whenever I can.'

'Dana?'

I looked down at him.

93

'I told Mama who you were. I mean that you were the one who saved me from the river. She said it wasn't true, but I think she really believed me. I told her because I thought it might make her like you better.'

'It hasn't that I've noticed.'

'I know.' He frowned. 'Why doesn't she like you? Did you do something to her?'

'Not likely! After all, what would happen to me if I did something to her?'

'Yeah. But why doesn't she like you?'

'You'll have to ask her.'

'She won't tell me.' He looked up solemnly. 'I keep thinking you're going to go home – that somebody will come and tell me you and Kevin are gone. I don't want you to go. But I don't want you to get hurt here either.'

I said nothing.

'You be careful,' he said softly.

I nodded and left the room. Just as I reached the stairs, Tom Weylin came out of his bedroom.

'What are you doing up here?' he demanded.

'Visiting Mister Rufus,' I said. 'He asked to see me.'

'You were reading to him!'

Now I knew how he happened to come out just in time to catch me. He had been eavesdropping, for Godsake. What had he expected to hear? Or rather, what had he heard that he shouldn't have? About Alice, perhaps. What would he make of that? For a moment my mind raced, searching for excuses, explanations. Then I realized I wouldn't need them. I would have met him outside Rufus's door if he had stayed long enough to hear about Alice. He had probably heard me addressing Rufus a little too familiarly. Nothing worse. I had deliberately not said anything damaging about Margaret because I thought her own attitude would damage her more in her son's eyes than anything I could say. I made myself face Weylin calmly.

'Yes, I was reading to him,' I admitted. 'He asked me to do that too. I think he was bored lying in there with nothing to do.'

94

'I didn't ask you what you thought,' he said.

I said nothing.

He walked me farther from Rufus's door, then stopped and turned to look hard at me. His eyes went over me like a man sizing up a woman for sex, but I got no message of lust from him. His eyes, I noticed, not for the first time, were almost as pale as Kevin's. Rufus and his mother had bright green eyes. I liked the green better, somehow.

'How old are you?' he asked.

'Twenty-six, sir.'

'You say that like you're sure.'

'Yes, sir. I am.'

'What year were you born?'

'Seventeen ninety-three.' I had figured that out days ago thinking that it wasn't a part of my personal history I should hesitate over if someone asked. At home, a person who hesitated over his birthdate was probably about to lie. As I spoke though, I realized that here, a person might hesitate over his birthdate simply because he didn't know it. Sarah didn't know hers.

'Twenty-six then,' said Weylin. 'How many children have you had?'

'None.' I kept my face impassive, but I couldn't keep myself from wondering where these questions were leading.

'No children by now?' He frowned. 'You must be barren then.'

I said nothing. I wasn't about to explain anything to him. My fertility was none of his business, anyway.

He stared at me a little longer, making me angry and uncomfortable, but I concealed my feelings as well as I could.

'You like children though, don't you?' he asked. 'You like my boy.'

'Yes, sir, I do.'

'Can you cipher too – along with your reading and writing?'

'Yes, sir.'

'How'd you like to be the one to do the teaching?'

'Me?' I managed to frown . . . managed not to laugh aloud with relief. Tom Weylin wanted to buy me. In spite of all his warnings to Kevin of the dangers of owning educated, Northern-born slaves, he wanted to buy me. I pretended not to understand. 'But that's Mr Franklin's job.'

'Could be your job.'

'Could it?'

'I could buy you. Then you'd live here instead of traveling around the country without enough to eat or a place to sleep.'

I lowered my eyes. 'That's for Mr Franklin to say.'

'I know it is, but how do you feel about it?'

'Well . . . no offense, Mr Weylin, I'm glad we stopped here, and as I said, I like your son. But I'd rather stay with Mr Franklin.'

He gave me an unmistakable look of pity. 'If you do, girl, you'll live to regret it.' He turned and walked away.

I stared after him believing in spite of myself that he really felt sorry for me.

That night I told Kevin what had happened, and he wondered too.

'Be careful, Dana,' he said, unwittingly echoing Rufus. 'Be as careful as you can.'

6

I was careful. As the days passed, I got into the habit of being careful. I played the slave, minded my manners probably more than I had to because I wasn't sure what I could get away with. Not much, as it turned out.

Once I was called over to the slave cabins – the quarter – to watch Weylin punish a field hand for the crime of answering back. Weylin ordered the man stripped naked and tied to the trunk of a dead tree. As this was being done – by other slaves – Weylin stood whirling his whip and biting his thin lips. Suddenly, he brought the whip down across the slave's back.

The slave's body jerked and strained against its ropes. I watched the whip for a moment wondering whether it was like the one Weylin had used on Rufus years before. If it was, I understood completely why Margaret Weylin had taken the boy and fled. The whip was heavy and at least six feet long, and I wouldn't have used it on anything living. It drew blood and screams at every blow. I watched and listened and longed to be away. But Weylin was making an example of the man. He had ordered all of us to watch the beating – all the slaves. Kevin was in the main house somewhere, probably not even aware of what was happening.

The whipping served its purpose as far as I was concerned. It scared me, made me wonder how long it would be before I made a mistake that would give someone reason to whip me. Or had I already made that mistake?

I had moved into Kevin's room, after all. And though that would be perceived as Kevin's doing, I could be made to suffer for it. The fact that the Weylins didn't seem to notice my move gave me no real comfort. Their lives and mine were so separate that it might take them several days to realize that I had abandoned my place in the attic. I always got up before they did to get water and live coals from the cookhouse to start Kevin's fire. Matches had apparently not been invented yet. Neither Sarah nor Rufus had ever heard of them.

By now, the manservant Weylin had assigned to Kevin ignored him completely, and Kevin and his room were left to me. It took us twice as long to get a fire started, and it took me longer to carry water up and down the stairs, but I didn't care. The jobs I had assigned myself gave me legitimate reason for going in and out of Kevin's room at all hours, and they kept me from being assigned more disagreeable work. Most important to me, though, they gave me a chance to preserve a little of 1976 amid the slaves and slaveholders.

After washing and watching Kevin bloody his face with the straight razor he had borrowed from Weylin, I would go down to help Sarah with breakfast. Whole mornings went by without my seeing either of the Weylins. At night, I helped clean up after supper and prepare for the next day. So, like Sarah and Carrie, I rose before the Weylins and went to bed after them. That gave me several days of peace before Margaret Weylin discovered that she had another reason to dislike me.

She cornered me one day as I swept the library. If she had walked in two minutes earlier, she would have caught me reading a book. 'Where did you sleep last night?' she demanded in the strident, accusing voice she reserved for slaves.

I straightened to face her, rested my hands on the broom. How lovely it would have been to say, *None of your business, bitch!* Instead, I spoke softly, respectfully. 'In Mr Franklin's room, ma'am.' I didn't bother to lie because all the house servants knew. It might even have been one of them who alerted Margaret. So now what would happen?

Margaret slapped me across the face.

I stood very still, gazed down at her with frozen calm. She was three or four inches shorter than I was and proportionately smaller. Her slap hadn't hurt me much. It had simply made me want to hurt her. Only my memory of the whip kept me still.

'You filthy black whore!' she shouted. 'This is a Christian house!'

I said nothing.

'I'll see you sent to the quarter where you belong!'

Still I said nothing. I looked at her.

'I won't have you in my house!' She took a step back from me. 'You stop looking at me that way!' She took another step back.

It occurred to me that she was a little afraid of me. I was an unknown, after all – an unpredictable new slave. And maybe I was a little too silent. Slowly, deliberately, I turned my back and went on sweeping.

I kept an eye on her, though, without seeming to. After all, she was as unpredictable as I was. She could pick up a candlestick or a vase and hit me with it. And whip or no whip, I wasn't going to stand passively and let her really hurt me.

But she made no move toward me. Instead, she turned and rushed away. It was a hot day, muggy and uncomfortable. No one else was moving very fast except to wave away flies. But Margaret Weylin still rushed everywhere. She had little or nothing to do. Slaves kept her house clean, did much of her sewing, all her cooking and washing. Carrie even helped her put her clothes on and take them off. So Margaret supervised – ordered people to do work they were already doing, criticized their slowness and laziness even when they were quick and industrious, and in general, made trouble. Weylin had married a poor, uneducated, nervous, startlingly pretty young woman who was determined to be the kind of person she thought of as a lady. That meant she didn't do 'menial' work, or any work at all, apparently. I had no one to compare her to except her guests who seemed, at least, to be calmer. But I suspected that most women of her time found enough to do to keep themselves comfortably busy whether they thought of themselves as 'ladies' or not. Margaret, in her boredom, simply rushed around and made a nuisance of herself.

I finished my work in the library, wondering all the while whether Margaret had gone to her husband about me. Her husband, I feared. I remembered the expression on his face when he had beaten the field hand. It hadn't been gleeful or angry or even particularly interested. He could have been chopping wood. He wasn't sadistic, but he didn't shrink from his 'duties' as master of the plantation. He would beat me bloody if he thought I had given him reason, and Kevin might not even find out until too late.

I went up to Kevin's room, but he wasn't there. I heard him when I passed Rufus's room and I would have gone in, but a moment later, I heard Margaret's voice. Repelled, I went back downstairs and out to the cookhouse.

Sarah and Carrie were alone when I went in, and I was glad of that. Sometimes old people and children lounged there, or house servants or even field hands stealing a few moments of leisure. I liked to listen to them talk sometimes and fight my way through their accents to find out more about how they survived lives of slavery. Without knowing it, they prepared me to survive. But now I wanted only Sarah and Carrie. I could say what I felt around them, and it wouldn't get back to either of the Weylins.

'Dana,' Sarah greeted me, 'you be careful. I spoke for you today. I don't want you making me out to be a liar!'

I frowned. 'Spoke for me? To Miss Margaret?'

Sarah gave a short harsh laugh. 'No! You know I don't say no more to her than I can help. She's got her house, and I got my kitchen.'

I smiled and my own trouble receded a little. Sarah was right. Margaret Weylin kept out of her way. Talk between them was brief and confined usually to meal planning.

'Why do you dislike her so if she doesn't bother you?' I asked.

Sarah gave me the look of silent rage that I had not seen since my first day on the plantation. 'Whose idea you think it was to sell my babies?'

'Oh.' She had not mentioned her lost children since that first day either.

'She wanted new furniture, new china dishes, fancy things you see in that house now. What she had was good enough for Miss Hannah, and Miss Hannah was a real lady. Quality. But it wasn't good enough for white-trash Margaret. So she made Marse Tom sell my three boys to get money to buy things she didn't even need!'

'Oh.' I couldn't think of anything else to say. My trouble seemed to shrink and become not worth mentioning. Sarah was silent for a while, her hands kneading bread dough automatically, maybe with a little more vigor than necessary. Finally she spoke again.

'It was Marse Tom I spoke to for you.'

I jumped. 'Am I in trouble?'

'Not by anything I said. He just wanted to know how you work and are you lazy. I told him you wasn't lazy. Told him

100

you didn't know how to do some things – and, girl, you come here not knowing how to do *nothing*, but I didn't tell him that. I said if you don't know how to do something, you find out. And you work. I tell you to do something, I know it's going to be done. Marse Tom say he might buy you.'

'Mr Franklin won't sell me.'

She lifted her head a little and literally looked down her nose at me. 'No. Guess he won't. Anyway, Miss Margaret don't want you here.'

I shrugged.

'Bitch,' muttered Sarah monotonously. Then, 'Well, greedy and mean as she is, at least she don't bother Carrie much.'

I looked at the mute girl eating stew and corn bread left over from the table of the whites. 'Doesn't she, Carrie?'

Carrie shook her head and kept eating.

'Course,' said Sarah, turning away from the bread dough, 'Carrie don't have nothing Miss Margaret wants.'

I just looked at her.

'You're caught between,' she said. 'You know that don't you?'

'One man ought to be enough for her.'

'Don't matter what ought to be. Matters what is. Make him let you sleep in the attic again.'

'Make him!'

'Girl . . .' She smiled a little. 'I see you and him together sometimes when you think nobody's looking. You can make him do just about anything you want him to do.'

Her smile surprised me. I would have expected her to be disgusted with me – or with Kevin.

'Fact,' she continued, 'if you got any sense, you'll try to get him to free you now while you still young and pretty enough for him to listen.'

I looked at her appraisingly – large dark eyes set in a full unlined face several shades lighter than my own. She had been pretty herself not long ago. She was still an attractive woman. I spoke to her softly. 'Were you sensible, Sarah? Did you try when you were younger?'

101

She stared hard at me, her large eyes suddenly narrowed. Finally, she walked away without answering.

7

I didn't move to the quarter. I took some cookhouse advice that I'd once heard Luke give to Nigel. 'Don't argue with white folks,' he had said. 'Don't tell them "no." Don't let them see you mad. Just say "yes, sir." Then go 'head and do what you want to do. Might have to take a whippin' for it later on, but if you want it bad enough, the whippin' won't matter much.'

There were a few whip marks on Luke's back, and I'd twice heard Tom Weylin swear to give them company. But he hadn't. And Luke went about his business, doing pretty much as he pleased. His business was keeping the field hands in line. Called the driver, he was a kind of black overseer. And he kept this relatively high position in spite of his attitude. I decided to develop a similar attitude – though with less risk to myself, I thought. I had no intention of taking a whipping if I could avoid it, and I was sure Kevin could protect me if he was nearby when I needed him.

Anyway, I ignored Margaret's ravings and continued to disgrace her Christian house.

And nothing happened.

Tom Weylin was up early one morning and he caught me stumbling, still half-asleep, out of Kevin's room. I froze, then made myself relax.

'Morning, Mr Weylin.'

He almost smiled – came as near to smiling as I'd ever seen. And he winked.

That was all. I knew then that if Margaret got me kicked out, it wouldn't be for doing a thing as normal as sleeping with my master. And somehow, that disturbed me. I felt almost as though I really was doing something shameful, happily playing whore for my supposed owner. I went away feeling uncomfortable, vaguely ashamed.

102

Time passed. Kevin and I became more a part of the household, familiar, accepted, accepting. That disturbed me too when I thought about it. How easily we seemed to acclimatize. Not that I wanted us to have trouble, but it seemed as though we should have had a harder time adjusting to this particular segment of history – adjusting to our places in the household of a slaveholder. For me, the work could be hard, but was usually more boring than physically wearing. And Kevin complained of boredom, and of having to be sociable with a steady stream of ignorant pretentious guests who visited the Weylin house. But for drop-ins from another century, I thought we had had a remarkably easy time. And I was perverse enough to be bothered by the ease.

'This could be a great time to live in,' Kevin said once. 'I keep thinking what an experience it would be to stay in it – go West and watch the building of the country, see how much of the Old West mythology is true.'

'West,' I said bitterly. 'That's where they're doing it to the Indians instead of the blacks!'

He looked at me strangely. He had been doing that a lot lately.

Tom Weylin caught me reading in his library one day. I was supposed to be sweeping and dusting. I looked up, found him watching me, closed the book, put it away, and picked up my dust cloth. My hand was shaking.

'You read to my boy,' he said. 'I let you do that. But that's enough reading for you.'

There was a long silence and I said tardily, 'Yes, sir.'

'In fact, you don't even have to be in here. Tell Carrie to do this room.'

'Yes, sir.'

'And stay away from the books!'

'Yes, sir.'

Hours later in the cookhouse, Nigel asked me to teach him to read.

The request surprised me, then I was ashamed of my surprise.

It seemed such a natural request. Years before, Nigel had been chosen to be Rufus's companion. If Rufus had been a better student, Nigel might already know how to read. As it was, Nigel had learned to do other things. At a husky thirteen, he could shoe a horse, build a cabinet, and plot to escape to Pennsylvania someday. I should have offered to teach him to read long before he asked me.

'You know what's going to happen to both of us if we get caught?' I asked him.

'You scared?' he asked.

'Yes. But that doesn't matter. I'll teach you. I just wanted to be sure you knew what you were getting into.'

He turned away from me, lifted his shirt in the back so that I could see his scars. Then he faced me again. 'I know,' he said.

That same day, I stole a book and began to teach him.

And I began to realize why Kevin and I had fitted so easily into this time. We weren't really in. We were observers watching a show. We were watching history happen around us. And we were actors. While we waited to go home, we humored the people around us by pretending to be like them. But we were poor actors. We never really got into our roles. We never forgot that we were acting.

This was something I tried to explain to Kevin on the day the children broke through my act. It suddenly became very important that he understand.

The day was miserably hot and muggy, full of flies, mosquitoes, and the bad smells of soapmaking, the outhouses, fish someone had caught, unwashed bodies. Everybody smelled, black and white. Nobody washed enough or changed clothes often enough. The slaves worked up a sweat and the whites sweated without working. Kevin and I didn't have enough clothes or any deodorant at all, so often, we smelled too. Surprisingly, we were beginning to get used to it.

Now we were walking together away from the house and the quarter. We weren't heading for our oak tree because by then, if Margaret Weylin saw us there, she sent someone with a job for me. Her husband may have stopped her from throwing me out of the house, but he hadn't stopped her from becoming a worse nuisance than ever. Sometimes Kevin countermanded her orders, claiming that he had work for me. That was how I got a little rest and gave Nigel some extra tutoring. Now, though, we were headed for the woods to spend some time together.

But before we got away from the buildings, we saw a group of slave children gathered around a tree stump. These were the children of the field hands, children too young to be of much use in the fields themselves. Two of them were standing on the wide flat stump while others stood around watching.

'What are they doing?' I asked.

'Playing some game, probably.' Kevin shrugged.

'It looks as though . . .'

'What?'

'Let's get closer. I want to hear what they're saying.'

We approached them from one side so that neither the children on the tree stump nor those on the ground were facing us. They went on with their play as we watched and listened.

'Now here a likely wench,' called the boy on the stump. He gestured toward the girl who stood slightly behind him. 'She cook and wash and iron. Come here, gal. Let the folks see you.' He drew the girl up beside him. 'She young and strong,' he continued. 'She worth plenty money. Two hundred dollars. Who bid two hundred dollars?'

The little girl turned to frown at him. 'I'm worth more than two hundred dollars, Sammy!' she protested. 'You sold Martha for five hundred dollars!'

'You shut your mouth,' said the boy. 'You ain't supposed to say nothing. When Marse Tom bought Mama and me, we didn't say nothing.'

I turned and walked away from the arguing children, feeling tired and disgusted. I wasn't even aware that Kevin was following me until he spoke.

'That's the game I thought they were playing,' he said. 'I've seen them at it before. They play at field work too.'

I shook my head. 'My God, why can't we go home? This place is diseased.'

He took my hand. 'The kids are just imitating what they've seen adults doing,' he said. 'They don't understand . . .'

'They don't have to understand. Even the games they play are preparing them for their future – and that future will come whether they understand it or not.'

'No doubt.'

I turned to glare at him and he looked back calmly. It was a what-do-you-want-me-to-do-about-it kind of look. I didn't say anything because, of course, there was nothing he could do about it.

I shook my head, rubbed my hand across my brow. 'Even knowing what's going to happen doesn't help,' I said. 'I know some of those kids will live to see freedom – after they've slaved away their best years. But by the time freedom comes to them, it will be too late. Maybe it's already too late.'

'Dana, you're reading too much into a kids' game.'

'And you're reading too little into it. Anyway . . . anyway, it's not their game.'

'No.' He glanced at me. 'Look, I won't say I understand how you feel about this because maybe that's something I can't under-stand. But as you said, you know what's going to happen. It already has happened. We're in the middle of history. We surely can't change it. If anything goes wrong, we might have all we can do just to survive it. We've been lucky so far.'

'Maybe.' I drew a deep breath and let it out slowly. 'But I can't close my eyes.'

Kevin frowned thoughtfully. 'It's surprising to me that there's so little to see. Weylin doesn't seem to pay much attention to what his people do, but the work gets done.'

'You think he doesn't pay attention. Nobody calls you out to see the whippings.'

'How many whippings?'

'One that I've seen. One too goddamn many!'

'One is too many, yes, but still, this place isn't what I would have imagined. No overseer. No more work than the people can manage . . .'

'. . . no decent housing,' I cut in. 'Dirt floors to sleep on, food so inadequate they'd all be sick if they didn't keep gardens in what's supposed to be their leisure time and steal from the cookhouse when Sarah lets them. And no rights and the possibility of being mistreated or sold away from their families for any reason – or no reason. Kevin, you don't have to beat people to treat them brutally.'

'Wait a minute,' he said. 'I'm not minimizing the wrong that's being done here. I just . . .'

'Yes you are. You don't mean to be, but you are.' I sat down against a tall pine tree, pulling him down beside me. We were in the woods now. Not far to one side of us was a group of Weylin's slaves who were cutting down trees. We could hear them, but we couldn't see them. I assumed that meant they couldn't see us either – or hear us over the distance and their own noise. I spoke to Kevin again.

'You might be able to go through this whole experience as an observer,' I said. 'I can understand that because most of the time, I'm still an observer. It's protection. It's nineteen seventy-six shielding and cushioning eighteen nineteen for me. But now and then, like with the kids' game, I can't maintain the distance. I'm drawn all the way into eighteen nineteen, and I don't know what to do. I ought to be doing something though. I know that.'

'There's nothing you could do that wouldn't eventually get you whipped or killed!'

I shrugged.

'You . . . you haven't already done anything, have you?'

'Just started to teach Nigel to read and write,' I said. 'Nothing more subversive than that.'

'If Weylin catches you and I'm not around . . .'

'I know. So stay close. The boy wants to learn, and I'm going to teach him.'

He raised one leg against his chest and leaned forward looking at me. 'You think someday he'll write his own pass and head North, don't you?'

'At least he'll be able to.'

'I see Weylin was right about educated slaves.'

I turned to look at him.

'Do a good job with Nigel,' he said quietly. 'Maybe when you're gone, he'll be able to teach others.'

I nodded solemnly.

'I'd bring him in to learn with Rufus if people weren't so good at listening at doors in that house. And Margaret is always wandering in and out.'

'I know. That's why I didn't ask you.' I closed my eyes and saw the children playing their game again. 'The ease seemed so frightening,' I said. 'Now I see why.'

'What?'

'The ease. Us, the children . . . I never realized how easily people could be trained to accept slavery.'

8

I said good-bye to Rufus the day my teaching finally did get me into trouble. I didn't know I was saying good-bye, of course – didn't know what trouble was waiting for me in the cookhouse where I was to meet Nigel. I thought there was trouble enough in Rufus's room.

I was there reading to him. I had been reading to him regularly since his father caught me that first time. Tom Weylin didn't want me reading on my own, but he had ordered me to read to his son. Once he had told Rufus in my presence, 'You ought to be ashamed of yourself! A nigger can read better than you!'

'She can read better than you too,' Rufus had answered.

His father had stared at him coldly, then ordered me out of the room. For a second I was afraid for Rufus, but Tom Weylin left the room with me.

'Don't go to him again until I say you can,' he told me.

Four days passed before he said I could. And again he chastised Rufus before me.

'I'm no schoolmaster,' he said, 'but I'll teach you if you can be taught. I'll teach you respect.'

Rufus said nothing.

'You want her to read to you?'

'Yes, sir.'

'Then you got something to say to me.'

'I . . . I'm sorry, Daddy.'

'Read,' said Weylin to me. He turned and left the room.

'What exactly are you supposed to be sorry for?' I asked when Weylin was gone. I spoke very softly.

'Talking back,' said Rufus. 'He thinks everything I say is talking back. So I don't say very much to him.'

'I see.' I opened the book and began to read.

We had finished *Robinson Crusoe* long ago, and Kevin had chosen a couple of other familiar books from the library. We had already gone through the first, *Pilgrim's Progress*. Now we were working on *Gulliver's Travels*. Rufus's own reading was improving slowly under Kevin's tutoring, but he still enjoyed being read to.

On my last day with him, though, as on a few others, Margaret came in to listen – and to fidget and to fiddle with Rufus's hair and to pet him while I was reading. As usual, Rufus put his head on her lap and accepted her caresses silently. But today, apparently, that was not enough.

'Are you comfortable?' she asked Rufus when I had been reading for a few moments. 'Does your leg hurt?' His leg was not healing as I thought it should have. After nearly two months, he still couldn't walk.

'I feel all right, Mama,' he said.

Suddenly, Margaret twisted around to face me. 'Well?' she demanded.

I had paused in my reading to give her a chance to finish. I lowered my head and began to read again.

About sixty seconds later, she said, 'Baby, you hot? You want me to call Virgie up here to fan you?' Virgie was about ten – one of the small house servants often called to fan the whites, run errands for them, carry covered dishes of food between the cookhouse and the main house, and serve the whites at their table.

'I'm all right, Mama,' said Rufus.

'Why don't you go on?' snapped Margaret at me. 'You're supposed to be here to read, so read!'

I began to read again, biting off the words a little.

'Are you hungry, baby?' asked Margaret a moment later. 'Aunt Sarah's just made a cake. Wouldn't you like a piece?'

I didn't stop this time. I just lowered my voice a little and read automatically, tonelessly.

'I don't know why you want to listen to her,' Margaret said to Rufus. 'She's got a voice like a fly buzzing.'

'I don't want no cake, Mama.'

'You sure? You ought to see the fine white icing Sarah put on it.'

'I want to hear Dana read, that's all.'

'Well, there she is, reading. If you can call it that.'

I let my voice grow progressively softer as they talked.

'I can't hear her with you talking,' Rufus said.

'Baby, all I said was . . .'

'Don't say nothing!' Rufus took his head off her lap. 'Go away and stop bothering me!'

'Rufus!' She sounded hurt rather than angry. And in spite of the situation, this sounded like real disrespect to me. I stopped reading and waited for the explosion. It came from Rufus.

'Go away, Mama!' he shouted. 'Just leave me alone!'

'Be still,' she whispered. 'Baby, you'll make yourself sick.'

Rufus turned his head and looked at her. The expression on his face startled me. For once, the boy looked like a smaller replica of his father. His mouth was drawn into a thin straight line and his eyes were coldly hostile. He spoke quietly now as Weylin sometimes did when he was angry. 'You're making me sick, Mama. Get away from me!'

Margaret got up and dabbed at her eyes. 'I don't see how you can talk to me that way,' she said. 'Just because of some nigger . . .'

Rufus just looked at her, and finally she left the room.

He relaxed against his pillows and closed his eyes. 'I get so tired of her sometimes,' he said.

'Rufe . . .?'

He opened weary, friendly eyes and looked at me. The anger was gone.

'You'd better be careful,' I said. 'What if your mother told your father you talked to her that way?'

'She never tells.' He grinned. 'She'll be back after 'while to bring me a piece of cake with fine white icing.'

'She was crying.'

'She always cries. Read, Dana.'

'Do you talk to her that way often?'

'I have to, or she won't leave me alone. Daddy does it too.'

I took a deep breath, shook my head, and plunged back into *Gulliver's Travels*.

Later, as I left Rufus, I passed Margaret on her way back to his room. Sure enough, she was carrying a large slice of cake on a plate.

I went downstairs and out to the cookhouse to give Nigel his reading lesson.

Nigel was waiting. He already had our book out of its hiding place and was spelling out words to Carrie. That surprised me because I had offered Carrie a chance to learn with him, and she had refused. Now though, the two of them, alone in the cookhouse, were so involved in what they were doing that they didn't even notice me until I shut the door. They looked up then, wide-eyed with fear. But they relaxed when they saw it was only me. I went over to them.

'Do you want to learn?' I asked Carrie.

The girl's fear seemed to return and she glanced at the door.

'Aunt Sarah's afraid for her to learn,' said Nigel. 'Afraid if she learns, she might get caught at it, and then be whipped or sold.'

111

I lowered my head, sighed. The girl couldn't talk, couldn't communicate at all except in the inadequate sign language she had invented – a language even her mother only half-understood. In a more rational society, an ability to write would be of great help to her. But here, the only people who could read her writing would be those who might punish her for being able to write. And Nigel. And Nigel.

I looked from the boy to the girl. 'Shall I teach you, Carrie?' If I did and her mother caught me, I might be in more trouble than if Tom Weylin caught me. I was afraid to teach her both for her sake and for mine. Her mother wasn't a woman I wanted to offend or to hurt, but my conscience wouldn't let me refuse her if she wanted to learn.

Carrie nodded. She wanted to learn all right. She turned away from us for a moment, did something to her dress, then turned back with a small book in her hand. She too had stolen from the library. Her book was a volume of English history illustrated with a few drawings which she pointed out to me.

I shook my head. 'Either hide it or put it back,' I told her. 'It's too hard for you to begin with. The one Nigel and I are using was written for people just starting to learn.' It was an old speller – probably the one Weylin's first wife had been taught from.

Carrie's fingers caressed one of the drawings for a moment. Then she put the book back into her dress.

'Now,' I said, 'find something to do in case your mother comes in. I can't teach you in here. We'll have to find someplace else to meet.'

She nodded, looking relieved, and went over to sweep the other side of the room.

'Nigel,' I said softly when she was gone, 'I surprised you when I came in here, didn't I?'

'Didn't know it was you.'

'Yes. It could have been Sarah, couldn't it?'

He said nothing.

'I teach you in here because Sarah said I could, and because the Weylins never seem to come out here.'

'They don't. They send us out here to tell Sarah what they want. Or to tell her to come to them.'

'So you can learn here, but Carrie can't. We might have trouble no matter how careful we are, but we don't have to ask for it.'

He nodded.

'By the way, what does your father think of my teaching you?'

'I don't know. I didn't tell him you was.'

Oh God. I took a shaky breath. 'But he does know, doesn't he?'

'Aunt Sarah probably told him. He never said nothing to me though.'

If anything went wrong, there would be blacks to take their revenge on me when the whites finished. When would I ever go home? *Would* I ever go home? Or if I had to stay here, why couldn't I just turn these two kids away, turn off my conscience, and be a coward, safe and comfortable?

I took the book from Nigel and handed him my own pencil and a piece of paper from my tablet. 'Spelling test,' I said quietly.

He passed the test. Every word right. To my surprise as well as his, I hugged him. He grinned, half-embarrassed, half-pleased. Then I got up and put his test paper into the hot coals of the hearth. It burst into flames and burned completely. I was always careful about that, and I always hated being careful. I couldn't help contrasting Nigel's lessons with Rufus's. And the contrast made me bitter.

I turned to go back to the table where Nigel was waiting. In that moment, Tom Weylin opened the door and stepped in.

It wasn't supposed to happen. For as long as I had been on the plantation, it had not happened – no white had come into the cookhouse. Not even Kevin. Nigel had just agreed with me that it didn't happen.

But there stood Tom Weylin staring at me. He lowered his gaze a little and frowned. I realized that I was still holding the old speller. I'd gotten up with it in my hand and I hadn't put it down. I even had one finger in it holding my place.

113

I withdrew my finger and let the book close. I was in for a beating now. Where was Kevin? Somewhere inside the house, probably. He might hear me if I screamed – and I would be screaming shortly, anyway. But it would be better if I could just get past Weylin and run into the house.

Weylin stood squarely in front of the door. 'Didn't I tell you I didn't want you reading!'

I said nothing. Clearly, nothing I could say would help. I felt myself trembling, and I tried to be still. I hoped Weylin couldn't see. And I hoped Nigel had had the sense to get the pencil off the table. So far, I was the only one in trouble. If it could just stay that way . . .

'I treated you good,' said Weylin quietly, 'and you pay me back by stealing from me! Stealing my books! Reading!'

He snatched the book from me and threw it on the floor. Then he grabbed me by the arm and dragged me toward the door. I managed to twist around to face Nigel and mouth the words, 'Get Kevin.' I saw Nigel stand up.

Then I was out of the cookhouse. Weylin dragged me a few feet, then pushed me hard. I fell, knocked myself breathless. I never saw where the whip came from, never even saw the first blow coming. But it came – like a hot iron across my back, burning into me through my light shirt, searing my skin . . .

I screamed, convulsed. Weylin struck again and again, until I couldn't have gotten up at gunpoint.

I kept trying to crawl away from the blows, but I didn't have the strength or the coordination to get far. I may have been still screaming or just whimpering, I couldn't tell. All I was really aware of was the pain. I thought Weylin meant to kill me. I thought I would die on the ground there with a mouth full of dirt and blood and a white man cursing and lecturing as he beat me. By then, I almost wanted to die. Anything to stop the pain.

I vomited. And I vomited again because I couldn't move my face away.

I saw Kevin, blurred, but somehow still recognizable. I saw

him running toward me in slow motion, running. Legs churning, arms pumping, yet he hardly seemed to be getting closer.

Suddenly, I realized what was happening and I screamed – I think I screamed. He had to reach me. He had to!

And I passed out.

The Fight

1

We never really moved in together, Kevin and I. I had a sardine-can sized apartment on Crenshaw Boulevard and he had a bigger one on Olympic not too far away. We both had books shelved and stacked and boxed and crowding out the furniture. Together, we would never have fitted into either of our apartments. Kevin did suggest once that I get rid of some of my books so that I'd fit into his place.

'You're out of your mind!' I told him.

'Just some of that book-club stuff that you don't read.'

We were at my apartment then, so I said, 'Let's go to your place and I'll help you decide which of your books you don't read. I'll even help you throw them out.'

He looked at me and sighed, but he didn't say anything else. We just sort of drifted back and forth between our two apartments and I got less sleep than ever. But it didn't seem to bother me as much as it had before. Nothing seemed to bother me much. I didn't love the agency now, but, on the other hand, I didn't kick the furniture in the morning anymore, either.

'Quit,' Kevin told me. 'I'll help you out until you find a better job.'

If I hadn't already loved him by then, that would have done

116

it. But I didn't quit. The independence the agency gave me was shaky, but it was real. It would hold me together until my novel was finished and I was ready to look for something more demanding. When that time came, I could walk away from the agency not owing anybody. My memory of my aunt and uncle told me that even people who loved me could demand more of me than I could give – and expect their demands to be met simply because I owed them.

I knew Kevin wasn't that way. The situation was completely different. But I kept my job.

Then about four months after we'd met, Kevin said, 'How would you feel about getting married?'

I shouldn't have been surprised, but I was. 'You want to marry me?'

'Yeah, don't you want to marry me?' He grinned. 'I'd let you type all my manuscripts.'

I was drying our dinner dishes just then, and I threw the dish towel at him. He really had asked me to do some typing for him three times. I'd done it the first time, grudgingly, not telling him how much I hated typing, how I did all but the final drafts of my stories in longhand. That was why I was with a blue-collar agency instead of a white-collar agency. The second time he asked, though, I told him, and I refused. He was annoyed. The third time when I refused again, he was angry. He said if I couldn't do him a little favor when he asked, I could leave. So I went home.

When I rang his doorbell the next day after work, he looked surprised. 'You came back.'

'Didn't you want me to?'

'Well . . . sure. Will you type those pages for me now?'

'No.'

'Damnit, Dana . . .!'

I stood waiting for him to either shut the door or let me in. He let me in.

And now he wanted to marry me.

I looked at him. Just looked, for a long moment. Then I looked away because I couldn't think while I was watching him. 'You, uh . . . don't have any relatives or anything who'll give you a hard time about me, do you?' As I spoke, it occurred to me that one of the reasons his proposal surprised me was that we had never talked much about our families, about how his would react to me and mine to him. I hadn't been aware of us avoiding the subject, but somehow, we'd never gotten around to it. Even now, he looked surprised.

'The only close relative I've got left is my sister,' he said. 'She's been trying to marry me off and get me "settled down" for years. She'll love you, believe me.'

I didn't, quite. 'I hope she does,' I said. 'But I'm afraid my aunt and uncle won't love you.'

He turned to face me. 'No?'

I shrugged. 'They're old. Sometimes their ideas don't have very much to do with what's going on now. I think they're still waiting for me to come to my senses, move back home, and go to secretarial school.'

'Are we going to get married?'

I went to him. 'You know damn well we are.'

'You want me to go with you when you talk to your aunt and uncle?'

'No. Go talk to your sister if you want to. Brace yourself though. She might surprise you.'

She did. And braced or not, he wasn't ready for his sister's reaction.

'I thought I knew her,' he told me afterward. 'I mean, I did know her. But I guess we've lost touch more than I thought.'

'What did she say?'

'That she didn't want to meet you, wouldn't have you in her house – or me either if I married you.' He leaned back on the shabby purple sofa that had come with my apartment and looked up at me. 'And she said a lot of other things. You don't want to hear them.'

'I believe you.'

He shook his head. 'The thing is, there's no reason for her to react this way. She didn't even believe the garbage she was

118

handing me – or didn't used to. It's as though she was quoting someone else. Her husband, probably. Pompous little bastard. I used to try to like him for her sake.'

'Her husband is prejudiced?'

'Her husband would have made a good Nazi. She used to joke about it – though never when he could hear.'

'But she married him.'

'Desperation. She would have married almost anybody.' He smiled a little. 'In high school, she and this friend of hers spent all their time together because neither of them could get a boyfriend. The other girl was black and fat and homely, and Carol was white and fat and homely. Half the time, we couldn't figure out whether she lived at the girl's house or the girl lived with us. My friends knew them both, but they were too young for them – Carol's three years older than I am. Anyway, she and this girl sort of comforted each other and fell off their diets together and planned to go to the same college so they wouldn't have to break up the partnership. The other girl really went, but Carol changed her mind and trained to become a dental assistant. She wound up marrying the first dentist she ever worked for – a smug little reactionary twenty years older than she was. Now she lives in a big house in La Canada and quotes clichéd bigotry at me for wanting to marry you.'

I shrugged, not knowing what to say. I-told-you-so? Hardly. 'My mother's car broke down in La Canada once,' I told him. 'Three people called the police on her while she was waiting for my uncle to come and get her. Suspicious character. Five-three, she was. About a hundred pounds. Real dangerous.'

'Sounds like the reactionary moved to the right town.'

'I don't know, that was back in nineteen sixty just before my mother died. Things may have improved by now.'

'What did your aunt and uncle say about me, Dana?'

I looked at my hands, thinking about all they had said, paring it down wearily. 'I think my aunt accepts the idea of my marrying you because any children we have will be light. Lighter than I am, anyway. She always said I was a little too "highly visible."'

He stared at me.

'You see? I told you they were old. She doesn't care much for white people, but she prefers light-skinned blacks. Figure that out. Anyway, she "forgives" me for you. But my uncle doesn't. He's sort of taken this personally.'

'Personally, how?'

'He . . . well, he's my mother's oldest brother, and he was like a father to me even before my mother died because my father died when I was a baby. Now . . . it's as though I've rejected him. Or at least that's the way he feels. It bothered me, really. He was more hurt than mad. Honestly hurt. I had to get away from him.'

'But, he knew you'd marry some day. How could a thing as natural as that be a rejection?'

'I'm marrying you.' I reached up and twisted a few strands of his straight gray hair between my fingers. 'He wants me to marry someone like him – someone who looks like him. A black man.'

'Oh.'

'I was always close to him. He and my aunt wanted kids, and they couldn't have any. I was their kid.'

'And now?'

'Now . . . well, they have a couple of apartment houses over in Pasadena – small places, but nice. The last thing my uncle said to me was that he'd rather will them to his church than leave them to me and see them fall into white hands. I think that was the worst thing he could think of to do to me. Or he thought it was the worst thing.'

'Oh hell,' muttered Kevin. 'Look, are you sure you still want to marry me?'

'Yes. I wish . . . never mind, just yes. Definitely, yes.'

'Then let's go to Vegas and pretend we haven't got relatives.'

So we drove to Las Vegas, got married, and gambled away a few dollars. When we came home to our bigger new apartment, we found a gift – a blender – from my best friend, and

120

a check from *The Atlantic* waiting for us. One of my stories had finally made it.

2

I awoke.

I was lying flat on my stomach, my face pressed uncomfortably against something cold and hard. My body below the neck rested on something slightly softer. Slowly, I became aware of sunlight and shadow, of shapes.

I lifted my head, started to sit up, and my back suddenly caught fire. I fell forward, hit my head hard on the bare floor of the bathroom. My bathroom. I was home.

'Kevin?'

I listened. I could have looked around, but I didn't want to.

'Kevin?'

I got up, aware that my eyes were streaming muddy tears, aware of the pain. God, the pain! For several seconds, all I could do was lean against the wall and bear it.

Slowly, I discovered that I wasn't as weak as I had thought. In fact, by the time I was fully conscious, I wasn't weak at all. It was only the pain that made me move slowly, carefully, like a woman three times my age.

I could see now that I had been lying with my head in the bathroom and my body in the bedroom. Now I went into the bathroom and turned on the water to fill the tub. Warm water. I don't think I could have stood hot. Or cold.

My blouse was stuck to my back. It was cut to pieces, really, but the pieces were stuck to me. My back was cut up pretty badly too from what I could feel. I had seen old photographs of the backs of people who had been slaves. I could remember the scars, thick and ugly. Kevin had always told me how smooth my skin was . . .

I took off my pants and shoes and got into the tub still wearing my blouse. I would let the water soften it until I could ease it from my back.

121

In the tub, I sat for a long while without moving, without thinking, listening for what I knew I would not hear elsewhere in the house. The pain was a friend. Pain had never been a friend to me before, but now it kept me still. It forced reality on me and kept me sane.

But Kevin . . .

I leaned forward and cried into the dirty pink water. The skin of my back stretched agonizingly, and the water got pinker.

And it was all pointless. There was nothing I could do. I had no control at all over anything. Kevin might as well be dead. Abandoned in 1819, Kevin *was* dead. Decades dead, perhaps a century dead.

Maybe I would be called back again, and maybe he would still be there waiting for me and maybe only a few years would have passed for him, and maybe he would be all right . . . But what had he said once about going West watching history happen?

By the time my wounds had softened and my rag of a blouse had come unstuck from them, I was exhausted. I felt the weakness now that I hadn't felt before. I got out of the tub and dried myself as best I could, then stumbled into the bedroom and fell across the bed. In spite of the pain, I fell asleep at once.

The house was dark when I awoke, and the bed was empty except for me. I had to remember why all over again. I got up stiffly, painfully, and went to find something that would make me sleep again quickly. I didn't want to be awake. I barely wanted to be alive. Kevin had gotten a prescription for some pills once when he was having trouble sleeping.

I found what was left of them. I was about to take two of them when I got a look at myself in the medicine cabinet mirror. My face had swollen and was puffy and old-looking. My hair was in tangled patches, brown with dirt and matted with blood. In my semi-hysterical state earlier, I had not thought to wash it.

I put the pills down and climbed back into the tub. This time I turned on the shower and somehow managed to wash my hair. Raising my arms hurt. Bending forward hurt. The shampoo that got into my cuts hurt. I started slowly, wincing, grimacing. Finally I got angry and moved vigorously in spite of the pain.

When I looked passably human again, I took some aspirins. They didn't help much, but I was sane enough now to know that I had something to do before I could afford to sleep again.

I needed a replacement for my lost canvas bag. Something that didn't look too good for a 'nigger' to be carrying. I finally settled on an old denim gym bag that I'd made and used back in high school. It was tough and roomy like the canvas bag, and faded enough to look properly shabby.

I would have put in a long dress this time if I'd had one. All I had, though, were a couple of bright filmy evening dresses that would have drawn attention to me, and, under the circumstances, made me look ridiculous. Best to go on being the woman who dressed like a man.

I rolled up a couple of pairs of jeans and stuffed them into the bag. Then shoes, shirts, a wool sweater, comb, brush, toothpaste and toothbrush – Kevin and I had really missed those – two large cakes of soap, my washcloth, the bottle of aspirins – if Rufus called me while my back was sore, I would need them – my knife. The knife had come back with me because I happened to be wearing it in a makeshift leather sheath at my ankle. I didn't know whether to be glad or not that I hadn't had a chance to use it against Weylin. I might have killed him. I had been angry enough, frightened enough, humiliated enough to try. Then if Rufus called me again, I would have to answer for the killing. Or maybe Kevin would have to answer for it. I was suddenly very glad that I had left Weylin alive. Kevin was in for enough trouble. And, too, when I saw Rufus again – if I saw him again – I would need his help. I wouldn't be likely to get it if I had killed his father – even a father he didn't like.

I stuffed another pencil, pen, and scratch pad into the bag. I was slowly emptying Kevin's desk. All my things were still packed. And I found a compact paperback history of slavery in America that might be useful. It listed dates and events that I should be aware of, and it contained a map of Maryland.

123

The bag was too full to close completely by the time everything was in, but I tied it shut with its own rope drawstring, and tied the drawstring around my arm. I couldn't have stood anything tied around my waist.

Then, incongruously, I was hungry. I went to the kitchen and found half-a-box of raisins and a full can of mixed nuts. To my surprise, I finished both, then slept again easily.

It was morning when I awoke, and I was still at home. My back hurt whenever I moved. I managed to spray it with an ointment Kevin had used for sunburn. The whip lacerations hurt like burns. The ointment cooled them and seemed to help. I had the feeling I should have used something stronger, though. Heaven knew what kind of infection you could get from a whip kept limber with oil and blood. Tom Weylin had ordered brine thrown onto the back of the field hand he had whipped. I could remember the man screaming as the solution hit him. But his wounds had healed without infection.

As I thought of the field hand, I felt strangely disoriented. For a moment, I thought Rufus was calling me again. Then I realized that I wasn't really dizzy – only confused. My memory of a field hand being whipped suddenly seemed to have no place here with me at home.

I came out of the bathroom into the bedroom and looked around. Home. Bed – without canopy – dresser, closet, electric light, television, radio, electric clock, books. Home. It didn't have anything to do with where I had been. It was real. It was where I belonged.

I put on a loose dress and went out to the front yard. The tiny blue-haired woman who lived next door noticed me and wished me a good morning. She was on her hands and knees digging in her flower garden and obviously enjoying herself. She reminded me of Margaret Weylin who also had flowers. I had heard Margaret's guests compliment her on her flowers. But, of course, she didn't take care of them herself . . .

Today and yesterday didn't mesh. I felt almost as strange as I had after my first trip back to Rufus – caught between his home and mine.

124

There was a Volvo parked across the street and there were powerlines overhead. There were palm trees and paved streets. There was the bathroom I had just left. Not a hole-in-the-ground privy toilet that you had to hold your breath to go into, but a bathroom.

I went back into the house and turned the radio on to an all-news station. There, eventually, I learned that it was Friday, June 11, 1976. I'd gone away for nearly two months and come back yesterday – the same day I left home. Nothing was real.

Kevin could be gone for years even if I went after him today and brought him back tonight.

I found a music station and turned the radio up loud to drown out my thinking.

The time passed and I did more unpacking, stopping often, taking too many aspirins. I began to bring some order to my own office. Once I sat down at my typewriter and tried to write about what had happened, made about six attempts before I gave up and threw them all away. Someday when this was over, if it was ever over, maybe I would be able to write about it.

I called my favorite cousin in Pasadena – my father's sister's daughter – and had her buy groceries for me. I told her I was sick and Kevin wasn't around. Something about my tone must have reached her. She didn't ask any questions.

I was still afraid to leave the house, walking or driving. Driving, I could easily kill myself, and the car could kill other people if Rufus called me from it at the wrong time. Walking, I could get dizzy and fall while crossing the street. Or I could fall on the sidewalk and attract attention. Someone could come to help me – a cop, anyone. Then I could be guilty of taking someone else back with me and stranding them.

My cousin was a good friend. She took one look at me and recommended a doctor she knew. She also advised me to send the police after Kevin. She assumed that my bruises were his work. But when I swore her to silence, I knew she would be silent. She and I had grown up keeping each other's secrets.

'I never thought you'd be fool enough to let a man beat you,' she said as she left. She was disappointed in me, I think.

'I never thought I would either,' I whispered when she was gone.

I waited inside the house with my denim bag always nearby. The days passed slowly, and sometimes I thought I was waiting for something that just wasn't going to happen. But I went on waiting.

I read books about slavery, fiction and nonfiction. I read everything I had in the house that was even distantly related to the subject – even *Gone With the Wind*, or part of it. But its version of happy darkies in tender loving bondage was more than I could stand.

Then, somehow, I got caught up in one of Kevin's World War II books – a book of excerpts from the recollections of concentration camp survivors. Stories of beatings, starvation, filth, disease, torture, every possible degradation. As though the Germans had been trying to do in only a few years what the Americans had worked at for nearly two hundred.

The books depressed me, scared me, made me stuff Kevin's sleeping pills into my bag. Like the Nazis, ante bellum whites had known quite a bit about torture – quite a bit more than I ever wanted to learn.

3

I had been at home for eight days when the dizziness finally came again. I didn't know whether to curse it for my own sake or welcome it for Kevin's – not that it mattered what I did.

I went to Rufus's time fully clothed, carrying my denim bag, wearing my knife. I arrived on my knees because of the dizziness, but I was immediately alert and wary.

I was in the woods either late in the day or early in the morning. The sun was low in the sky and surrounded as I was by trees, I had no reference point to tell me whether it was rising or setting. I could see a stream not far from me, running between tall trees. Off to my opposite side was a woman, black, young – just a girl, really – with her dress torn down the front. She was holding it together as she watched a black man and a white man fighting.

The white man's red hair told me who he must be. His face was already too much of a mess to tell me. He was losing his fight – had already lost it. The man he was fighting was his size with the same slender build, but in spite of the black man's slenderness, he looked wiry and strong. He had probably been conditioned by years of hard work. He didn't seem much affected when Rufus hit him, but he was killing Rufus.

Then it occurred to me that he might really be doing just that – killing the only person who might be able to help me find Kevin. Killing my ancestor. What had happened here seemed obvious. The girl, her torn dress. If everything was as it seemed, Rufus had earned his beating and more. Maybe he had grown up to be even worse than I had feared. But no matter what he was, I needed him alive – for Kevin's sake and for my own.

I saw him fall, get up, and be knocked down again. This time, he got up more slowly, but he got up. I had a feeling he'd done a lot of getting up. He wouldn't be doing much more.

I went closer, and the woman saw me. She called out something I didn't quite understand, and the man turned his head to look at her. Then he followed her gaze to me. Just then, Rufus hit him on the jaw.

Surprisingly, the black man stumbled backward, almost fell. But Rufus was too tired and hurt to follow up his advantage. The black man hit him one more solid blow, and Rufus collapsed. There was no question of his getting up this time. He was out cold.

As I approached, the black man reached down and caught Rufus by the hair as though to hit him again. I stepped up to the man quickly. 'What will they do to you if you kill him?' I said.

The man twisted around to glare at me.

'What will they do to the woman if you kill him?' I asked.

That seemed to reach him. He released Rufus and stood straight to face me. 'Who's going to say I did anything to him?' His voice was low and threatening, and I began to wonder whether I might wind up joining Rufus unconscious on the ground.

I made myself shrug. 'You'll say yourself what you did if they ask you right. So will the woman.'

'What are you going to say?'

'Not a word if I can help it. But . . . I'm asking you not to kill him.'

'You belong to him?'

'No. It's just that he might know where my husband is. And I might be able to get him to tell me.'

'Your husband . . .?' He looked me over from head to foot. 'Why you go 'round dressed like a man?'

I said nothing. I was so tired of answering that question that I wished I had risked going out to buy a long dress. I looked down at Rufus's bloody face and said, 'If you leave him here now, it will be a long while before he can send anyone after you. You'll have time to get away.'

'You think you'd want him alive if you was her?' He gestured toward the woman.

'Is she your wife?'

'Yeah.'

He was like Sarah, holding himself back, not killing in spite of anger I could only imagine. A lifetime of conditioning could be overcome, but not easily. I looked at the woman. 'Do you want your husband to kill this man?'

She shook her head and I saw that her face was swollen on one side. ''While ago, I could have killed him myself,' she said. 'Now . . . Isaac, let's just get away!'

'Get away and leave *her* here?' He stared at me, suspicious and hostile. 'She sure don't talk like no nigger I ever heard. Talks like she been mighty close with the white folks – for a long time.'

'She talks like that 'cause she comes from a long way off,' said the girl.

128

I looked at her in surprise. Tall and slender and dark, she was. A little like me. Maybe a lot like me.

'You're Dana, aren't you?' she asked.

'Yes . . . how did you know?'

'He told me about you.' She nudged Rufus with her foot. 'He used to talk about you all the time. And I saw you once, when I was little.'

I nodded. 'You're Alice, then. I thought so.'

She nodded and rubbed her swollen face. 'I'm Alice.' And she looked at the black man with pride. 'Alice Jackson now.'

I tried to see her again as the thin, frightened child I remembered – the child I had seen only two months before. It was impossible. But I should have been used to the impossible by now – just as I should have been used to white men preying on black women. I had Weylin as my example, after all. But somehow, I had hoped for better from Rufus. I wondered whether the girl was pregnant with Hagar already.

'My name was Greenwood when you saw me last,' Alice continued. 'I married Isaac last year . . . just before Mama died.'

'She died then?' I caught myself visualizing a woman my age dying, even though I knew that was wrong. But still, the woman must have died fairly young. 'I'm sorry,' I said. 'She tried to help me.'

'She helped lot of folks,' said Isaac. 'She used to treat this little no-good bastard better than his own people treated him.' He kicked Rufus hard in the side.

I winced and wished I could move Rufus out of his reach. 'Alice,' I said, 'wasn't Rufus a friend of yours? I mean . . . did he just grow out of the friendship or what?'

'Got to where he wanted to be more friendly than I did,' she said. 'He tried to get Judge Holman to sell Isaac South to keep me from marrying him.'

'You're a slave?' I said to Isaac, surprised. 'My God, you'd better get out of here.'

Isaac gave Alice a look that said very clearly, *You talk too much*. Alice answered the look.

'Isaac, she's all right. She got a whipping once for teaching a slave how to read. Tom Weylin was the one whipped her.'

'I want to know what she's going to do when we leave,' said Isaac.

'I'm going to stay with Rufus,' I told him. 'When he comes to, I'm going to help him home – as slowly as possible. I'm not going to tell him where you went because I won't know.'

Isaac looked at Alice, and she tugged at his arm. 'Let's go!' she urged.

'But . . .'

'You can't whip everybody! Let's go!'

He seemed on the verge of going when I said, 'Isaac, if you want me to, I can write you a pass. It doesn't have to be to where you're really going, but it might help you if you're stopped.'

He looked at me with no trust at all, then turned and walked away without answering.

Alice hesitated, spoke softly to me. 'Your man went away,' she said. 'He waited a long time for you, then he left.'

'Where did he go?'

'Somewhere North. I don't know. Mister Rufe knows. You got to be careful, though. Mister Rufe gets mighty crazy sometimes.'

'Thank you.'

She turned and followed Isaac, leaving me alone with the unconscious Rufus – alone to wonder where she and Isaac would go. North to Pennsylvania? I hoped so. And where had Kevin gone? Why had he gone anywhere? What if Rufus wouldn't help me find him? Or what if I didn't stay in this time long enough to find him? Why couldn't he have waited . . .?

4

I knelt down beside Rufus and rolled him over onto his back. His nose was bleeding. His split lip was bleeding. I thought he had probably lost a few teeth, but I didn't look closely enough

130

to be sure. His face was a lumpy mess, and he would be looking out of a couple of black eyes for a while. All in all, though, he probably looked worse off than he was. No doubt he had some bruises that I couldn't see without undressing him, but I didn't think he was badly hurt. He would be in some pain when he came to, but he had earned that.

I sat on my knees, watching him, first wishing he would hurry and regain consciousness, then wanting him to stay unconscious so that Alice and her husband could get a good start. I looked at the stream, thinking that a little cold water might bring him around faster. But I stayed where I was. Isaac's life was at stake. If Rufus was vindictive enough, he could surely have the man killed. A slave had no rights, and certainly no excuse for striking a white man.

If it was possible, if Rufus was in any way still the boy I had known, I would try to keep him from going after Isaac at all. He looked about eighteen or nineteen now. I would be able to bluff and bully him a little. It shouldn't take him long to realize that he and I needed each other. We would be taking turns helping each other now. Neither of us would want the other to hesitate. We would have to learn to co-operate with each other – to make compromises.

'Who's there?' said Rufus suddenly. His voice was weak, barely audible.

'It's Dana, Rufe.'

'Dana?' He opened his swollen eyes a little wider. 'You came back!'

'You keep trying to get yourself killed. I keep coming back.'

'Where's Alice?'

'I don't know. I don't even know where we are. I'll help you get home, though, if you'll point the way.'

'Where did she go?'

'I don't know, Rufe.'

He tried to sit up, managed to raise himself about six inches before he fell back, groaning. 'Where's Isaac?' he muttered. 'That's the son-of-a-bitch I want to catch up with.'

131

'Rest awhile,' I said. 'Get your strength back. You couldn't catch him now if he was standing next to you.'

He moaned and felt his side gingerly. 'He's going to pay!'

I got up and walked toward the stream.

'Where are you going?' he called.

I didn't answer.

'Dana? Come back here! Dana!'

I could hear his increasing desperation. He was hurt and alone except for me. He couldn't even get up, and I seemed to be abandoning him. I wanted him to experience a little of that fear.

'*Dana!*'

I dug the washcloth out of my denim bag, wet it, and took it back to him. Kneeling beside him, I began wiping blood from his face.

'Why didn't you tell me that's where you were going?' he said petulantly. He was panting and holding his side.

I watched him, wondering how much he had really grown up.

'Dana, say something!'

'I want you to say something.'

He squinted at me. 'What?' I was leaning close to him, and I caught a whiff of his breath when he spoke. He had been drinking. He didn't seem drunk, but he had definitely been drinking. That worried me, but there was nothing I could do about it. I didn't dare wait until he was completely sober.

'I want you to tell me about the men who attacked you,' I said.

'What men? Isaac . . .'

'The men you were drinking with,' I improvised. 'They were strangers – white men. They got you drinking, then tried to rob you.' Kevin's old story was coming in handy.

'What in hell are you talking about? You know Isaac Jackson did this to me!' The words came out in a harsh whisper.

'All right, Isaac beat you up,' I agreed. 'Why?'

He glared at me without answering.

'You raped a woman – or tried to – and her husband beat

132

you up,' I said. 'You're lucky he didn't kill you. He would have if Alice and I hadn't talked him out of it. Now what are you going to do to repay us for saving your life?'

The bewilderment and anger left his face, and he stared at me blankly. After a while, he closed his eyes and I went over to rinse my washcloth. When I got back to him, he was trying – and failing – to stand up. Finally, he collapsed back panting and holding his side. I wondered whether he was hurt more than he appeared to be – hurt inside. His ribs, perhaps.

I knelt beside him again and wiped the rest of the blood and dirt from his face. 'Rufe, did you manage to rape that girl?'

He looked away guiltily.

'Why would you do such a thing? She used to be your friend.'

'When we were little, we were friends,' he said softly. 'We grew up. She got so she'd rather have a buck nigger than me!'

'Do you mean her husband?' I asked. I managed to keep my voice even.

'Who in hell else would I mean!'

'Yes.' I gazed down at him bitterly. Kevin had been right. I'd been foolish to hope to influence him. 'Yes,' I repeated. 'How dare she choose her own husband. She must have thought she was a free woman or something.'

'What's that got to do with it?' he demanded. Then his voice dropped to almost a whisper. 'I would have taken better care of her than any field hand could. I wouldn't have hurt her if she hadn't just kept saying no.'

'She had the right to say no.'

'We'll see about her rights!'

'Oh? Are you planning to hurt her more? She just helped me save your life, remember?'

'She'll get what's coming to her. She'll get it whether I give it to her or not.' He smiled. 'If she ran off with Isaac, she'll get plenty.'

'Why? What do you mean?'

'She did run off with Isaac, then?'

'I don't know. Isaac figured I was on your side so he didn't trust me enough to tell me what they were going to do.'

133

'He didn't have to. Isaac just attacked a white man. He's not going back to Judge Holman after doing that. Some other nigger might, but not Isaac. He's run away, and Alice is with him, helping him to escape. Or at least, that's the way the Judge will see it.'

'What will happen to her?'

'Jail. A good whipping. Then they'll sell her.'

'She'll be a slave?'

'Her own fault.'

I stared at him. Heaven help Alice and Isaac. Heaven help me. If Rufus could turn so quickly on a life-long friend, how long would it take him to turn on me?

'I don't want her being sold South, though,' he whispered. 'Her fault or not, I don't want her dying in some rice swamp.'

'Why not?' I asked bitterly. 'Why should it matter to you?'

'I wish it didn't.'

I frowned down at him. His tone had changed suddenly. Was he going to show a little humanity then? Did he have any left to show?

'I told her about you,' he said.

'I know. She recognized me.'

'I told her everything. Even about you and Kevin being married. Especially about that.'

'What will you do, Rufe, if they bring her back?'

'Buy her. I've got some money.'

'What about Isaac?'

'To hell with Isaac!' He said it too vehemently and hurt his side. His face twisted in pain.

'So you'll be rid of the man and have possession of the woman just as you wanted,' I said with disgust. 'Rape rewarded.'

He turned his head toward me and peered at me through swollen eyes. 'I begged her not to go with him,' he said quietly. 'Do you hear me, *I begged her!*'

I said nothing. I was beginning to realize that he loved the woman – to her misfortune. There was no shame in raping a black woman, but there could be shame in loving one.

'I didn't want to just drag her off into the bushes,' said Rufus. 'I never wanted it to be like that. But she kept saying no. I could have had her in the bushes years ago if that was all I wanted.'

'I know,' I said.

'If I lived in your time, I would have married her. Or tried to.' He began trying to get up again. He seemed stronger now, but in pain. I sat watching him, but not helping. I was not eager for him to recover and go home – not until I was sure what story he would tell when he got there.

Finally, the pain seemed to overwhelm him and he lay down again. 'What did that bastard do to me?' he whispered.

'I could go and get help for you,' I said. 'If you tell me which way to go.'

'Wait.' He caught his breath and coughed and the coughing hurt him badly. 'Oh God,' he moaned.

'I think you've got broken ribs,' I said.

'I wouldn't be surprised. I guess you'd better go.'

'All right. But, Rufe . . . white men attacked you. You hear?'

He said nothing.

'You said people would be going after Isaac anyway. All right then, so be it. But let him – and Alice – have a chance. They've given you one.'

'It won't make any difference whether I tell or not. Isaac's a runaway. They'll have to answer for that, no matter what.'

'Then your silence won't matter.'

'Except to give them the start you want them to have.'

I nodded. 'I do want them to have it.'

'You'll trust me, then?' He was watching me very closely. 'If I say I won't tell, you'll believe me?'

'Yes.' I paused for a moment. 'We should never lie to each other, you and I. It wouldn't be worthwhile. We both have too much opportunity for retaliation.'

He turned his face away from me. 'You talk like a damn book.'

'Then I hope Kevin did a good job of teaching you to read.'

'You . . .!' He caught my arm in a grip I could have broken, but I let him hold on. 'You threaten me, I'll threaten you. Without me, you'll never find Kevin.'

'I know that.'

'Then don't threaten me!'

'I said we were dangerous to each other. That's more a reminder than a threat.' Actually, it was more a bluff.

'I don't need reminders or threats from you.'

I said nothing.

'Well? Are you going to go get some help for me?'

Still I said nothing. I didn't move.

'You go through those trees,' he said pointing. 'There's a road out there, not too far away. Go left on the road and then just follow it until you come to our place.'

I listened to his directions knowing that I would use them sooner or later. But we had to have an understanding first, he and I. He didn't have to admit that we had one. He could keep his pride if that was what he thought was at stake. But he did have to behave as though he understood me. If he refused, he was going to get a lot more pain now. And maybe later when Kevin was safe and Hagar had at least had a chance to be born – I might never find out about that – I would walk away from Rufus and leave him to get out of his own trouble.

'Dana!'

I looked at him. I had let my attention wander.

'I said she'll . . . they'll get their time. White men attacked me.'

'Good, Rufe.' I laid a hand on his shoulder. 'Look, your father will listen to me, won't he? I don't know what he saw last time I went home.'

'He doesn't know what he saw either. Whatever it was, he's seen it before – that time at the river – and he didn't believe it then, either. But he'll listen to you. He might even be a little afraid of you.'

'That's better than the other way around. I'll get back as quickly as I can.'

The road was farther away than I had expected. As it got darker – the sun was setting, not rising – I tore pages from my scratch pad and stuck them on trees now and then to mark my trail. Even then I worried that I might not be able to find my way back to Rufus.

When I reached the road, I pulled up some bushes and made a kind of barricade speckled with bits of white paper. That would stop me at the right place when I came back – if no one moved it meanwhile.

I followed the road until it was dark, followed it through woods, through fields, past a large house much finer than Weylin's. No one bothered me. I hid behind a tree once when two white men rode past. They might not have paid any attention to me, but I didn't want to take the chance. And there were three black women walking with large bundles balanced on their heads.

'Evenin',' they said as I passed them.

I nodded and wished them a good evening. And I walked faster, wondering suddenly what the years had done to Luke and Sarah, to Nigel and Carrie. The children who had played at selling each other might already be working in the fields now. And what would time have done to Margaret Weylin? I doubted that it had made her any easier to live with.

Finally, after more woods and fields, the plain square house was before me, its downstairs windows full of yellow light. I was startled to catch myself saying wearily, 'Home at last.'

I stood still for a moment between the fields and the house and reminded myself that I was in a hostile place. It didn't look alien any longer, but that only made it more dangerous, made me more likely to relax and make a mistake.

I rubbed my back, touched the several long scabs to remind myself that I could not afford to make mistakes. And the scabs forced me to remember that I had been away from this place for only a few days. Not that I had forgotten – exactly. But it was as though during my walk I had been getting used to the idea that years had passed for these people since I had seen them last. I had begun to feel – feel, not think – that a great deal of time had passed for me too. It was a vague feeling, but it seemed right and comfortable. More comfortable than trying to keep in mind what was really happening. Some part of me had apparently given up on time-distorted reality and smoothed things out. Well, that was all right, as long as it didn't go too far.

I continued on toward the house, mentally prepared now, I hoped, to meet Tom Weylin. But as I approached, a tall thin shadow of a white man came toward me from the direction of the quarter.

'Hey there,' he called. 'What are you doing out here?' His long steps closed the distance between us quickly, and in a moment, he stood peering down at me. 'You don't belong here,' he said. 'Who's your master?'

'I've come to get help for Mister Rufus,' I said. And then, feeling suddenly doubtful because he was a stranger, I asked, 'This is still where he lives, isn't it?'

The man did not answer. He continued to peer at me. I wondered whether it was my sex or my accent that he was trying to figure out. Or maybe it was the fact that I hadn't called him sir or master. I'd have to begin that degrading nonsense again. But who was this man, anyway?

'He lives here.' An answer, finally. 'What's wrong with him?'

'Some men beat him. He can't walk.'

'Is he drunk?'

'Uh . . . no, sir, not quite.'

'Worthless bastard.'

I jumped a little. The man had spoken softly, but there was no mistaking what he had said. I said nothing.

'Come on,' he ordered, and led me into the house. He left me standing in the entrance hall and went to the library where I supposed Weylin was. I looked at the wooden bench a few steps from me, the settee, but although I was tired, I didn't sit down. Margaret Weylin had once caught me sitting there tying my shoe. She had screamed and raged as though she'd caught me stealing her jewelry. I didn't want to renew my acquaintance with her in another scene like that. I didn't want to renew my acquaintance with her at all, but it seemed inevitable.

There was a sound behind me and I turned in quick apprehension. A young slave woman stood staring at me. She was light-skinned, blue-kerchiefed, and very pregnant.

'Carrie?' I asked.

She ran to me, caught me by the shoulders for a moment, and looked into my face. Then she hugged me.

The white stranger chose that moment to come out of the library with Tom Weylin.

'What's going on here?' demanded the stranger.

Carrie moved away from me quickly, head down, and I said, 'We're old friends, sir.'

Tom Weylin, grayer, thinner, grimmer-looking than ever, came over to me. He stared at me for a moment, then turned to face the stranger. 'When did you say his horse came in, Jake?'

'About an hour ago.'

'That long . . . you should have told me.'

'He's taken that long and longer before.'

Weylin sighed, glanced at me. 'Yes. But I think it might be more serious this time. Carrie!'

The mute woman had been walking away toward the back door. Now, she turned to look at Weylin.

'Have Nigel bring the wagon around front.'

She gave the half-nod, half-curtsey that she reserved for whites and hurried away.

Something occurred to me as she was going and I spoke to Weylin. 'I think Mister Rufus might have broken ribs. He wasn't coughing blood so his lungs are probably all right, but it might be a good idea for me to bandage him a little before you move him.' I had never bandaged anything worse than a cut finger in my life, but I did remember a little of the first aid I had learned in school. I hadn't thought to act when Rufus broke his leg, but I might be able to help now.

'You can bandage him when we get him here,' said Weylin. And to the stranger, 'Jake, you send somebody for the doctor.'

Jake took a last disapproving look at me and went out the back door after Carrie.

Weylin went out the front door without another word to me and I followed, trying to remember how important it was to bandage broken ribs – that is, whether it was worth 'talking back' to Weylin about. I didn't want Rufus badly injured, even though he deserved to be. Any injury could be dangerous. But from what I could remember, bandaging the ribs was done mostly to relieve pain. I wasn't sure whether I remembered that because it was true or because I wanted to avoid any kind of confrontation with Weylin. I didn't have to touch the scabs on my back to be conscious of them.

A tall stocky slave drove a wagon around to us and I got on the back while Weylin took the seat beside the driver. The driver glanced back at me and said softly, 'How are you, Dana?'

'Nigel?'

'It's me,' he said grinning. 'Grown some since you seen me last, I guess.'

He had grown into another Luke – a big handsome man bearing little resemblance to the boy I remembered.

'You keep your mouth shut and watch the road,' said Weylin. Then to me, 'You've got to tell us where to go.'

It would have been a pleasure to tell him where to go, but I spoke civilly. 'It's a long way from here,' I said. 'I had to pass someone else's house and fields on my way to you.'

'The judge's place. You could have got help there.'

'I didn't know.' And wouldn't have tried if I had known. I wondered, though, whether this was the Judge Holman who would soon be sending men out to chase Isaac. It seemed likely.

'Did you leave Rufus by the side of the road?' Weylin asked.

'No, sir. He's in the woods.'

'You sure you know where in the woods?'

'Yes, sir.'

'You'd better.'

He said nothing else.

I found Rufus with no particular difficulty and Nigel lifted him as gently and as easily as Luke once had. On the wagon, he held his side, then he held my hand. Once, he said, 'I'll keep my word.'

I nodded and touched his forehead in case he couldn't see me nodding. His forehead was hot and dry.

'He'll keep his word about what?' asked Weylin.

He was looking back at me, so I frowned and looked perplexed and said, 'I think he has a fever as well as broken ribs, sir.'

Weylin made a sound of disgust. 'He was sick yesterday, puking all over. But he would get up and go out today. Damn fool!'

And he fell silent again until we reached his house. Then, as Nigel carried Rufus inside and up the stairs, Weylin steered me into his forbidden library. He pushed me close to a whale-oil lamp, and there, in the bright yellow light, he stared at me silently, critically until I looked toward the door.

'You're the same one, all right,' he said finally. 'I didn't want to believe it.'

I said nothing.

'Who are you?' he demanded. 'What are you?'

I hesitated not knowing what to answer because I didn't know how much he knew. The truth might make him decide I was out of my mind, but I didn't want to be caught in a lie.

'Well!'

'I don't know what you want me to say,' I told him. 'I'm Dana. You know me.'

'Don't tell me what I know!'

I stood silent, confused, frightened. Kevin wasn't here now. There was no one for me to call if I needed help.

'I'm someone who may have just saved your son's life,' I said softly. 'He might have died out there sick and injured and alone.'

'And you think I ought to be grateful?'

Why did he sound angry? And why shouldn't he be grateful? 'I can't tell you how you ought to feel, Mr Weylin.'

'That's right. You can't.'

There was a moment of silence that he seemed to expect me to fill. Eagerly, I changed the subject. 'Mr Weylin, do you know where Mr Franklin went?'

Oddly, that seemed to reach him. His expression softened a little. 'Him,' he said. 'Damn fool.'

'Where did he go?'

'Somewhere North. I don't know. Rufus has some letters from him.' He gave me another long stare. 'I guess you want to stay here.'

He sounded as though he was giving me a choice, which was surprising because he didn't have to. Maybe gratitude meant something to him after all.

'I'd like to stay for a while,' I said. Better to try to reach Kevin from here than go wandering around some Northern city trying to find him. Especially since I had no money, and since I was still so ignorant of this time.

'You got to work for your keep,' said Weylin. 'Like you did before.'

'Yes, sir.'

'That Franklin comes back, he'll stop here. He came back once – hoping to find you, I think.'

'When?'

'Last year sometime. You go up and stay with Rufus until the doctor comes. Take care of him.'

'Yes, sir.' I turned to go.

'That seems to be what you're for, anyway,' he muttered.

I kept going, glad to get away from him. He had known more about me than he wanted to talk about. That was clear from the questions he hadn't asked. He had seen me vanish twice now. And Kevin and Rufus had probably told him at least something about me. I wondered how much. And I wondered what Kevin had said or done that made him a 'damn fool.'

Whatever it was, I'd learn about it from Rufus. Weylin was too dangerous to question.

I sponged Rufus off as best I could and bandaged his ribs with pieces of cloth that Nigel brought me. The ribs were very tender on the left side. Rufus said the bandage made breathing a little less painful, though, and I was glad of that. But he was still sick. His fever was still with him. And the doctor didn't come. Rufus had fits of coughing now and then, and that seemed to be agonizing to him because of his ribs. Sarah came in to see him – and to hug me – and she was more alarmed at the marks of his beating than at his ribs or his fever. His face was black and blue and deformed-looking with its lumpy swellings.

'He will fight,' she said angrily. Rufus opened his puffy slits of eyes and looked at her, but she went on anyway. 'I've seen him pick a fight just out of meanness,' she said. 'He's out to get himself killed!'

She could have been his mother, caught between anger and concern and not knowing which to express. She took away the basin Nigel had brought me and returned it full of clean cool water.

'Where's his mother?' I asked her softly as she was leaving.

She drew back from me a little. 'Gone.'

'Dead?'

'Not yet.' She glanced at Rufus to see whether he was listening. His face was turned away from us. 'Gone to Baltimore,' she whispered. 'I'll tell you 'bout it tomorrow.'

I let her go without questioning her further. It was enough to know that I would not be suddenly attacked. For once, there would be no Margaret to protect Rufus from me.

He was thrashing about weakly when I went back to him. He cursed the pain, cursed me, then remembered himself enough to say he didn't mean it. He was burning up.

'Rufe?'

He moved his head from side to side and did not seem to

hear me. I dug into my denim bag and found the plastic bottle of aspirin – a big bottle nearly full. There was enough to share.

'Rufe!'

He squinted at me.

'Listen, I have medicine from my own time.' I poured him a glass of water from the pitcher beside his bed, and shook out two aspirin tablets. 'These could lower your fever,' I said. 'They might ease your pain too. Will you take them?'

'What are they?'

'They're called aspirin. In my time, people use them against headache, fever, other kinds of pain.'

He looked at the two tablets in my hand, then at me. 'Give them to me.'

He had trouble swallowing them and had to chew them up a little.

'My Lord,' he muttered. 'Anything tastes that bad must be good for you.'

I laughed and wet a cloth in the basin to bathe his face. Nigel came in with a blanket and told me the doctor was held up at a difficult childbirth. I was to stay the night with Rufus.

I didn't mind. Rufus was in no condition to take an interest in me. I would have thought it would be more natural, though, for Nigel to stay. I asked him about it.

'Marse Tom knows about you,' said Nigel softly. 'Marse Rufe and Mister Kevin both told him. He figures you know enough to do some doctoring. More than doctoring, maybe. He saw you go home.'

'I know.'

'I saw it too.'

I looked up at him – he was a head taller than me now – and saw nothing but curiosity in his eyes. If my vanishing had frightened him, the fear was long dead. I was glad of that. I wanted his friendship.

'Marse Tom says you s'pose to take care of him and you better do a good job. Aunt Sarah says you call her if you need help.'

'Thanks. Thank her for me.'

He nodded, smiled a little. 'Good thing for me you showed up. I want to be with Carrie now. It's so close to her time.'

I grinned. 'Your baby, Nigel? I thought it might be.'

'Better be mine. She's my wife.'

'Congratulations.'

'Marse Rufe paid a free preacher from town to come and say the same words they say for white folks and free niggers. Didn't have to jump no broomstick.'

I nodded, remembering what I'd read about the slaves' marriage ceremonies. They jumped broomsticks, sometimes backward, sometimes forward, depending on local custom; or they stood before their master and were pronounced husband and wife; or they followed any number of other practices even to hiring a minister and having things done as Nigel had. None of it made any difference legally, though. No slave marriage was legally binding. Even Alice's marriage to Isaac was merely an informal agreement since Isaac was a slave, or had been a slave. I hoped now that he was a free man well on his way to Pennsylvania.

'Dana?'

I looked up at Nigel. He had whispered my name so softly I had hardly heard him.

'Dana, was it white men?'

Startled, I put a finger to my lips, cautioning, and waved him away. 'Tomorrow,' I promised.

But he wasn't as co-operative as I had been with Sarah. 'Was it Isaac?'

I nodded, hoping he would be satisfied and let the subject drop.

'Did he get away?'

Another nod.

He left me, looking relieved.

I stayed up with Rufus until he managed to fall asleep. The aspirins did seem to help. Then I wrapped myself in the blanket, pulled the room's two chairs together in front of the fireplace, and settled in as comfortably as I could. It wasn't bad.

The doctor arrived late the next morning to find Rufus's fever gone. The rest of his body was still bruised and sore, and his ribs still kept him breathing shallowly and struggling not to cough, but even with that, he was much less miserable. I had gotten him a breakfast tray from Sarah, and he had invited me to share the large meal she had prepared. I ate hot biscuits with butter and peach preserve, drank some of his coffee, and had a little cold ham. It was good and filling. He had the eggs, the rest of the ham, the corn cakes. There was too much of everything, and he didn't feel like eating very much. Instead, he sat back and watched me with amusement.

'Daddy'd do some cussin' if he came in here and found us eating together,' he said.

I put down my biscuit and reined in whatever part of my mind I'd left in 1976. He was right.

'What are you doing then? Trying to make trouble?'

'No. He won't bother us. Eat.'

'The last time someone told me he wouldn't bother me, he walked in and beat the skin off my back.'

'Yeah. I know about that. But I'm not Nigel. If I tell you to do something, and he doesn't like it, he'll come to me about it. He won't whip you for following *my* orders. He's a fair man.'

I looked at him, startled.

'I said fair,' he repeated. 'Not likable.'

I kept quiet. His father wasn't the monster he could have been with the power he held over his slaves. He wasn't a monster at all. Just an ordinary man who sometimes did the monstrous things his society said were legal and proper. But I had seen no particular fairness in him. He did as he pleased. If you told him he wasn't being fair, he would whip you for talking back. At least the Tom Weylin I had known would have. Maybe he had mellowed.

'Stay,' said Rufus. 'No matter what you think of him, I won't let him hurt you. And it's good to eat with someone I can talk to for a change.'

That was nice. I began to eat again, wondering why he was in such a good mood this morning. He had come a long way

146

from his anger the night before – from threatening not to tell me where Kevin was.

'You know,' said Rufus thoughtfully, 'you still look mighty young. You pulled me out of that river thirteen or fourteen years ago, but you look like you would have been just a kid back then.'

Uh-oh. 'Kevin didn't explain that part, I guess.'

'Explain what?'

I shook my head. 'Just . . . let me tell you how it's been for me. I can't tell you why things are happening as they are, but I can tell you the order of their happening.' I hesitated, gathering my thoughts. 'When I came to you at the river, it was June ninth, nineteen seventy-six for me. When I got home, it was still the same day. Kevin told me I had only been gone a few seconds.'

'Seconds . . .?'

'Wait. Let me tell it all to you at once. Then you can have all the time you need to digest it and ask questions. Later, on that same day, I came to you again. You were three or four years older and busy trying to set the house afire. When I went home, Kevin told me only a few minutes had passed. The next morning, June tenth, I came to you because you'd fallen out of a tree . . . Kevin and I came to you. I was here nearly two months. But when I went home, I found that I had lost only a few minutes or hours of June tenth.'

'You mean after two months, you . . .'

'I arrived home on the same day I had left. Don't ask me how. I don't know. After eight days at home, I came back here.' I faced him silently for a moment. 'And, Rufe, now that I'm here, now that you're safe, I want to find my husband.'

He absorbed this slowly, frowning as though he was translating it from another language. Then he waved vaguely toward his desk – a new larger desk than he had had on my last visit. The old one had been nothing more than a little table. This one had a roll-top and plenty of drawer space both above and below the work surface.

'His letters are in the middle drawer there. You can have them if you want them. They have his addresses . . . But Dana, you're saying while I've been growing up, somehow, time has been almost standing still for you.'

I was at the desk hunting through the cluttered drawer for the letters. 'It hasn't stood still,' I said. 'I'm sure my last two visits here have aged me quite a bit, no matter what my calendar at home says.' I found the letters. Three of them – short notes on large pieces of paper that had been folded, sealed with sealing wax, and mailed without an envelope. 'Here's my Philadelphia address,' Kevin said in one. 'If I can get a decent job, I'll be here for a while.' That was all, except for the address. Kevin wrote books, but he'd never cared much for writing letters. At home he tried to catch me in a good mood and get me to take care of his correspondence for him.

'I'll be an old man,' said Rufus, 'and you'll still come to me looking just like you do now.'

I shook my head. 'Rufe, if you don't start being more careful, you'll never live to be an old man. Now that you're grown up, I might not be able to help you much. The kind of trouble you get into as a man might be as overwhelming to me as it is to you.'

'Yes. But this time thing . . .'

I shrugged.

'Damnit, there must be something mighty crazy about both of us, Dana. I never heard of anything like this happening to anybody else.'

'Neither have I.' I looked at the other two letters. One from New York, and one from Boston. In the Boston one, he was talking about going to Maine. I wondered what was driving him farther and farther north. He had been interested in the West, but Maine . . .?

'I'll write to him,' said Rufus. 'I'll tell him you're here. He'll come running back.'

'I'll write him, Rufe.'

'I'll have to mail the letter.'

'All right.'

'I just hope he hasn't already taken off for Maine.'

Weylin opened the door before I could answer. He brought in another man who turned out to be the doctor, and my leisure time was over. I put Kevin's letters back into Rufus's desk – that seemed the best place to keep them – took away the breakfast tray, brought the doctor the empty basin he asked for, stood by while the doctor asked Weylin whether I had any sense or not and whether I could be trusted to answer simple questions accurately.

Weylin said yes twice without looking at me, and the doctor asked his questions. Was I sure Rufus had had a fever? How did I know? Had he been delirious? Did I know what delirious meant? Smart nigger, wasn't I?

I hated the man. He was short and slight, black-haired and black-eyed, pompous, condescending, and almost as ignorant medically as I was. He guessed he wouldn't bleed Rufus since the fever seemed to be gone – bleed him! He guessed a couple of ribs were broken, yes. He rebandaged them sloppily. He guessed I could go now; he had no more use for me.

I escaped to the cookhouse.

'What's the matter with you?' asked Sarah when she saw me.

I shook my head. 'Nothing important. Just a stupid little man who may be one step up from spells and good luck charms.'

'What?'

'Don't pay any attention to me, Sarah. Do you have anything for me to do out here? I'd like to stay out of the house for a while.'

'Always something to do out here. You have anything to eat?'

I nodded.

She lifted her head and gave me one of her down-the-nose looks. 'Well, I put enough on his tray. Here. Knead this dough.'

She gave me a bowl of bread dough that had risen and was ready to be kneaded down. 'He all right?' she asked.

'He's healing.'

'Was Isaac all right?'

I glanced at her. 'Yes.'

'Nigel said he didn't think Marse Rufe told what happened.'

'He didn't. I managed to talk him out of it.'

She laid a hand on my shoulder for a moment. 'I hope you stay around for a while, girl. Even his daddy can't talk him out of much these days.'

'Well, I'm glad I was able to. But look, you promised to tell me about his mother.'

'Not much to tell. She had two more babies – twins. Sickly little things. They lingered awhile, then died one after the other. She almost died too. She went kind of crazy. The birth had left her pretty bad off anyhow – sick, hurt inside. She fought with Marse Tom, got so she'd scream at him every time she saw him – cussin' and goin' on. She was hurtin' most of the time, couldn't get out of bed. Finally, her sister came and got her, took her to Baltimore.'

'And she's still there?'

'Still there, still sick. Still crazy, for all I know. I just hope she stays there. That overseer, Jake Edwards, he's a cousin of hers, and he's all the mean low white trash we need around here.'

Jake Edwards was the overseer then. Weylin had begun hiring overseers. I wondered why. But before I could ask, two house servants came in and Sarah deliberately turned her back to me, ending the conversation. I began to understand what had happened later, though, when I asked Nigel where Luke was.

'Sold,' said Nigel quietly. And he wouldn't say anything more. Rufus told me the rest.

'You shouldn't have asked Nigel about that,' he told me when I mentioned the incident.

'I wouldn't have, if I'd known.' Rufus was still in bed. The doctor had given him a purgative and left. Rufus had poured the purgative into his chamber pot and ordered me to tell his father he'd taken it. He had had his father send me back to him so that I could write my letter to Kevin. 'Luke did his work,' I said. 'How could your father sell him?'

150

'He worked all right. And the hands would work hard for him – mostly without the cowhide. But sometimes he didn't show much sense.' Rufus stopped, began a deep breath, caught himself and grimaced in pain. 'You're like Luke in some ways,' he continued. 'So you'd better show some sense yourself, Dana. You're on your own this time.'

'But what did he do wrong? What am I doing wrong?'

'Luke . . . he would just go ahead and do what he wanted to no matter what Daddy said. Daddy always said he thought he was white. One day maybe two years after you left, Daddy got tired of it. New Orleans trader came through and Daddy said it would be better to sell Luke than to whip him until he ran away.'

I closed my eyes remembering the big man, hearing again his advice to Nigel on how to defy the whites. It had caught up with him. 'Do you think the trader took him all the way to New Orleans?' I asked.

'Yeah. He was getting a load together to ship them down there.'

I shook my head. 'Poor Luke. Are there cane fields in Louisiana now?'

'Cane, cotton, rice, they grow plenty down there.'

'My father's parents worked in the cane fields there before they went to California. Luke could be a relative of mine.'

'Just make sure you don't wind up like him.'

'I haven't done anything.'

'Don't go teaching nobody else to read.'

'Oh.'

'Yes, oh. I might not be able to stop Daddy if he decided to sell you.'

'Sell me! He doesn't own me. Not even by the law here. He doesn't have any papers saying he owns me.'

'Dana, don't talk stupid!'

'But . . .'

'In town, once, I heard a man brag how he and his friends had caught a free black, tore up his papers, and sold him to a trader.'

151

I said nothing. He was right, of course. I had no rights – not even any papers to be torn up.

'Just be careful,' he said quietly.

I nodded. I thought I could escape from Maryland if I had to. I didn't think it would be easy, but I thought I could do it. On the other hand, I didn't see how even someone much wiser than I was in the ways of the time could escape from Louisiana, surrounded as they would be by water and slave states. I would have to be careful, all right, and be ready to run if I seemed to be in any danger of being sold.

'I'm surprised Nigel is still here,' I said. Then I realized that might not be a very bright thing to say even to Rufus. I would have to learn to keep more of my thoughts to myself.

'Oh, Nigel ran away,' said Rufus. 'Patrollers brought him back, though, hungry and sick. They had whipped him, and Daddy whipped him some more. Then Aunt Sarah doctored him and I talked Daddy into letting me keep him. I think my job was harder. I don't think Daddy relaxed until Nigel married Carrie. Man marries, has children, he's more likely to stay where he is.'

'You sound like a slaveholder already.'

He shrugged.

'Would you have sold Luke?'

'No! I liked him.'

'Would you sell anyone?'

He hesitated. 'I don't know. I don't think so.'

'I hope not,' I said watching him. 'You don't have to do that kind of thing. Not all slaveholders do it.'

I took my denim bag from where I had hidden it under his bed, and sat down at his desk to write the letter, using one of his large sheets of paper with my pen. I didn't want to bother dipping the quill and steel pen on his desk into ink.

'Dear Kevin, I'm back. And I want to go North too . . .'

'Let me see your pen when you're finished,' said Rufus.

'All right.'

I went on writing, feeling myself strangely near tears. It was

152

as though I was really talking to Kevin. I began to believe I would see him again.

'Let me see the other things you brought with you,' said Rufus.

I swung the bag onto his bed. 'You can look,' I said, and continued writing. Not until I was finished with the letter did I look up to see what he was doing.

He was reading my book.

'Here's the pen,' I said casually, and I waited to grab the book the moment he put it down. But instead of putting it down, he ignored the pen and looked up at me.

'This is the biggest lot of abolitionist trash I ever saw.'

'No it isn't,' I said. 'That book wasn't even written until a century after slavery was abolished.'

'Then why the hell are they still complaining about it?'

I pulled the book down so that I could see the page he had been reading. A photograph of Sojourner Truth stared back at me solemn-eyed. Beneath the picture was part of the text of one of her speeches.

'You're reading history, Rufe. Turn a few pages and you'll find a white man named J. D. B. DeBow claiming that slavery is good because, among other things, it gives poor whites someone to look down on. That's history. It happened whether it offends you or not. Quite a bit of it offends me, but there's nothing I can do about it.' And there was other history that he must not read. Too much of it hadn't happened yet. Sojourner Truth, for instance, was still a slave. If someone bought her from her New York owners and brought her South before the Northern laws could free her, she might spend the rest of her life picking cotton. And there were two important slave children right here in Maryland. The older one, living here in Talbot County, would be called Frederick Douglass after a name change or two. The second, growing up a few miles south in Dorchester County was Harriet Ross, eventually to be Harriet Tubman. Someday, she was going to cost Eastern Shore plantation owners a huge amount of money by guiding three hundred of their runaway slaves to freedom. And farther down in Southampton, Virginia, a man named Nat Turner was biding his time. There were more. I had said I couldn't do anything to change history. Yet, if history could be changed, this book in the hands of a white man – even a sympathetic white man – might be the thing to change it.

'History like this could send you down to join Luke,' said Rufus. 'Didn't I tell you to be careful!'

'I wouldn't have let anyone else see it.' I took it from his hand, spoke more softly. 'Or are you telling me I shouldn't trust you either?'

He looked startled. 'Hell, Dana, we have to trust each other. You said that yourself. But what if my daddy went through that bag of yours. He could if he wanted to. You couldn't stop him.'

I said nothing.

'You've never had a whipping like he'd give you if he found that book. Some of that reading . . . He'd take you to be another Denmark Vesey. You know who Vesey was?'

'Yes.' A freedman who had plotted to free others violently.

'You know what they did to him?'

'Yes.'

'Then put that book in the fire.'

I held the book for a moment, then opened it to the map of Maryland. I tore the map out.

'Let me see,' said Rufus.

I handed him the map. He looked at it and turned it over. Since there was nothing on the back but a map of Virginia, he handed it back to me. 'That will be easier to hide,' he said. 'But you know if a white man sees it, he'll figure you mean to use it to escape.'

'I'll take my chances.'

He shook his head in disgust.

I tore the book into several pieces and threw it onto the hot coals in his fireplace. The fire flared up and swallowed the dry paper, and I found my thoughts shifting to Nazi book burnings.

154

Repressive societies always seemed to understand the danger of 'wrong' ideas.

'Seal your letter,' said Rufus. 'There's wax and a candle on the desk there. I'll send the letter as soon as I can get to town.'

I obeyed inexpertly, dripping hot wax on my fingers.

'Dana . . .?'

I glanced at him, caught him watching me with unexpected intensity. 'Yes?'

His eyes seemed to slide away from mine. 'That map is still bothering me. Listen, if you want me to get that letter to town soon, you put the map in the fire too.'

I turned to face him, dismayed. More blackmail. I had thought that was over between us. I had hoped it was over; I needed so much to trust him. I didn't dare stay with him if I couldn't trust him.

'I wish you hadn't said that, Rufe,' I told him quietly. I went over to him, fighting down anger and disappointment and began putting the things that he had scattered back into my bag.

'Wait a minute.' He caught my hand. 'You get so damned cold when you're mad. Wait!'

'For what?'

'Tell me what you're mad about.'

What, indeed? Could I make him see why I thought his blackmail was worse than my own? It was. He threatened to keep me from my husband if I did not submit to his whim and destroy a paper that might help me get free. I acted out of desperation. He acted out of whimsy or anger. Or so it seemed.

'Rufe, there are things we just can't bargain on. This is one of them.'

'You're going to tell me what we can't bargain on?' He sounded more surprised than indignant.

'You're damn right I am.' I spoke very softly. 'I won't bargain away my husband or my freedom!'

'You don't have either to bargain.'

'Neither do you.'

He stared at me with at least as much confusion as anger, and that was encouraging. He could have let his temper flare,

155

could have driven me from the plantation very quickly. 'Look,' he said through his teeth, 'I'm trying to help you!'

'Are you?'

'What do you think I'm doing? Listen, I know Kevin tried to help you. He made things easier for you by keeping you with him. But he couldn't really protect you. He didn't know how. He couldn't even protect himself. Daddy almost had to shoot him when you disappeared. He was fighting and cursing . . . at first Daddy didn't even know why. I'm the one who helped Kevin get back on the place.'

'You?'

'I talked Daddy into seeing him again – and it wasn't easy. I may not be able to talk him into anything for you if he sees that map.'

'I see.'

He waited, watching me. I wanted to ask him what he would do with my letter if I didn't burn the map. I wanted to ask, but I didn't want to hear an answer that might send me out to face another patrol or earn another whipping. I wanted to do things the easy way if I could. I wanted to stay here and let a letter go to Boston and bring Kevin back to me.

So I told myself the map was more a symbol than a necessity anyway. If I had to go, I knew how to follow the North Star at night. I had made a point of learning. And by day, I knew how to keep the rising sun to my right and the setting sun to my left.

I took the map from Rufus's desk and dropped it into the fireplace. It darkened, then burst into flame.

'I can manage without it, you know,' I said quietly.

'No need for you to,' said Rufus. 'You'll be all right here. You're home.'

7

Isaac and Alice had four days of freedom together. On the fifth day, they were caught. On the seventh day, I found out about it. That was the day Rufus and Nigel took the wagon into town to mail my letter and take care of some business of their own. I had heard nothing of the runaways and Rufus seemed to have forgotten about them. He was feeling better, looking better. That seemed to be enough for him. He came to me just before he left and said, 'Let me have some of your aspirins. I might need them the way Nigel drives.'

Nigel heard and called out, 'Marse Rufe, you can drive. I'll just sit back and relax while you show me how to go smooth over a bumpy road.'

Rufus threw a clod of dirt at him, and he caught it, laughing, and threw it back just missing Rufus. 'See there?' Rufus told me. 'Here I am all crippled up and he's taking advantage.'

I laughed and got the aspirins. Rufus never took anything from my bag without asking – though he could have easily done so.

'You sure you feel well enough to go to town?' I asked as I gave them to him.

'No,' he said, 'but I'm going.' I didn't find out until later that a visitor had brought him word of Alice and Isaac's capture. He was going to get Alice.

And I went to the laundry yard to help a young slave named Tess to beat and boil the dirt out of a lot of heavy smelly clothes. She had been sick, and I had promised her I would help. My work was still pretty much whatever I wanted it to be. I felt a little guilty about that. No other slave – house or field – had that much freedom. I worked where I pleased, or where I saw that others needed help. Sarah sent me to do one job or another sometimes, but I didn't mind that. In Margaret's absence, Sarah ran the house – and the house servants. She spread the work fairly and managed the house as efficiently as Margaret had, but without much of the tension and strife Margaret generated. She was resented, of course, by slaves who made every effort to avoid jobs they didn't like. But she was also obeyed.

'Lazy niggers!' she would mutter when she had to get after someone.

I stared at her in surprise when I first heard her say it. 'Why should they work hard?' I asked. 'What's it going to get them?'

'It'll get them the cowhide if they don't,' she snapped. 'I ain't goin' to take the blame for what they don't do. Are you?'

'Well, no, but . . .'

'I work. You work. Don't need somebody behind us all the time to make us work.'

'When the time comes for me to stop working and get out of here, I'll do it.'

She jumped, looked around quickly. 'You got no sense sometimes! Just talk all over your mouth!'

'We're alone.'

'Might not be alone as we look. People listen around here. And they talk too.'

I said nothing.

'You do what you want to do – or think you want to do. But you keep it to yourself.'

I nodded. 'I hear.'

She lowered her voice to a whisper. 'You need to look at some of the niggers they catch and bring back,' she said. 'You need to see them – starving, 'bout naked, whipped, dragged, bit by dogs . . . You need to see them.'

'I'd rather see the others.'

'What others?'

'The ones who make it. The ones living in freedom now.'

'If any do.'

'They do.'

'Some say they do. It's like dying, though, and going to heaven. Nobody ever comes back to tell you about it.'

'Come back and be enslaved again?'

'Yeah. But still . . . This is dangerous talk! No point to it anyway.'

'Sarah, I've seen books written by slaves who've run away and lived in the North.'

'Books!' She tried to sound contemptuous but sounded uncertain instead. She couldn't read. Books could be awesome

158

mysteries to her, or they could be dangerous time-wasting nonsense. It depended on her mood. Now her mood seemed to flicker between curiosity and fear. Fear won. 'Foolishness!' she said. 'Niggers writing books!'

'But it's true. I've seen . . .'

'Don't want to hear no more 'bout it!' She had raised her voice sharply. That was unusual, and it seemed to surprise her as much as it surprised me. 'Don't want to hear no more,' she repeated softly. 'Things ain't bad here. I can get along.'

She had done the safe thing – had accepted a life of slavery because she was afraid. She was the kind of woman who might have been called 'mammy' in some other household. She was the kind of woman who would be held in contempt during the militant nineteen sixties. The house-nigger, the handkerchief-head, the female Uncle Tom – the frightened powerless woman who had already lost all she could stand to lose, and who knew as little about the freedom of the North as she knew about the hereafter.

I looked down on her myself for a while. Moral superiority. Here was someone even less courageous than I was. That comforted me somehow. Or it did until Rufus and Nigel drove into town and came back with what was left of Alice.

It was late when they got home – almost dark. Rufus ran into the house shouting for me before I realized he was back. 'Dana! Dana, get down here!'

I came out of his room – my new refuge when he wasn't in it – and hurried down the stairs.

'Come on, come on!' he urged.

I said nothing, followed him out the front door not knowing what to expect. He led me to the wagon where Alice lay bloody, filthy, and barely alive.

'Oh my God,' I whispered.

'Help her!' demanded Rufus.

I looked at him, remembering why Alice needed help. I didn't say anything, and I don't know what expression I was wearing, but he took a step back from me.

159

'Just help her!' he said. 'Blame me if you want to, but help her!'

I turned to her, straightened her body gently, feeling for broken bones. Miraculously, there didn't seem to be any. Alice moaned and cried out weakly. Her eyes were open, but she didn't seem to see me.

'Where will you put her?' I asked Rufus. 'In the attic?'

He lifted her gently, carefully, and carried her up to his bedroom.

Nigel and I followed him up, saw him place the girl on his bed. Then he looked up at me questioningly.

'Tell Sarah to boil some water,' I told Nigel. 'And tell her to send some clean cloth for bandages. Clean cloth.' How clean would it be? Not sterile, of course, but I had just spent the day cooking clothes in lye soap and water. That surely got them clean.

'Rufe, get me something to cut these rags off her.'

Rufus hurried out, came back with a pair of his mother's scissors.

Most of Alice's wounds were new, and the cloth came away from them easily. Those that had dried and stuck to the cloth, I left alone. Warm water would soften them.

'Rufe, have you got any kind of antiseptic?'

'Anti-what?'

I looked at him. 'You've never heard of it?'

'No. What is it?'

'Never mind. I could use a salt solution, I guess.'

'Brine? You want to use that on her back?'

'I want to use it wherever she's hurt.'

'Don't you have anything in your bag better than that?'

'Just soap, which I intend to use. Find it for me, will you? Then . . . hell, I shouldn't be doing this. Why didn't you take her to the doctor?'

He shook his head. 'The judge wanted her sold South – for spite, I guess. I had to pay near twice what she's worth to get her. That's all the money I had, and Daddy won't pay for a doctor to fix niggers. Doc knows that.'

'You mean your father just lets people die when maybe they could be helped?'

'Die or get well. Aunt Mary – you know, the one who watches the kids?'

'Yes.' Aunt Mary didn't watch the kids. Old and crippled, she sat in the shade with a switch and threatened them with gory murder if they happened to misbehave right in front of her. Otherwise, she ignored them and spent her time sewing and mumbling to herself, contentedly senile. The children cared for each other.

'Aunt Mary does some doctoring,' said Rufus. 'She knows herbs. But I thought you'd know more.'

I turned to look at him in disbelief. Sometimes the poor woman barely knew her name. Finally I shrugged. 'Get me some brine.'

'But . . . that's what Daddy uses on field hands,' he said. 'It hurts them worse than the beating sometimes.'

'It won't hurt her as badly as an infection would later.'

He frowned, came to stand protectively close to the girl. 'Who fixed up your back?'

'I did. No one else was around.'

'What did you do?'

'I washed it with plenty of soap and water, and I put medicine on it. Here, brine will have to be my medicine. It should be just as good.' Please, heaven, let it be as good. I only half knew what I was doing. Maybe old Mary and her herbs weren't such a bad idea after all – if I could be sure of catching her in one of her saner moments. But no. Ignorant as I knew I was, I trusted myself more than I trusted her. Even if I couldn't do any more good than she could, I was at least less likely to do harm.

'Let me see your back,' said Rufus.

I hesitated, swallowed a few indignant words. He spoke out of love for the girl – a destructive love, but a love, nevertheless. He needed to know that it was necessary to hurt her more and that I had some idea what I was doing. I turned my back to

161

him and raised my shirt a little. My cuts were healed or nearly healed.

He didn't speak or touch me. After a moment, I put my shirt down.

'You didn't get the big thick scars some of the hands get,' he observed.

'Keloids. No, thank God, I'm not subject to them. What I've got is bad enough.'

'Not as bad as she'll have.'

'Get the salt, Rufe.'

He nodded and went away.

8

I did my best for Alice, hurt her as little as possible, got her clean and bandaged the worst of her injuries – the dog bites.

'Looks like they just let the dogs chew on her,' said Rufus angrily. He had to hold her for me while I cleaned the bites, gave them special attention. She struggled and wept and called for Isaac, until I was almost sick at having to cause her more pain. I swallowed and clenched my teeth against threatening nausea. When I spoke to Rufus, it was more to calm myself than to get information.

'What did they do with Isaac, Rufe? Give him back to the judge?'

'Sold him to a trader-fellow taking slaves overland to Mississippi.'

'Oh God.'

'He'd be dead if I'd spoken up.'

I shook my head, located another bite. I wanted Kevin. I wanted desperately to go home and be out of this. 'Did you mail my letter, Rufe?'

'Yeah.'

Good. Now if only Kevin would come quickly.

I finished with Alice and gave her, not aspirins, but sleeping pills. She needed rest after days of running, after the dogs and the whipping. After Isaac.

Rufus left her in his bed. He simply climbed in beside her.

'Rufe, for Godsake!'

He looked at me, then at her. 'Don't talk foolishness. I'm not going to put her on the floor.'

'But . . .'

'And I'm sure not going to bother her while she's hurt like this.'

'Good,' I said relieved, believing him. 'Don't even touch her if you can help it.'

'All right.'

I cleaned up the mess I had made and left them. Finally, I made my way to my pallet in the attic, and lay down wearily.

But tired as I was, I couldn't sleep. I thought of Alice, and then of Rufus, and I realized that Rufus had done exactly what I had said he would do: gotten possession of the woman without having to bother with her husband. Now, somehow, Alice would have to accept not only the loss of her husband, but her own enslavement. Rufus had caused her trouble, and now he had been rewarded for it. It made no sense. No matter how kindly he treated her now that he had destroyed her, it made no sense.

I lay turning, twisting, holding my eyes closed and trying first to think, then not to think. I was tempted to squander two more of my sleeping pills to buy myself relief.

Then Sarah came in. I could see her vaguely outlined in the moonlight that came through the window. I whispered her name, trying not to awaken anyone.

She stepped over the two children who slept nearest to me and made her way over to my corner. 'How's Alice?' she asked softly.

'I don't know. She'll probably be all right. Her body will anyway.'

Sarah sat down on the end of my pallet. 'I'd have come in to see her,' she said, 'but then I'd have to see Marse Rufe too. Don't want to see him for a while.'

'Yeah.'

'They cut off the boy's ears.'

I jumped. 'Isaac?'

'Yeah. Cut them both off. He fought. Strong boy, even if he

163

didn't show much sense. The judge's son hit him, and he struck back. And he said some things he shouldn't have said.'

'Rufus said they sold him to a Mississippi trader.'

'Did. After they got through with him. Nigel told me 'bout it – how they cut him, beat him. He'll have to do some healing 'fore he can go to Mississippi or anywhere else.'

'Oh God. All because our little jackass here drank too much and decided to rape somebody!'

She hushed me with a sharp hiss. 'You got to learn to watch what you say! Don't you know there's folks in this house who love to carry tales?'

I sighed. 'Yes.'

'You ain't no field nigger, but you still a nigger. Marse Rufe can get mad and make things mighty hard for you.'

'I know. All right.' Luke's being sold must have frightened her badly. He used to be the one who hushed her.

'Marse Rufe keeping Alice in his room?'

'Yes.'

'Lord, I hope he'll let her 'lone. Tonight, anyway.'

'I think he will. Hell, I think he'll be gentle and patient with her now that he's got her.'

'Huh!' A sound of disgust. 'What'll you do now?'

'Me? Try to keep the girl clean and comfortable until she gets well.'

'I don't mean that.'

I frowned. 'What do you mean?'

'She'll be in. You'll be out.'

I stared at her, tried to see her expression. I couldn't, but I decided she was serious. 'It's not like that, Sarah. She's the only one he seems to want. And me, I'm content with my husband.'

There was a long silence. 'Your husband . . . was that Mister Kevin?'

'Yes.'

'Nigel said you and him was married. I didn't believe it.'

'We kept quiet about it because it's not legal here.'

'Legal!' Another sound of disgust. 'I guess what Marse Rufe done to that girl is legal.'

I shrugged.

'Your husband . . . he'd get in trouble every now and then 'cause he couldn't tell the difference 'tween black and white. Guess now I know why.'

I grinned. 'I'm not why. He was like that when I married him – or I wouldn't have married him. Rufus just sent him a letter telling him to come back and get me.'

She hesitated. 'You sure Marse Rufe sent it?'

'He said he did.'

'Ask Nigel.' She lowered her voice. 'Sometimes Marse Rufe says what will make you feel good – not what's true.'

'But . . . he'd have no reason to lie about it.'

'Didn't say he was lyin'. Just said ask Nigel.'

'All right.'

She was silent for a moment, then, 'You think he'll come back for you, Dana, your . . . husband?'

'I know he will.' He would. Surely he would.

'He ever beat you?'

'No! Of course not!'

'My man used to. He'd tell me I was the only one he cared about. Then, next thing I knew, he'd say I was looking at some other man, and he'd go to hittin'.'

'Carrie's father?'

'No . . . my oldest boy's father. Miss Hannah, her father. He always said he'd free me in his will, but he didn't. It was just another lie.' She stood up, joints creaking. 'Got to get some rest.' She started away. 'Don't you forget now, Dana. Ask Nigel.'

'Yes.'

9

I asked Nigel the next day, but he didn't know. Rufus had sent him on an errand. When Nigel saw Rufus again, it was at the jail where Rufus had just bought Alice.

'She was standing up then,' he said remembering. 'I don't

165

know how. When Marse Rufe was ready to go, he took her by the arm, and she fell over and everybody around laughed. He had paid way too much for her and anybody could see she was more dead than alive. Folks figured he didn't have much sense.'

'Nigel, do you know how long it would take a letter to reach Boston?' I asked.

He looked up from the silver he was polishing. 'How would I know that?' He began rubbing again. 'Like to find out though – follow it and see.' He spoke very softly.

He said things like that now and then when Weylin gave him a hard time, or when the overseer, Edwards, tried to order him around. This time, I thought it was Edwards. The man had stomped out of the cookhouse as I was going in. He would have knocked me down if I hadn't jumped out of his way. Nigel was a house servant and Edwards wasn't supposed to bother him, but he did.

'What happened?' I asked.

'Old bastard swears he'll have me out in the field. Says I think too much of myself.'

I thought of Luke and shuddered. 'Maybe you'd better take off some time soon.'

'Carrie.'

'Yes.'

'Tried to run once. Followed the Star. If not for Marse Rufe, I would have been sold South when they caught me.' He shook his head. 'I'd probably be dead by now.'

I went away from him not wanting to hear any more about running away – and being caught. It was pouring rain outside, but before I reached the house I saw that the hands were still in the fields, still hoeing corn.

I found Rufus in the library going over some papers with his father. I swept the hall until his father left the room. Then I went in to see Rufus.

Before I could open my mouth, he said, 'Have you been up to check on Alice?'

'I'll go in a moment. Rufe, how long does it take for a letter to go from here to Boston?'

He lifted an eyebrow. 'Someday, you're going to call me Rufe down here and Daddy is going to be standing right behind you.'

I looked back in sudden apprehension and Rufus laughed. 'Not today,' he said. 'But someday, if you don't remember.'

'Hell,' I muttered. 'How long?'

He laughed again. 'I don't know, Dana. A few days, a week, two weeks, three . . .' He shrugged.

'His letters were dated,' I said. 'Can you remember when you received the one from Boston?'

He thought about it, finally shook his head. 'No, Dana, I just didn't pay any attention. You better go look in on Alice.'

I went, annoyed, but silent. I thought he could have given me a decent estimate if he had wanted to. But it didn't really matter. Kevin would receive the letter and he could come to get me. I couldn't really doubt that Rufus had sent it. He didn't want to lose my good will anymore than I wanted to lose his. And this was such a small thing.

Alice became a part of my work – an important part. Rufus had Nigel and a young field hand move another bed into Rufus's room – a small low bed that could be pushed under Rufus's bed. We had to move Alice from Rufus's bed for his comfort as well as hers, because for a while, Alice was a very young child again, incontinent, barely aware of us unless we hurt her or fed her. And she did have to be fed – spoonful by spoonful.

Weylin came in to look at her once, while I was feeding her. 'Damn!' he said to Rufus. 'Kindest thing you could do for her would be to shoot her.'

I think the look Rufus gave him scared him a little. He went away without saying anything else.

I changed Alice's bandages, always checking for signs of infection, always hoping not to find any. I wondered what the incubation period was for tetanus or – or for rabies. Then I tried to make myself stop wondering. The girl's body seemed to be healing slowly, but cleanly. I felt superstitious about even

167

thinking about diseases that would surely kill her. Besides, I had enough real worries just keeping her clean and helping her grow up all over again. She called me Mama for a while.

'Mama, it hurts.'

She knew Rufus, though. Mister Rufus. Her friend. He said she crawled into his bed at night.

In one way, that was all right. She was using the pot again. But in another . . .

'Don't look at me like that,' said Rufus when he told me. 'I wouldn't bother her. It would be like hurting a baby.'

Later it would be like hurting a woman. I suspected that wouldn't bother him at all.

As Alice progressed, she became a little more reserved with him. He was still her friend, but she slept in her trundle bed all night. And I ceased to be 'Mama.'

One morning when I brought her breakfast, she looked at me and said, 'Who are you?'

'I'm Dana,' I said. 'Remember?' I always answered her questions.

'No.'

'How do you feel?'

'Kind of stiff and sore.' She put a hand down to her thigh where a dog had literally torn away a mouthful. 'My leg hurts.'

I looked at the wound. She would have a big ugly scar there for the rest of her life, but the wound still seemed to be healing all right – no unusual darkening or swelling. It was as though she had just noticed this specific pain in the same way she had just noticed me.

'Where is this?' she asked.

The way she was just really noticing a lot of things. 'This is the Weylin house,' I said. 'Mister Rufus's room.'

'Oh.' She seemed to relax, content, no longer curious. I didn't push her. I had already decided I wouldn't. I thought she would return to reality when she was strong enough to face it. Tom Weylin, in his loud silence, clearly thought she was hopeless. Rufus never said what he thought. But like me, he didn't push her.

'I almost don't want her to remember,' he said once. 'She could be like she was before Isaac. Then maybe . . .' He shrugged.

'She remembers more every day,' I said. 'And she asks questions.'

'Don't answer her!'

'If I don't, someone else will. She'll be up and around soon.'

He swallowed. 'All this time, it's been so good . . .'

'Good?'

'She hasn't hated me!'

10

Alice continued to heal and to grow. She came down to the cookhouse with me for the first time on the day Carrie had her baby.

Alice had been with us for three weeks. She might have been twelve or thirteen mentally now. That morning, she had told Rufus she wanted to sleep in the attic with me. To my surprise, Rufus had agreed. He hadn't wanted to, but he had done it. I thought, not for the first time, that if Alice could manage to go on not hating him, there would be very little she couldn't ask of him. If.

Now, slowly, cautiously, she followed me down the stairs. She was weak and thinner than ever, looking like a child in one of Margaret Weylin's old dresses. But boredom had driven her from her bed.

'I'll be glad when I get well,' she muttered as she paused on a step. 'I hate to be like this.'

'You're getting well,' I said. I was a little ahead of her, watching to see that she did not stumble. I had taken her arm at the top of the stairs, but she had tried to pull away.

'I can walk.'

I let her walk.

We got to the cookhouse just as Nigel did, but he was in a

bigger hurry. We stood aside and let him rush through the door ahead of us.

'Huh!' said Alice as he went by. ''Scuse me!'

He ignored her. 'Aunt Sarah,' he called, 'Aunt Sarah, Carrie's having pains!'

Old Mary had been the midwife of the plantation before her age caught up with her. Now, the Weylins may have expected her to go on doctoring the slaves, but the slaves knew better. They helped each other as best they could. I hadn't seen Sarah called to help with a birth before, but it was natural that she should be called to this one. She dropped a pan of corn meal and started to follow Nigel out.

'Can I help?' I asked.

She looked at me as though she'd just noticed me. 'See to the supper,' she said. 'I was going to send somebody in to finish cooking, but you can, can't you?'

'Yes.'

'Good.' She and Nigel hurried away. Nigel had a cabin away from the quarter, not far from the cookhouse. A neat wood-floored brick-chimneyed cabin that he had built for himself and Carrie. He had shown it to me. 'Don't have to sleep on rags up in the attic no more,' he'd said. He'd built a bed and two chairs. Rufus had let him hire his time, work for other whites in the area, until he had money enough to buy the things he couldn't make. It had been a good investment for Rufus. Not only did he get part of Nigel's earnings, but he got the assurance that Nigel, his only valuable piece of property, was not likely to run away again soon.

'Can I go see?' Alice asked me.

'No,' I said reluctantly. I wanted to go myself, but Sarah didn't need either of us getting in her way. 'No, you and I have work to do here. Can you peel potatoes?'

'Sure.'

I sat her down at the table and gave her a knife and some potatoes to peel. The scene reminded me of my own first time in the cookhouse when I had sat peeling potatoes until Kevin

170

called me away. Kevin might have my letter by now. He almost surely did. He might already be on his way here.

I shook my head and began cutting up a chicken. No sense tormenting myself.

'Mama used to make me cook,' said Alice. She frowned as though trying to remember. 'She said I'd have to be cooking for my husband.' She frowned again, and I almost cut myself trying to watch her. What was she remembering?

'Dana?'

'Yes?'

'Don't you have a husband? I remember once . . . something about you having a husband.'

'I do. He's up North now.'

'He free?'

'Yes.'

'Good to marry a freeman. Mama always said I should.'

Mama was right, I thought. But I said nothing.

'My father was a slave, and they sold him away from her. She said marrying a slave is almost bad as being a slave.' She looked at me. 'What's it like to be a slave?'

I managed not to look surprised. It hadn't occurred to me that she didn't realize she was a slave. I wondered how she had explained her presence here to herself.

'Dana?'

I looked at her.

'I said what's it like to be a slave?'

'I don't know.' I took a deep breath. 'I wonder how Carrie is doing – in all that pain, and not even able to scream.'

'How could you not know what it's like to be a slave. You are one.'

'I haven't been one for very long.'

'You were free?'

'Yes.'

'And you let yourself be made a slave? You should run away.'

I glanced at the door. 'Be careful how you say things like that. You could get into trouble.' I felt like Sarah, cautioning.

'Well it's true.'

'Sometimes it's better to keep the truth to yourself.'

She stared at me with concern. 'What will happen to you?'

'Don't worry about me, Alice. My husband will help me get free.' I went to the door to look out toward Carrie's cabin. Not that I expected to see anything. I just wanted to distract Alice. She was getting too close, 'growing' too fast. Her life would change so much for the worse when she remembered. She would be hurt more, and Rufus would do much of the hurting. And I would have to watch and do nothing.

'Mama said she'd rather be dead than be a slave,' she said.

'Better to stay alive,' I said. 'At least while there's a chance to get free.' I thought of the sleeping pills in my bag and wondered just how great a hypocrite I was. It was so easy to advise other people to live with their pain.

Suddenly, she threw the potato she had been peeling into the fire.

I jumped, looked at her. 'Why'd you do that?'

'There's things you ain't saying.'

I sighed.

'I'm here too,' she said. 'Been here a long time.' She narrowed her eyes. 'Am I a slave too?'

I didn't answer.

'I said am I a slave?'

'Yes.'

She had risen half off the bench, her whole body demanding that I answer her. Now that I had, she sat down again heavily, her back and shoulders rounded, her arms crossed over her stomach hugging herself. 'But I'm supposed to be free. I was free. Born free!'

'Yes.'

'Dana, tell me what I don't remember. Tell me!'

'It will come back to you.'

'No, you tell—'

'Oh, hush, will you!'

She drew back a little in surprise. I had shouted at her. She probably thought I was angry – and I was. But not at her. I wanted to pull her back from the edge of a cliff. It was too late though. She would have to take her fall.

'I'll tell you whatever you want to know,' I said wearily. 'But believe me, you don't want to know as much as you think you do.'

'Yes I do!'

I sighed. 'All right. What do you want to know?'

She opened her mouth, then frowned and closed it again. Finally, 'There's so much . . . I want to know everything, but I don't know where to start. Why am I a slave?'

'You committed a crime.'

'A crime? What'd I do?'

'You helped a slave to escape.' I paused. 'Do you realize that in all the time you've been here, you never asked me how you were hurt?'

That seemed to touch something in her. She sat blank-faced for several seconds, then frowned and stood up. I watched her carefully. If she was going to have hysterics, I wanted her to have them where she was, out of sight of the Weylins. There were too many things she could say that Tom Weylin in particular would resent.

'They beat me,' she whispered. 'I remember. The dogs, the rope . . . They tied me behind a horse and I had to run, but I couldn't . . . Then they beat me . . . But . . . but . . .'

I walked over to her, stood in front of her, but she seemed to look through me. She had that same look of pain and confusion she'd had when Rufus brought her from town.

'Alice?'

She seemed not to hear me. 'Isaac?' she whispered. But it was more a soundless moving of her lips than a whisper. Then,

'*Isaac!*' An explosion of sound. She bolted for the door. I let her take about three steps before I grabbed her.

'Let go of me! Isaac! *Isaac!*'

'Alice, stop. You'll make me hurt you.' She was struggling against me with all her feeble strength.

173

'They cut him! They cut off his ears!'

I had been hoping she hadn't seen that. 'Alice!' I held her by the shoulders and shook her.

'I've got to get away,' she wept. 'Find Isaac.'

'Maybe. When you can walk more than ten steps without getting tired.'

She stopped her struggles, stared at me through streaming tears. 'Where'd they send him?'

'Mississippi.'

'Oh Jesus . . .' She collapsed against me, crying. She would have fallen if I hadn't held her and half-dragged and half-carried her back to the bench. She sat slumped where I put her, crying, praying, cursing. I sat with her for a while, but she didn't tire, or at least, she didn't stop. I had to leave her to finish preparing supper. I was afraid I would anger Weylin and get Sarah into trouble if I didn't. There would be trouble enough in the house now that Alice had her memory back, and somehow, it had become my job to ease troubles – first Rufus's, now Alice's – as best I could.

I finished the meal somehow, though my mind wasn't on it. There was the soup that Sarah had left simmering; fish to fry; ham that had been rock-hard before Sarah soaked it, then boiled it; chicken to fry and corn bread and gravy to make; Alice's forgotten potatoes to finish; bread to bake in the little brick oven alongside the fireplace; vegetables, including salad; a sugary peach dessert – Weylin raised peaches; a cake that Sarah had already made, thank God; and both coffee and tea. There would be company to help eat it all. There usually was. And they would all eat too much. It was no wonder the main medicines of this era were laxatives.

I got the food ready, almost on time, then had to hunt down the two little boys whose job it was to ferry it from cookhouse to table and then serve it. When I found them, they wasted some time staring at the now silent Alice, then they grumbled because I made them wash. Finally, my washhouse friend Tess, who also worked in the main house, ran out and said, 'Marse Tom say get food on the table!'

174

'Is the table set?'

'Been set! Even though you didn't say nothin'.'

Oops. 'I'm sorry, Tess. Here, help me out.' I thrust a covered dish of soup into her hands. 'Carrie is having her baby now and Sarah's gone to help her. Take that in, would you?'

'And come back for more?'

'Please.'

She hurried away. I had helped her with the washing several times – had done as much of it as I could myself recently because Weylin had casually begun taking her to bed, and had hurt her. Apparently, she paid her debts.

I went out to the well and got the boys just as they were starting a water fight.

'If you two don't get yourselves into the house with that food . . .!'

'You sound just like Sarah.'

'No I don't. You know what she'd be saying. You know what she'd be doing too. Now move! Or I'll get a switch and really be like her.'

Dinner was served. Somehow. And it was all edible. There may have been more of it if Sarah had been cooking, but it wouldn't have tasted any better. Sarah had managed to overcome my uncertainty, my ignorance of cooking on an open hearth and teach me quite a bit.

As the meal progressed and the leftovers began to come back, I tried to get Alice to eat. I fixed her a plate but she pushed it away, turned her back to me.

She had sat either staring into space or resting her head on the table for hours. Now, finally, she spoke.

'Why didn't you tell me?' she asked bitterly. 'You could have said something, got me out of his room, his bed . . . Oh Lord, his bed! And he may as well have cut my Isaac's ears off with his own hand.'

'He never told anyone Isaac beat him.'

'Shit!'

'It's true. He never did because he didn't want you to get

hurt. I know because I was with him until he got back on his feet. I took care of him.'

'If you had any sense, you would have let him die!'

'If I had, it wouldn't have kept you and Isaac from being caught. It might have gotten you both killed though if anyone guessed what Isaac had done.'

'Doctor-nigger,' she said with contempt. 'Think you know so much. Reading-nigger. *White-nigger!* Why didn't you know enough to let me die?'

I said nothing. She was getting angrier and angrier, shouting at me. I turned away from her sadly, telling myself it was better, safer for her to vent her feelings on me than on anyone else.

Along with her shouting now, I could hear the thin faint cries of a baby.

11

Carrie and Nigel named their thin, wrinkled, brown son, Jude. Nigel did a lot of strutting and happy babbling until Weylin told him to shut up and get back to work on the covered passageway he was supposed to be building to connect the house and the cookhouse. A few days after the baby's birth, though, Weylin called him into the library and gave him a new dress for Carrie, a new blanket, and a new suit of clothes for himself.

'See,' Nigel told me later with some bitterness. ''Cause of Carrie and me, he's one nigger richer.' But before the Weylins, he was properly grateful.

'Thank you, Marse Tom. Yes, sir. Sure do thank you. Fine clothes, yes, sir . . .'

Finally he escaped back to the covered passageway.

Meanwhile, in the library, I heard Weylin tell Rufus, 'You should have been the one to give him something – instead of wasting all your money on that worthless girl.'

'She's well!' Rufus answered. 'Dana got her well. Why do you say she's worthless?'

'Because you're going to have to whip her sick again to get what you want from her!'

Silence.

'Dana should have been enough for you. She's got some sense.' He paused. 'Too much sense for her own good, I'd say, but at least she wouldn't give you trouble. She's had that Franklin fellow to teach her a few things.'

Rufus walked away from him without answering. I had to get away from the library door where I had been eavesdropping very quickly as I heard him approach. I ducked into the dining room and came out again just as he was passing by.

'Rufe.'

He gave me a look that said he didn't want to be bothered, but he stopped anyway.

'I want to write another letter.'

He frowned. 'You've got to be patient, Dana. It hasn't been that long.'

'It's been over a month.'

'Well . . . I don't know. Kevin could have moved again, could have done anything. I think you should give him a little more time to answer.'

'Answer what?' asked Weylin. He'd done what Rufus had predicted – come up behind us so silently that I hadn't noticed him.

Rufus glanced at his father sourly. 'Letter to Kevin Franklin telling him she's here.'

'She wrote a letter?'

'I told her to write it. Why should I do it when she can?'

'Boy, you don't have the sense you—' He cut off abruptly. 'Dana, go do your work!'

I left wondering whether Rufus had shown lack of sense by letting me write the letter – instead of writing it himself – or by sending it. After all, if Kevin never came back for me, Weylin's property was increased by one more slave. Even if I proved not to be very useful, he could always sell me.

177

I shuddered. I had to talk Rufus into letting me write another letter. The first one could have been lost or destroyed or sent to the wrong place. Things like that were still happening in 1976. How much worse might they be in this horse-and-buggy era? And surely Kevin would give up on me if I went home without him again – left him here for more long years. If he hadn't already given up on me.

I tried to put that thought out of my mind. It came to me now and then even though everything people told me seemed to indicate that he was waiting. Still waiting.

I went out to the laundry yard to help Tess. I had come to almost welcome the hard work. It kept me from thinking. White people thought I was industrious. Most blacks thought I was either stupid or too intent on pleasing the whites. I thought I was keeping my fears and doubts at bay as best I could, and managing to stay relatively sane.

I caught Rufus alone again the next day – in his room this time where we weren't likely to be interrupted. But he wouldn't listen when I brought up the letter. His mind was on Alice. She was stronger now, and his patience with her was gone. I had thought that eventually, he would just rape her again – and again. In fact, I was surprised that he hadn't already done it. I didn't realize that he was planning to involve me in that rape. He was, and he did.

'Talk to her, Dana,' he said once he'd brushed aside the matter of my letter. 'You're older than she is. She thinks you know a lot. Talk to her!'

He was sitting on his bed staring into the cold fireplace. I sat at his desk looking at the clear plastic pen I had loaned him. He'd used half its ink already. 'What the hell have you been writing with this?' I asked.

'Dana, listen to me!'

I turned to face him. 'I heard you.'

'Well?'

'I can't stop you from raping the woman, Rufe, but I'm not going to help you do it either.'

'You want her to get hurt?'

'Of course not. But you've already decided to hurt her, haven't you?'

He didn't answer.

'Let her go, Rufe. Hasn't she suffered enough because of you?' He wouldn't. I knew he wouldn't.

His green eyes glittered. 'She'll never get away from me again. Never!' He drew a deep breath, let it out slowly. 'You know, Daddy wants me to send her to the fields and take you.'

'Does he?'

'He thinks all I want is a woman. Any woman. So you, then. He says you'd be less likely to give me trouble.'

'Do you believe him?'

He hesitated, managed to smile a little. 'No.'

I nodded. 'Good.'

'I know you, Dana. You want Kevin the way I want Alice. And you had more luck than I did because no matter what happens now, for a while he wanted you too. Maybe I can't ever have that – both wanting, both loving. But I'm not going to give up what I can have.'

'What do you mean, "no matter what happens now?"'

'What in hell do you think I mean? It's been five years! You want to write another letter. Did you ever think maybe he threw the first letter out? Maybe he got like Alice – wanted to be with one of his own kind.'

I said nothing. I knew what he was doing – trying to share his pain, hurt me as he was hurting. And of course, he knew just where I was vulnerable. I tried to keep a neutral expression, but he went on.

'He told me once that you two had been married for four years. That means he's been here away from you even longer than you've been together. I doubt if he'd have waited as long as he did if you weren't the only one who could get him back to his home time. But now . . . who knows. The right woman could make this time mighty sweet to him.'

'Rufe, nothing you say to me is going to ease your way with Alice.'

'No? How about this: you talk to her – talk some sense into her – or you're going to watch while Jake Edwards beats some sense into her!'

I stared at him in revulsion. 'Is that what you call love?'

He was on his feet and across the room to me before I could take another breath. I sat where I was, watching him, feeling frightened, and suddenly very much aware of my knife, of how quickly I could reach it. He wasn't going to beat me. Not him, not ever.

'Get up!' he ordered. He didn't order me around much, and he'd never done it in that tone. 'Get up, I said!'

I didn't move.

'I've been too easy on you,' he said. His voice was suddenly low and ugly. 'I treated you like you were better than the ordinary niggers. I see I made a mistake!'

'That's possible,' I said. 'I'm waiting for you to show me I made a mistake.'

For several seconds, he stood frozen, towering over me, glaring down as though he meant to hit me. Finally, though, he relaxed, leaned against his desk. 'You think you're white!' he muttered. 'You don't know your place any better than a wild animal.'

I said nothing.

'You think you own me because you saved my life!'

And I relaxed, glad not to have to take the life I had saved – glad not to have to risk other lives, including my own.

'If I ever caught myself wanting you like I want her, I'd cut my throat,' he said.

I hoped that problem would never arise. If it did, one of us would do some cutting all right.

'Help me, Dana.'

'I can't.'

'You can! You and nobody else. Go to her. Send her to me. I'll have her whether you help or not. All I want you to do is fix it so I don't have to beat her. You're no friend of hers if you won't do that much!'

Of hers! He had all the low cunning of his class. No, I couldn't refuse to help the girl – help her avoid at least some pain. But she wouldn't think much of me for helping her this way. I didn't think much of myself.

'Do it!' hissed Rufus.

I got up and went out to find her.

She was strange now, erratic, sometimes needing my friendship, trusting me with her dangerous longings for freedom, her wild plans to run away again; and sometimes hating me, blaming me for her trouble.

One night in the attic, she was crying softly and telling me something about Isaac. She stopped suddenly and asked, 'Have you heard from your husband yet, Dana?'

'Not yet.'

'Write another letter. Even if you have to do it in secret.'

'I'm working on it.'

'No sense in you losing your man too.'

Yet moments later for no reason that I could see, she attacked me, 'You ought to be ashamed of yourself, whining and crying after some poor white trash of a man, black as you are. You always try to act so white. White nigger, turning against your own people!'

I never really got used to her sudden switches, her attacks, but I put up with them. I had taken her through all the other stages of healing, and somehow, I couldn't abandon her now. Most of the time, I couldn't even get angry. She was like Rufus. When she hurt, she struck out to hurt others. But she had been hurting less as the days passed, and striking out less. She was healing emotionally as well as physically. I had helped her to heal. Now I had to help Rufus tear her wounds open again.

She was at Carrie's cabin watching Jude and two other older babies someone had left with her. She had no regular duties yet, but like me, she had found her own work. She liked children, and she liked sewing. She would take the coarse blue cloth Weylin bought for the slaves and make neat sturdy clothing of it while small children played around her feet. Weylin

181

complained that she was like old Mary with the children and the sewing, but he brought her his clothing to be mended. She worked better and faster than the slave woman who had taken over much of old Mary's sewing – and if she had an enemy on the plantation, it was that woman, Liza, who was now in danger of being sent to more onerous work.

I went into the cabin and sat down with Alice before the cold fireplace. Jude slept beside her in the crib Nigel had made for him. The other two babies were awake lying naked on blankets on the floor quietly playing with their feet.

Alice looked up at me, then held up a long blue dress. 'This is for you,' she said. 'I'm sick of seeing you in them pants.'

I looked down at my jeans. 'I'm so used to dressing like this, I forget sometimes. At least it keeps me from having to serve at the table.'

'Serving ain't bad.' She'd done it a few times. 'And if Mister Tom wasn't so stingy, you'd have had a dress a long time ago. Man loves a dollar more than he loves Jesus.'

That, I believed literally. Weylin had dealings with banks. I knew because he complained about them. But I had never known him to have any dealings with churches or hold any kind of prayer meeting in his home. The slaves had to sneak away in the night and take their chances with the patrollers if they wanted to have any kind of religious meeting.

'Least you can look like a woman when your man comes for you,' Alice said.

I drew a deep breath. 'Thanks.'

'Yeah. Now tell me what you come here to say . . . that you don't want to say.'

I looked at her, startled.

'You think I don't know you after all this time? You got a look that says you don't want to be here.'

'Yes. Rufus sent me to talk to you.' I hesitated. 'He wants you tonight.'

Her expression hardened. 'He sent *you* to tell me that?'

'No.'

182

She waited, glaring at me, silently demanding that I tell her more.

I said nothing.

'Well! What did he send you for then?'

'To talk you into going to him quietly, and to tell you you'd be whipped this time if you resist.'

'Shit! Well, all right, you told me. Now get out of here before I throw this dress in the fireplace and light it.'

'I don't give a damn what you do with that dress.'

Now it was her turn to be startled. I didn't usually talk to her that way, even when she deserved it.

I leaned back comfortably in Nigel's homemade chair. 'Message delivered,' I said. 'Do what you want.'

'I mean to.'

'You might look ahead a little though. Ahead and in all three directions.'

'What are you talking about?'

'Well, it looks as though you have three choices. You can go to him as he orders; you can refuse, be whipped, and then have him take you by force; or you can run away again.'

She said nothing, bent to her sewing and drew the needle in quick neat tiny stitches even though her hands were shaking. I bent down to play with one of the babies – one who had forgotten his own feet and crawled over to investigate my shoe. He was a fat curious little boy of several months who began trying to pull the buttons off my blouse as soon as I picked him up.

'He go' pee all over you in a minute,' said Alice. 'He likes to let go just when somebody's holding him.'

I put the baby down quickly – just in time, as it turned out. 'Dana?'

I looked at her.

'What am I going to do?'

I hesitated, shook my head. 'I can't advise you. It's your body.'

'Not mine.' Her voice had dropped to a whisper. 'Not mine, his. He paid for it, didn't he?'

'Paid who? You?'

'You know he didn't pay me! Oh, what's the difference? Whether it's right or wrong, the law says he owns me now. I don't know why he hasn't already whipped the skin off me. The things I've said to him . . .'

'You know why.'

She began to cry. 'I ought to take a knife in there with me and cut his damn throat.' She glared at me. 'Now go tell him that! Tell him I'm talking 'bout killing him!'

'Tell him yourself.'

'Do your job! Go tell him! That's what you for – to help white folks keep niggers down. That's why he sent you to me. They be calling you mammy in a few years. You be running the whole house when the old man dies.'

I shrugged and stopped the curious baby from sucking on my shoe string.

'Go tell on me, Dana. Show him you the kind of woman he needs, not me.'

I said nothing.

'One white man, two white men, what difference do it make?'

'One black man, two black men, what difference does that make?'

'I could have ten black men without turning against my own.'

I shrugged again, refusing to argue with her. What could I win?

She made a wordless sound and covered her face with her hands. 'What's the matter with you?' she said wearily. 'Why you let me run you down like that? You done everything you could for me, maybe even saved my life. I seen people get lockjaw and die from way less than I had wrong with me. Why you let me talk about you so bad?'

'Why do you do it?'

She sighed, bent her body into a 'c' as she crouched in the chair. 'Because I get so mad . . . I get so mad I can taste it in my mouth. And you're the only one I can take it out on – the only one I can hurt and not be hurt back.'

184

'Don't keep doing it,' I said. 'I have feelings just like you do.'

'Do you want me to go to him?'

'I can't tell you that. You have to decide.'

'Would you go to him?'

I glanced at the floor. 'We're in different situations. What I'd do doesn't matter.'

'*Would you go to him?*'

'No.'

'Even though he's just like your husband?'

'He isn't.'

'But . . . All right, even though you don't . . . don't hate him like I do?'

'Even so.'

'Then I won't go either.'

'What will you do?'

'I don't know. Run away?'

I got up to leave.

'Where you going?' she asked quickly.

'To stall Rufus. If I really work at it, I think I can get him to let you off tonight. That will give you a start.'

She dropped the dress to the floor and came out of her chair to grab me. 'No, Dana! Don't go.' She drew a deep breath, then seemed to sag. 'I'm lying. I can't run again. I can't. You be hungry and cold and sick out there, and so tired you can't walk. Then they find you and set dogs on you . . . My Lord, the dogs . . .' She was silent for a moment. 'I'm going to him. He knew I would sooner or later. But he don't know how I wish I had the nerve to just kill him!'

12

She went to him. She adjusted, became a quieter more subdued person. She didn't kill, but she seemed to die a little.

Kevin didn't come to me, didn't write. Rufus finally let me write another letter – payment for services rendered, I supposed – and he mailed it for me. Yet another month went by, and Kevin didn't reply.

'Don't worry about it,' Rufus told me. 'He probably did move again. We'll be getting a letter from him in Maine any day now.'

I didn't say anything. Rufus had become talkative and happy, openly affectionate to a quietly tolerant Alice. He drank more than he should have sometimes, and one morning after he'd really overdone it, Alice came downstairs with her whole face swollen and bruised.

That was the morning I stopped wondering whether I should ask him to help me go North to find Kevin. I wouldn't have expected him to give me money, but he could have gotten me some damned official-looking free papers. He could even have gone with me, at least to the Pennsylvania State Line. Or he could have stopped me cold.

He had already found the way to control me – by threatening others. That was safer than threatening me directly, and it worked. It was a lesson he had no doubt learned from his father. Weylin, for instance, had known just how far to push Sarah. He had sold only three of her children – left her one to live for and protect. I didn't doubt now that he could have found a buyer for Carrie, afflicted as she was. But Carrie was a useful young woman. Not only did she work hard and well herself, not only had she produced a healthy new slave, but she had kept first her mother, and now her husband in line with no effort at all on Weylin's part. I didn't want to find out how much Rufus had learned from his father's handling of her.

I longed for my map now. It contained names of towns I could write myself passes to. No doubt some of the towns on it didn't exist yet, but at least it would have given me a better idea of what was ahead. I would have to take my chances without it.

Well, at least I knew that Easton was a few miles to the north, and that the road that ran past the Weylin house would take me to it. Unfortunately, it would also take me through a lot of open fields – places where it would be nearly impossible to hide. And pass or no pass, I would hide from whites if I could.

I would have to carry food – johnnycake, smoked meat, dried fruit, a bottle of water. I had access to what I needed. I had heard of runaway slaves starving before they reached freedom, or poisoning themselves because they were as ignorant as I was about which wild plants were edible.

In fact, I had read and heard enough scare stories about the fate of runaways to keep me with the Weylins for several days longer than I meant to stay. I might not have believed them, but I had the example of Isaac and Alice before me. Fittingly, then, it was Alice who gave me the push I needed.

I was helping Tess with the wash – sweating and stirring dirty clothes as they boiled in their big iron pot – when Alice came to me, crept to me, looking back over her shoulder, her eyes wide with what I read as fear.

'You look at this,' she said to me, not even glancing at Tess who had stopped pounding a pair of Weylin's pants to watch us. She trusted Tess. 'See,' she said. 'I been looking where I wasn't s'pose to look – in Mister Rufe's bed chest. But what I found don't look like it ought to be there.'

She took two letters from her apron pocket. Two letters, their seals broken, their faces covered with my handwriting.

'Oh my God,' I whispered.

'Yours?'

'Yes.'

'Thought so. I can read some words. Got to take these back now.'

'Yes.'

She turned to go.

'Alice.'

'Yeah?'

'Thanks. Be careful when you put them back.'

'You be careful too,' she said. Our eyes met and we both knew what she was talking about.

I left that night.

I collected the food and 'borrowed' one of Nigel's old hats, to pull down over my hair – which wasn't very long, luckily. When I asked Nigel for the hat, he just looked at me for a long moment, then got it for me. No questions. I didn't think he expected to see it again.

I stole a pair of Rufus's old trousers and a worn shirt. My jeans and shirts were too well known to Rufus's neighbors, and the dress Alice had made me looked too much like the dresses every other slave woman on the place wore. Besides, I had decided to become a boy. In the loose, shabby, but definitely male clothing I had chosen, my height and my contralto voice would get me by. I hoped.

I packed everything I could into my denim bag and left it in its place on my pallet where I normally used it as a pillow. My freedom of movement was more useful to me now than it had ever been. I could go where I wanted to and no one said, 'What are you doing here? Why aren't you working?' Everyone assumed I was working. Wasn't I the industrious stupid one who always worked?

So I was left alone, allowed to make my preparations. I even got a chance to prowl through Weylin's library. Finally, at day's end, I went to the attic with the other house servants and lay down to wait until they were asleep. That was my mistake.

I wanted the others to be able to say they saw me go to bed. I wanted Rufus and Tom Weylin to waste time looking around the plantation for me tomorrow when they realized they hadn't seen me for a while. They wouldn't do that if some house servant – one of the children, perhaps – said, 'She never went to bed last night.'

Overplanning.

I got up when the others had been quiet for some time. It was about midnight, and I knew I could be past Easton before morning. I had talked to others who had walked the distance. Before the sun rose, though, I'd have to find a place to hide and sleep. Then I could write myself a pass to one of the other places whose names and general locations I had learned in Weylin's library. There was a place near the county line called Wye Mills. Beyond that, I would veer northeast, slanting toward the plantation of a cousin of Weylin's and toward Delaware to travel up the highest part of the peninsula. In that way, I hoped to avoid many of the rivers. I had a feeling they were what would make my trip long and difficult.

I crept away from the Weylin house, moving through the darkness with even less confidence than I had felt when I fled to Alice's house months before. Years before. I hadn't known quite as well then what there was to fear. I had never seen a captured runaway like Alice. I had never felt the whip across my own back. I had never felt a man's fists.

I felt almost sick to my stomach with fear, but I kept walking. I stumbled over a stick that lay in the road and first cursed it, then picked it up. It felt good in my hand, solid. A stick like this had saved me once. Now, it quenched a little of my fear, gave me confidence. I walked faster, moving into the woods alongside the road as soon as I passed Weylin's fields.

The way was north toward Alice's old cabin, toward the Holman plantation, toward Easton which I would have to skirt. The walking was easy, at least. This was flat country with only a few barely noticeable rolling hills to break the monotony. The road ran through thick dark woods that were probably full of good places to hide. And the only water I saw flowed in streams so tiny they barely wet my feet. That wouldn't last, though. There would be rivers.

I hid from an old black man who drove a wagon pulled by a mule. He went by humming tunelessly, apparently fearing neither patrollers nor any other dangers of the night. I envied his calmness.

I hid from three white men who rode by on horseback. They had a dog with them, and I was afraid it would smell me and give me away. Luckily, the wind was in my favor, and it went on its way. Another dog found me later, though. It came racing toward me through a field and over a rail fence, barking and growling. I turned to meet it almost without thinking, and clubbed it down as it lunged at me.

I wasn't really afraid. Dogs with white men frightened me, or dogs in packs – Sarah had told me of runaways who had been torn to pieces by the packs of dogs used to hunt them. But one lone dog didn't seem to be much of a threat.

As it turned out, the dog was no threat at all. I hit it, it fell, then got up and limped away yelping. I let it go, glad I hadn't had to hurt it worse. I liked dogs normally.

I hurried on, wanting to be out of sight if the dog's noise brought people out to investigate. The experience did make me a little more confident of my ability to defend myself, though, and the natural night noises disturbed me less.

I reached the town and avoided what I could see of it – a few shadowy buildings. I walked on, beginning to tire, beginning to worry that dawn was not far away. I couldn't tell whether my worrying was legitimate or came from my desire to rest. Not for the first time, I wished I had been wearing a watch when Rufus called me.

I pushed myself on until I could see that the sky really was growing light. Then, as I looked around wondering where I could find shelter for the day, I heard horses. I moved farther from the road and crouched in a thick growth of bushes, grasses, and young trees. I was used to hiding now, and no more afraid than I had been when I'd hidden before. No one had spotted me yet.

There were two horsemen moving slowly up the road toward me. Very slowly. They were looking around, peering through the dimness into the trees. I could see that one of them was riding a light colored horse. A gray horse, I saw as it drew closer, a . . .

I jumped. I managed not to gasp, but I did make that one small involuntary movement. And a twig that I hadn't noticed snapped under me.

The horsemen stopped almost in front of me, Rufus on the gray he usually rode, and Tom Weylin on a darker animal. I could see them clearly now. They were looking for me – already! They shouldn't even have known yet that I was gone. They couldn't have known – unless someone told them. Someone must have seen me leaving, someone other than Rufus or Tom Weylin. They would simply have stopped me. It must have been one of the slaves. Someone had betrayed me. And now, I had betrayed myself.

'I heard something,' said Tom Weylin.

And Rufus, 'So did I. She's around here somewhere.'

I shrank down, tried to make myself smaller without moving enough to make more noise.

'Damn that Franklin,' I heard Rufus say.

'You're damning the wrong man,' said Weylin.

Rufus let that go unanswered.

'Look over there!' Weylin was pointing away from me, pointing into the woods ahead of me. He headed his horse over to investigate what he had seen – and frightened out a large bird.

Rufus's eyes were better. He ignored his father and headed straight for me. He couldn't have seen me, couldn't have seen anything other than a possible hiding place. He plunged his horse into the bushes that hid me, plunged it in to either trample me or drive me out.

He drove me out. I threw myself to one side away from the horse's hooves.

Rufus let out a whoop and swung down literally on top of me. I fell under his weight, and the fall twisted my club out of my hand, set it in just the right position for me to fall on.

I heard my stolen shirt tear, felt the splintered wood scrape my side . . .

'She's here!' called Rufus. 'I've got her!'

He would get something else too if I could reach my knife. I twisted downward toward the ankle sheath with him still on top of me. My side was suddenly aflame with pain.

'Come help me hold her,' he called.

His father strode over and kicked me in the face.

That held me, all right. From far away, I could hear Rufus shout – strangely soft shouting – 'You didn't have to do that!'

Weylin's reply was lost to me as I drifted into unconsciousness.

13

I awoke tied hand and foot, my side throbbing rhythmically, my jaw not throbbing at all. The pain there was a steady scream. I probed with my tongue and found that two teeth on the right side were gone.

I had been thrown over Rufus's horse like a grain sack, head and feet hanging, blood dripping from my mouth onto the familiar boot that let me know it was Rufus I rode with.

I made a noise, a kind of choked moan, and the horse stopped. I felt Rufus move, then I was lifted down, placed in the tall grass beside the road. Rufus looked down at me.

'You damn fool,' he said softly. He took his handkerchief and wiped blood from my face. I winced away, tears suddenly filling my eyes at the startlingly increased pain.

'Fool!' repeated Rufus.

I closed my eyes and felt the tears run back into my hair.

'You give me your word you won't fight me, and I'll untie you.'

After a while, I nodded. I felt his hands at my wrists, at my ankles.

'What's this?'

He had found my knife, I thought. Now he would tie me again. That's what I would have done in his place. I looked at him.

He was untying the empty sheath from my ankle. Just a piece of rough-cut, poorly sewn leather. I had apparently lost the knife in my struggle with him. No doubt, though, the shape of the sheath told him what it had held. He looked at it, then at me. Finally, he nodded grimly and, with a sharp motion, threw the sheath away.

'Get up.'

I tried. In the end, he had to help me. My feet were numb from being tied, and were just coming back to painful life. If Rufus decided to make me run behind his horse, I would be dragged to death.

He noticed that I was holding my side as he half-carried me back to his horse, and he stopped to move my hand and look at the wound.

'Scratch,' he pronounced. 'You were lucky. Going to hit me with a stick, were you? And what else were you going to do?'

I said nothing, thought of him sending his horse charging over the spot I had barely leaped from in time.

As I leaned against his horse, he wiped more blood from my face, one hand firmly holding the top of my head so that I couldn't wince away. I bore it somehow.

'Now you've got a gap in your teeth,' he observed. 'Well, if you don't laugh big, nobody'll notice. They weren't the teeth right in front.'

I spat blood and he never realized that I had made my comment on such good luck.

'All right,' he said, 'let's go.'

I waited for him to tie me behind the horse or throw me over it grain-sack fashion again. Instead, he put me in front of him in the saddle. Not until then did I see Weylin waiting for us a few paces down the road.

'See there,' the old man said. 'Educated nigger don't mean smart nigger, do it?' He turned away as though he didn't expect an answer. He didn't get one.

I sat stiffly erect, holding my body straight somehow until Rufus said, 'Will you lean back on me before you fall off! You got more pride than sense.'

He was wrong. At that moment, I couldn't manage any pride at all. I leaned back against him, desperate for any support I could find, and closed my eyes.

He didn't say anything more for a long while – not until we were nearing the house. Then,

'You awake, Dana?'

I sat straight. 'Yes.'

'You're going to get the cowhide,' he said. 'You know that.'

Somehow, I hadn't known. His gentleness had lulled me. Now the thought of being hurt even more terrified me. The whip, again. 'No!'

Without thinking about it or intending to do it, I threw one leg over and slid from the horse. My side hurt, my mouth hurt, my face was still bleeding, but none of that was as bad as the whip. I ran toward the distant trees.

Rufus caught me easily and held me, cursing me, hurting me. 'You take your whipping!' he hissed. 'The more you fight, the more he'll hurt you.'

He? Was Weylin to whip me, then, or the overseer, Edwards?

'Act like you've got some sense!' demanded Rufus as I struggled.

What I acted like was a wild woman. If I'd had my knife, I would surely have killed someone. As it was, I managed to leave scratches and bruises on Rufus, his father, and Edwards who was called over to help. I was totally beyond reasoning. I had never in my life wanted so desperately to kill another human being.

They took me to the barn and tied my hands and raised whatever they had tied them to high over my head. When I was barely able to touch the floor with my toes, Weylin ripped my clothes off and began to beat me.

He beat me until I swung back and forth by my wrists, half-crazy with pain, unable to find my footing, unable to stand the pressure of hanging, unable to get away from the steady slashing blows . . .

He beat me until I tried to make myself believe he was going to kill me. I said it aloud, screamed it, and the blows seemed to emphasize my words. He would kill me. Surely, he would kill me if I didn't get away, save myself, *go home!*

It didn't work. This was only punishment, and I knew it. Nigel had borne it. Alice had borne worse. Both were alive and healthy. I wasn't going to die – though as the beating went on,

194

I wanted to. Anything to stop the pain! But there was nothing. Weylin had ample time to finish whipping me.

I was not aware of Rufus untying me, carrying me out of the barn and into Carrie's and Nigel's cabin. I was not aware of him directing Alice and Carrie to wash me and care for me as I had cared for Alice. That, Alice told me about later – how he demanded that everything used on me be clean, how he insisted on the deep ugly wound in my side – the scratch – being carefully cleaned and bandaged.

He was gone when I awoke, but he left me Alice. She was there to calm me and feed me pills that I saw were my own inadequate aspirins, and to assure me that my punishment was over, that I was all right. My face was almost too swollen for me to ask for salt water to wash my mouth. After several tries, though, she understood and brought it to me.

'Just rest,' she said. 'Carrie and me'll take care of you as good as you took care of me.'

I didn't try to answer. Her words touched something in me, though, started me crying silently. We were both failures, she and I. We'd both run and been brought back, she in days, I in only hours. I probably knew more than she did about the general layout of the Eastern Shore. She knew only the area she'd been born and raised in, and she couldn't read a map. I knew about towns and rivers miles away – and it hadn't done me a damned bit of good! What had Weylin said? That educated didn't mean smart. He had a point. Nothing in my education or knowledge of the future had helped me to escape. Yet in a few years an illiterate runaway named Harriet Tubman would make nineteen trips into this country and lead three hundred fugitives to freedom. What had I done wrong? Why was I still slave to a man who had repaid me for saving his life by nearly killing me. Why had I taken yet another beating. And why . . . why was I so frightened now – frightened sick at the thought that sooner or later, I would have to run again?

I moaned and tried not to think about it. The pain of my body was enough for me to contend with. But now there was a question in my mind that had to be answered.

Would I really try again? Could I?

I moved, twisted myself somehow, from my stomach onto my side. I tried to get away from my thoughts, but they still came.

See how easily slaves are made? they said.

I cried out as though from the pain of my side, and Alice came to ease me into a less agonizing position. She wiped my face with a cool damp cloth.

'I'll try again,' I said to her. And I wondered why I was saying it, boasting, maybe lying.

'What?' she asked.

My swollen face and mouth were still distorting my speech. I would have to repeat the words. Maybe they would give me courage if I said them often enough.

'I'll try again.' I spoke as slowly and as clearly as I could.

'You rest!' Her voice was suddenly rough, and I knew she had understood. 'Time enough later for talking. Go to sleep.'

But I couldn't sleep. The pain kept me awake; my own thoughts kept me awake. I caught myself wondering whether I would be sold to some passing trader this time . . . or next time . . . I longed for my sleeping pills to give me oblivion, but some small part of me was glad I didn't have them. I didn't quite trust myself with them just now. I wasn't quite sure how many of them I might take.

14

Liza, the sewing woman, fell and hurt herself. Alice told me all about it. Liza was bruised and battered. She lost some teeth. She was black and blue all over. Even Tom Weylin was concerned.

'Who did it to you?' he demanded. 'Tell me, and they'll be punished!'

'I fell,' she said sullenly. 'Fell on the stairs.'

Weylin cursed her for a fool and told her to get out of his sight.

And Alice, Tess, and Carrie concealed their few scratches and gave Liza quiet meaningful glances. Glances that Liza turned away from in anger and fear.

'She heard you get up in the night,' Alice told me. 'She got up after you and went straight to Mister Tom. She knew better than to go to Mister Rufe. He might have let you go. Mister Tom never let a nigger go in his life.'

'But why?' I asked from my pallet. I was stronger now, but Rufus had forbidden me to get up. For once, I was glad to obey. I knew that when I got up, Tom Weylin would expect me to work as though I were completely well. Thus, I had missed Liza's 'accident' completely.

'She did it to get at me,' said Alice. 'She would have liked it better if I had been the one slipping out at night, but she hates you too – almost as much. She figures I would have died if not for you.'

I was startled. I had never had a serious enemy – someone who would go out of her way to get me hurt or killed. To slaveholders and patrollers, I was just one more nigger, worth so many dollars. What they did to me didn't have much to do with me personally. But here was a woman who hated me and who, out of sheer malice, had nearly killed me.

'She'll keep her mouth shut next time,' said Alice. 'We let her know what would happen to her if she didn't. Now she's more scared of us than of Mister Tom.'

'Don't get yourselves into trouble over me,' I said.

'Don't be telling us what to do,' she replied.

15

The first day I was up, Rufus called me to his room and handed me a letter – from Kevin to Tom Weylin.

'Dear Tom,' it said, 'There may be no need for this letter since I hope to reach you ahead of it. If I'm held up, however, I want you – and Dana – to know that I'm coming. Please tell her I'm coming.'

197

It was Kevin's handwriting – slanted, neat, clear. In spite of the years of note taking and longhand drafts, his writing had never gone to hell the way mine had. I looked blankly at Rufus.

'I said once that Daddy was a fair man,' he said. 'You all but laughed out loud.'

'He wrote to Kevin about me?'

'He did after . . . after . . .'

'After he learned that you hadn't sent my letters?'

His eyes widened with surprise, then slowly took on a look of understanding. 'So that's why you ran. How did you find out?'

'By being curious.' I glanced at the bed chest. 'By satisfying my curiosity.'

'You could be whipped for snooping through my things.'

I shrugged, and small pains shot through my scabby shoulders.

'I never even saw that they had been moved. I'll have to watch you better from now on.'

'Why? Are you planning to hide more lies from me?'

He jumped, started to get up, then sat back down heavily and rested one polished boot on his bed. 'Watch what you say, Dana. There are things I won't take, even from you.'

'You lied,' I repeated deliberately. 'You lied to me over and over. *Why*, Rufe?'

It took several seconds for his anger to dissolve and be replaced by something else. I watched him at first, then looked away, uncomfortably. 'I wanted to keep you here,' he whispered. 'Kevin hates this place. He would have taken you up North.'

I looked at him again and let myself understand. It was that destructive single-minded love of his. He loved me. Not the way he loved Alice, thank God. He didn't seem to want to sleep with me. But he wanted me around – someone to talk to, someone who would listen to him and care what he said, care about him.

And I did. However little sense it made, I cared. I must have. I kept forgiving him for things . . .

I stared out the window guiltily, feeling that I should have been more like Alice. She forgave him nothing, forgot nothing, hated him as deeply as she had loved Isaac. I didn't blame her. But what good did her hating do? She couldn't bring herself to run away again or to kill him and face her own death. She couldn't do anything at all except make herself more miserable. She said, 'My stomach just turns every time he puts his hands on me!' But she endured. Eventually, she would bear him at least one child. And as much as I cared for him, I would not have done that. I couldn't have. Twice, he had made me lose control enough to try to kill him. I could get that angry with him, even though I knew the consequences of killing him. He could drive me to a kind of unthinking fury. Somehow, I couldn't take from him the kind of abuse I took from others. If he ever raped me, it wasn't likely that either of us would survive.

Maybe that was why we didn't hate each other. We could hurt each other too badly, kill each other too quickly in hatred. He was like a younger brother to me. Alice was like a sister. It was so hard to watch him hurting her – to know that he had to go on hurting her if my family was to exist at all. And, at the moment, it was hard for me to talk calmly about what he had done to me.

'North,' I said finally. 'Yes, at least there I could keep the skin on my back.'

He sighed. 'I never wanted Daddy to whip you. But hell, don't you know you got off easy! He didn't hurt you nearly as much as he's hurt others.'

I said nothing.

'He couldn't let a runaway go without some punishment. If he did, there'd be ten more taking off tomorrow. He was easy on you, though, because he figured your running away was my fault.'

'It was.'

'It was your own fault! If you had waited . . .'

'For what! You were the one I trusted. I did wait until I found out what a liar you were!'

199

He took the charge without anger this time. 'Oh hell, Dana . . . all right! I should have sent the letters. Even Daddy said I should have sent them after I promised you I would. Then he said I was a damn fool for promising.' He paused. 'But that promise was the only thing that made him send for Kevin. He didn't do it out of gratitude to you for helping me. He did it because I had given my word. If not for that, he would have kept you here until you went home. If you're going to go home this time.'

We sat together in silence for a moment.

'Daddy's the only man I know,' he said softly, 'who cares as much about giving his word to a black as to a white.'

'Does that bother you?'

'No! It's one of the few things about him I can respect.'

'It's one of the few things about him you should copy.'

'Yeah.' He took his foot off the bed. 'Carrie's bringing a tray up here so we can eat together.'

That surprised me, but I just nodded.

'Your back doesn't hurt much, does it?'

'Yes.'

He stared out the window miserably until Carrie arrived with the tray.

16

I went back to helping Sarah and Carrie the next day. Rufus said I didn't have to, but as tedious as the work was, I could stand it easier than I could stand more long hours of boredom. And now that I knew Kevin was coming, my back and side didn't seem to hurt as much.

Then Jake Edwards came in to destroy my new-found peace. It was amazing how much misery the man could cause doing the same job Luke had managed to do without hurting anyone.

'You!' he said to me. He knew my name. 'You go do the wash. Tess is going to the fields today.'

Poor Tess. Weylin had tired of her as a bed mate and passed her casually to Edwards. She had been afraid Edwards would send her to the fields where he could keep an eye on her. With Alice and I in the house, she knew she could be spared. She had cried with the fear that she would be spared. 'You do everything they tell you,' she wept, 'and they still treat you like an old dog. Go here, open your legs; go there, bust your back. What they care! I ain't s'pose to have no feelin's!' She had sat with me crying while I lay on my stomach sweating and hurting and knowing I wasn't as bad off as I thought I was.

I would be a lot worse off now, though, if I obeyed Edwards. He had no right to give me orders, and he knew it. His authority was over the field hands. But today, Rufus and Tom Weylin had gone into town leaving Edwards in charge, leaving him several hours to show us how 'important' he was. I'd heard him outside the cookhouse trying to bully Nigel. And I'd heard Nigel's answer, first placating – 'I'm just doing what Marse Tom told me to do.' Finally threatening – 'Marse Jake, you put your hands on me, you go' get hurt. Now that's all!'

Edwards backed off. Nigel was big and strong and not one to make idle threats. Also, Rufus tended to back Nigel, and Weylin tended to back Rufus. Edwards had cursed Nigel, then come into the cookhouse to bother me. I had neither the size nor the strength to frighten him, especially now. But I knew what a day of washing would do to my back and side. I'd had enough pain, surely.

'Mr Edwards, I'm not supposed to be washing. Mister Rufus told me not to.' It was a lie, but Rufus would back me too. In some ways, I could still trust him.

'You lyin' nigger, you do what *I* tell you to do!' Edwards loomed over me. 'You think you been whipped? You don't know what a whippin' is yet!' He carried his whip around with him. It was like part of his arm – long and black with its lead-weighted butt. He dropped the coil of it free.

And I went out, God help me, and tried to do the wash. I couldn't face another beating so soon. I just couldn't.

When Edwards was gone, Alice came out of Carrie's cabin and began to help me. I felt sweat on my face mingling with silent tears of frustration and anger. My back had already begun to ache dully, and I felt dully ashamed. Slavery was a long slow process of dulling.

'You stop beatin' them clothes 'fore you fall over,' Alice told me. 'I'll do this. You go back to the cookhouse.'

'He might come back,' I said. 'You might get in trouble.' It wasn't her trouble I was worried about; it was mine. I didn't want to be dragged out of the cookhouse and whipped again.

'Not me,' she said. 'He knows where I sleep at night.'

I nodded. She was right. As long as she was under Rufus's protection, Edwards might curse her, but he wouldn't touch her. Just as he hadn't touched Tess – until Weylin was finished with her . . .

'Thanks, Alice, but . . .'

'Who's that?'

I looked around. There was a white man, gray-bearded and dusty, riding around the side of the main house toward us. I thought at first that it was the Methodist minister. He was a friend and sometime dinner guest of Tom Weylin in spite of Weylin's indifference to religion. But no children gathered around this man as he rode. The kids always mobbed the minister – and his wife too when he brought her along. The couple dispensed candy and 'safe' Bible verses ('Servants, be obedient to them that are your masters . . .'). The kids got candy for repeating the verses.

I saw two little girls staring at the gray-bearded stranger, but no one approached him or spoke to him. He rode straight back to us, stopped, sat looking at both of us uncertainly.

I opened my mouth to tell him the Weylins weren't home, but in that moment, I got a good look at him. I dropped one of Rufus's good white shirts into the dirt and stumbled over to the fence.

'Dana?' he said softly. The question mark in his voice scared me. Didn't he know me? Had I changed so much? He hadn't, beard or no beard.

'Kevin, get down. I can't reach you up there.'

And he was off the horse and over the laundry yard fence, pulling me to him before I could take another breath.

The dull ache in my back and shoulders roared to life. Suddenly, I was struggling to get away from him. He let me go, confused.

'What the . . .?'

I went to him again because I couldn't keep away, but I caught his arms before he could get them around me. 'Don't. My back is sore.'

'Sore from what?'

'From running away to find you. Oh, Kevin . . .'

He held me – gently now – for several seconds, and I thought if we could just go home then, at that moment, everything would be all right.

Finally, Kevin stood back from me a little, looked at me without letting me go. 'Who beat you?' he asked quietly.

'I told you, I ran away.'

'Who?' he insisted. 'Was it Weylin again?'

'Kevin, forget it.'

'Forget . . .?'

'Yes! Please forget it. I might have to live here again someday.' I shook my head. 'Hate Weylin all you want to. I do. But don't do anything to him. Let's just get out of here.'

'It was him then.'

'Yes!'

He turned slowly and stared toward the main house. His face was lined and grim where it wasn't hidden by the beard. He looked more than ten years older than when I had last seen him. There was a jagged scar across his forehead – the remnant of what must have been a bad wound. This place, this time, hadn't been any kinder to him than it had been to me. But what had it made of him? What might he be willing to do now that he would not have done before?

'Kevin, please, let's just go.'

He turned that same hard stare on me.

'Do anything to them and I'll suffer for it,' I whispered urgently. 'Let's go! Now!'

He stared at me a moment longer, then sighed, rubbed his hand across his forehead. He looked at Alice, and because he didn't speak to her, just kept looking, I turned to look at her too.

She was watching us – watching dry-eyed, but with more pain than I had ever seen on another person's face. My husband had come to me, finally. Hers would not be coming to her. Then the look was gone and her mask of toughness was in place again.

'You better do like she says,' she told Kevin softly. 'Get her out of here while you can. No telling what our "good masters" will do if you don't.'

'You're Alice, aren't you?' asked Kevin.

She nodded as she would not have to Weylin or Rufus. They would have gotten a dull dry 'yes, sir.' 'Used to see you 'round here sometimes,' she said. 'Back when things made sense.'

He made a sound, not quite a laugh. 'Was there ever such a time?' He glanced at me, then back at her again, comparing. 'Good Lord,' he murmured to himself. Then to her, 'You going to be all right here, finishing this work by yourself?'

''Go' be fine,' she said. 'Just get her out of here.'

He finally seemed convinced. 'Get your things,' he told me.

I almost told him to forget about my things. Extra clothing, medicine, toothbrush, pens, paper, whatever. But here, some of those things were irreplaceable. I climbed the fence, went to the house and up to the attic as quickly as I could and stuffed everything into my bag. Somehow, I got out again without being seen, without having to answer questions.

At the laundry yard fence, Kevin waited, feeding something to his mare. I looked at the mare, wondering how tired she was. How far could she carry two people before she had to rest? How far could Kevin go before he had to rest? I looked at him as I reached him and could read weariness now in the dusty lines of his face. I wondered how fast he had traveled to reach me. When had he slept last?

204

For a moment, we stood wasting time, staring at each other. We couldn't help it – I couldn't anyway. New lines and all, he was so damned beautiful.

'It's been five years for me,' he said.

'I know,' I whispered.

Abruptly, he turned away. 'Let's go! Let's put this place behind us for good.'

Please, God. But not very likely. I turned to say good-bye to Alice, called her name once. She was beating a pair of Rufus's pants, and she kept beating them with no break in her rhythm to indicate that she had heard me.

'Alice!' I called louder.

She did not turn, did not stop her beating and beating of those pants, though I was certain now that she heard me. Kevin laid a hand on my shoulder and I glanced at him, then again at her. 'Good-bye, Alice,' I said, this time not expecting any answer. There was none.

Kevin mounted and helped me up behind him. As we headed away, I leaned against Kevin's sweaty back and waited for the regular thump of her beating to fade. But we could still hear it faintly when we met Rufus on the road.

Rufus was alone. I was glad of that, at least. But he stopped a few feet ahead of us, frowning, deliberately blocking our way.

'Oh hell,' I muttered.

'You were just going to leave,' Rufus said to Kevin. 'No thanks, nothing at all, just take her and go.'

Kevin stared at him silently for several seconds – stared until Rufus began to look uncomfortable instead of indignant.

'That's right,' Kevin said.

Rufus blinked. 'Look,' he said in a milder tone, 'look, why don't you stay for dinner. My father will be back by then. He'd want you to stay.'

'You can tell your father—!'

I dug my fingers into Kevin's shoulder, cutting off the rush of words before they became insulting in content as well as in tone. 'Tell him we were in a hurry,' Kevin finished.

Rufus did not move from blocking our path. He looked at me.

'Good-bye, Rufe,' I said quietly.

And without warning, with no perceptible change in mood, Rufus turned slightly and trained his rifle on us. I knew a little about firearms now. It wasn't wise for any but the most trusted slaves to show an interest in them, but then I had been trusted before I ran away. Rufus's gun was a flintlock, a long slender Kentucky rifle. He had even let me fire it a couple of times . . . before. And I had looked down the barrel of one like it for his sake. This one, however, was aimed more at Kevin. I stared at it, then at the young man holding it. I kept thinking I knew him, and he kept proving to me that I didn't.

'Rufe, what are you doing!' I demanded.

'Inviting Kevin to dinner,' he said. And to Kevin, 'Get down. I think Daddy might want to talk to you.'

People kept warning me about him, dropping hints that he was meaner than he seemed to be. Sarah had warned me and most of the time, she loved him like one of the sons she had lost. And I had seen the marks he occasionally left on Alice. But he had never been that way with me – not even when he was angry enough to be. I had never feared him as I'd feared his father. Even now, I wasn't as frightened as I probably should have been. I wasn't frightened for myself. That was why I challenged him.

'Rufe, if you shoot anybody, it better be me.'

'Dana, shut up!' said Kevin.

'You think I won't?' said Rufus.

'I think if you don't, I'll kill you.'

Kevin got down quickly and hauled me down. He didn't understand the kind of relationship Rufus and I had – how dependent we were on each other. Rufus understood though.

'No need for any talk of killing,' he said gently – as though he was quieting an angry child. And then to Kevin in a more normal tone, 'I just think Daddy might have something to say to you.'

'About what?' Kevin asked.

'Well . . . about her keep, maybe.'

'My keep!' I exploded, pulling away from Kevin. 'My keep! I've worked, worked hard every day I've been here until your father beat me so badly I couldn't work! You people owe me! And you, Goddamnit, owe me more than you could ever pay!'

He swung the rifle to where I wanted it. Straight at me. Now I would either goad him into shooting me or shame him into letting us go – or possibly, I would go home. I might go home wounded, or even dead, but one way or another, I would be away from this time, this place. And if I went home, Kevin would go with me. I caught his hand and held it.

'What are you going to do, Rufe? Keep us here at gun point so you can rob Kevin?'

'Get back to the house,' he said. His voice had gone hard.

Kevin and I looked at each other, and I spoke softly.

'I already know all I ever want to find out about being a slave,' I told him. 'I'd rather be shot than go back in there.'

'I won't let them keep you,' Kevin promised. 'Come on.'

'No!' I glared at him. 'You stay or go as you please. I'm not going back in that house!'

Rufus cursed in disgust. 'Kevin, put her over your shoulder and bring her in.'

Kevin didn't move. I would have been amazed if he had.

'Still trying to get other people to do your dirty work for you, aren't you, Rufe?' I said bitterly. 'First your father, now Kevin. To think I wasted my time saving your worthless life!' I stepped toward the mare and caught her reins as though to remount. At that moment, Rufus's composure broke.

'You're not leaving!' he shouted. He sort of crouched around the gun, clearly on the verge of firing. 'Damn you, you're not leaving me!'

He was going to shoot. I had pushed him too far. I was Alice all over again, rejecting him. Terrified in spite of myself, I dove past the mare's head, not caring how I fell as long as I put something between myself and the rifle.

I hit the ground – not too hard – tried to scramble up, and found that I couldn't. My balance was gone. I heard shouting – Kevin's voice, Rufus's voice . . . Suddenly, I saw the gun, blurred, but seemingly only inches from my head. I hit at it and missed. It wasn't quite where it appeared to be. Everything was distorted, blurred.

'Kevin!' I screamed. I couldn't leave him behind again – not even if my scream made Rufus fire.

Something landed heavily on my back and I screamed again, this time in pain. Everything went dark.

The Storm

1

Home.

I couldn't have been unconscious for more than a minute. I came to on the living-room floor to find Kevin bending over me. There was no one for me to mistake him for this time. It was him, and he was home. We were home. My back felt as though I'd taken another beating, but it didn't matter. I'd gotten us home without either of us being shot.

'I'm sorry,' said Kevin.

I focused on him clearly. 'Sorry about what?'

'Doesn't your back hurt?'

I lowered my head, rested it on my hand. 'It hurts.'

'I fell on you. Between Rufus and the horse and you screaming, I don't know how it happened, but . . .'

'Thank God it did happen. Don't be sorry, Kevin, you're here. You'd be stranded again if you hadn't fallen on me.'

He sighed, nodded. 'Can you get up? I think I'd hurt you more by lifting you than you'd hurt yourself by walking.'

I got up slowly, cautiously, found that it didn't hurt any more to stand than it did to lie down. My head was clear now, and I could walk without trouble.

'Go to bed,' said Kevin. 'Get some rest.'

'Come with me.'

Something of the expression he'd had when we met in the laundry yard came back to him and he took my hands.

'Come with me,' I repeated softly.

'Dana, you're hurt. Your back . . .'

'Hey.'

He stopped, pulled me closer.

'Five years?' I whispered.

'That long. Yes.'

'They hurt you.' I fingered the scar on his forehead.

'That's nothing. It healed years ago. But you . . .'

'Please come with me.'

He did. He was so careful, so fearful of hurting me. He did hurt me, of course. I had known he would, but it didn't matter. We were safe. He was home. I'd brought him back. That was enough.

Eventually, we slept.

He wasn't in the room when I awoke. I lay still listening until I heard him opening and closing doors in the kitchen. And I heard him cursing. He had a slight accent, I realized. Nothing really noticeable, but he did sound a little like Rufus and Tom Weylin. Just a little.

I shook my head and tried to put the comparison out of my mind. He sounded as though he were looking for something, and after five years didn't know where to find it. I got up and went to help.

I found him fiddling with the stove, turning the burners on, staring into the blue flame, turning them off, opening the oven, peering in. He had his back to me and didn't see or hear me. Before I could say anything, he slammed the oven door and stalked away shaking his head. 'Christ,' he muttered. 'If I'm not home yet, maybe I don't have a home.'

He went into the dining room without noticing me. I stayed where I was, thinking, remembering.

I could recall walking along the narrow dirt road that ran past the Weylin house and seeing the house, shadowy in twilight, boxy and familiar, yellow light showing from some of the windows – Weylin was surprisingly extravagant with his candles and oil. I had heard that other people were not. I could recall feeling relief at seeing the house, feeling that I had come home. And having to stop and correct myself, remind myself that I was in an alien, dangerous place. I could recall being surprised that I would come to think of such a place as home.

That was more than two months ago when I went to get help for Rufus. I had been home to 1976, to this house, and it hadn't felt that homelike. It didn't now. For one thing, Kevin and I had lived here together for only two days. The fact that I'd had eight extra days here alone didn't really help. The time, the year, was right, but the house just wasn't familiar enough. I felt as though I were losing my place here in my own time. Rufus's time was a sharper, stronger reality. The work was harder, the smells and tastes were stronger, the danger was greater, the pain was worse . . . Rufus's time demanded things of me that had never been demanded before, and it could easily kill me if I did not meet its demands. That was a stark, powerful reality that the gentle conveniences and luxuries of this house, of *now*, could not touch.

And if I felt that way after spending only short periods in the past, what must Kevin be feeling after five years. His white skin had saved him from much of the trouble I had faced, but still, he couldn't have had an easy time.

I found him in the living room trying knobs on the television set. It was new to us, that television, like the house. The on/off switch was under the screen out of sight, and Kevin clearly didn't remember.

I went to it, reached under, and switched the set on. There was a public service announcement on advising women to see their doctors and take care of themselves while they were pregnant.

'Turn it off,' said Kevin.

I obeyed.

'I saw a woman die in childbirth once,' he said.

I nodded. 'I never saw it, but I kept hearing about it happening. It was pretty common back then, I guess. Poor medical care or none at all.'

'No, medical care had nothing to do with the case I saw. This woman's master strung her up by her wrists and beat her until the baby came out of her – dropped onto the ground.'

I swallowed, looked away, rubbing my wrists. 'I see.' Would Weylin have done such a thing to one of his pregnant slave women, I wondered. Probably not. He had more business sense than that. Dead mother, dead baby – dead loss. I'd heard stories, though, about other slaveholders who didn't care what they did. There was a woman on Weylin's plantation whose former master had cut three fingers from her right hand when he caught her writing. She had a baby nearly every year, that woman. Nine so far, seven surviving. Weylin called her a good breeder, and he never whipped her. He was selling off her children, though, one by one.

Kevin stared at the blank TV screen, then turned away with a bitter laugh. 'I feel like this is just another stopover,' he said. 'A little less real than the others, maybe.'

'Stopover?'

'Like Philadelphia. Like New York and Boston. Like that farm in Maine . . .'

'You did get to Maine, then?'

'Yes. Almost bought a farm there. Would have been a stupid mistake. Then a friend in Boston forwarded me Weylin's letter. Home at last, I thought, and you . . .' He looked at me. 'Well. I got half of what I wanted. You're still you.'

I went to him with relief that surprised me. I hadn't realized how much I'd worried, even now, that I might not be 'still me' as far as he was concerned.

'Everything is so soft here,' he said, 'so easy . . .'

'I know.'

'It's good. Hell, I wouldn't go back to some of the pestholes I've lived in for pay. But still . . .'

We were walking through the dining room, through the hall.

212

We stopped at my office and he went in to look at the map of the United States that I had on the wall. 'I kept going farther and farther up the east coast,' he said. 'I guess I would have wound up in Canada next. But in all my traveling, do you know the only time I ever felt relieved and eager to be going to a place?'

'I think so,' I said quietly.

'It was when . . .' He stopped, realizing what I had said, and frowned at me.

'It was when you went back to Maryland,' I said. 'When you visited the Weylins to see whether I was there.'

He looked surprised, but strangely pleased. 'How could you know that?'

'It's true, isn't it?'

'It's true.'

'I felt it the last time Rufus called me. I've got no love at all for that place, but so help me, when I saw it again, it was so much like coming home that it scared me.'

Kevin stroked his beard. 'I grew this to come back.'

'Why?'

'To disguise myself. You ever hear of a man named Denmark Vesey?'

'The freedman who plotted rebellion down in South Carolina.'

'Yes. Well, Vesey never got beyond the planning stage, but he scared the hell out of a lot of white people. And a lot of black people suffered for it. Around that time, I was accused of helping slaves to escape. I barely got out ahead of the mob.'

'Were you at the Weylins' then?'

'No, I had a job teaching school.' He rubbed the scar on his forehead. 'I'll tell you all about it, Dana, but some other time. Now, somehow, I've got to fit myself back into nineteen seventy-six. If I can.'

'You can.'

He shrugged.

'One more thing. Just one.'

He looked at me questioningly.

'Were you helping slaves to escape?'

'Of course I was! I fed them, hid them during the day, and when night came, I pointed them toward a free black family who would feed and hide them the next day.'

I smiled and said nothing. He sounded angry, almost defensive about what he had done.

'I guess I'm not used to saying things like that to people who understand them,' he said.

'I know. It's enough that you did what you did.'

He rubbed his head again. 'Five years is longer than it sounds. So much longer.'

We went on to his office. Both our offices were ex-bedrooms in the solidly built old frame house we had bought. They were big comfortable rooms that reminded me a little of the rooms in the Weylin house.

No. I shook my head, denying the impression. This house was nothing like the Weylin house. I watched Kevin look around his office. He circled the room, stopping at his desk, at the file cabinets, at the bookcases. He stood for a moment looking at the shelf filled with copies of *The Water of Meribah*, his most successful novel – the novel that had bought us this house. He touched a copy as though to take it down, then left it and drifted back to his typewriter. He fumbled with that for a moment, remembered how to turn it on, then looked at the stack of blank paper beside it and turned it off again. Abruptly, he brought his fist down hard on it.

I jumped at the sudden sound. 'You'll break it, Kevin.'

'What difference would that make?'

I winced, remembered my own attempts to write when I'd been home last. I had tried and tried and only managed to fill my wastebasket.

'What am I going to do?' said Kevin, turning his back on the typewriter. 'Christ, if I can't feel anything even in here . . .'

'You will. Give yourself time.'

He picked up his electric pencil sharpener, examined it as though he did not know what it was, then seemed to remember.

He put it down, took a pencil from a china cup on the desk, and put it in the sharpener. The little machine obligingly ground the pencil to a fine point. Kevin stared at the point for a moment, then at the sharpener.

'A toy,' he said. 'Nothing but a damned toy.'

'That's what I said when you bought it,' I told him. I tried to smile and make it a joke, but there was something in his voice that scared me.

With a sudden slash of his hand, he knocked both the sharpener and the cup of pencils from his desk. The pencils scattered and the cup broke. The sharpener bounced hard on the bare floor, just missing the rug. I unplugged it quickly.

'Kevin . . .' He stalked out of the room before I could finish. I ran after him, caught his arm. 'Kevin!'

He stopped, glared at me as though I was some stranger who had dared to lay hands on him.

'Kevin, you can't come back all at once any more than you can leave all at once. It takes time. After a while, though, things will fall into place.'

His expression did not change.

I took his face between my hands and looked into his eyes, now truly cold. 'I don't know what it was like for you,' I said, 'being gone so long, having so little control over whether you'd ever get back. I can't really know, I guess. But I do know . . . that I almost didn't want to be alive when I thought I'd left you behind for good. But now that you're back . . .'

He pulled away from me and walked out of the room. The expression on his face was like something I'd seen, something I was used to seeing on Tom Weylin. Something closed and ugly.

I didn't go after him when I left his office. I didn't know what to do to help him, and I didn't want to look at him and see things that reminded me of Weylin. But because I went to the bedroom, I found him.

He was standing beside the dresser looking at a picture of himself – himself as he had been. He had always hated having his picture taken, but I had talked him into this one, a close-up of the young face under a cap of thick gray hair, dark brows, pale eyes . . .

I was afraid he would throw the picture down, smash it as he had tried to smash the pencil sharpener. I took it from his hand. He let it go easily and turned to look at himself in the dresser mirror. He ran a hand through his hair, still thick and gray. He would probably never be bald. But he looked old now; the young face had changed more than could be accounted for by the new lines in his face or the beard.

'Kevin?'

He closed his eyes. 'Leave me alone for a while, Dana,' he said softly. 'I just need to be by myself and get used to . . . to things again.'

There was suddenly a loud, house-shaking sonic boom and Kevin jumped back against the dresser looking around wildly.

'Just a jet passing overhead,' I told him.

He gave me what almost seemed to be a look of hatred, then brushed past me, went to his office and shut the door.

I left him alone. I didn't know what else to do – or even whether there was anything I could do. Maybe this was something he had to work out for himself. Maybe it was something that only time could help. Maybe anything. But I felt so damned helpless as I looked down the hall at his closed door. Finally, I went to bathe, and that hurt enough to hold my attention for a while. Then I checked my denim bag, put in a bottle of antiseptic, Kevin's large bottle of Excedrin, and an old pocket knife to replace the switchblade. The knife was large and easily as deadly as the switchblade I had lost, but I wouldn't be able to use it as quickly, and I would have a harder time surprising an opponent with it. I considered taking a kitchen knife of some kind instead, but I thought one big enough to be effective would be too hard to hide. Not that any kind of knife had been very effective for me so far. Having one just made me feel safer.

I dropped the knife into the bag and replaced soap, toothpaste, some clothing, a few other things. My thoughts went back to

Kevin. Did he blame me for the five years he had lost, I wondered. Or if he didn't now, would he when he tried to write again? He would try. Writing was his profession. I wondered whether he had been able to write during the five years, or rather, whether he had been able to publish. I was sure he had been writing. I couldn't imagine either of us going for five years without writing. Maybe he'd kept a journal or something. He had changed – in five years he couldn't help changing. But the markets he wrote for hadn't changed. He might have a frustrating time for a while. And he might blame me.

It had been so good seeing him again, loving him, knowing his exile was ended. I had thought everything would be all right. Now I wondered if anything would be all right.

I put on a loose dress and went to the kitchen to see what we could make a meal of – if I could get Kevin to eat. The chops I had put out to defrost over two months ago were still icy. How long had we been away, then? What day was it? Somehow, neither of us had bothered to find out.

I turned on the radio and found a news station – tuned in right in the middle of a story about the war in Lebanon. The war there was worse. The President was ordering an evacuation of nonofficial Americans. That sounded like what he had been ordering on the day Rufus called me. A moment later, the announcer mentioned the day, confirming what I had thought. I had been away for only a few hours. Kevin had been away for eight days. Nineteen seventy-six had not gone on without us.

The news switched to a story about South Africa – blacks rioting there and dying wholesale in battles with police over the policies of the white supremacist government.

I turned off the radio and tried to cook the meal in peace. South African whites had always struck me as people who would have been happier living in the nineteenth century, or the eighteenth. In fact, they were living in the past as far as their race relations went. They lived in ease and comfort supported by huge numbers of blacks whom they kept in poverty

217

and held in contempt. Tom Weylin would have felt right at home.

After a while, the smell of food brought Kevin out of his office, but he ate in silence.

'Can't I help?' I asked finally.

'Help with what?'

There was an edge to his voice that made me wary. I didn't answer.

'I'm all right,' he said grudgingly.

'No you're not.'

He put his fork down. 'How long were you away this time?'

'A few hours. Or just over two months. Take your pick.'

'There was a newspaper in my office. I was reading it. I don't know how old it is, but . . .'

'It's today's paper. It came the morning Rufus called me last. That's this morning if you want to believe the calendar. June eighteenth.'

'It doesn't matter. I wasted my time reading that paper. I didn't know what the hell it was talking about most of the time.'

'It's like I said. The confusion doesn't go away all at once. It doesn't for me either.'

'It was so good coming home at first.'

'It was good. It still is.'

'I don't know. I don't know anything.'

'You're in too much of a hurry. You . . .' I stopped, realized I was swaying a little on my chair. 'Oh God, no!' I whispered.

'I suppose I am,' said Kevin. 'I wonder how people just out of prison manage to readjust.'

'Kevin, go get my bag. I left it in the bedroom.'

'What? Why . . .?'

'Go, Kevin!'

He went, understanding finally. I sat still, praying that he would come back in time. I could feel tears streaming down my face. So soon, so soon . . . Why couldn't I have had just a few days with him – a few days of peace at home?

218

I felt something pressed into my hands and I grasped it. My bag. I opened my eyes to the dark blur of it, and the larger blur of Kevin standing near me. I was suddenly afraid of what he might do.

'Get away, Kevin!'

He said something, but suddenly, there was too much noise for me to hear him – even if he had still been there.

2

There was water, rain pouring down on me. I was sitting in mud clutching my bag.

I got up sheltering my bag as much as I could so that eventually, I'd have something dry to change into. I looked around grimly for Rufus.

I couldn't find him. I peered through the dim gray light, looked around until I realized where I was. I could see the familiar boxy Weylin house in the distance, yellow light at one window. At least there would be no long walk for me this time. In this storm, that was something to be grateful for. But where was Rufus? If he was in trouble inside the house, why had I arrived outside?

I shrugged and started toward the house. If he was there, it would be stupid for me to waste time out here. Not that I could get any wetter.

I tripped over him.

He was lying face down in a puddle so deep the water almost covered his head. Face down.

I grabbed him and pulled him out of the water and over to a tree that would shelter us a little from the rain. A moment later, there was thunder and a flash of lightning, and I dragged him away from the tree again. With his ability to draw bad luck I didn't want to take chances.

He was alive. As I moved him, he threw up on himself and partly on me. I almost joined him. He began to cough and mutter and I realized that he was either drunk or sick. More probably drunk. He was also heavy. He didn't look any bigger than he had when I saw him last, but he was soaking wet now, and he was beginning to struggle feebly.

I had been dragging him toward the house while he was still. Now, I dropped him in disgust and went to the house alone. Some stronger, more tolerant person could drag or carry him the rest of the way.

Nigel answered the door, stood peering down at me. 'Who the devil . . .?'

'It's Dana, Nigel.'

'Dana?' He was suddenly alert. 'What happened? Where's Marse Rufe?'

'Out there. He was too heavy for me.'

'Where?'

I looked back the way I had come and could not see Rufus. If he had flipped himself over again . . .

'Damn!' I muttered. 'Come on.' I led him back to the gray lump – still face up – that was Rufus. 'Watch it,' I said. 'He threw up on me.'

Nigel picked Rufus up like a sack of grain, threw him over his shoulder, and strode back to the house in such quick long strides that I had to run to keep up. Rufus threw up again down Nigel's back, but Nigel paid no attention. The rain washed them both fairly clean before we reached the house.

Inside, we met Weylin who was coming down the stairs. He stopped short as he saw us. 'You!' he said, staring at me.

'Hello, Mr Weylin,' I said wearily. He looked bent and old – thinner than ever. He walked with a cane.

'Is Rufus all right? Is he . . .?'

'He's alive,' I said. 'I found him unconscious, face down in a ditch. A little more and he would have drowned.'

'If you're here, I suppose he would have.' The old man looked at Nigel. 'Take him up to his room and put him to bed. Dana, you . . .' He stopped, looked at my dripping, clinging – to him – immodestly short dress. It was the kind of loose smocklike

220

garment that little children of both sexes wore before they were old enough to work. It clearly offended Weylin more than my pants ever had. 'Haven't you got something decent to put on?' he asked.

I looked at my wet bag. 'Decent, maybe, but probably not dry.'

'Go put on what you've got, then come back down to the library.'

He wanted to talk to me, I thought. Just what I needed at the end of a long jumbled day. Weylin didn't talk to me normally except to give orders. When he did, it was always harrowing. There was so much that I couldn't say; he took offense so easily.

I followed Nigel up the stairs, then went on to the narrow, ladderlike attic stairs. My old corner was empty so I went there to put my bag down and search through it. I found a nearly dry shirt and a pair of Levi's that were wet only at the ankles. I dried myself, changed, combed my hair, and spread out some of my wettest clothing to dry. Then I went down to Weylin. I had learned not to worry about leaving my things in the attic. Other house servants examined them. I knew that because I had caught them at it now and then. But nothing was ever missing.

Apprehensively, I went through the library door.

'You look as young as you ever did,' Weylin complained sourly when he saw me.

'Yes, sir.' I'd agree with anything he said if it would get me away from him sooner.

'What happened to you there? Your face.'

I touched the scab. 'That's where you kicked me, Mr Weylin.'

He had been sitting in a worn old armchair, but now he surged out of it like a young man, his cane a blunt wooden sword before him. 'What are you talking about! It's been six years since I've seen you.'

'Yes, sir.'

'Well!'

'For me, it's only been a few hours.' I thought Rufus and

221

Kevin had probably told him enough to enable him to understand, whether he believed or not. And perhaps he did understand. He seemed to get angrier.

'Who in hell ever said you were an educated nigger? You can't even tell a decent lie. Six years for me is six years for you!'

'Yes, sir,' Why did he bother to ask me questions? Why did I bother to answer them?

He sat down again and leaned forward, one hand resting on his cane. His voice was softer, though, when he spoke. 'That Franklin get back home all right?'

'Yes, sir.' What would happen if I asked him where he thought that home was? But no, he had done at least one decent thing for Kevin and me, no matter what he was. I met his eyes for a moment. 'Thank you.'

'I didn't do it for you.'

My temper flared suddenly. 'I don't give a damn why you did it! I'm just telling you, one human being to another, that I'm grateful. Why can't you leave it at that!'

The old man's face went pale. 'You want a good whipping!' he said. 'You must not have had one for a while.'

I said nothing. I realized then, though, that if he ever hit me again, I would break his scrawny neck. I would not endure it again.

Weylin leaned back in his chair. 'Rufus always said you didn't know your place any better than a wild animal,' he muttered. 'I always said you were just another crazy nigger.'

I stood watching him.

'Why'd you help my son again?' he asked.

I settled down a little, shrugged. 'Nobody ought to die the way he would have – lying in a ditch, drowning in mud and whiskey and his own vomit.'

'Stop it!' Weylin shouted. 'I'll take the cowhide to you myself! I'll . . .' He fell silent, gasped for breath. His face was still dead white. He'd make himself really sick if he didn't regain some of his old control.

222

I dropped back into indifference. 'Yes, sir.'

After a moment he had control of himself. In fact, he sounded perfectly calm again. 'You and Rufus had some trouble when you saw him last.'

'Yes, sir.' Having Rufus try to shoot me had been troublesome.

'I hoped you would go on helping him. You know there's always a home for you here if you do.'

I smiled a little in spite of myself. 'Bad nigger that I am, eh?'

'Is that the way you think of yourself?'

I laughed bitterly. 'No. I don't kid myself much. Your son is still alive, isn't he?'

'You're bad enough. I don't know any other white man who would put up with you.'

'If you can manage to put up with me a little more humanely, I'll go on doing what I can for Mister Rufus.'

He frowned. 'Now what are you talking about?'

'I'm saying the day I'm beaten just once more, your son is on his own.'

His eyes widened, perhaps in surprise. Then he began to tremble. I had never before seen a man literally trembling with anger. 'You're threatening him!' he stammered. 'By God, you are crazy!'

'Crazy or sane, I mean what I say.' My back and side ached as though to warn me, but for the moment, I wasn't afraid. He loved his son no matter how he behaved toward him, and he knew I could do as I threatened. 'At the rate Mister Rufus has accidents,' I said, 'he might live another six or seven years without me. I wouldn't count on more than that.'

'You damned black bitch!' He shook his cane at me like an extended forefinger. 'If you think you can get away with making threats . . . giving orders . . .' He ran out of breath and began gasping again. I watched without sympathy, wondering whether he was already sick. 'Get out!' he gasped. 'Go to Rufus. Take care of him. If anything happens to him, I'll flay you alive!'

My aunt used to say things like that to me when I was little and did something to annoy her – 'Girl, I'm going to skin you alive!' And she'd get my uncle's belt and use it on me. But it had never occurred to me that anyone could make such a threat and mean it literally as Weylin meant it now. I turned and left him before he could see that my courage had vanished. He could get help from his neighbors, from the patrollers, probably even from whatever police officials the area had. He could do anything he wanted to to me, and I had no enforceable rights. None at all.

3

Rufus was sick again. When I reached his room I found him lying in bed shaking violently while Nigel tried to keep him wrapped in blankets.

'What's wrong with him?' I asked.

'Nothing,' said Nigel. 'Got the ague again, I guess.'

'Ague?'

'Yeah, he's had it before. He'll be all right.'

He didn't look all right to me. 'Has anyone gone for the doctor?'

'Marse Tom don't hardly get Doc West for ague. He says all the doc knows is bleeding and blistering and purging and puking and making folks sicker than they was to start.'

I swallowed, remembered the pompous little man I had disliked so. 'Is the doctor really that bad, Nigel?'

'He gave me some stuff once, nearly killed me. From then on, I just let Sarah doctor me when I'm sick. 'Least she don't dose niggers like they was horses or mules.'

I shook my head and went close to Rufus's bed. He looked miserable, seemed to be in pain. I tried to think what the ague might be; the word was familiar, but I couldn't remember what I'd heard or read about it.

Rufus looked up at me, red-eyed, and tried to smile, though

the grimace he managed was far from pleasant. To my surprise, his attempt touched me. I hadn't expected to still care about him except for my own and my family's sake. I didn't want to care.

'Idiot,' I muttered down at him.

He managed to look hurt.

I looked at Nigel, wondered whether the disease could be as unimportant as he thought. Would he think it was important if he had been the one on his back shaking?

Nigel was busy plucking his wet shirt away from his skin. No one had given him a chance to change his clothes, I realized.

'Nigel, I'll stay here if you want to go dry off,' I said.

He looked up, smiled at me. 'You go away for six years,' he said, 'then come back and fit right in. It's like you never left.'

'Every time I go I keep hoping I'll never come back.'

He nodded. 'But at least you get some time of freedom.'

I looked away, feeling strangely guilty that, yes, I did get some time of freedom. Not enough, but probably more than Nigel would ever know. I didn't like feeling guilty about it. Then something bit me on my ear and I forgot my guilt. As I slapped at my ear, I remembered, finally, what the ague was.

Malaria.

I wondered dully whether the mosquito that had just bitten me was carrying the disease. In my reading I'd come across a lot of information on malaria and none of it led me to believe the disease was as harmless as Nigel seemed to think. It might not kill, but it weakened and it recurred and it could lower one's resistance to other diseases. Also, with Rufus lying exposed as he was to new mosquito attacks, the disease could be spread over the plantation and beyond.

'Nigel, is there anything we can hang up to keep the mosquitoes off him?'

'Mosquitoes! He wouldn't feel it if twenty mosquitoes bit him now.'

'No, but the rest of us would be feeling it eventually.'

'What do you mean?'

'Does anyone else have it now?'

'Don't think so. Some of the children are sick, but I think they have something wrong with their faces – one side all swollen up.'

Mumps? Never mind. 'Well, let's see if we can keep this from spreading. Is there any kind of mosquito netting – or whatever people use here?'

'Sure, for white folks. But . . .'

'Would you get some? With the help of the canopy, we should be able to enclose him completely.'

'Dana, listen!'

I looked at him.

'What do mosquitoes have to do with the ague?'

I blinked, stared at him in surprise. He didn't know. Of course he didn't. Doctors of the day didn't know. Which probably meant that Nigel wouldn't believe me when I told him. After all, how could a thing as tiny as a mosquito make anybody sick? 'Nigel, you know where I'm from, don't you?'

He gave me something that wasn't quite a smile. 'Not New York.'

'No.'

'I know where Marse Rufe said you was from.'

'It shouldn't be that hard for you to believe him. You've seen me go home at least once.'

'Twice.'

'Well?'

He shrugged. 'I can't say. If I hadn't seen . . . the way you go home, I'd just figure you were one crazy nigger. But I haven't ever seen anybody do what you did. I don't want to believe you, but I guess I do.'

'Good.' I took a deep breath. 'Where I'm from, people have learned that mosquitoes carry ague. They bite someone who's sick with it, then later they bite healthy people and give them the disease.'

'How?'

226

'They suck blood from the sick and . . . pass on some of that blood when they bite a healthy person. Like a mad dog that bites a man and drives the man mad.' No talk about micro-organisms. Nigel not only wouldn't believe me, he might decide I really was crazy.

'Doc says it's something in the air that spreads ague – something off bad water and garbage. A miasma, he called it.'

'He's wrong. He's wrong about the bleeding and purging and the rest, he was wrong when he dosed you, and he's wrong now. It's a wonder any of his patients survive.'

'I heard he was good and quick when it comes to cutting off legs or arms.'

I had to look at Nigel to see whether he was making a grisly joke. He wasn't. 'Get the mosquito net,' I said wearily. 'Let's do what we can to keep that butcher away from here.'

He nodded and went away. I wondered whether or not he believed me, but it didn't really matter. It wouldn't cost anyone anything to take this small precaution.

I looked down at Rufus to see that he had stopped trembling and closed his eyes. His breathing was regular and I thought he was asleep.

'Why do you keep trying to kill yourself?' I said softly.

I hadn't expected an answer so I was surprised when he spoke quietly. 'Most of the time, living just isn't worth the trouble.'

I sat down next to his bed. 'It never occurred to me that you might really want to die.'

'I don't.' He opened his eyes, looked at me, then shut them again and covered them with his hands. 'But if your eyes and your head and your leg hurt the way mine do, dying might start to look good.'

'Your eyes hurt?'

'When I look around.'

'Did they hurt before when you had ague?'

'No. This isn't ague. Ague is bad enough. My leg feels like it's coming off, and my head . . .!'

He scared me. His pain seemed to increase and he twisted

227

his body as though to move away from it, then untwisted quickly and lay panting.

'Rufe, I'm going to get your father. If he sees how sick you are, he'll send for the doctor.'

He seemed to be too involved with his own pain to answer. I didn't want to leave him until Nigel came back, though I had no idea what I could do for him. My problem was solved when Weylin came in with Nigel.

'What is all this about mosquitoes giving people ague?' he demanded.

'We may be able to forget about that,' I said. 'This doesn't look like malaria. Ague. He's in a lot of pain. I think someone should go for the doctor.'

'You're doctor enough for him.'

'But . . .' I stopped, took a deep breath, made myself calm down. Rufus was groaning behind me. 'Mr Weylin, I'm no doctor. I don't have any idea what's wrong with him. Whatever professional help is available, you should get it for him.'

'Should I now?'

'His life may be at stake.'

Weylin's mouth was set in a straight hard line. 'If he dies, you die, and you won't die easy.'

'You already said that. But no matter what you do to me, your son will still be dead. Is that what you want?'

'You do your job,' he said stubbornly, 'and he'll live. You're something different. I don't know what – witch, devil, I don't care. Whatever you are, you just about brought a girl back to life when you came here last, and she wasn't even the one you came to help. You come out of nowhere and go back into nowhere. Years ago, I would have sworn there couldn't even be anybody like you. You're not natural! But you can feel pain – and you can die. Remember that and do your job. Take care of your master.'

'But, I tell you . . .'

He walked out of the room and shut the door behind him.

228

4

We got the mosquito netting and used it, just in case. Nigel said Weylin didn't really mind letting us have it. He just didn't want to hear any more damned nonsense about mosquitoes. He didn't like to be taken for a fool.

'He's as close to being scared of you as he's ever been of anything,' said Nigel. 'I think he'd rather try to kill you than admit it though.'

'I don't see any sign of fear in him.'

'You don't know him the way I do.' Nigel paused. 'Could he kill you, Dana?'

'I don't know. It's possible.'

'We better get Marse Rufe well then. Sarah has a kind of tea she makes that kind of helps the ague. Maybe it will help whatever Marse Rufe has now.'

'Would you ask her to brew up a pot?'

He nodded and went out.

Sarah came upstairs with Nigel to bring Rufus the tea and to see me. She looked old now. Her hair was streaked with gray and her face lined. She walked with a limp.

'Dropped a kettle on my foot,' she said. 'Couldn't walk at all for a while.' She gave me the feeling that everyone was getting older, passing me by. She brought me roast beef and bread to eat.

Rufus had a fever now. He didn't want the tea, but I coaxed and bullied until he swallowed it. Then we all waited, but all that happened was that Rufus's other leg began to hurt. His eyes bothered him most because moving them hurt him, and he couldn't help following my movements or Nigel's around the room. Finally, I put a cool damp cloth over them. That seemed to help. He still had a lot of pain in his joints – his arms, his legs, everywhere. I thought I could ease that, so I took his candle and went up to the attic for my bag. I was just in time to catch a little girl trying

229

to get the top off my Excedrin bottle. It scared me. She could just as easily have chosen the sleeping pills. The attic wasn't as safe a place as I had thought.

'No, honey, give those to me.'

'They yours?'

'Yes.'

'They candy?'

Good Lord. 'No, they're medicine. Nasty medicine.'

'Ugh!' she said, and handed them back to me. She went back to her pallet next to another child. They were new children. I wondered whether the two little boys who had preceded them had been sold or sent to the fields.

I took the Excedrin, what was left of the aspirin, and the sleeping pills back down with me. I would have to keep them somewhere in Rufus's room or eventually one of the kids would figure out how to get the safety caps off.

Rufus had thrown off the damp cloth and was knotted on his side in pain when I got back to him. Nigel had lain down on the floor before the fireplace and gone to sleep. He could have gone back to his cabin, but he had asked me if I wanted him to stay since this was my first night back, and I'd said yes.

I dissolved three aspirins in water and tried to get Rufus to drink it. He wouldn't even open his mouth. So I woke Nigel, and Nigel held him down while I held his nose and poured the bad-tasting solution into his mouth as he gasped for air. He cursed us both, but after a while he began to feel a little better. Temporarily.

It was a bad night. I didn't get much sleep. Nor was I to get much for six days and nights following. Whatever Rufus had, it was terrible. He was in constant pain, he had fever – once I had to call Nigel to hold him while I tied him down to keep him from hurting himself. I gave him aspirins – too many, but not as many as he wanted. I made him take broth and soup and fruit and vegetable juices. He didn't want them. He never wanted to eat, but he didn't want Nigel holding him down either. He ate.

Alice came in now and then to relieve me. Like Sarah, she looked older. She also looked harder. She was a cool, bitter older sister to the girl I had known.

'Folks treat her bad because of Marse Rufe,' Nigel told me. 'They figure if she's been with him this long, she must like it.'

And Alice said contemptuously, 'Who cares what a bunch of niggers think!'

'She lost two babies,' Nigel told me. 'And the one she's got left is sickly.'

'White babies,' Alice said. 'Look more like him than me. Joe is even red-headed.' Joe was the single survivor. I almost cried when I heard that. No Hagar yet. I was so tired of this going back and forth; I wanted so much for it to be over. I couldn't even feel sorry for the friend who had fought for me and taken care of me when I was hurt. I was too busy feeling sorry for myself.

On the third day of his illness, Rufus's fever left him. He was weak and several pounds lighter, but so relieved to be rid of the fever and the pain that nothing else mattered. He thought he was getting well. He wasn't.

The fever and the pain returned for three more days and he got a rash that itched and eventually peeled . . .

At last, he got well and stayed well. I prayed that whatever his disease had been, I wouldn't get it, wouldn't ever have to care for anyone else who had it. A few days after the worst of his symptoms had disappeared, I was allowed to sleep in the attic. I collapsed gratefully onto the pallet Sarah had made me there, and it felt like the world's softest bed. I didn't awaken until late the next morning after long hours of deep, unbroken sleep. I was still a little groggy when Alice came running up the steps and into the attic to get me.

'Marse Tom is sick,' she said. 'Marse Rufe wants you to come.'

'Oh no,' I muttered. 'Tell him to send for the doctor.'

'Already sent for. But Marse Tom is having bad pains in his chest.'

The significance of that filtered through to me slowly. 'Pains in his chest?'

'Yeah. Come on. They in the parlor.'

'God, that sounds like a heart attack. There's nothing I can do.'

'Just come. They want you.'

I pulled on a pair of pants and threw on a shirt as I ran. What did these people want from me? Magic? If Weylin was having a heart attack, he was going to either recover or die without my help.

I ran down the stairs and into the parlor where Weylin lay on a sofa, ominously still and silent.

'Do something!' Rufus pleaded. 'Help him!' His voice sounded as thin and weak as he looked. His sickness had left its marks on him. I wondered how he had gotten downstairs.

Weylin wasn't breathing, and I couldn't find a pulse. For a moment, I stared at him, undecided, repelled, not wanting to touch him again, let alone breathe into him. Then quelling disgust, I began mouth to mouth resuscitation and external heart massage – what did they call it? Cardiopulmonary resuscitation. I knew the name, and I'd seen someone doing it on television. Beyond that, I was completely ignorant. I didn't even know why I was trying to save Weylin. He wasn't worth it. And I didn't know if CPR could do any good in an era when there was no ambulance to call, no one to take over for me even if I somehow got Weylin's heart going – which I didn't expect to do.

Which I didn't do.

Finally, I gave up. I looked around to see Rufus on the floor near me. I didn't know whether he had sat down or fallen, but I was glad he was sitting now.

'I'm sorry, Rufe. He's dead.'

'You let him die?'

'He was dead when I got here. I tried to bring him back the way I brought you back when you were drowning. I failed.'

'You let him die.'

He sounded like a child about to cry. His illness had weakened him so, I thought he might cry. Even healthy people cried and said irrational things when their parents died.

232

'I did what I could, Rufe. I'm sorry.'

'Damn you to hell, you let him die!' He tried to lunge at me, succeeded only in falling over. I moved to help him up, but stopped when he tried to push me away.

'Send Nigel to me,' he whispered. 'Get Nigel.'

I got up and went to find Nigel. Behind me, I heard Rufus say once more, 'You just let him die.'

5

Things were happening too fast for me. I was almost glad to find myself put back to work with Sarah and Carrie, ignored by Rufus. I needed time to catch up with myself – and catch up with life on the plantation. Carrie and Nigel had three sons now, and Nigel had never mentioned it to me because the youngest was two years old. He had forgotten that I didn't know. I was with him once, as he watched them playing. 'It's good to have children,' he said softly. 'Good to have sons. But it's so hard to see them be slaves.'

I met Alice's thin pale little boy and saw with relief that in spite of the way she talked, she obviously loved the child.

'I keep thinking I might wake up and find him cold like the others,' she said one day in the cookhouse.

'What did they die of?' I asked.

'Fevers. The doctor came and bled them and purged them, but they still died.'

'He bled and purged babies?'

'They were two and three. He said it would break the fever. And it did. But they . . . they died anyway.'

'Alice, if I were you, I wouldn't ever let that man near Joe.'

She looked at her son sitting on the floor of the cookhouse eating mush and milk. He was five years old and he looked almost white in spite of Alice's dark skin. 'I never wanted no doctor near the other two,' said Alice. 'Marse Rufe sent for him – sent for him and made me let him kill my babies.'

233

Rufus's intentions had been good. Even the doctor's intentions had probably been good. But all Alice knew was that her children were dead and she blamed Rufus. Rufus himself was to teach me about that attitude.

On the day after Weylin was buried, Rufus decided to punish me for letting the old man die. I didn't know whether he honestly believed I had done such a thing. Maybe he just needed to hurt someone. He did lash out at others when he was hurt; I had already seen that.

So on the morning after the funeral, he sent the current overseer, a burly man named Evan Fowler, to get me from the cookhouse. Jake Edwards had either quit or been fired sometime during my six-year absence. Fowler came to tell me I was to work in the fields.

I didn't believe it, even when the man pushed me out of the cookhouse. I thought he was just another Jake Edwards throwing his weight around. But outside, Rufus stood waiting, watching. I looked at him, then back at Fowler.

'This the one?' Fowler asked Rufus.

'That's her,' said Rufus. And he turned and went back into the main house.

Stunned, I took the sicklelike corn knife Fowler thrust into my hands and let myself be herded out toward the cornfield. Herded. Fowler got his horse and rode a little behind me as I walked. It was a long walk. The cornfield wasn't where I'd left it. Apparently, even in this time, planters practiced some form of crop rotation. Not that that mattered to me. What in the world could I do in a cornfield?

I glanced back at Fowler. 'I've never done field work before,' I told him. 'I don't know how.'

'You'll learn,' he said. He used the handle of his whip to scratch his shoulder.

I began to realize that I should have resisted, should have refused to let Fowler bring me out here where only other slaves could see what happened to me. Now it was too late. It was going to be a grim day.

Slaves were walking down rows of corn, chopping the stalks down with golf-swing strokes of their knives. Two slaves worked a row, moving toward each other. Then they gathered the stalks they had cut and stood them in bunches at opposite ends of the row. It looked easy, but I suspected that a day of it could be backbreaking.

Fowler dismounted and pointed toward a row.

'You chop like the others,' he said. 'Just do what they do. Now get to work.' He shoved me toward the row. There was already someone at the other end of it working toward me. Someone quick and strong, I hoped, because I doubted that I would be quick or strong for a while. I hoped that the washing and the scrubbing at the house and the factory and warehouse work back in my own time had made me strong enough just to survive.

I raised the knife and chopped at the first stalk. It bent over, partially cut.

At almost the same moment, Fowler lashed me hard across the back.

I screamed, stumbled, and spun around to face him, still holding my knife. Unimpressed, he hit me across the breasts.

I fell to my knees and doubled over in a blaze of pain. Tears ran down my face. Even Tom Weylin hadn't hit slave women that way – any more than he'd kicked slave men in the groin. Fowler was an animal. I glared up at him in pain and hatred.

'Get up!' he said.

I couldn't. I didn't think anything could make me get up just then – until I saw Fowler raising his whip again.

Somehow, I got up.

'Now do what the others do,' he said. 'Chop close to the ground. Chop hard!'

I gripped the knife, felt myself much more eager to chop him.

'All right,' he said. 'Try it and get it over with. I thought you was supposed to be smart.'

He was a big man. He hadn't impressed me as being very quick, but he was strong. I was afraid that even if I managed to hurt him, I wouldn't hurt him enough to keep him from killing me. Maybe I should make him try to kill me. Maybe it would get me out of this Godawful place where people punished you for helping them. Maybe it would get me home. But in how many pieces? Fowler would take the knife away from me and give it back edge first.

I turned and slashed furiously at the corn stalk, then at the next. Behind me, Fowler laughed.

'Maybe you got some sense after all,' he said.

He watched me for a while, urging me on, literally cracking the whip. By the time he left, I was sweating, shaking, humiliated. I met the woman who had been working toward me and she whispered, 'Slow down! Take a lick or two if you have to. You kill yourself today, he'll push you to kill yourself every day.'

There was sense in that. Hell, if I went on the way I had been, I wouldn't even last through today. My shoulders were already beginning to ache.

Fowler came back as I was gathering the cut stalks. 'What the devil do you think you're doing!' he demanded. 'You ought to be halfway down the next row by now.' He hit me across the back as I bent down. 'Move! You're not in the cookhouse getting fat and lazy now. Move!'

He did that all day. Coming up suddenly, shouting at me, ordering me to go faster no matter how fast I went, cursing me, threatening me. He didn't hit me that often, but he kept me on edge because I never knew when a blow would fall. It got so just the sound of his coming terrified me. I caught myself cringing, jumping at the sound of his voice.

The woman in my row explained, 'He's always hard on a new nigger. Make 'em go fast so he can see how fast they can work. Then later on if they slow down, he whip 'em for gettin' lazy.'

I made myself slow down. It wasn't hard. I didn't think my shoulders could have hurt much worse if they'd been broken. Sweat ran down into my eyes and my hands were beginning to blister. My back hurt from the blows I'd taken as well as from sore muscles. After a while, it was more painful for me to push myself than it was for me to let Fowler hit me. After a while, I was so tired, I didn't care either way. Pain was pain. After a while, I just wanted to lie down between the rows and not get up again.

I stumbled and fell, got up and fell again. Finally, I lay face-down in the dirt, unable to get up. Then came a welcome blackness. I could have been going home or dying or passing out; it made no difference to me. I was going away from the pain. That was all.

6

I was on my back when I came to and there was a white face floating just above me. For a wild moment, I thought it was Kevin, thought I was home. I said his name eagerly.

'It's me, Dana.'

Rufus's voice. I was still in hell. I closed my eyes, not caring what would happen next.

'Dana, get up. You'll be hurt more if I carry you than if you walk.'

The words echoed strangely in my head. Kevin had said something like that to me once. I opened my eyes again to be sure it was Rufus.

It was. I was still in the cornfield, still lying in the dirt.

'I came to get you,' said Rufus. 'Not soon enough, I guess.'

I struggled to my feet. He offered a hand to help me, but I ignored it. I brushed myself off a little and followed him down the row toward his horse. From there, we rode together back to the house without a word passing between us. At the house, I went straight to the well, got a bucket of water, carried it up the stairs somehow, then washed, spread antiseptic on my new cuts, and put on clean clothes. I had a headache that eventually drove me down to Rufus's room for some Excedrin. Rufus had used all the aspirins.

Unfortunately, he was in his room.

'Well, you're no good in the fields,' he said when he saw me. 'That's clear.'

I stopped, turned, and stared at him. Just stared. He had been sitting on his bed, leaning back against the headboard, but now he straightened, faced me.

'Don't do anything stupid, Dana.'

'Right,' I said softly. 'I've done enough stupid things. How many times have I saved your life so far?' My aching head sent me to his desk where I had left the Excedrin. I shook three of them into my hand. I had never taken so many before. I had never needed so many before. My hands were trembling.

'Fowler would have given you a good whipping if I hadn't stopped him,' said Rufus. 'That's not the first beating I've saved you from.'

I had my Excedrin. I turned to leave the room.

'Dana!'

I stopped, looked at him. He was thin and weak and hollow-eyed; his illness had left its marks on him. He probably couldn't have carried me to his horse if he'd tried. And he couldn't stop me from leaving now – I thought.

'You walk away from me, Dana, you'll be back in the fields in an hour!'

The threat stunned me. He meant it. He'd send me back out. I stood straring at him, not with anger now, but with surprise – and fear. He could do it. Maybe later, I would have a chance to make him pay, but for now, he could do as he pleased. He sounded more like his father than himself. In that moment, he even looked like his father.

'Don't you ever walk away from me again!' he said. Strangely, he began to sound a little afraid. He repeated the words, spacing them, emphasizing each one. '*Don't you ever walk away from me again!*'

I stood where I was, my head throbbing, my expression as neutral as I could make it. I still had some pride left.

'Get back in here!' he said.

I stood there for a moment longer, then went back to his desk and sat down. And he wilted. The look I associated with his father vanished. He was himself again – whoever that was.

'Dana, don't make me talk to you like that,' he said wearily. 'Just do what I tell you.'

I shook my head, unable to think of anything safe to say. And I guess I wilted. To my shame, I realized I was almost crying. I needed desperately to be alone. Somehow, I kept back the tears.

If he noticed, he didn't say anything. I remembered I still had the Excedrin tablets in my hand, and I took them, swallowed them without water, hoping they'd work quickly, steady me a little. Then I looked at Rufus, saw that he'd lain back again. Was I supposed to stay and watch him sleep?

'I don't see how you can swallow those things like that,' he said, rubbing his throat. There was a long silence, then another command. 'Say something! Talk to me!'

'Or what?' I asked. 'Are you going to have me beaten for not talking to you?'

He muttered something I didn't quite hear.

'What?'

Silence. Then a rush of bitterness from me.

'I saved your life, Rufus! Over and over again.' I stopped for a moment, caught my breath. 'And I tried to save your father's life. You know I did. You know I didn't kill him or let him die.'

He moved uncomfortably, wincing a little. 'Give me some of your medicine,' he said.

Somehow, I didn't throw the bottle at him. I got up and handed it to him.

'Open it,' he said. 'I don't want to be bothered with that damn top.'

I opened it, shook one tablet into his hand, and snapped the top back on.

He looked at the tablet. 'Only one?'

'These are stronger than the others,' I said. And also, I wanted to hang on to them for as long as I could. Who knew how

239

many more times he would make me need them. The ones I had taken were beginning to help me already.

'You took three,' he said petulantly.

'I needed three. No one has been beating you.'

He looked away from me, put the one into his mouth. He still had to chew tablets before he could swallow them. 'This tastes worse than the others,' he complained.

I ignored him, put the bottle away in the desk.

'Dana?'

'What?'

'I know you tried to help Daddy. I know.'

'Then why did you send me to the field? Why did I have to go through all that, Rufe?'

He shrugged, winced, rubbed his shoulders. He still had plenty of sore muscles, apparently. 'I guess I just had to make somebody pay. And it seemed that . . . well, people don't die when you're taking care of them.'

'I'm not a miracle worker.'

'No. Daddy thought you were, though. He didn't like you, but he thought you could heal better than a doctor.'

'Well I can't. Sometimes I'm less likely to kill than the doctor, that's all.'

'Kill?'

'I don't bleed or purge away people's strength when they need it most. And I know enough to try to keep a wound clean.'

'Is that all?'

'That's enough to save a few lives around here, but no, it's not all. I know a little about some diseases. Only a little.'

'What do you know about . . . about a woman who's been hurt in childbearing?'

'Been hurt how?' I wondered whether he meant Alice.

'I don't know. The doctor said she wasn't to have any more and she did. The babies died and she almost died. She hasn't been well since.'

Now I knew who he was talking about. 'Your mother?'

'Yes. She's coming home. I want you to take care of her.'

'My God! Rufe, I don't know anything about problems like that! Believe me, nothing at all.' What if the woman died in my care. He'd have me beaten to death!

'She wants to come home, now that . . . She wants to come home.'

'I can't care for her. I don't know how.' I hesitated. 'Your mother doesn't like me anyway, Rufe. You know that as well as I do.' She hated me. She'd make my life hell out of pure spite.

'There's no one else I'd trust,' he said. 'Carrie's got her own family now. I'd have to take her out of her cabin away from Nigel and the boys . . .'

'Why?'

'Mama has to have someone with her through the night. What if she needed something?'

'You mean I'd have to sleep in her room?'

'Yes. She'd never have a servant sleep in her room before. Now, though, she's gotten used to it.'

'She won't get used to me. I'm telling you, she won't have me.' Please heaven!

'I think she will. She's older now, not so full of fire. You give her her laudanum when she needs it and she won't give you much trouble.'

'Laudanum?'

'Her medicine. She doesn't need it so much for pain anymore, Aunt May says. But she still needs it.'

Since laudanum was an opium extract, I didn't doubt that she still needed it. I was going to have a drug addict on my hands. A drug addict who hated me. 'Rufe, couldn't Alice . . .'

'No!' A very sharp no. It occurred to me that Margaret Weylin had more reason to hate Alice than she did to hate me.

'Alice will be having another baby in a few months anyway,' said Rufus.

'She will? Then maybe . . .' I shut my mouth, but the thought went on. Maybe this one would be Hagar. Maybe for once, I had something to gain by staying here. If only . . .

'Maybe what?'

'Nothing. It doesn't matter. Rufe, I'm asking you not to put your mother in my care, for her sake and for mine.'

He rubbed his forehead. 'I'll think about it, Dana, and talk to her. Maybe she remembers someone she'd like. Let me sleep now. I'm still so damn weak.'

I started out of the room.

'Dana.'

'Yes?' What now?

'Go read a book or something. Don't do any more work today.'

'Read a book?'

'Do whatever you want to.'

In other words, he was sorry. He was always sorry. He would have been amazed, uncomprehending if I refused to forgive him. I remembered suddenly the way he used to talk to his mother. If he couldn't get what he wanted from her gently, he stopped being gentle. Why not? She always forgave him.

7

Margaret Weylin wanted me. She was thin and pale and weak and older than her years. Her beauty had gone to a kind of fragile gauntness. As I was reintroduced to her, she sipped at her little bottle of dark brownish-red liquid and smiled beneficently.

Nigel carried her up to her room. She could walk a little, but she couldn't manage the stairs. Sometime later, she wanted to see Nigel's children. She was sugary sweet with them. I couldn't remember her being that way with anyone but Rufus before. Slave children hadn't interested her unless her husband had fathered them. Then her interest had been negative. But she gave Nigel's sons candy and they loved her.

She asked to see another slave – one I didn't know – and then wept a little when she heard that one had been sold. She was full of sweetness and charity. It scared me a little. I couldn't quite believe she'd changed that much.

'Dana, can you still read the way you used to?' she asked me.

'Yes, ma'am.'

'I wanted you because I remembered how well you read.'

I kept my expression neutral. If she didn't remember what she had thought of my reading, I did.

'Read the Bible to me,' she said.

'Now?' She had just had her breakfast. I hadn't had anything yet, and I was hungry.

'Now, yes. Read the Sermon on the Mount.'

That was the beginning of my first full day with her. When she was tired of hearing me read, she thought of other things for me to do. Her laundry, for instance. She wouldn't trust anyone else to do it. I wondered whether she had already found out that Alice generally did the laundry. And there was cleaning. She didn't believe her room had been swept and dusted until she saw me do it. She didn't believe Sarah understood how she wanted dinner prepared until I went down, got Sarah, and brought her back with me to receive instructions. She had to talk to Carrie and Nigel about the cleaning. She had to inspect the boy and girl who served at the table. In short, she had to prove that she was running her own house again. It had gone along without her for years, but she was back now.

She decided to teach me to sew. I had an old Singer at home and I could sew well enough with it to take care of my needs and Kevin's. But I thought sewing by hand, especially sewing for 'pleasure' was slow torture. Margaret Weylin never asked me whether I wanted to learn though. She had time to fill, and it was my job to help her fill it. So I spent long tedious hours trying to imitate her tiny, straight, even stitches, and she spent minutes ripping out my work and lecturing me none too gently on how bad it was.

As the days passed, I learned to take longer than necessary when she sent me on errands. I learned to tell lies to get away

243

from her when I thought I was about to explode. I learned to listen silently while she talked and talked and talked . . . mostly about how much better things were in Baltimore than here. I never learned to like sleeping on the floor of her room, but she wouldn't permit the trundle bed to be brought in. She honestly didn't see that it was any hardship for me to sleep on the floor. Niggers always slept on the floor.

Troublesome as she was, though, Margaret Weylin had mellowed. She didn't have the old bursts of temper any more. Maybe it was the laudanum.

'You're a good girl,' she said to me once as I sat near her bed stitching at a slip cover. 'Much better than you used to be. Someone must have taught you to behave.'

'Yes, ma'am.' I didn't even look up.

'Good. You were impudent before. There's nothing worse than an impudent nigger.'

'Yes, ma'am.'

She depressed me, bored me, angered me, drove me crazy. But my back healed completely while I was with her. The work wasn't hard and she never complained about anything but my sewing. She never threatened me or tried to have me whipped. Rufus said she was pleased with me. That seemed to surprise even him. So I endured her quietly. By now, I knew enough to realize when I was well off. Or I thought I did.

'You ought to see yourself,' Alice told me one day as I was hiding out in her cabin – the cabin Rufus had had Nigel build her just before the birth of her first child.

'What do you mean?' I asked.

'Marse Rufe really put the fear of God in you, didn't he?'

'Fear of . . . What are you talking about?'

'You run around fetching and carrying for that woman like you love her. And half a day in the fields was all it took.'

'Hell, Alice, leave me alone. I've been listening to nonsense all morning. I don't need yours.'

'You don't want to hear me, get out of here. The way you always suck-in' up to that woman is enough to make anybody sick.'

I got up and went to the cookhouse. There were times when it was stupid to expect reason from Alice, times when it did no good to point out the obvious.

There were two field hands in the cookhouse. One young man who had a broken leg splinted and obviously healing crooked, and one old man who didn't do much work any more. I could hear them before I went in.

'I know Marse Rufe'll get rid of me if he can,' said the young man. 'I ain't no good to him. His daddy would have got rid of me.'

'Won't nobody buy me,' said the old man. 'I was burnt out long time ago. It's you young ones got to worry.'

I went into the cookhouse and the young man who had his mouth open to speak closed it quickly, looking at me with open hostility. The old man simply turned his back. I'd seen slaves do that to Alice. I hadn't noticed them doing it to me before. Suddenly, the cookhouse was no more comfortable than Alice's cabin had been. It might have been different if Sarah or Carrie had been there, but they weren't. I left the cookhouse and went back toward the main house, feeling lonely.

Once I was inside, though, I wondered why I had crept away like that. Why hadn't I fought back? Alice accusing me was ridiculous, and she knew it. But the field hands . . . They just didn't know me, didn't know how loyal I might be to Rufus or Margaret, didn't know what I might report.

And if I told them, how likely would they be to believe me? But still . . .

I went down the hall and toward the stairs slowly, wondering why I hadn't tried to defend myself – at least tried. Was I getting so used to being submissive?

Upstairs, I could hear Margaret Weylin thumping on the floor with her cane. She didn't use the cane much for walking because she hardly ever walked. She used it to call me.

I turned and went back out of the house, out toward the woods. I had to think. I wasn't getting enough time to myself. Once – God knows how long ago – I had worried that I was

245

keeping too much distance between myself and this alien time. Now, there was no distance at all. When had I stopped acting? Why had I stopped?

There were people coming toward me through the woods. Several people. They were on the road, and I was several feet off it. I crouched in the trees to wait for them to pass. I was in no mood to answer some white man's stupid inevitable questions: 'What are you doing here? Who's your master?'

I could have answered without trouble. I was nowhere near the edge of Weylin land. But just for a while, I wanted to be my own master. Before I forgot what it felt like.

A white man went by on horseback leading two dozen black men chained two by two. Chained. They wore handcuffs and iron collars with chains connecting the collars to a central chain that ran between the two lines. Behind the men walked several women roped together neck to neck. A coffle – slaves for sale.

At the end of the procession rode a second white man with a gun in his belt. They were all headed for the Weylin house.

I realized suddenly that the slaves in the cookhouse had not been speculating idly about the possibility of being sold. They had known that there was a sale coming. Field hands who never set foot in the main house, and they had known. I hadn't heard a thing.

Lately, Rufus spent his time either straightening out his father's affairs, or sleeping. The weakness left over from his illness was still with him, and he had no time for me. He barely had time for his mother. But he had time to sell slaves. He had time to make himself that much more like his father.

I let the coffle reach the house far ahead of me. By the time I got there, three slaves were already being added to the line. Two men, one grim-faced, one openly weeping; and one woman who moved as though she were sleepwalking. As I got closer, the woman began to look familiar to me. I stopped, almost not wanting to know who it was. A tall, strongly built, handsome woman.

Tess.

I'd seen her only two or three times this trip. She was still working in the fields, still serving the overseer at night. She'd had no children, and that may have been why she was being sold. Or maybe this was something Margaret Weylin had arranged. She might be that vindictive if she knew of her husband's temporary interest in Tess.

I started toward Tess and the white man who had just tied a rope around her neck, fastening her into the line, saw me. He turned to face me, gun drawn.

I stopped, alarmed, confused . . . I had made no threatening move. 'I just wanted to say good-bye to my friend,' I told him. I was whispering for some reason.

'Say it from there. She can hear you.'

'Tess?'

She stood, head down, shoulders rounded, a little red bundle hanging from one hand. She should have heard me, but I didn't think she had.

'Tess, it's Dana.'

She never looked up.

'Dana!' Rufus's voice from near the steps where he was talking with the other white man. 'You get away from here. Go inside.'

'Tess?' I called once more, willing her to answer. She knew my voice, surely. Why wouldn't she look up? Why wouldn't she speak? Why wouldn't she even move? It was as though I didn't exist for her, as though I wasn't real.

I stepped toward her. I think I would have gone to her, taken the rope from her neck or gotten shot trying. But at that moment, Rufus reached me. He grabbed me, hustled me into the house, into the library.

'Stay here!' he ordered. 'Just stay . . .' He stopped, suddenly stumbled against me, clutching at me now, not to hold me where I was, but to keep himself upright. 'Damn!'

'How could you do it!' I hissed as he straightened. 'Tess . . . those others . . .'

'They're my property!'

247

I stared at him in disbelief. 'Oh my God . . .!'

He passed a hand over his face, turned away. 'Look, this sale is something my father arranged before he died. You can't do anything about it, so just stay out of the way!'

'Or what? You going to sell me too? You might as well!'

He went back outside without answering. After a while, I sat down in Tom Weylin's worn armchair and put my head down on his desk.

8

Carrie covered for me with Margaret Weylin. She wanted me to know that when she caught me heading back upstairs. Actually, I don't know why I was heading upstairs, except that I didn't want to see Rufus again for a while, and there was nowhere else to go.

Carrie stopped me on the stairs, looked at me critically, then took my arm and led me back down and out to her cabin. I didn't know or care what she had in mind, but I did understand when she told me through gestures that she had told Margaret Weylin I was sick. Then she circled her neck with the thumbs and forefingers of both hands and looked at me.

'I saw,' I said. 'Tess and two others.' I drew a ragged breath. 'I thought that was over on this plantation. I thought it died with Tom Weylin.'

Carrie shrugged.

'I wish I had left Rufus lying in the mud,' I said. 'To think I saved him so he could do something like this . . .!'

Carrie caught my wrist and shook her head vigorously.

'What do you mean, no? He's no good. He's all grown up now, and part of the system. He could feel for us a little when his father was running things – when he wasn't entirely free himself. But now, he's in charge. And I guess he had to do something right away, to prove it.'

Carrie clasped her hands around her neck again. Then she

drew closer to me and clasped them around my neck. Finally, she went over to the crib that her youngest child had recently outgrown and there, symbolically, clasped her hands again, leaving enough of an open circle for a small neck.

She straightened and looked at me.

'Everybody?' I asked.

She nodded, gestured widely with her arms as though gathering a group around her. Then, once again, her hands around her neck.

I nodded. She was almost surely right. Margaret Weylin could not run the plantation. Both the land and the people would be sold. And if Tom Weylin was any example, the people would be sold without regard for family ties.

Carrie stood looking down at the crib as though she had read my thought.

'I was beginning to feel like a traitor,' I said. 'Guilty for saving him. Now . . . I don't know what to feel. Somehow, I always seem to forgive him for what he does to me. I can't hate him the way I should until I see him doing things to other people.' I shook my head. 'I guess I can see why there are those here who think I'm more white than black.'

Carrie made quick waving-aside gestures, her expression annoyed. She came over to me and wiped one side of my face with her fingers – wiped hard. I drew back, and she held her fingers in front of me, showed me both sides. But for once, I didn't understand.

Frustrated, she took me by the hand and led me out to where Nigel was chopping firewood. There, before him, she repeated the face-rubbing gesture, and he nodded.

'She means it doesn't come off, Dana,' he said quietly. 'The black. She means the devil with people who say you're anything but what you are.'

I hugged her and got away from her quickly so that she wouldn't see that I was close to tears. I went up to Margaret Weylin and she'd just had her laudanum. Being with her at such times was like being alone. And being alone was just what I needed.

I avoided Rufus for three days after the sale. He made it easy for me. He avoided me too. Then on the fourth day he came looking for me. He found me in his mother's room yes-ma'aming her and changing her bed while she sat looking thin and frail beside the window. She barely ate. I had actually caught myself coaxing her to eat. Then I realized that she enjoyed being coaxed. She could forget to be superior sometimes, and just be someone's old mother. Rufus's mother. Unfortunately.

He came in and said, 'Let Carrie finish that, Dana. I have something else for you to do.'

'Oh, do you have to take her now?' said Margaret. 'She was just . . .'

'I'll send her back later, Mama. And Carrie'll be up to finish your bed in a minute.'

I left the room silently, not looking forward to whatever he had in mind.

'Down to the library,' he said right behind me.

I glanced back at him, trying to gauge his mood, but he only looked tired. He ate well and got twice the rest he should have needed, but he always looked tired.

'Wait a minute,' he said.

I stopped.

'Did you bring another of those pens with the ink inside?'

'Yes.'

'Get it.'

I went up to the attic where I still kept most of my things. I'd brought a packet of three pens this time, but I only took one back down with me – in case he still took as much pleasure as he had last trip in wasting ink.

'You ever hear of dengue fever?' he asked as he went down the stairs.

'No.'

'Well, according to the doc in town, that's what I had. I told him about it.' He had been going back and forth to town often since his father's death. 'Doc said he didn't see how I'd made it without bleeding and a good emetic. Says I'm still weak because I didn't get all the poisons out of my body.'

'Put yourself in his hands,' I said quietly. 'And with a little luck, that will solve both our problems.'

He frowned uncertainly. 'What do you mean by that?'

'Not a thing.'

He turned and caught me by the shoulders in a grip that he probably meant to be painful. It wasn't. 'Are you trying to say you want me to die?'

I sighed. 'If I did, you would, wouldn't you?'

Silence. He let go of me and we went into the library. He sat down in his father's old armchair and motioned me into a hard Windsor chair nearby. Which was one step up from his father who had always made me stand before him like a school kid sent to the principal's office.

'If you think that little sale was bad – and Daddy really had already arranged it – you better make sure nothing happens to me.' Rufus leaned back and looked at me wearily. 'Do you know what would happen to the people here if I died?'

I nodded. 'What bothers me,' I said, 'is what's going to happen to them if you live.'

'You don't think I'm going to do anything to them, do you?'

'Of course you are. And I'll have to watch and remember and decide when you've gone too far. Believe me, I'm not looking forward to the job.'

'You take a lot on yourself.'

'None of it was my idea.'

He muttered something inaudible, and probably obscene. 'You ought to be in the fields,' he added. 'God knows why I didn't leave you out there. You would have learned a few things.'

'I would have been killed. You would have had to start taking very good care of yourself.' I shrugged. 'I don't think you have the knack.'

251

'Damnit, Dana . . . What's the good of sitting here trading threats? I don't believe you want to hurt me any more than I want to hurt you.'

I said nothing.

'I brought you down here to write a few letters for me, not fight with me.'

'Letters?'

He nodded. 'I'll tell you, I hate to write. Don't mind reading so much, but I hate to write.'

'You didn't hate it six years ago.'

'I didn't have to do it then. I didn't have eight or nine people all wanting answers, and wanting them now.'

I twisted the pen in my hands. 'You'll never know how hard I worked in my own time to avoid doing jobs like this.'

He grinned suddenly. 'Yes I do. Kevin told me. He told me about the books you wrote too. Your own books.'

'That's how he and I earn our living.'

'Yeah. Well, I thought you might miss it – writing your own things, I mean. So I got enough paper for you to write for both of us.'

I looked at him, not quite sure I'd heard right. I had read that paper in this time was expensive, and I had seen that Weylin had never had very much of it. But here was Rufus offering . . . Offering what? A bribe? Another apology?

'What's the matter?' he said. 'Seems to me, this is better than any offer I've made you so far.'

'No doubt.'

He got paper, made room for me at the desk.

'Rufe, are you going to sell anyone else?'

He hesitated. 'I hope not. I don't like it.'

'What's to hope? Why can't you just not do it?'

Another hesitation. 'Daddy left debts, Dana. He was the most careful man I know with money, but he still left debts.'

'But won't your crops pay them?'

'Some of them.'

'Oh. What are you going to do?'

'Get somebody who makes her living by writing to write some very persuasive letters.'

10

I wrote his letters. I had to read several of the letters he'd received first to pick up the stilted formal style of the day. I didn't want Rufus having to face some creditor that I had angered with my twentieth-century brevity – which could come across as nineteenth-century abruptness, even discourtesy. Rufus gave me a general idea of what he wanted me to say and then approved or disapproved of the way I said it. Usually, he approved. Then we started to go over his father's books together. I never did get back to Margaret Weylin.

And I wasn't ever to get back to her full time. Rufus brought a young girl named Beth in from the fields to help with the housework. That eventually freed Carrie to spend more time with Margaret. I continued to sleep in Margaret's room because I agreed with Rufus that Carrie belonged with her family, at least at night. That meant I had to put up with Margaret waking me up when she couldn't sleep and complaining bitterly that Rufus had taken me away just when she and I were beginning to get on so well . . .

'What does he have you doing?' she asked me several times – suspiciously.

I told her.

'Seems as though he could do that himself. Tom always did it himself.'

Rufus could have done it himself too, I thought, though I never said it aloud. He just didn't like working alone. Actually, he didn't like working at all. But if he had to do it, he wanted company. I didn't realize how much he preferred my company in particular until he came in one night a little drunk and found Alice and I eating together in her cabin. He had been away eating with a family in town – 'Some people with daughters they want to get rid of,' Alice had told me. She had said it with no concern at all even though she knew her life could become much harder if Rufus married. Rufus had property and slaves and was apparently quite eligible.

He came home, and not finding either of us in the house, came out to Alice's cabin. He opened the door and saw us both looking up at him from the table, and he smiled happily.

'Behold the woman,' he said. And he looked from one to the other of us. 'You really are only one woman. Did you know that?'

He tottered away.

Alice and I looked at each other. I thought she would laugh because she took any opportunity she could find to laugh at him – though not to his face because he would beat her when he decided she needed it.

She didn't laugh. She shuddered, then got up, not too gracefully – her pregnancy was showing now – and looked out the door after him.

After a while, she asked, 'Does he ever take you to bed, Dana?'

I jumped. Her bluntness could still startle me. 'No. He doesn't want me and I don't want him.'

She glanced back at me over one shoulder. 'What you think your wants got to do with it?'

I said nothing because I liked her. And no answer I could give could help sounding like criticism of her.

'You know,' she said, 'you gentle him for me. He hardly hits me at all when you're here. And he never hits you.'

'He arranges for other people to hit me.'

'But still . . . I know what he means. He likes me in bed, and you out of bed, and you and I look alike if you can believe what people say.'

'We look alike if we can believe our own eyes!'

'I guess so. Anyway, all that means we're two halves of the same woman – at least in his crazy head.'

11

The time passed slowly, uneventfully, as I waited for the birth of the child I hoped would be Hagar. I went on helping Rufus and his mother. I kept a journal in shorthand. ('What the devil are these chicken marks?' Rufus asked me when he looked over my shoulder one day.) It was such a relief to be able to say what I felt, even in writing, without worrying that I might get myself or someone else into trouble. One of my secretarial classes had finally come in handy.

I tried husking corn and blistered my slow clumsy hands while experienced field hands sped through the work effortlessly, enjoying themselves. There was no reason for me to join them, but they seemed to be making a party of the husking – Rufus gave them a little whiskey to help them along – and I needed a party, needed anything that would relieve my boredom, take my mind off myself.

It was a party, all right. A wild rough kind of party that nobody modified because 'the master's women' – Alice and I – were there. People working near me around the small mountain of corn laughed at my blisters and told me I was being initiated. A jug went around and I tasted it, choked, and drew more laughter. Surprisingly companionable laughter. A man with huge muscles told me it was too bad I was already spoken for, and that earned me hostile looks from three women. After the work, there were great quantities of food – chicken, pork, vegetables, corn bread, fruit – better food than the herring and corn meal field hands usually saw so much of. Rufus came out to play hero for providing such a good meal, and the people gave him the praise he wanted. Then they made gross jokes about him behind his back. Strangely, they seemed to like him, hold him in contempt, and fear him all at the same time. This confused me because I felt just about the same mixture of emotions for him myself. I had thought my feelings were complicated because he and I had such a strange relationship. But then, slavery of any kind fostered strange relationships. Only the overseer drew simple, unconflicting emotions of hatred and fear when he appeared briefly. But then, it was part of the overseer's job to be hated and feared while the master kept his hands clean.

Young people began disappearing in pairs after a while, and some of the older ones stopped their eating or drinking or singing or talking long enough to give them looks of disapproval – or more understanding wistful looks. I thought about Kevin and missed him and knew I wasn't going to sleep well that night.

At Christmas, there was another party – dancing, singing, three marriages.

'Daddy used to make them wait until corn shucking or Christmas to marry,' Rufus told me. 'They like parties when they marry, and he made a few parties do.'

'Anything to pinch a few pennies,' I said tactlessly.

He glanced at me. 'You'd better be glad he didn't waste money. You're the one who gets upset when some quick money has to be raised.'

My mind had caught up with my mouth by then, and I kept quiet. He hadn't sold anyone else. The harvest had been good and the creditors patient.

'Found anybody you want to jump the broom with?' he asked me.

I looked at him startled and saw that he wasn't serious. He was smiling and watching the slaves do a bowing, partner-changing dance to the music of a banjo.

'What would you do if I had found someone?' I asked.

'Sell him,' he said. His smile was still in place, but there was no longer any humor in it. I noticed, now, that he was watching the big muscular man who had tried to get me to dance – the same man who had spoken to me at the corn husking. I would have to ask Sarah to tell him not to speak to me again. He didn't mean anything, but that wouldn't save him if Rufus got angry.

256

'One husband is enough for me,' I said.

'Kevin?'

'Of course, Kevin.'

'He's a long way off.'

There was something in his tone that shouldn't have been there. I turned to face him. 'Don't talk stupid.'

He jumped and looked around quickly to see whether anyone had heard.

'You watch your mouth,' he said.

'Watch yours.'

He stalked away angrily. We'd been working together too much lately, especially now that Alice was so advanced in her pregnancy. I was grateful when Alice herself created another job for me – a job that got me away from him regularly. Sometime during the week-long Christmas holiday, Alice persuaded him to let me teach their son Joe to read and write.

'It was my Christmas present,' she told me. 'He asked me what I wanted, and I told him I wanted my son not to be ignorant. You know, I had to fight with him all week to get him to say yes!'

But he had said it, finally, and the boy came to me every day to learn to draw big clumsy letters on the slate Rufus bought him and read simple words and rhymes from the books Rufus himself had used. But unlike Rufus, Joe wasn't bored with what he was learning. He fastened onto the lessons as though they were puzzles arranged for his entertainment – puzzles he loved solving. He could get so intense – throw screaming kicking tantrums when something seemed to be eluding him. But not all that much eluded him.

'You've got a damn bright little kid there,' I told Rufus. 'You ought to be proud.'

Rufus looked surprised – as though it had never occurred to him that there might be anything special about the under-sized runny-nosed child. He had spent his life watching his father ignore, even sell the children he had had with black women. Apparently, it had never occurred to Rufus to break that tradition. Until now.

Now, he began to take an interest in his son. Perhaps he was only curious at first, but the boy captured him. I caught them together once in the library, the boy sitting on one of Rufus's knees and studying a map that Rufus had just brought home. The map was spread on Rufus's desk.

'Is this our river?' the boy was asking.

'No, that's the Miles River, northeast of here. This map doesn't show our river.'

'Why not?'

'It's too small.'

'What is?' The boy peered up at him. 'Our river or this map?'

'Both, I suspect.'

'Let's draw it in, then. Where does it go?'

Rufus hesitated. 'Just about here. But we don't have to draw it in.'

'Why? Don't you want the map to be right?'

I made a noise and Rufus looked up at me. I thought he looked almost ashamed for a moment. He put the boy down quickly and shooed him away.

'Nothing but questions,' Rufus complained to me.

'Enjoy it, Rufe. At least he's not out setting fire to the stable or trying to drown himself.'

He couldn't quite keep from laughing. 'Alice said something like that.' He frowned a little. 'She wants me to free him.'

I nodded. Alice had already told me she meant to ask for the boy's freedom.

'You put her up to it, I guess.'

I stared at him. 'Rufe, if there's a woman on the place who makes up her own mind, it's Alice. I didn't put her up to a thing.'

'Well . . . now she's got something else to make up her mind about.'

'What?'

'Nothing. Nothing to you. I just mean to make her earn what she wants for a change,' he said.

I couldn't get any more out of him than that. Eventually, though, Alice told me what he wanted.

'He wants me to like him,' she said with heavy contempt. 'Or maybe even love him. I think he wants me to be more like you!'

'I guarantee you he doesn't.'

She closed her eyes. 'I don't care what he wants. If I thought it would make him free my children, I'd try to do it. But he lies! And he won't put it down on no paper.'

'He likes Joe,' I said. 'He ought to. Joe looks like a slightly darker version of him at that age. Anyway, he might decide on his own to free the boy.'

'And this one?' She patted her stomach. 'And the others? He'll make sure there're others.'

'I don't know. I'll push him whenever I can.'

'I should have took Joe and tried to run before I got pregnant again.'

'You're still thinking about running?'

'Wouldn't you be if you didn't have another way to get free?'

I nodded.

'I don't mean to spend my life here watching my children grow up as slaves and maybe get sold.'

'He wouldn't . . .'

'You don't know what he would do! He don't treat you the way he treats me. When I'm strong again after I have this baby, I'm going.'

'With the baby?'

'You don't think I'm going to leave it here, do you?'

'But . . . I don't see how you can make it.'

'I know more now than I did when Isaac and me left. I can make it.'

I drew a deep breath. 'When the time comes, if I can help you, I will.'

'Get me a bottle of laudanum,' she said.

'Laudanum!'

'I'll have the baby to keep quiet. Old Mama won't let me near her, but she likes you. Get it.'

259

'All right.' I didn't like it. Didn't like the idea of her trying to run with a baby and a small child, didn't like the idea of her trying to run at all. But she was right. In her place, I would have tried. I would have tried sooner and gotten killed sooner, but I would have done it alone.

'You think about this awhile longer,' I said. 'You'll get the laudanum and anything else I can supply, but you think.'

'I've already thought.'

'Not enough. I shouldn't say this, but think what's going to happen if the dogs catch Joe, or if they pull you down and get the baby.'

12

The baby was a girl, born in the second month of the new year. She was her mother's daughter, born darker skinned than Joe would probably ever be.

''Bout time I had a baby to look like me,' said Alice when she saw her.

'You could have at least tried for red hair,' said Rufus. He was there too, peering at the baby's wrinkled little face, peering with even more concern at Alice's face, sweat-streaked and weary.

For the first and only time, I saw her smile at him – a real smile. No sarcasm, no ridicule. It silenced him for several seconds.

Carrie and I had helped with the birth. Now, we left quietly, both of us probably thinking the same thing. That if Alice and Rufus were going to make peace, finally, neither of us wanted to break their mood.

They called the baby Hagar. Rufus said that was the ugliest name he had ever heard, but it was Alice's choice, and he let it stand. I thought it was the most beautiful name I had ever heard. I felt almost free, half-free if such a thing was possible, half-way home. I was gleeful at first – secretly elated. I even kidded Alice about the names she chose for her children. Joseph

260

and Hagar. And the two others whose names I thought silently – Miriam and Aaron. I said, 'Someday Rufus is going to get religion and read enough of the Bible to wonder about those children's names.'

Alice shrugged. 'If Hagar had been a boy, I would have called her Ishmael. In the Bible, people might be slaves for a while, but they didn't have to stay slaves.'

My mood was so good, I almost laughed. But she wouldn't have understood that, and I couldn't have explained. I kept it all in somehow, and congratulated myself that the Bible wasn't the only place where slaves broke free. Her names were only symbolic, but I had more than symbols to remind me that freedom was possible – probable – and for me, very near.

Or was it?

Slowly, I began to calm down. The danger to my family was past, yes. Hagar had been born. But the danger to me personally . . . the danger to me personally still walked and talked and sometimes sat with Alice in her cabin in the evening as she nursed Hagar. I was there with them a couple of times, and I felt like an intruder.

I was not free. Not any more than Alice was, or her children with their names. In fact, it looked as though Alice might get free before I did. She caught me alone one evening and pulled me into her cabin. It was empty except for the sleeping Hagar. Joe was out collecting cuts and bruises from sturdier children.

'Did you get the laudanum?' she demanded.

I peered at her through the semidarkness. Rufus kept her well supplied with candles, but at the moment, the only light in the room came from the window and from a low fire over which two pots simmered. 'Alice, are you sure you still want it?'

I saw her frown. 'Sure I want it! 'Course I want it! What's the matter with you?'

I hedged a little. 'It's so soon . . . The baby's only a few weeks old.'

'You get me that stuff so I can leave when I want to!'

'I've got it.'

'Give it to me!'

'Goddamnit, Alice, will you slow down! Look, you keep working on him the way you have been, and you can get whatever you want and live to enjoy it.'

To my surprise, her stony expression crumbled, and she began to cry. 'He'll never let any of us go,' she said. 'The more you give him, the more he wants.' She paused, wiped her eyes, then added softly, 'I got to go while I still can — before I turn into just what people call me.' She looked at me and did the thing that made her so much like Rufus, though neither of them recognized it. 'I got to go before I turn into what you are!' she said bitterly.

Sarah had cornered me once and said, 'What you let her talk to you like that for? She can't get away with it with nobody else.'

I didn't know. Guilt, maybe. In spite of everything, my life was easier than hers. Maybe I tried to make up for that by taking her abuse. Everything had its limits, though.

'You want my help, Alice, you watch your mouth!'

'Watch yours,' she mocked.

I stared at her in astonishment, remembering, knowing exactly what she had overheard.

'If I talked to him the way you do, he'd have me hangin' in the barn,' she said.

'If you go on talking to me the way you do, I won't care what he does to you.'

She looked at me for a long time without saying anything. Finally, she smiled. 'You'll care. And you'll help me. Else, you'd have to see yourself for the white nigger you are, and you couldn't stand that.'

Rufus never called my bluff. Alice did it automatically — and because I was bluffing, she got away with it. I got up and walked away from her. Behind me, I thought I heard her laugh.

Some days later, I gave her the laudanum. Later that same

262

day, Rufus began talking about sending Joe to school up North when he was a little older.

'Do you mean to free the boy, Rufe?'

He nodded.

'Good. Tell Alice.'

'When I get around to it.'

I didn't argue with him; I told her myself.

'It don't matter what he says,' she told me. 'Did he show you any free papers?'

'No.'

'When he does, and you read them to me, maybe I'll believe him. I'm tellin' you, he uses those children just the way you use a bit on a horse. I'm tired of havin' a bit in my mouth.'

I didn't blame her. But still, I didn't want her to go, didn't want her to risk Joe and Hagar. Hell, I didn't even want her to risk herself. Elsewhere, under other circumstances, I would probably have disliked her. But here, we had a common enemy to unite us.

13

I planned to stay on the Weylin plantation long enough to see Alice leave, to find out whether she would be able to keep her freedom this time. I managed to talk her into waiting until early summer to go. And I was prepared to wait that long myself before I tried some dangerous trick that might get me home. I was homesick and Kevinsick and damned sick of Margaret Weylin's floor and Alice's mouth, but I could wait a few more months. I thought.

I talked Rufus into letting me teach Nigel's two older sons and the two children who served at the table along with Joe. Surprisingly, the children liked it. I couldn't recall having liked school much when I was their ages. Rufus liked it because Joe was as bright as I had said – bright and competitive. He had a head start on the others, and he didn't intend to lose it.

'Why weren't you like that about learning?' I asked Rufus.

'Don't bother me,' he muttered.

Some of his neighbors found out what I was doing and offered him fatherly advice. It was dangerous to educate slaves, they warned. Education made blacks dissatisfied with slavery. It spoiled them for field work. The Methodist minister said it made them disobedient, made them want more than the Lord intended them to have. Another man said educating slaves was illegal. When Rufus replied that he had checked and that it wasn't illegal in Maryland, the man said it should have been. Talk. Rufus shrugged it off without ever saying how much of it he believed. It was enough that he sided with me, and my school continued. I got the feeling that Alice was keeping him happy – and maybe finally enjoying herself a little in the process. I guessed from what she had told me that this was what was frightening her so, driving her away from the plantation, causing her to lash out at me. She was trying to deal with guilt of her own.

But she was waiting and using some discretion. I relaxed, spent my spare moments trying to think of a way to get home. I didn't want to depend on someone else's chance violence again – violence that, if it came, could be more effective than I wanted.

Then Sam James stopped me out by the cookhouse and my complacency was brought to an end.

I saw him waiting for me beside the cookhouse door – a big young man. I mistook him for Nigel at first. Then I recognized him. Sarah had told me his name. He had spoken to me at the corn husking, and again at Christmas. Then Sarah had spoken to him for me and he had said nothing else. Until now.

'I'm Sam,' he said. 'Remember at Christmas?'

'Yes. But I thought Sarah told you . . .'

'She did. Look, it ain't that. I just wanted to see if maybe you'd teach my brother and sister to read.'

'Your . . . Oh. How old are they?'

'Sister was born the year you came here last . . . brother, the year before that.'

'I'll have to get permission. Ask Sarah about it in a few days but don't come to me again.' I thought of the expression I had seen on Rufus's face as he looked at this man. 'Maybe I'm too cautious, but I don't want you getting in trouble because of me.'

He gave me a long searching look. 'You want to be with that white man, girl?'

'If I were anywhere else, no black child on the place would be learning anything.'

'That ain't what I mean.'

'Yes it is. It's all part of the same thing.'

'Some folks say . . .'

'Hold on.' I was suddenly angry. 'I don't want to hear what "some folks" say. "Some folks" let Fowler drive them into the fields every day and work them like mules.'

'*Let* him . . .?'

'Let him! They do it to keep the skin on their backs and breath in their bodies. Well, they're not the only ones who have to do things they don't like to stay alive and whole. Now you tell me why that should be so hard for "some folks" to understand?'

He sighed. 'That's what I told them. But you better off than they are, so they get jealous.' He gave me another of his long searching looks. 'I still say it's too bad you already spoke for.'

I grinned. 'Get out of here, Sam. Field hands aren't the only ones who can be jealous.'

He went. That was all. Innocent – completely innocent. But three days later, a trader led Sam away in chains.

Rufus never said a word to me. He didn't accuse me of anything. I wouldn't have known Sam had been sold if I hadn't glanced out the window of Margaret Weylin's room and seen the coffle.

I told Margaret some hasty lie, then ran out of her room, down the stairs, and out the door. I ran headlong into Rufus, and felt him steady me, hold me. The weakness that his dengue fever had left was finally gone. His grip was formidable.

'Get back in the house!' he hissed.

I saw Sam beyond him being chained into line. There were people a few feet away from him crying loudly. Two women, a boy and a girl. His family.

'Rufe,' I pleaded desperately, 'don't do this. There's no need!'

He pushed me back toward the door and I struggled against him.

'Rufe, please! Listen, he came to ask me to teach his brother and sister to read. That's all!'

It was like talking to the wall of the house. I managed to break away from him for a moment just as the younger of the two weeping women spotted me.

'You whore!' she screamed. She had not been permitted to approach the coffle, but she approached me. 'You no-'count nigger whore, why couldn't you leave my brother alone!'

She would have attacked me. And field hand that she was, strengthened by hard work, she would probably have given me the beating she thought I deserved. But Rufus stepped between us.

'Get back to work, Sally!'

She didn't move, stood glaring at him until the older woman, probably her mother, reached her and pulled her away.

I caught Rufus by the hand and spoke low to him. 'Please, Rufe. If you do this, you'll destroy what you mean to preserve. Please don't . . .'

He hit me.

It was a first, and so unexpected that I stumbled backward and fell.

And it was a mistake. It was the breaking of an unspoken agreement between us – a very basic agreement – and he knew it.

I got up slowly, watching him with anger and betrayal.

'Get in the house and stay there,' he said.

I turned my back and went to the cookhouse, deliberately disobeying. I could hear one of the traders say, 'You ought to sell that one too. Troublemaker!'

266

At the cookhouse, I heated water, got it warm, not hot. Then I took a basin of it up to the attic. It was hot there, and empty except for the pallets and my bag in its corner. I went over to it, washed my knife in antiseptic, and hooked the drawstring of my bag over my shoulder.

And in the warm water I cut my wrists.

The Rope

1

I awoke in darkness and lay still for several seconds trying to think where I was and when I had gone to sleep.

I was lying on something unbelievably soft and comfortable . . . My bed. Home. Kevin?

I could hear regular breathing beside me now. I sat up and reached out to turn on the lamp – or I tried to. Sitting up made me faint and dizzy. For a moment, I thought Rufus was pulling me back to him before I could even see home. Then I became aware that my wrists were bandaged and throbbing – and I remembered what I had done.

The lamp on Kevin's side of the bed went on and I could see him beardless now, but with his thatch of gray hair uncut.

I lay flat and looked up at him happily. 'You're beautiful,' I said. 'You look a little like a heroic portrait I saw once of Andrew Jackson.'

'No way,' he said. 'Man was skinny as hell. I've seen him.'

'But you haven't seen my heroic portrait.'

'Why the hell did you cut your wrists? You could have bled to death! Or did you cut them yourself?'

'Yes. It got me home.'

'There must be a safer way.'

I rubbed my wrists gingerly. 'There isn't any safe way to almost kill yourself. I was afraid of the sleeping pills. I took them with me because I wanted to be able to die if . . . if I wanted to die. But I was afraid that if I used them to get home, I might die before you or some doctor figured out what was wrong with me. Or that if I didn't die, I'd have some grisly side-effect – like gangrene.'

'I see,' he said after a while.

'Did you bandage me?'

'Me? No, I thought this was too serious for me to handle alone. I stopped the bleeding as best I could and called Lou George. He bandaged you.' Louis George was a doctor friend Kevin had met through his writing. Kevin had interviewed George for an article once, and the two had taken a liking to each other. They wound up doing a nonfiction book together.

'Lou said you managed to miss the main arteries in both arms,' Kevin told me. 'Said you didn't do much more than scratch yourself.'

'With all that blood!'

'It wasn't that much. You were probably too frightened to cut as deeply as you could have.'

I sighed. 'Well . . . I guess I'm glad I didn't do much damage – as long as I got home.'

'How would you feel about seeing a psychiatrist?'

'Seeing a . . . Are you kidding?'

'I am, but Lou wasn't. He says if you're doing things like this, you need help.'

'Oh God. Do I have to? The lies I'd have to invent!'

'No, this time you probably won't have to. Lou is a friend. You do it again, though, and . . . well, you could be locked up for psychiatric treatment whether you like it or not. The law tries to protect people like you from themselves.'

I found myself laughing, almost crying. I put my head on his shoulder and wondered whether a little time in some sort of mental institution would be worse than several months of slavery. I doubted it.

'How long was I gone this time?' I asked.

'About three hours. How long was it for you?'

'Eight months.'

'Eight . . .' He put his arm over me, holding me. 'No wonder you cut your wrists.'

'Hagar has been born.'

'Has she?' There was silence for a moment, then, 'What's that going to mean?'

I twisted uncomfortably and, by accident, put pressure on one of my wrists. The sudden pain made me gasp.

'Be careful,' he said. 'Treat yourself gently for a change.'

'Where's my bag?'

'Here.' He pulled the blanket aside and let me see that I was securely tied to my denim bag. 'What are you going to do, Dana?'

'I don't know.'

'What's he like now?'

He. Rufus. He had become such a fixture in my life that it wasn't even necessary to say his name. 'His father died,' I said. 'He's running things now.'

'Well?'

'I don't know. How do you do well at owning and trading in slaves?'

'Not well,' Kevin decided. He got up and went to the kitchen, came back with a glass of water. 'Did you want anything to eat? I can get you something.'

'I'm not hungry.'

'What did he do to you, finally, to make you cut your wrists?'

'Nothing to me. Nothing important. He sold a man away from his family when there was no need for him to. He hit me when I objected. Maybe he'll never be as hard as his father was, but he's a man of his time.'

'Then . . . it doesn't seem to me that you have such a difficult decision ahead of you.'

'But I do. I talked to Carrie about it once, and she said . . .'

'Carrie?' He looked at me strangely.

'Yes. She said . . . Oh. She gets her meaning across, Kevin. Weren't you around the place long enough to find that out?'

'She never tried to get much across to me. I used to wonder whether she was a little retarded.'

'God, no! Far from it. If you had gotten to know her, you wouldn't even suspect.'

He managed to shrug. 'Well, anyway, what did she tell you?'

'That if I had let Rufus die, everyone would have been sold. More families would have been separated. She has three children now.'

He was silent for several seconds. Then, 'She might be sold with her children if they're young. But I doubt that anyone would bother to keep her and her husband together. Someone would buy her and breed her to a new man. It is breeding, you know.'

'Yes. So you see, my decision isn't as easy as you thought.'

'But . . . they're being sold anyway.'

'Not all of them. Good Lord, Kevin, their lives are hard enough.'

'What about your life?'

'It's better than anything most of them will ever know.'

'It may not be as he gets older.'

I sat up, trying to ignore my own weakness. 'Kevin, tell me what you want me to do.'

He looked away, said nothing. I gave him several seconds, but he kept silent.

'It's real now, isn't it,' I said softly. 'We talked about it before – God knows how long ago – but somehow, it was abstract then. Now . . . Kevin, if you can't even say it, how can you expect me to do it?'

2

We had fifteen full days together this time. I marked them off on the calendar – June 19, through July 3. With some kind of reverse symbolism, Rufus called me back on July 4. But at least Kevin and I had a chance to grow back into the twentieth century. We

271

didn't seem to have to grow back into each other. The separations hadn't been good for us, but they hadn't hurt us that much either. It was easy for us to be together, knowing we shared experiences no one else would believe. It wasn't as easy, though, for us to be with other people.

My cousin came over, and when Kevin answered the door, she didn't recognize him.

'What's the matter with him?' she whispered later when she and I were alone.

'He's been sick,' I lied.

'With what?'

'The doctor isn't sure what it was. Kevin is much better now, though.'

'He looks just like my girl friend's father did, and he had cancer.'

'Julie, for Godsake!'

'I'm sorry, but . . . never mind. He hasn't hit you again, has he?'

'No.'

'Well, that's something. You'd better take care of yourself. You don't look so good either.'

Kevin tried driving – his first time after five years of horses and buggies. He said the traffic confused him, made him more nervous than he could see any reason for. He said he'd almost killed a couple of people. Then he put the car in the garage and left it there.

Of course, I wouldn't drive, wouldn't even ride with someone else while there was still a chance of Rufus snatching me away. After the first week, though, Kevin began to doubt that I would be called again.

I didn't doubt it. For the sake of the people whose lives Rufus controlled, I didn't wish him dead, but I wouldn't rest easy until I knew he was. As things stood now, sooner or later, he would get himself into trouble again and call me. I kept my denim bag nearby.

'You know, someday, you're going to have to stop dragging

that thing around with you and come back to life,' Kevin said after two weeks. He had just tried driving again, and when he came in, his hands were shaking. 'Hell, half the time I wonder if you're not eager to go back to Maryland anyway.'

I had been watching television – or at least, the television was on. Actually, I was looking over some journal pages I had managed to bring home in my bag, wondering whether I could weave them into a story. Now, I looked up at Kevin. 'Me?'

'Why not? Eight months, after all.'

I put my journal pages down and got up to turn off the television.

'Leave it on,' said Kevin.

I turned it off. 'I think you've got something to say to me,' I said. 'And I think I should hear it clearly.'

'You don't want to hear anything.'

'No, I don't. But I'm going to, aren't I?'

'My God, Dana, after two weeks . . .'

'It was eight days, time before last. And about three hours last time. The intervals between trips don't mean anything.'

'How old was he last time?'

'He turned twenty-five when I was there last. And, though I'll never be able to prove it, I turned twenty-seven.'

'He's grown up.'

I shrugged.

'Do you remember what he said just before he tried to shoot you?'

'No. I had other things on my mind.'

'I had forgotten it myself, but it's come back to me. He said, "You're not going to leave me!"'

I thought for a moment. 'Yes, that sounds about right.'

'It doesn't sound right to me.'

'I mean it sounds like what he said! I don't have any control over what he says.'

'But still . . .' He paused, looked at me as though he expected me to say something. I didn't. 'It sounded more like what I might say to you if you were leaving.'

'Would you?'

'You know what I mean.'

'Say what you mean. I can't answer you unless you say it.'

He drew a deep breath. 'All right. You've said he was a man of his time, and you've told me what he's done to Alice. What's he done to you?'

'Sent me to the field, had me beaten, made me spend nearly eight months sleeping on the floor of his mother's room, sold people . . . He's done plenty, but the worst of it was to other people. He hasn't raped me, Kevin. He understands, though you don't seem to, that for him that would be a form of suicide.'

'You mean there's something he could do to make you kill him, after all?'

I sighed, went over to him, and sat down on the arm of his chair. I looked down at him. 'Tell me you believe I'm lying to you.'

He looked at me uncertainly. 'Look, if anything did happen, I could understand it. I know how it was back then.'

'You mean you could forgive me for having been raped?'

'Dana, I lived there. I know what those people were like. And Rufus's attitude toward you . . .'

'Was sensible most of the time. He knew I could kill him just by turning my back at the right moment. And he believed that I wouldn't have him because I loved you. He said something like that once. He was wrong, but I never told him so.'

'Wrong?'

'At least partly. Of course I love you, and I don't want anyone else. But there's another reason, and when I'm back there it's the most important reason. I don't think Rufus would have understood it. Maybe you won't either.'

'Tell me.'

I thought for a moment, tried to find the right words. If I could make him understand, then surely he would believe me. He had to believe. He was my anchor here in my own time. The only person who had any idea what I was going through.

'You know what I thought,' I said, 'when I saw Tess tied into

274

that coffle?' I had told him about Tess and about Sam – that I had known them, that Rufus had sold them. I hadn't told him the details though – especially not the details of Sam's sale. I had been trying for two weeks to avoid sending his thoughts in the direction they had taken now.

'What does Tess have to do with . . .?'

'I thought, that could be me – standing there with a rope around my neck waiting to be led away like someone's dog!' I stopped, looked down at him, then went on softly. 'I'm not property, Kevin. I'm not a horse or a sack of wheat. If I have to seem to be property, if I have to accept limits on my freedom for Rufus's sake, then he also has to accept limits – on his behavior toward me. He has to leave me enough control of my own life to make living look better to me than killing and dying.'

'If your black ancestors had felt that way, you wouldn't be here,' said Kevin.

'I told you when all this started that I didn't have their endurance. I still don't. Some of them will go on struggling to survive, no matter what. I'm not like that.'

He smiled a little. 'I suspect that you are.'

I shook my head. He thought I was being modest or something. He didn't understand.

Then I realized that he had smiled. I looked down at him questioningly.

He sobered. 'I had to know.'

'And do you, now?'

'Yes.'

That felt like truth. It felt enough like truth for me not to mind that he had only half understood me.

'Have you decided what you're going to do about Rufus?' he asked.

I shook my head. 'You know, it's not only what will happen to the slaves that worries me . . . if I turn my back on him. It's what might happen to me.'

'You'll be finished with him.'

'I might be finished period. I might not be able to get home.'

275

'Your coming home has never had anything to do with him. You come home when your life is in danger.'

'But how do I come home? Is the power mine, or do I tap some power in him? All this started with him, after all. I don't know whether I need him or not. And I won't know until he's not around.'

3

A couple of Kevin's friends came over on the Fourth of July and tried to get us to go to the Rose Bowl with them for the fireworks. Kevin wanted to go – more to get out of the house than for any other reason, I suspected. I told him to go ahead, but he wouldn't go without me. As it turned out, there was no chance for me to go, anyway. As Kevin's friends left the house, I began to feel dizzy.

I stumbled toward my bag, fell before I reached it, crawled toward it, grabbed it just as Kevin came in from saying good-bye to his friends.

'Dana,' he was saying, 'we can't stay cooped up in this house any longer waiting for something that isn't . . .'

He was gone.

Instead of lying on the floor of my living room, I was lying on the ground in the sun, almost directly over a hill of large black ants.

Before I could get up, someone kicked me, fell on me heavily. I had the breath knocked out of me for a moment.

'Dana!' said Rufus's voice. 'What the hell are you doing here?'

I looked up, saw him sprawled across me where he had fallen. We got up just as something began to bite me – the ants, probably. I brushed myself off quickly.

'I said what are you doing here!' He sounded angry. He looked no older than he had been when I'd last seen him, but something was wrong with him. He looked haggard and weary – looked as though it had been too long since he'd slept last, looked as though it would be even longer before he was able to sleep again.

'I don't know what I'm doing here, Rufe. I never do until I find out what's wrong with you.'

He stared at me for a long moment. His eyes were red and under them were dark smudges. Finally, he grabbed me by the arm and led me back the way he had come. We were on the plantation not far from the house. Nothing looked changed. I saw two of Nigel's sons wrestling, rolling around on the ground. They were the two I had been teaching, and they were no bigger than they had been when I saw them last.

'Rufe, how long have I been gone?'

He didn't answer. He was leading me toward the barn, I saw, and apparently I wasn't going to learn anything until I got there.

He stopped at the barn door and pushed me through it. He didn't follow me in.

I looked around, seeing very little at first as my eyes became accustomed to the dimmer light. I turned to the place where I had been strung up and whipped – and jumped back in surprise when I saw that someone was hanging there. Hanging by the neck. A woman.

Alice.

I stared at her not believing, not wanting to believe . . . I touched her and her flesh was cold and hard. The dead gray face was ugly in death as it had never been in life. The mouth was open. The eyes were open and staring. Her head was bare and her hair loose and short like mine. She had never liked to tie it up the way other women did. It was one of the things that had made us look even more alike – the only two consistently bareheaded women on the place. Her dress was dark red and her apron clean and white. She wore shoes that Rufus had had made specifically for her, not the rough heavy shoes or boots other slaves wore. It was as though she had dressed up and combed her hair and then . . .

I wanted her down.

I looked around, saw that the rope had been tied to a wall peg, thrown over a beam. I broke my fingernails, trying to untie it until I remembered my knife. I got it from my bag and cut Alice down.

She fell stiffly like something that would break when it hit the floor. But she landed without breaking and I took the rope from her neck and closed her eyes. For a time, I just sat with her, holding her head and crying silently.

Eventually, Rufus came in. I looked up at him and he looked away.

'Did she do this to herself?' I asked.

'Yes. To herself.'

'Why?'

He didn't answer.

'Rufe?'

He shook his head slowly from side to side.

'Where are her children?'

He turned and walked out of the barn.

I straightened Alice's body and her dress and looked around for something to cover her with. There was nothing.

I left the barn and went across an expanse of grass to the cookhouse. Sarah was there chopping meat with that frightening speed and coordination of hers. I had told her once that it always looked as though she was about to cut off a finger or two, and she had laughed. She still had all ten.

'Sarah?' There was such a difference in our ages now that everyone else my age called her 'Aunt Sarah.' I knew it was a title of respect in this culture, and I respected her. But I couldn't quite manage 'Aunt' any more than I could have managed 'Mammy.' She didn't seem to mind.

She looked up. 'Dana! Girl, what are you doing back here? What Marse Rufe done now?'

'I'm not sure. But, Sarah, Alice is dead.'

Sarah put down her cleaver and sat on the bench next to the table. 'Oh Lord. Poor child. He finally killed her.'

'I don't know,' I said. I went over and sat beside her. 'I think she did it to herself. Hung herself. I just took her down.'

'He did it!' she hissed. 'Even if he didn't put the rope on her, he drove her to it. He sold her babies!'

I frowned. Sarah had spoken clearly enough, loudly enough,

278

but for a moment, I didn't understand. 'Joe and Hagar? His children?'

'What he care 'bout that?'

'But . . . he did care. He was going to . . . Why would he do such a thing?'

'She run off.' Sarah faced me. 'You must have known she was goin'. You and her was like sisters.'

I didn't need the reminder. I got up, feeling that I had to move around, distract myself, or I would cry again.

'You sure fought like sisters,' said Sarah. 'Always fussin' at each other, stompin' away from each other, comin' back. Right after you left, she knocked the devil out of a field hand who was runnin' you down.'

Had she? She would. Insulting me was her prerogative. No trespassing. I paced from the table to the hearth to a small work table. Back to Sarah.

'Dana, where is she?'

'In the barn.'

'He'll give her a big funeral.' Sarah shook her head. 'It's funny. I thought she was finally settlin' down with him – getting not to mind so much.'

'If she was, I don't think she could have forgiven herself for it.' Sarah shrugged.

'When she ran . . . did he beat her?'

'Not much. 'Bout much as old Marse Tom whipped you that time.'

That gentle spanking, yes.

'The whipping didn't matter much. But when he took away her children, I thought she was go' die right there. She was screaming and crying and carrying on. Then she got sick and I had to take care of her.' Sarah was silent for a moment. 'I didn't want to even be close to her. When Marse Tom sold my babies, I just wanted to lay down and die. Seeing her like she was brought all that back.'

Carrie came in then, her face wet with tears. She came up to me without surprise, and hugged me.

'You know?' I asked.

She nodded, then made her sign for white people and pushed me toward the door. I went.

I found Rufus at his desk in the library fondling a hand gun.

He looked up and saw me just as I was about to withdraw. It had occurred to me suddenly, certainly, that this was where he had been heading when he called me. What had his call been, then? A subconscious desire for me to stop him from shooting himself?

'Come in, Dana.' His voice sounded empty and dead.

I pulled my old Windsor chair up to his desk and sat down. 'How could you do it, Rufe?'

He didn't answer.

'Your son and your daughter . . . How could you sell them?'

'I didn't.'

That stopped me. I had been prepared for almost any other answer – or no answer. But a denial . . . 'But . . . but . . .'

'She ran away.'

'I know.'

'We were getting along. You know. You were here. It was good. Once, when you were gone, she came to my room. She came on her own.'

'Rufe . . .?'

'Everything was all right. I even went on with Joe's lessons. Me! I told her I would free both of them.'

'She didn't believe you. You wouldn't put anything into writing.'

'I would have.'

I shrugged. 'Where are the children, Rufe?'

'In Baltimore with my mother's sister.'

'But . . . why?'

'To punish her, scare her. To make her see what could happen if she didn't . . . if she tried to leave me.'

'Oh God! But you could have at least brought them back when she got sick.'

'I wish I had.'

'Why didn't you?'

'I don't know.'

I turned away from him in disgust. 'You killed her. Just as though you had put that gun to her head and fired.'

He looked at the gun, put it down quickly.

'What are you going to do now?'

'Nigel's gone to get a coffin. A decent one, not just a homemade box. And he'll hire a minister to come out tomorrow.'

'I mean what are you going to do for your son and your daughter?'

He looked at me helplessly.

'Two certificates of freedom,' I said. 'You owe them that, at least. You've deprived them of their mother.'

'Damn you, Dana! Stop saying that! Stop saying I killed her.'

I just looked at him.

'Why did you leave me! If you hadn't gone, she might not have run away!'

I rubbed my face where he had hit me when I begged him not to sell Sam.

'You didn't have to go!'

'You were turning into something I didn't want to stay near.'

Silence.

'Two certificates of freedom, Rufe, all legal. Raise them free. That's the least you can do.'

4

There was an outdoor funeral the next day. Everyone attended – field hands, house servants, even the indifferent Evan Fowler.

The minister was a tall coal-black deep-voiced freedman with a face that reminded me of a picture I had of my father who had died before I was old enough to know him. The minister was literate. He held a Bible in his huge hands and read from Job and Ecclesiastes until I could hardly stand to listen. I had shrugged off my aunt and uncle's strict Baptist teachings years before. But even now, especially now, the bitter melancholy words of Job could still reach me. 'Man that is born of a woman is of few days, and full of trouble. He cometh forth like a flower, and is cut down: he fleeth also as a shadow, and continueth not . . .'

I kept quiet somehow, wiped away silent tears, beat away flies and mosquitoes, heard the whispers.

'She gone to hell! Don't you know folks kills theyself goes to hell!'

'Shut your mouth! Marse Rufe'll make you think you down there with her!'

Silence.

They buried her.

There was a big dinner afterward. My relatives at home had dinners after funerals too. I had never thought about how far back the custom might go.

I ate a little, then went away to the library where I could be alone, where I would write. Sometimes I wrote things because I couldn't say them, couldn't sort out my feelings about them, couldn't keep them bottled up inside me. It was a kind of writing I always destroyed afterward. It was for no one else. Not even Kevin.

Rufus came in later when I was nearly written out. He came to the desk, sat down in my old Windsor – I was in his chair – and put his head down. We didn't say anything, but we sat together for a while.

The next day, he took me to town with him, took me to the old brick Court House, and let me watch while he had certificates of freedom drawn up for his children.

'If I bring them back,' he said on the ride home, 'will you take care of them?'

I shook my head. 'It wouldn't be good for them, Rufe. This isn't my home. They'd get used to me, then I'd be gone.'

'Who, then?'

'Carrie. Sarah will help her.'

He nodded listlessly.

Early one morning a few days later, he left for Easton Point where he could catch a steamboat to Baltimore. I offered to go with him to help with the children, but all that got me was a look of suspicion – a look I couldn't help understanding.

'Rufe, I don't have to go to Baltimore to escape from you. I really want to help.'

'Just stay here,' he said. And he went out to talk to Evan Fowler before he left. He knew how I had gone home last. He had asked me, and I had told him.

'But why?' he had demanded. 'You could have killed yourself.'

'There're worse things than being dead,' I had said.

He had turned and walked away from me.

Now he watched more than he had before. He couldn't watch me all the time, of course, and unless he wanted to keep me chained, he couldn't prevent me from taking one route or another out of his world if that was what I wanted to do. He couldn't control me. That clearly bothered him.

Evan Fowler was in the house more than he had to be while Rufus was gone. He said little to me, gave me no orders. But he was there. I took refuge in Margaret Weylin's room, and she was so pleased she talked endlessly. I found myself laughing and actually holding conversations with her as though we were just a couple of lonely people talking without the extra burden of stupid barriers.

Rufus came back, came to the house carrying the dark little girl and leading the boy who seemed to look even more like him. Joe saw me in the hall and ran to me.

'Aunt Dana, Aunt Dana!' And a hug later, 'I can read better now. Daddy's been teaching me. Wanna hear?'

'Sure I do.' I looked up at Rufus. *Daddy?*

He glared at me tight-lipped as though daring me to speak. All I had wanted to say, though, was, 'What took you so long?' The boy had spent his short life calling his father 'Master.' Well, now that he no longer had a mother, I supposed Rufus thought it was time he had a father. I managed to smile at Rufus – a real smile. I didn't want him feeling embarrassed or defensive for finally acknowledging his son.

He smiled back, seemed to relax.

'How about my getting classes going again?'

He nodded. 'I guess the others haven't had time to forget much.'

They hadn't. As it turned out, I had only been away for three months. The children had had a kind of early summer vacation. Now they went back to school. And I, slowly, delicately, went to work on Rufus, began to push him toward freeing a few more of them, perhaps several more of them – perhaps in his will, all of them. I had heard of slaveholders doing such things. The Civil War was still thirty years away. I might be able to get some of the adult slaves freed while they were still young enough to build new lives. I might be able to do some good for everyone, finally. At least, I felt secure enough to try, now that my own freedom was within reach.

Rufus had been keeping me with him more than he needed me now. He called me to share his meals openly, and he seemed to listen when I talked to him about freeing the slaves. But he made no promises. I wondered whether he thought making a will was foolish at his age – or maybe it was freeing more slaves that he thought was foolish. He didn't say anything, so I couldn't tell.

Finally, though, he did answer me, told me much more than I wanted to know. None of it should have surprised me at all.

'Dana,' he said one afternoon in the library, 'I'd have to be crazy to make a will freeing these people and then tell you about it. I could die damn young for that kind of craziness.'

I had to look at him to see whether he was serious. But looking at him confused me even more. He was smiling, but I got the feeling he was completely serious. He believed I would kill him to free his slaves. Strangely, the idea had not occurred to me. My suggestion had been innocent. But he might have a point. Eventually, it would have occurred to me.

'I used to have nightmares about you,' he said. 'They started when I was little – right after I set fire to the draperies. Remember the fire?'

'Of course.'

'I'd dream about you and wake up in a cold sweat.'

'Dream . . . about me killing you?'

'Not exactly.' He paused, gave me a long unreadable look. 'I'd dream about you leaving me.'

I frowned. That was close to the thing Kevin had heard him say – the thing that had awakened Kevin's suspicions. 'I leave,' I said carefully. 'I have to. I don't belong here.'

'Yes you do! As far as I'm concerned, you do. But that's not what I mean. You leave, and sooner or later you come back. But in my nightmares, you leave without helping me. You walk away and leave me in trouble, hurting, maybe dying.'

'Oh. Are you sure those dreams started when you were little? They sound more like something you would have come up with after your fight with Isaac.'

'They got worse then,' he admitted. 'But they started way back at the fire – as soon as I realized you could help me or not, just as you chose. I had those nightmares for years. Then when Alice had been here awhile, they went away. Now they've come back.'

He stopped, looked at me as though he expected me to say something – to reassure him, perhaps, to promise him that I would never do such a thing. But I couldn't quite bring myself to say the words.

'You see?' he said quietly.

I moved uncomfortably in my chair. 'Rufe, do you know how many people live to ripe old ages without ever getting into the kind of trouble that causes you to need me? If you don't trust me, then you have more reason than ever to be careful.'

'Tell me I can trust you.'

More discomfort. 'You keep doing things that make it impossible for me to trust you – even though you know it has to work both ways.'

He shook his head. 'I don't know. I never know how to treat you. You confuse everybody. You sound too white to the field hands – like some kind of traitor, I guess.'

'I know what they think.'

'Daddy always thought you were dangerous because you knew too many white ways, but you were black. Too black, he said.

The kind of black who watches and thinks and makes trouble. I told that to Alice and she laughed. She said sometimes Daddy showed more sense than I did. She said he was right about you, and that I'd find out some day.'

I jumped. Had Alice really said such a thing?

'And my mother,' continued Rufus calmly, 'says if she closes her eyes while you and her are talking, she can forget you're black without even trying.'

'I'm black,' I said. 'And when you sell a black man away from his family just because he talked to me, you can't expect me to have any good feelings toward you.'

He looked away. We hadn't really discussed Sam before. We had talked around him, alluded to him without quite mentioning him.

'He wanted you,' said Rufus bluntly.

I stared at him, knowing now why we hadn't spoken of Sam. It was too dangerous. It could lead to speaking of other things. We needed safe subjects now, Rufus and I – the price of corn, supplies for the slaves, that sort of thing.

'Sam didn't do anything,' I said. 'You sold him for what you thought he was thinking.'

'He wanted you,' Rufus repeated.

So do you, I thought. No Alice to take the pressure off any more. It was time for me to go home. I started to get up.

'Don't leave, Dana.'

I stopped. I didn't want to hurry away – run away – from him. I didn't want to give him any indication that I was going to the attic to reopen the tender new scar tissue at my wrists. I sat down again. And he leaned back in his chair and looked at me until I wished I had taken the chance of hurrying away.

'What am I going to do when you go home this time?' he whispered.

'You'll survive.'

'I wonder . . . why I should bother.'

'For your children, at least,' I said. 'Her children. They're all you have left of her.'

He closed his eyes, rubbed one hand over them. 'They should be your children now,' he said. 'If you had any feelings for them, you'd stay.'

For them? 'You know I can't.'

'You could if you wanted to. I wouldn't hurt you, and you wouldn't have to hurt yourself . . . again.'

'You wouldn't hurt me until something frustrated you, made you angry or jealous. You wouldn't hurt me until someone hurt you. Rufe, I know you. I couldn't stay here even if I didn't have a home to go back to – and someone waiting for me there.'

'That Kevin!'

'Yes.'

'I wish I had shot him.'

'If you had, you'd be dead yourself by now.'

He turned his body so that he faced me squarely. 'You say that as though it means something.'

I got up to leave. There was nothing more to be said. He had asked for what he knew I could not give, and I had refused.

'You know, Dana,' he said softly, 'when you sent Alice to me that first time, and I saw how much she hated me, I thought, I'll fall asleep beside her and she'll kill me. She'll hit me with a candlestick. She'll set fire to the bed. She'll bring a knife up from the cookhouse . . .

'I thought all that, but I wasn't afraid. Because if she killed me, that would be that. Nothing else would matter. But if I lived, I would have her. And, by God, I had to have her.'

He stood up and came over to me. I stepped back, but he caught my arms anyway. 'You're so much like her, I can hardly stand it,' he said.

'Let go of me, Rufe!'

'You were one woman,' he said. 'You and her. One woman. Two halves of a whole.'

I had to get away from him. 'Let me go, or I'll make your dream real!' Abandonment. The one weapon Alice hadn't had. Rufus didn't seem to be afraid of dying. Now, in his grief, he seemed almost to want death. But he was afraid of dying alone, afraid of being deserted by the person he had depended on for so long.

He stood holding my arms, perhaps trying to decide what he should do. After a moment, I felt his grip loosen, and I pulled away. I knew I had to go now before he submerged his fear. He could do it. He could talk himself into anything.

I left the library, went up the main stairs, then the attic stairs. Over to my bag, my knife . . .

Footsteps on the stairs.

The knife!

I opened it, hesitated, then slipped the knife, blade still open, back into my bag.

He opened the door, came in, looked around the big hot empty room. He saw me at once, but still, he looked around – to see whether we were alone?

We were.

He came over and sat next to me on my pallet. 'I'm sorry, Dana,' he said.

Sorry? For what he had nearly done, or for what he was about to do? Sorry. He had apologized to me many times in many ways before, but his apologies had always been oblique, 'Eat with me, Dana. Sarah is cooking up something special.' Or, 'Here, Dana, here's a new book I bought for you in town.' Or, 'Here's some cloth, Dana. Maybe you can make yourself something from it.'

Things. Gifts given when he knew he had hurt or offended me. But he had never before said, 'I'm sorry, Dana.' I looked at him uncertainly.

'I've never felt so lonesome in my life,' he said.

The words touched me as no others could have. I knew about loneliness. I found my thoughts going back to the time I had gone home without Kevin – the loneliness, the fear, sometimes the hopelessness I had felt then. Hopelessness wouldn't be a sometime thing to Rufus, though. Alice was dead and buried. He had only his children left. But at least one of them had also loved Alice. Joe.

'Where'd my mama go?' he demanded on his first day home.

'Away,' Rufus had said. 'She went away.'

'When is she coming back?'

'I don't know.'

The boy came to me. 'Aunt Dana, where'd my mama go?'

'Honey . . . she died.'

'Died?'

'Yes. Like old Aunt Mary.' Who at last had drifted the final distance to her reward. She had lived over eighty years – had come over from Africa, people said. Nigel had made a box and Mary had been laid to rest near where Alice lay now.

'But Mama wasn't old.'

'No, she was sick, Joe.'

'Daddy said she went away.'

'Well . . . to heaven.'

'No!'

He had cried and I had tried to comfort him. I remembered the pain of my own mother's death – grief, loneliness, uncertainty in my aunt and uncle's house . . .

I had held the boy and told him he still had his daddy – please God. And that Sarah and Carrie and Nigel loved him. They wouldn't let anything happen to him – as though they had the power to protect him, or even themselves.

I let Joe go to his mother's cabin to be alone for a while. He wanted to. Then I told Rufus what I had done. And Rufus hadn't known whether to hit me or thank me. He had glared at me, the skin of his face drawn tight, intense. Then, finally, he had relaxed and nodded and gone out to find his son.

Now, he sat with me – being sorry and lonely and wanting me to take the place of the dead.

'You never hated me, did you?' he asked.

'Never for long. I don't know why. You worked hard to earn my hatred, Rufe.'

'She hated me. From the first time I forced her.'

'I don't blame her.'

'Until just before she ran. She had stopped hating me. I wonder how long it will take you.'

'What?'

'To stop hating.'

Oh God. Almost against my will, I closed my fingers around the handle of the knife still concealed in my bag. He took my other hand, held it between his own in a grip that I knew would only be gentle until I tried to pull away.

'Rufe,' I said, 'your children . . .'

'They're free.'

'But they're young. They need you to protect their freedom.'

'Then it's up to you, isn't it?'

I twisted my hand, tried to get it away from him in sudden anger. At once, his hold went from caressing to imprisoning. My right hand had become wet and slippery on the knife.

'It's up to you,' he repeated.

'No, Goddamnit, it isn't! Keeping you alive has been up to me for too long! Why didn't you shoot yourself when you started to? I wouldn't have stopped you!'

'I know.'

The softness of his voice made me look up at him.

'So what else do I have to lose?' he asked. He pushed me back on the pallet, and for a few moments, we lay there, still. What was he waiting for? What was I waiting for?

He lay with his head on my shoulder, his left arm around me, his right hand still holding my hand, and slowly, I realized how easy it would be for me to continue to be still and forgive him even this. So easy, in spite of all my talk. But it would be so hard to raise the knife, drive it into the flesh I had saved so many times. So hard to kill . . .

He was not hurting me, would not hurt me if I remained as I was. He was not his father, old and ugly, brutal and disgusting. He smelled of soap, as though he had bathed recently – for me? The red hair was neatly combed and a little damp. I would never be to him what Tess had been to his father – a thing passed around like the whiskey jug at a husking. He wouldn't do that to me or sell me or . . .

No.

290

I could feel the knife in my hand, still slippery with perspiration. A slave was a slave. Anything could be done to her. And Rufus was Rufus – erratic, alternately generous and vicious. I could accept him as my ancestor, my younger brother, my friend, but not as my master, and not as my lover. He had understood that once.

I twisted sharply, broke away from him. He caught me, trying not to hurt me. I was aware of him trying not to hurt me even as I raised the knife, even as I sank it into his side.

He screamed. I had never heard anyone scream that way – an animal sound. He screamed again, a lower ugly gurgle.

He lost his hold on my hand for a moment, but caught my arm before I could get away. Then he brought up the fist of his free hand to punch me once, and again as the patroller had done so long ago.

I pulled the knife free of him somehow, raised it, and brought it down again into his back.

This time he only grunted. He collapsed across me, somehow still alive, still holding my arm.

I lay beneath him, half conscious from the blows, and sick. My stomach seemed to twist, and I vomited on both of us.

'Dana?'

A voice. A man's voice.

I managed to turn my head and see Nigel standing in the doorway.

'Dana, what . . .? Oh no. God, no!'

'Nigel . . .' moaned Rufus, and he gave a long shuddering sigh. His body went limp and leaden across me. I pushed him away somehow – everything but his hand still on my arm. Then I convulsed with terrible, wrenching sickness.

Something harder and stronger than Rufus's hand clamped down on my arm, squeezing it, stiffening it, pressing into it – painlessly, at first – melting into it, meshing with it as though somehow my arm were being absorbed into something. Something cold and nonliving.

Something . . . paint, plaster, wood – a wall. The wall of my

291

living room. I was back at home – in my own house, in my own time. But I was still caught somehow, joined to the wall as though my arm were growing out of it – or growing into it. From the elbow to the ends of the fingers, my left arm had become a part of the wall. I looked at the spot where flesh joined with plaster, stared at it uncomprehending. It was the exact spot Rufus's fingers had grasped.

I pulled my arm toward me, pulled hard.

And suddenly, there was an avalanche of pain, red impossible agony! And I screamed and screamed.

Epilogue

We flew to Maryland as soon as my arm was well enough. There, we rented a car – Kevin was driving again, finally – and wandered around Baltimore and over to Easton. There was a bridge now, not the steamship Rufus had used. And at last I got a good look at the town I had lived so near and seen so little of. We found the courthouse and an old church, a few other buildings time had not worn away. And we found Burger King and Holiday Inn and Texaco and schools with black kids and white kids together and older people who looked at Kevin and me, then looked again.

We went into the countryside, into what was still woods and farmland, and found a few of the old houses. A couple of them could have been the Weylin house. They were well-kept and handsomer, but basically, they were the same red-brick Georgian Colonials.

But Rufus's house was gone. As nearly as we could tell, its site was now covered by a broad field of corn. The house was dust, like Rufus.

I was the one who insisted on trying to find his grave, questioning the farmer about it because Rufus, like his father, like old Mary and Alice, had probably been buried on the plantation.

But the farmer knew nothing – or at least, said nothing. The only clue we found – more than a clue, really – was an old newspaper article – a notice that Mr Rufus Weylin had been killed when his house caught fire and was partially destroyed. And in later papers, notice of the sale of the slaves from Mr Rufus Weylin's estate. These slaves were listed by their first names with their approximate ages and their skills given. All three of Nigel's sons were listed, but Nigel and Carrie were not. Sarah was listed, but Joe and Hagar were not. Everyone else was listed. Everyone.

I thought about that, put together as many pieces as I could. The fire, for instance. Nigel had probably set it to cover what I had done – and he had covered. Rufus was assumed to have burned to death. I could find nothing in the incomplete newspaper records to suggest that he had been murdered, or even that the fire had been arson. Nigel must have done a good job. He must also have managed to get Margaret Weylin out of the house alive. There was no mention of her dying. And Margaret had relatives in Baltimore. Also, Hagar's home had been in Baltimore.

Kevin and I went back to Baltimore to skim newspapers, legal records, anything we could find that might tie Margaret and Hagar together or mention them at all. Margaret might have taken both children. Perhaps with Alice dead she had accepted them. They were her grandchildren, after all, the son and daughter of her only child. She might have cared for them. She might also have held them as slaves. But even if she had, Hagar, at least, lived long enough for the Fourteenth Amendment to free her.

'He could have left a will,' Kevin told me outside one of our haunts, the Maryland Historical Society. 'He could have freed those people at least when he had no more use for them.'

'But there was his mother to consider,' I said. 'And he was only twenty-five. He probably thought he had plenty of time to make a will.'

'Stop defending him,' muttered Kevin.

I hesitated, then shook my head. 'I wasn't. I guess in a way, I was defending myself. You see, I know why he wouldn't make that kind of will. I asked him, and he told me.'

'Why?'

'Because of me. He was afraid I'd kill him afterwards.'

'You wouldn't even have had to know about it!'

'Yes, but I guess he wasn't taking any chances.'

'Was he right . . . to be afraid?'

'I don't know.'

'I doubt it, considering what you took from him. I don't think you were really capable of killing him until he attacked you.'

And barely then, I thought. Kevin would never know what those last moments had been like. I had outlined them for him, and he'd asked few questions. For that I was grateful. Now I said simply, 'Self-defense.'

'Yes,' he said.

'But the cost . . . Nigel's children, Sarah, all the others . . .'

'It's over,' he said. 'There's nothing you can do to change any of it now.'

'I know.' I drew a deep breath. 'I wonder whether the children were allowed to stay together – maybe stay with Sarah.'

'You've looked,' he said. 'And you've found no records. You'll probably never know.'

I touched the scar Tom Weylin's boot had left on my face, touched my empty left sleeve. 'I know,' I repeated. 'Why did I even want to come here. You'd think I would have had enough of the past.'

'You probably needed to come for the same reason I did.' He shrugged. 'To try to understand. To touch solid evidence that those people existed. To reassure yourself that you're sane.'

I looked back at the brick building of the Historical Society, itself a converted early mansion. 'If we told anyone else about this, anyone at all, they wouldn't think we were so sane.'

'We are,' he said. 'And now that the boy is dead, we have some chance of staying that way.'

Reading group guide

- 'There was no honest explanation I could give them – none they would believe.' How did the prologue shape your expectations of the book? Did you find that these changed as you read on?

- *Kindred* was first published in 1979 – for today's readers, Dana's present is now seen as the past. Does this influence your understanding of the book? How do the two different time strands in *Kindred* compare to your experience of the world now?

- Discuss the portrayal of the Weylin family. How does Rufus compare to his father as he grows up? To what extent can you empathise with Rufus, considering his upbringing?

- 'We're in the middle of history. We surely can't change it.' How does the use of time travel in this story affect our perception of the past and present? Could Dana and Kevin have chosen to act differently in the antebellum South? Should they?

Think about how Dana and Sarah's relationship develops throughout the novel. What is Sarah most driven by? And how does Dana's perception of her friend change over time?

 Discuss the presentation of love in the novel and how it motivates the different characters.

Likewise 'I never realized how easily people could be trained to accept slavery.' Were you surprised by Dana's observation here? Discuss the portrayal of complicity and choice in the novel.

What do you make of the way Rufus sees Dana and Alice as 'two halves of the same woman?' How is power connected to race, class, and gender?

 Back in their present day, what does the future hold for Dana and Kevin? How do you imagine their lives will continue in the wake of the extraordinary things they've experienced?

 'Octavia E. Butler's evocative, often troubling, novels explore far-reaching issues of race, sex, power and, ultimately, what it means to be human' – *New York Times*. How does *Kindred* encourage us to examine our own humanity and the relationships we have with others?

To what extent is the title *Kindred* significant to the events of the novel? Did you find it ironic?

'One of the most significant literary artists of the twentieth century. One cannot exaggerate the impact she has had'
– Junot Diaz.

Have you read any of these other extraordinary stories by Octavia E. Butler? Discover more about them in the following pages.

Available from

HEADLINE

PARABLE
OF THE SOWER

When unattended environmental and economic crises lead to social breakdown, no one is safe.

In a night of fire and death, Lauren Olamina, the young daughter of a minister, loses her family and home and ventures out from their ravaged gated community into the unprotected American landscape.

But what begins as a fight for survival soon leads to something much more: a startling vision of human destiny . . . and the birth of a new faith.

HEADLINE

PARABLE
OF THE TALENTS

(Winner of the Nebula Award for Best Novel)

Lauren Olamina's love is divided among her young daughter, her community and the revelation that led her to found a new faith that teaches 'God Is Change'.

But in the wake of environmental and economic chaos, the U.S. government turns a blind eye to the violent bigots who consider the mere existence of a black female leader a threat.

Soon Lauren must either sacrifice her child and her followers – or forsake the religion that can transform human destiny.

HEADLINE

DAWN

(Lilith's Brood – Book One)

In a world devastated by nuclear war with humanity on the edge of extinction, aliens finally make contact. They rescue those humans they can, keeping most survivors in suspended animation and begin the slow process of rehabilitating the planet.

When Lilith Iyapo is 'awakened', she finds that she has been chosen to revive her fellow humans in small groups by first preparing them to meet the utterly terrifying Oankali, then training them to survive on the wilderness that the planet has become.

But the Oankali cannot help humanity without altering it forever. Bonded to the aliens in ways no human has ever known, Lilith tries to fight them even as her own species comes to fear and loathe her.

HEADLINE

ADULTHOOD RITES

(Lilith's Brood – Book Two)

Lilith Iyapo has given birth to what looks like a normal human boy, Akin. But his genealogy is complicated and includes an alien race that rescued humanity from a devastating nuclear war. The price the Oankali exact is a high one – they are compelled to genetically merge their species with other races, drastically altering both in the process.

On a rehabilitated Earth, this new race is emerging, living alongside the 'pure' humans who choose to resist the aliens and the salvation they offer. These resisters are sterilized so that they cannot reproduce the genetic defect that drives humanity to destroy itself.

When the resisters kidnap young Akin, the Oankali choose to leave the child with his captors. Will Akin give the resisters back their fertility and freedom, even though they will only destroy themselves again?

HEADLINE

IMAGO

(Lilith's Brood – Book Three)

Child of the Earth and stars, Jodahs can shapeshift, heal the maimed, cure cancer . . . and create contagion with every breath. The child is an *ooloi*, a being beyond gender, born with the alien Oankali power to mix pure DNA within its body. But Jodahs is also the first ooloi born to a human mother, and its destiny is unknown.

The futures of both humans and Oankali rest in one young being's successful metamorphosis into adulthood.

Jodahs can become a mad, living plague – or a bridge of peace. Its challenge is to reconcile its galactic heritage of gene trading with the rage of a people facing a terrifying dilemma. For human children will inherit the universe only if they lose all that makes them human.

HEADLINE

FLEDGLING

Shori wakes up in the wilderness with extensive injuries and no memories. As she recovers, the realization that she has very unhuman needs and abilities leads to a shocking conclusion: Shori is a 53-year-old vampire.

To have a future, she must unravel her past . . . because the people that nearly killed her haven't given up.

HEADLINE

BLOODCHILD

(A novella: Winner of the Hugo, Locus, Nebula and Science Fiction Chronicle awards)

Years ago, a group known as the Terrans left Earth in search of a life free of persecution. Now they live alongside the Tlic, an alien race who face extinction; their only chance of survival is to plant their larvae inside the bodies of the humans.

When Gan, a young, boy, is chosen as a carrier of Tlic eggs, he faces an impossible dilemma: can he really help the species he has grown up with, even if it means sacrificing his own life?

HEADLINE

SEED TO HARVEST

The Patternist series, collected here in one edition, chart an epic secret history, the roots of which lie in the dawn of civilization, and whose tangled branches reach far into our future.

It begins when two immortals meet. Doro is an entity who changes bodies like clothes, killing his hosts; Anyanwu can change her very shape, absorbing bullets as easily as she can heal with a kiss. Their relationship, albeit as marked by hate as by love, will change the world.

After years of selected breeding, their 'Patternists' are becoming increasing harder to control, and harder to hide from society. They will eventually bring humanity to the brink of extinction and beyond, into a nightmare that Doro and Anyanwu could never have anticipated.

HEADLINE